Time Travelers
Back to New York City at the
End of the Roaring Twenties

Time Travelers

Back to New York City at the End of the Roaring Twenties

A Novel

Inspired by 1928 Editions of the New York Times

BEM P. ALLEN

iUniverse

TIME TRAVELERS
BACK TO NEW YORK CITY AT THE END
OF THE ROARING TWENTIES

iUniverse books may be ordered through booksellers or by contacting:

iUniverse
1663 Liberty Drive
Bloomington, IN 47403
www.iuniverse.com
1-800-Authors (1-800-288-4677)

ISBN: 978-1-4917-4225-9 (sc)
ISBN: 978-1-4917-4224-2 (e)

Library of Congress Control Number: 2014915625

Printed in the United States of America.

iUniverse rev. date: 1/15/2015

CONTENTS

ACKNOWLEDGEMENTS

Years ago my wife Paula and I were searching the shelves and tables of an old antique store near our town in Illinois. While Paula rummaged among various trinkets dating back to who-knows-when, I searched among books and other written materials. There on a table loaded down with "take your pick" items, all "on-sale" for no more than a few dollars, I found a collection of newspapers wrapped in cellophane. When I peeled away the plastic wrap, I was not surprised to find copies of local newspapers. Headlines of one heralded the destruction of Hiroshima and Nagasaki by atomic bombs. Another reported the assassination of John F. Kennedy. However, to my amazement, two late December 1928 New York Times editions were mixed in with the other papers. Scanning the front pages of these Times editions convinced me that I'd found something worth reading in depth. In particular, coverage of the 1928 American Association for the Advancement of Science Convention at Columbia University caught my attention. Provocative comments by psychologists attending the meetings dominated the front-page coverage.

Being immediately captivated by goings-on in New York City at the end of the Roaring Twenties, I plunked down the few bucks needed to purchase the newspapers.

Within the next few days, I perused the Times editions and found numerous fascinating accounts of life in New York City only months before the great market crash. At the time, it never occurred to me that the papers provided more than a brief glimpse into life in the world's greatest city during one of it's most fascinating epochs. Reading these old editions was entertaining and educational, nothing more. I carefully re-wrapped the papers and stored them in a closet.

Several times over the years while searching the closet I rediscovered the Times editions and explored them again. During a 2012 reading of the editions, the idea for a book about time travel materialized. The next year, partly in Illinois and partly in Michigan, I wrote the first draft of *Time Travelers*.

The characters in the 2010s are four PhD candidates in several science departments at a major university. They become obsessed with a rumor that the Computer Science College had successfully tested a time machine. After befriending a PhD student in that College, they ultimately trick him into allowing them access to the carefully guarded time machine. John is chosen by the other students to travel back to New York City at the end of 1928. His mission is to gain the confidence of science graduate students at Columbia University in order to plant suggestions into their minds concerning future developments in science. The hope is that these hints about future advances will speed up scientific progress.

His adventures in New York City include regular visits to the Savoy. John falls in love with a beautiful woman who works there and befriends two men who share his love of jazz and eventually become his business partners. He lives in the Hotel Theresa and does business at the beautiful Mount Morris Bank building. John's adventures include encounters with mobsters, shady business practitioners, and famous figures in entertainment and sports. He also has surprising experiences at the historic Lindy's Restaurant and installs a basketball rim in the Mount Morris Park for use by poor kids who have no other access to sports facilities.

It's clear to me that this book would not have happened had it not been for a chance encounter with late 1920s editions of the New York Times. The discussions among the book's main character and Columbia University graduate students contain many references to events reported in my collection of Times editions. A great city during arguably one it's most important periods was described by the Times with objectivity tempered by love. I hope my book captures that spirit.

Two of John's fellow present-time graduates, Martha and Joe, make brief trips to ancient Egypt and Chicago ten years into the future.

My wife Paula inspired, encouraged and gently corrected me during the course of writing Time Travelers. Norma Rosado-Blake, Archivist at the national headquarters of the American Association for the Advancement of Science (AAAS) in New York City, and AAAS Internist Brenda Aquilino, provided priceless information about the AAAS meeting in New York City 1928 (which lapsed over into 1929). They were even able to find a long-lost program for the 1928 convention, from which they provided information about presenters as well as titles and synopses of their presentations.

CHAPTER 1

Hail, Hail, The Gang's All Here

It was noon on Friday and John Albertstin, a psychology graduate student in a joint psychology/biology neuroscience program, was late to the weekly confab with fellow science aficionados. He was tall and lanky, sort of wiry strong. But how tall? His height had to be estimated because he refused to reveal it. If asked, he responded simply, "I don't know." Friends settled on "about 6' 3"." His deep brown eyes complimented skin with a rich ruddy tint, possibly owing to spending much time in the sun at his family's beach house. John's facial features fit his cowboy look. Cheekbones were prominent and accentuated the slope down to a broad chin, creased in the middle. His straight, dark hair fell unevenly about his neck and shoulders, giving him an unkept look.

As he approached their favorite watering hole, the Lion's Den, he saw Martha Aberre entering through a side door. At 5" 9 ½", Martha was tall for a woman. She was also unique in appearance. Her big brown eyes seemed to be fixed in a smiling shape, except when she was angered, which occurred periodically. The net effect was the look of someone who was teasingly hiding something. Her hair was

1

black and naturally straight, but she managed to curl the bottom of it from the back of her neck toward her chin. She enhanced this sly look with stylish clothes that accentuated her curvy profile. Martha was a bright, bubbly innovative thinker who found something laudable about everyone else's point of view. Nevertheless she was the unofficial leader of the gang. Martha was a graduate student in physics.

As John sat down at their table, they knowingly smiled at one another. His friends' view of him as not so serious-minded was reinforced by his habitual tardiness. Joseph von Haber, who corrected anyone daring to call him "Joe", icily intoned, "Got lost again? Well, if you can't find your ass, how are you going to find your way across campus." Joseph, who regularly put on his "better than thou" act, was, nevertheless, known to be a good and reliable friend. The periodic show of arrogance may have been to compensate for his ordinary looks, especially in comparison to John. Joseph was about Martha's height, unless she wore high heels. That's without factoring in the observation that he regularly wore what amounted to booster shoes. Joseph's hair was dirty blond in color and sort of sticking out everywhere. His pale face was a little too round to fit the macho male image he awkwardly and inconsistently tried to cultivate. Joseph did have attractive deep blue eyes. He was pursuing a doctorate in computer engineering.

Joseph and the others already had beers in front of them. Martha was approaching with John's and her favorite brand of suds. She carefully placed his beer on the table, and, while taking a seat, she whispered, "You now owe me ten bucks … pay up." He reached for his wallet.

Sarah Arredondo, was an honor student in mathematics who passed on PhD programs in that field to pursue a doctorate in philosophy. In terms of stature, she was petite and unimposing. Her svelte 5' 3" frame gave her an athletic look. That's not to say that she was plain. To the contrary, her clear brown eyes and neat brown hair fit well with a pleasantly shaped face and flawless complexion. Although friends regarded her as very smart, she didn't flaunt her high intelligence. Nevertheless she could be rough on people who speak more from emotion than reason and who belittle others. Her role, it seemed, was to promote rational thought about the issues they discussed and discourage oratories presented as "fact," but actually originating in emotions.

They chatted for a while about nothing in particular. After the group was properly lubricated by the beer, Joseph ended a brief silence with, "Well, fellow gangsters, what about John's hypothesis. He believes that knowing something extraordinarily innovative has been invented or discovered is enough for people who know about it to figure out its nature and usefulness."

Martha stole the floor by asserting, "His example was the so-called 'theft' of atomic bomb technology by the Soviets. The odds of them being able to steal the world's best-kept secret were near zero. However, knowing about the bombs effects from the world's media, they were able to manufacture their own nuclear weapon. That is, knowing that something of extraordinary value can be done, they set out to do it."

"So," interjected John, "having the knowledge that something of great value has been accomplished, may be enough to inspire others to discover how to do it."

"Then," Martha offered, "the question becomes, how do you test John's idea."

"I know," announced Sarah, who was more sober than the rest, "we could put someone in a time machine and send him or her back to sometime in the early 1900s where they could inform people of that time about modern discoveries."

They all burst into such raucous sounds of derision that everyone else in the joint turned to gape at them. When they recovered, Joseph rasped, "You know, that may not be so far-fetched. There's something going on in the Computer Science College that's very hush-hush and is garnering multiple millions in grant money. Only a few top faculty and doctoral students are privy to it, and I'm not yet one of them, though I'm working on it."

"What do you think they are doing?" asked John.

"I'm betting," returned Joseph, "they are trying to alter time in some way … that's the gist of the rumors that are circulating."

Martha chimed in, "that sounds absurd to me … compress or expand the time continuum? It's nonsense."

"I don't know," Joseph replied, "but I'm going to find out."

The next day after classes and chores in the lab, Joseph was sniffing around the area where the secret lab was rumored to be located. He probably wouldn't have been noticed had he not been trying doorknobs with the intent of sneaking peeks into rooms.

"What are you doing?" an official sounding voice asked from behind. Joseph wheeled around displaying the chagrined look of someone caught with a hand stuck in the door of a sweet-treat vending machine. He encountered the stern look and authoritarian posture of computer engineering department head, Professor Lawrence Silvers, who was known to have PhDs in physics and computer science. Because Joseph thought of himself as one of those born to lead the denizens, he had great deference for this fellow special-person, who was widely regarded as one of the world's most influential researchers in computer science.

Joseph pulled himself up to his full height and felt that he was repressing the need to salute. "Ah, Sir … Professor Silvers, I'm a computer science graduate student … I heard about this state of the art lab and had to take a look … I'm sorry, but anyone into computers would want to see it, possibly be a part of it."

The professor changed his expression to mere announce, and asked for Joseph's name and that of his major professor. Silvers responded with, "Yes, I know Professor Ranson … she has spoken to me about you. Regards you as very promising. However, I don't know whether she'd be willing to give you up, and I'm not sure you'd be right for our lab. Tell you what, send me your resume and if you have the right background, I'll ask Ranson about possibly splitting your research hours."

About a month later Ranson informed Joseph that she would release 75% of his research time to Silvers for a year, as she wouldn't need much of his time until her recently submitted research-grant proposals got through the maze of government agencies. Joseph was to report to Professor Chanault, one of the several bright young computer scientists working under Silvers. He would be provided with an office—actually more like a library cubicle than the small office he had been using—and, for the coming year he would receive his monthly stipend from one of Silvers' grants.

When Joseph first met with Associate Professor Frank Chanault he was almost as deferential as he had been with Professor Silvers, but was quickly told to call his new boss "Ron." Joseph began this adventure into informality with a barely audible, "Ok." But he nearly gasped when "Ron" inquired, "And can I call you Joe?" The response was a child-like, slow and partial nod.

Some weeks had lapsed since he told his science-wonk friends that he would "look into the secret lab." He had put off telling them that he had gotten an assistantship under the professor who managed the secret lab. He wanted to wait until he felt that he knew enough to suggest he might infiltrate the "time machine" lab. Now he had learned enough to call a meeting at the Lion's Den. He came early and waited patiently until they all arrived. For the next 15 minutes he silently sipped his beer and munched on free-be nuts, crackers and such, all heavily salted so as to increase the need for beer. Soon they were all "three sheets to the wind" and talking excitedly about the latest news of scientific advances. When they paused briefly to catch their collective breath, he suddenly shouted in a voice only a few decibels below the sound of a train passing nearby, "Guess what I did?"

They turned their heads to him, each with "What tha …." looks on their faces and waited to find out what kind of weirdness had overcome him. "I now have a research assistantship that could allow me total access to the 'time machine' computer lab."

They sobered up fast and asked him how he had managed such an extraordinary feat. Of course, though he would come to tolerate being called "Joe," he was still the same special person he had always been. Thus, he began with an oration about how clever he had been and how quickly he was accepted by the superior beings in the secret lab.

After a few minutes of this self-indulgence, Sarah lost patience and exclaimed, "Get to the part about the secret lab." Joseph was startled, as he always was when she pulled him away from himself, back to the conversation at hand.

He admitted that, even though he now worked in the restricted computer sciences labs, he had not been granted access to many labs. One had to have special credentials to be admitted into the certain labs that remained locked at all times. These sanctuaries were accessed only with a special card assigned to the most trusted graduate students of the privileged professors reporting directly to Professor Silvers. Furthermore, a card for one of these clandestine labs would not open the doors of other labs at the same level of restriction. But he was working on it.

Joseph knew that his direct supervisor, Professor Chanault, had cards to all the highly restricted rooms. His plan was to suck up to Chanault's top grad assistants and find out how they got access to cards that opened the portals to the most restricted labs. One such Chanault underling, Randy Blumquest, was a short, rotund guy with a congenial manner. He looked something like a large inflated ball with a head and appendages tacked on. Puffy cheeks almost hid his small nose and mouth. Randy's huge jowls overflowed onto the gobs of fat that constituted his shoulders and neck. Only his expressive brown eyes escaped the fate of his other facial features. Joe, as he had begun to think of himself, saw an easy mark. He and Randy were soon the best of buddies.

After several days of small talk, Joe began to query Randy about the restricted labs. At first, Randy was taken aback and only replied in an embarrassed tone, "I … I can't talk about that." Or, "I told you, I'm not supposed to say anything about those labs to anybody." However, the day arrived when Randy had to enter one of the restricted labs when Joe was accompanying him on his rounds. They paused in front of the lab door, and Randy awkwardly looked at Joe as if he was, somehow, supposed to disappear. Rather than retreating, Joe stood his ground and alternated glances from Randy's stricken face to the door-lock mechanism. Finally,

Randy snorted with uncommon aggressiveness, "Go stand over there!" as he pointed to nearby hallway intersection.

Sheepishly, Joe complied with the command, but he backed away to his assigned destination so he could watch Randy open the door and enter the restricted space. Unfortunately, Randy's rotund physique blocked the application of pass-card to the door-lock and even a glimpse of the room's content.

This scene was replayed repeatedly for the next few weeks, with Randy showing the inevitable desensitization that accompanies repetition of emotionally-tinged behaviors. Progressively, Randy began to reveal where he kept his pass-card—in the right-side pocket of his lab jacket—and some contents of the restricted labs. This process was accompanied by Joe's tendency to progressively shorten the distance between where he was supposed to stand and the restricted lab doors. This was accomplished by stopping short of where Randy 's now-automatic thrust of an index finger commanded him to stand. When Randy invariably turned away from him to address the door-locks, Joe simply stopped receding into the distance. In fact, he began to sneak a little bit forward as Randy fumbled with the pass-card. Soon he was standing nearby when Randy opened the restricted-lab doors.

But there was an exception to Randy's declining vigilance. At one particularly secluded hallway which contained only one lab entrance, Randy would look up two or three times as he addressed the door-lock and look menacingly at Joe if he was not at his assigned location far down the hall from the door. This was a special lab that apparently harbored a super-secret project. Joe was going to find a way to get inside this most guarded space.

While Joe and Randy continued to be best buds, Randy's behavior during the restricted lab rounds stabilized.

Occasionally, Randy even allowed Joe to look into some restricted labs. Sometimes he forgot the rules and, being in need of Joe's help, Randy actually called Joe into a few of the labs. But it became clear that Randy had allowed all the access to the restricted labs Joe was going to get. The labs Joe accessed appeared to be so ordinary he wondered why they were restricted.

After a while Joe was bored with Randy's ritual during lab inspections. Because he could devise no plan for getting into the ultra-restricted lab, he did the lab rounds only if Randy asked him. The two still spent time together. Joe would visit with Randy in the graduate student lounge, and occasionally they'd have lunch together. During one of their intermittent meetings, Randy seemed agitated and distracted. When Joe queried his friend about the reason for his angst, Randy just muttered, "It's nothing … just nothing." Joe backed off, but a few minutes later Randy burst forth with "I don't understand this software!" In the ensuing discussion, Randy revealed that he had to periodically check the functioning of the computer system in the lab that had it's own hallway—the super-secret lab. "This software" was a reference to the program that controlled a hub computer in the ultra-restricted lab.

"Why don't you just ask your major professor about using this software?" asked Joe. Randy's extreme embarrassment was revealed by his reddened face and slumped posture. "I can't tell a computer science professor that I don't know how to use a piece of software. I'll look incompetent."

"Look," returned Joe, "some software is made to be difficult so only trained, authorized personnel can use it. It's probably encrypted in some unique way."

"Well my professor assumed I could use the software, and I didn't want to discourage that assumption. When I tried to use it and couldn't, I kept it to myself. That worked until he asked me about the outcome of checking the system with the arcane software. I said that my check using the software revealed that all components of the lab were working effectively. But, what if that's not true? What if things are going from bad to worse? I'll be revealed as a fraud!"

Joe calmed his friend and began to seek a solution that would be mutually beneficial. During a pause in his therapy session with Randy, Joe mused to himself, "If I could find out about the software and use it to check the lab operations, I'd save Randy's butt and maybe discover the function of the lab."

"Ok, so let's figure out how to fix this problem. First, tell me what name or nickname it has and what sort of computer it was used on."

Randy, signed, straightened up and began with, "The computer was one of many built by computer engineers in our department. It is chained to others with the same or similar components. I know this, because I've gotten onto most of them to inspect or repair them. I could build them myself ... hardware is my thing. But the software is of unknown origin ... unknown to me at least. They call it Attila, as in Attila the Hun, because it's the biggest, badest piece of software around. It's also referred to as RD475 or Rude Dude because of the 'RD'."

"Oh yeah, I've heard of that ... in fact, I've used it" interjected Joe, who immediately blanched at the blatant lie to which he had just committed himself. Randy heaved a sigh of relief and excitedly asked, "Well tell me about it." Joe thought quickly and came up with "Uh, well, it's been awhile. I'll have to consult my notes. I'll get back to you very soon." With that he wheeled around and headed for the nearest exit. Randy was left with his mouth open, eyes wide, and a sinking feeling in his gut.

CHAPTER 2

Solving Problems

Joe decided it was time to take his findings to the next periodic meeting of fellow science wonks. He had been to many gatherings at their favorite watering hole since beginning his mission to discover what lay behind the electronically secured doors buried in the Computer Engineering building. But, at each get-together held since he met Randy, Joe parried his friend's excited requests for information with the claim that he didn't yet have enough to talk about.

Now that he was finally about to report on his invasion of the restricted labs, Sarah, Martha, and John were so excited that they neglected their beers in favor of throwing out wild speculations regarding what he would say. Sarah skeptically laughed at how ludicrous it would be if Joe reported that he had gotten access to the time machine. John mildly countered that they should hear Joe out before deciding on the credibility of his report. To Martha, everything is within the realm of possibility—and that includes everything in the realm of science, even if it's estimated probability is infinitesimally small (p = .00000 … 1). How many lifetimes would it take to walk through a solid wall for someone doing nothing else but attempting to breach the wall? Perhaps it would take hundreds or even thousands of lifetimes. So, she reminded the others, time machines are within the realm of possibilities as are innumerable feats, mostly not yet contemplated.

Joe immediately disappointed them all by declaring that he found no hard evidence of a time machine, but that he could access a super-secret lab with an extraordinary system of computers that must have some scientific goal never before conceived, much less approached. After he had filled them in about earning Randy's friendship and confidence, Joe revealed his plan to gain access to the most secretive lab. He now had the ability to follow Randy almost anywhere in the heavily secured part of the Computer Engineering building. That included the student locker room where Joe witnessed Randy carefully placing his lab coat into a locker. Randy's end-of-lab-tour ritual was to make sure the special card that opened the restricted labs was still in the breast pock of his lab-coat before he took his building access card out of the right coat pocket. Only then did he shove the building access card into his large and bulging wallet, hang the coat in the locker, and slam the locker door. Finally, he threaded a padlock into the door handle, spun its dial, yanked the lock downward and pulled it outward, all to make sure that the door was truly locked.

The significant exception to Joe's ability to see all parts of the restricted labs was a room in the most tightly secured lab. Randy made him stand at a location that was positioned so far from the mysterious room's door that Joe could not possibly see inside as Randy entered and closed the door behind him. "I believe that we'll find the time machine behind this door."

Joe's friends were now enthralled by his description of the "secret chamber," as they would come to call the putative home of the "time machine." To help them understand what they would face should they attempt to enter the secret room, he described how Randy opened its door. "He inserts the building access card into lock first, waits a few seconds, and then the swipes the restricted-lab card through the door lock. Obviously, this means we will need both of those cards to enter the time-machine room. I've been promised a building access card soon, but there is no way I will be granted a card to enter the restricted labs. Got any suggestions?"

"Yeah," exclaimed Martha, "why don't you hit your roly-poly friend over the head and steal his card?"

After the giggling subsided, Joe asserted, "We will have to break some rules. Maybe we'll break some laws. It's possible we'll commit so many transgressions that we will be thrown out of our doctoral programs."

The mood change was startling. They had not thought of the possibility that their quest for the time machine would destroy their careers before they were underway. Being able to finish their doctoral programs and land jobs in academe were their most cherished assumptions about their futures.

"But," continued Joe as if he had not seen the disconsolate expressions on their faces, "if we are going to get access to the time machine, we'll have to come up with a detailed, unassailable plan. Let's start with gaining access to the pass-cards?"

After a few somber moments Sarah quietly suggested, "Let's get this Randy guy on our side."

"Hold on, now," said Martha in a tone close to a growl, "are we going to seriously consider doings something that would very likely put an end to our lives as scientists?"

John, who would soon be granted a PhD in a joint psychology-biology neuroscience program, tried to give his friends a broader perspective. "Of course, we won't do this until we have considered all the ethical and practical implications of any plan we might devise. We have serious questions to answer. Can we develop a rationale for exploring the possibility of 'time travel,' a pursuit that would have to be so personally valuable and reasonably likely to succeed that we would risk everything for it? Can we become so enamored with traveling in time that we are willing to accept ultimately dire consequences: being caught trying to use the supposed 'time machine' and lose our careers? Or, given we succeed at time travel, would we become personas non grata in the scientific community because we can't prove our success? Can we justify risking the life of whoever becomes the first time traveler? What if infusing the past with ideas from today affects both time frames badly? Only when these questions are successfully addressed should we ever consider breaking into a secure building on campus in the hope that it contains a usable time machine."

A grim silence followed this heart-felt oration. John had never before spoken to them so ardently or with such clarity and impeccable grasp of the relevant issues. He generally let others do the talking. Though no one said a word in response to his comments, all understood that John had properly laid out the problems that must be solved before they even considered further talk of actually pursuing time travel. They left individually after Sarah suggested that they meet again after each of them had spent time thinking about what had transpired that day.

During the next several days the science gang communicated by email and texting. A plan began to take shape that revolved around getting Randy to be their new best friend. Joe had explained to them that Randy was beyond geek all the way to nerd. He was very smart when dealing with computers, but almost totally lacking in social skills. Consequently, he had no friends prior to meeting Joe. He seemed to be unable to talk about anything but computer issues. When it came to social issues, he was as backward as a toddler. The conversations he could not have were legion. Ask him about politics and he could go no further than naming the current President of the US. If religion comes up, he, like most people, could say "I believe in God," but he could not describe the nature of God or the practices of major religions. When it came to popular culture he couldn't tell you the difference between hip-hop and b-bop. As to Randy's knowledge of how someone of his gender and age should dress, well, all one had to do was look at him. He had worn the same pair of pants everyday that Joe had laid eyes on him. Looking behind all the rips, tears and dirt or food splotches one could make out what looked like army surplus trousers. His belt was made of some kind of elastic material with a buckle that was large and rusted. Fortunately, one could rarely see the buckle, as his ample belly usually hid it from view. He did have a collection of t-shirts dating to the 1990s between which he alternated on a daily basis. These tattered shirts were adorned with everything from peace symbols to Disney characters. Footwear was one pair of sandals worn with heavy socks in the winter and some grungy flip-flops that seemed to have become integrated with the soles of his feet. His only coat looked like it had been ripped off Chairman Mao.

When Joe first met Randy, he had to stand a few feet away from computer engineering PhD candidate. The scent Randy emitted was high on the barnyard smell-scale. To deal with this problem, over a period of time, Joe gently convinced Randy that people would approach him more closely and be more willing to talk with him if he bathed at least a few times a week and washed his clothes at least weekly. Joe even gave his new pal some of his infrequently worn clothes. Sadly, Randy still favored his usual attire over the gifted outfits. He said that he was saving the latter for "special occasions."

Ah, but Randy's awkwardness in the presence of women truly intrigued Joe. On several occasions, he caught Randy sneaking a peak at some woman. But if caught in the act by a target of his glance, he quickly turned away and seemed to be looking for a place to hide. After a few displays of this timid behavior, Joe bluntly asked, "Don't you like women?" Randy blushed and muttered that he very much liked women, but they "don't like me." Joe tried to help by modeling some "striking up a conversation" behavior. When that effort failed to inspire Randy to approach women, Joe concentrated on helping the awkward young man develop rudimentary social skills.

After everyone had time to contemplate the issues raised by plans to invade restricted university facilities, a meeting was held at the Lion's Den. The usual gregariousness was absent when the group settled into seats near the bar. Beers and munches were neglected as each person waited for someone else to speak. Finally, Sarah broke the silence with a question: "Joe, tell us all you know about this guy, Randy." Joe described Randy's deficiencies in social skills, personal hygiene, relating to the opposite gender and knowledge of proper attire. He went on to suggest that Randy longed for friendships, but almost certainly had none. 'Well, none until he met me."

"So," said Martha, "we should hover around him and pretend to be his friends so we can use him to gain access to the putative time machine?"

"I hope that is not what we end up doing," interjected John. "We have to get to know Randy so we can make a proposal to him including outcomes that would be good for him. We should also inform him about the risks he may face should he choose to work with us."

"And just how would we benefit him?" queried Martha.

John, the psychological science representative in the group, paused for a moment and then firmly stated, "We can't make him into Prince Charming ... his deficiencies are too well established. However, some of us may actually become friends with him. Joe considers him a friend. If he gains other friends from our group, it could immensely improve the quality of his life."

"And how about the serious problems we may create for him?" offered Sarah. "If he helps us and the whole thing blows up in our faces, he will join us in the academic bone yard."

John responded, "We will have to make sure Randy understands the dangers he will face should he agree to cooperate with us. If he is not willing to accept the risks, we will have to step down and that will be the end of this whole 'time travel' pipe dream. Further, once he learns what we plan to do, he could decide to report us to his professors. If he does, we will be dismissed from our programs and may even face criminal charges. Recruiting Randy is fraught with dangers for all of us."

"So, now where are we?" asked Sarah. "This whole thing is not making sense to me."

"Me either," returned John, "but there is a way we can find out whether he would willing join us. Maybe Joe could talk Randy into allowing me to accompany the two of them during inspections of the restrictive computer science labs.

Randy wants friends. I have been able to offer my friendship to almost anyone."

"Ok with me," said Joe, "but he is very suspicious and cautious. We will have to come up with some reason for you to accompany us as we inspect the ...."

"I think I have a reason that might work," interrupted John. "You talked earlier about how frustrated Randy was with the RD475 software used to check on the computer systems in the most restricted lab. I happened to understand it as we used it in some brain research. RD is difficult and counter-intuitive, but since I used it repeatedly, I know it quite well. It was essential to our research into the coordination of brain systems during the performance of prospective memory tasks. That's, for example, trying to remember a grocery list you composed at home after you arrive at the grocery store without it. The Rude Dude software allowed us to coordinate fMRI images so that we could plot relationships between brain systems involved in prospective memory. I can show him how to get around the quirks of the RD software."

The faces of John's friends revealed enhanced respect for him. Joe, who previously had little interest in "whatever psychological researchers do" was clearly impressed. After getting over his amazement, Joe accepted John's offer without hesitation. "I'll talk to Randy about it tomorrow."

Martha mischievously offered a quip to close the conservation: "Hey Joe, why didn't you decipher the RD software for Randy?"

With a malicious look that was once characteristic of Joseph, Joe growled, "Hardware is my thing, as is also true of Randy."

"So," continued Martha, who never tired of needling haughty people, "you concede that a psychological scientist knows software better than you, a computer scientist?"

Before Joe fully completed his transition back to Joseph, John intervened: "Hold on now. I'm not claiming to be good at software. In fact, there were people on our project who taught me the RD software and were available to help when I got lost in its complexities. I only know it well because I used it for hundreds of hours over many months."

As the gang gathered up their belongings and prepared to leave the Den, Martha facial expression reflected mock irritation with John for spoiling her fun. He flashed her his partial smile showing no teeth and eyes closed to slits. It was his way of telling her "enough of your mischief making." Laughing about it later opened a conversation that centered on how Joseph was becoming a better person after being forced to allow people to call him Joe and becoming Randy's friend and mentor. Alternatively, perhaps Joe's pretentiousness had more to do with how he was raised by his plutocratic parents than with his more basic nature. Working with Randy may have brought out Joe's more socially sensitive self. In fact, John was impressed with Joe's social skills. He revealed himself to be so socially adept that he could not only win over a friendless person, but also instruct him regarding productive ways to behave during encounters with other people. "I'm an experimental psychologist, and thus, don't know much about clinical psychology. But, I know enough to believe that Joe might have been an effective clinical psychologist. He has subtle sensitivities and genuine concerns about people, along with the smarts that one needs to be a good clinical psychologist."

"Aw, you're saying that Joe could become one of the true psychologists, people who do some kind of psychotherapy."

"That's the public view of psychologists, but it's inaccurate. Clinical psychologists—those who help people with mental and emotional problems—constitute about half of all psychologists. However, a great many of us are either experimentalists actively involved in research, or professionals who teach and/or apply the findings of experimental psychology. But, because of public figures like Joyce Brothers, Bob Newhart and Dr. Phil, most people think of us as therapists."

"Now I get it," exclaimed Martha. "Most of you experimental psychologists run rats in mazes, plant electrodes in brains, secretly measure people's prejudices or use results of these pursuits in practical applications or teaching."

John threw up his hands and announced, "I teach you and teach you, but, as smart as you are, there are some things you'll never get."

"I could inform you about some of the dumb things physicists do, if it will make you feel better," offered Martha as she started to run for the door. John pretended to chase her for a few steps, but stopped and waved goodbye to her.

John and Joe began immediately working on how to convince Randy to let John join them on their visits to the restricted labs. Joe believed just telling Randy that John could end his problems with the RD software wouldn't be enough. Something else was needed and Joe knew that John would have reservations about what he had in mind: Joe would have to sell Randy on "making a new friend." Just as everyone who knew John would expect, when told about Randy's plan, John backed away and exclaimed, "I won't pretend to be someone's friend in order to use him."

Joe countered with a remainder that Randy was really a good person who needed and deserved friends. The problem was, he didn't know how to make friends. Anyone who helped him with that skill by befriending him would be performing an act of kindness and gaining a loyal and true friend. "If you get to know him you'll like him. There is a certain innocence and lack of guile about him that is rare and fetching."

CHAPTER 3

Getting Ready to Get Ready

Joe waited patiently for Randy to bring up the RD software so he could suggest how the vexing problem could be solved. One day during rounds in the restricted lab area, upon entering the super-secret lab, Randy was cursing under his breath about checking the lab systems using the RD software. "I'll never know how to get this right," he mumbled as he approached the master computer to bring up the RD software. He fiddled around for few minutes then left the computer with a sour look on his face.

"Having trouble again?" asked Joe in a sympathetic voice. Randy sheepishly nodded.

Joe slipped into this opening very quickly. "Let me get this guy I know to help you figure out the hateful RD software."

"Ok," sighed Randy, "When can you take me to his lab so he can tell me what I'm doing wrong?"

"Oh, we can't do that ... his research using the RD software is done and the lab where the research was completed doesn't exist anymore. He'll need to come here to show you how to use the software."

Randy, turned very pale and gasped, "We can't bring him here! It's bad enough that I'm letting you into these labs. I can't take any more chances."

"Look, this guy is very trustworthy. You trust me, right? I trust him and know him very well. You can count on him to keep quiet about what little he'll see as he helps you with the software."

"No. Forget it," Randy replied in a sad whisper. "I'll just have to face the humiliation when my professors find out that I can't really use the software."

"There's no need to do that," exclaimed Joe. "Look at the other side of the coin. If you master this software, you can look very good in the eyes of your professors, instead of very bad, if they happen to be around while you are using it."

"I can't! I can't!" he moaned as his hands covered the sides of his head.

Joe thought better of continuing his persuasive efforts. He would wait until Randy was more in control of his emotions.

Over the course of the next week, the topic of the RD software came up several times. On each occasion Randy froze up and refused to consider Joe's proposal. However, in time, the repeated allusion to John's trustworthiness and his RD software expertise caused Randy to become desensitized to the threat of introducing yet another outsider into the most secret lab. Finally, Randy relented and suggested that John could join them during the next session of lab checks.

When Joe introduced Randy to John at the entrance to the computer science building, John extended his hand in greeting. Randy carefully wiped his hand on his pants and offered it to John, who noted that it was clammy and quivered noticeable. Gaining Randy's trust him would be a challenge.

John's first few rounds of the restricted labs with Randy and Joe were a replay of Joe's initiation into the secret recesses of the science building. Although Joe now routinely followed Randy into all of the secret labs, John was made to wait outside. This replay of Joe's early days in the restricted lab portion of the computer science building lasted many days, but felt like weeks to John. Partly due to Joe's badgering—"This is absurd. We're wasting time. Don't you want to get help with the RD software?"—Randy relented earlier for John than had been the case for Joe.

Randy was particularly nervous when John entered the most secret lab for the first time. Although the new initiate was allowed into the main room of this mysterious lab, Randy altered his usual routine of slipping into the adjoining room where Joe believed the time machine was housed. Instead Randy led John straight to the computer that ran the RD software. After bringing up the cranky software, he told John what he needed to do with it. John stepped forward and made a show of moving the cursor around the screen and activating various components of the software. After several minutes of this contrived exhibition, he pointed to the monitor screen where an announcement indicated that all systems governed by the computer were operating up to specifications. He then tutored Randy on how to use the RD software to check out the computer systems. Randy's problem had been his assumption that, like other software, RD should be intuitively easy to figure out. John disabused him of this reasonable assumption with the declaration, "This software includes some illogical sequences of steps that one can only learn by being told about them and going through them repeatedly. That's what I had to do to master the Rude Dude. Making it is difficult to learn is probably by design: it's arcane nature would discourage unauthorized people from using it, much less trying to figure out how to replicate it." Several lessons later Randy was checking out the computer systems quickly and effectively.

At the next meeting, after the usual libations had been laid out in front of them, the conservation shifted to what else had to be accomplished before it became possible to attempt use of the time machine. "Well," began Sarah, "all of us will have to become involved in the most secret lab. But, do we first induce Randy to allow all of us into that inner-sanctum and then tell him about our plan to use the machine, or do we tell him about the plan first?"

"Martha responded with, "Let's just tell him the whole thing up front and get it over with."

"Absolutely not," responded Joe. "He'll freak-out and probably slam the door on all of us. I think that we should introduce just one more to him for now, and, after he's acclimated to her, bring in the last of us. Then we'll bring up the time-travel plan."

"Yeah, I think Joe's right," offered John. "There's a bit of irony here. Randy would love to get to know a woman, but he's scared to death of doing it. My suggestion is to bring in Sarah first, because she's easy going and speaks likes a logician, which will appeal to Randy."

Martha's mouth flew open, her eyes bulged and she flung her hands out in front of her, palms up. The hurt in her voice was obvious when she asked, "Would you leave me behind?"

"No, no," John was almost shouting, "you'll be included, but initially it would be better not to threaten Randy. He might melt down in the presence of you and Sarah at the same time."

Now Martha was steaming. She growled, "Let me see if I've got this right. You want to introduce Sarah first because, unlike me, she's emotionally stable and she is also much more rational than me."

In utter exasperation John exclaimed, "I'm not saying that she is better than you, Martha, just different in a way that fits our situation here: keeping Randy from imploding and getting on his good side."

Sarah interrupted at this point. "Look, John, you're making too much of this. Why don't both of us meet him at the same time. We'll make it work."

John interjected, "Now Sarah, you don't know this guy like Joe and I do. He's very threatened by people in general and women in particular. He'll freak out … we've seen him do it."

"Ok," returned Sarah, "I'll wait … Martha can meet him first."

"That won't work," returned Joe. "I agree with John, you will be less threatening than Martha."

Martha stomped off, head down, arms limp at her side. John ran after her. She heard him coming and wheeled around. With hands clinched into fists she shouted, "I hate you!" He stopped in his tracks. Past experience told him that trying to reason with her now would only make matters worse.

It took a couple of days for Joe and John to convince Randy that Sarah would be a good addition to their lab-checking team. They assured him that she was real smart and could help them figure out any problems that arose. Randy responded, "What problems?".

"Well," returned Joe, "remember when you couldn't figure out why one of the restricted labs looked different and worried that some unauthorized person had gotten past the security system?"

Randy responded, "Yeah, I do remember that."

"I took the problem to Sarah, without, of course, revealing anything about the top secret equipment and research records contained in the labs. She said, 'Aren't there other people with keys who might have entered the rooms?' We talked about it some more and she concluded that it must be one of the computer science professors accessing the secret rooms late at night or early in the morning to do some work or to check on something."

"So, it was this Sarah, not you, who figured it out?"

"Yes," gulped Joe. Once again he had constructed a fib to get himself out of a tight spot.

"Can we trust her?"

"Of course," said Joe with emphasis. "I've known her for a long time. She'll be an asset and won't tell anyone about what she sees. But here's something you will have to understand: You can't test her like you did with John and I. You'll just have to let her into the rooms with the rest of us. If you don't, well, it could get dicey."

Randy's pupils dilated for a moment and he looked alarmed. But he didn't protest.

Randy steeled himself in advance for the day when Sarah would accompany Joe and John to the computer science building. He wanted to feel relaxed, nonchalant, even laidback when she showed up, but he knew that, in all likelihood, he would be rattled. When Sarah arrived with Joe and John, they were surprised that she had relatively little effect on Randy. Her soft tone of voice and relaxed posture assured him that she was the kind of person who accepted people no matter who they were. She extended her hand and introduced herself with "Hello. I'm Sarah. Pleased to meet you." Randy hesitated only for a moment before he grasped her hand gently. He was surprised at how soft it was and he held it for a moment before reluctantly releasing it.

In only a few days Sarah was fully integrated into the circle of Randy's only friends. During rounds, she asked him questions about the labs—mostly what kinds of research was done in them and about the equipment. Randy loved informing her about the labs and their functions. He was providing her with information that had never been offered to John and Joe in response to their questions. In a very short time, her questions got more information out of Randy than they had accumulated over months. Outside the labs, such as at lunch, Randy opened up about himself and chatted enthusiastically during any topic that came up. Sarah's mere presence was transforming Randy from a social dud to a reasonably proficient conversationalist.

At the gang's next get-together, despite the late-Spring temperatures outdoors and in the Lion's Den, there was a chill in the air. It was hard to carry on a discussion when Martha would not sit near or talk to John, much less acknowledge anything he said or was addressed to him. John sat rigidly on the edge of his chair and said nothing except to answer questions. Finally, just before he felt his head would part company with his torso, John cut into the conversation to announce that it was time to introduce Martha to Randy. Martha immediately rose from her chair as if to leave. Sensing an embarrassing public melee was seconds away, Joe and Sarah grabbed Martha's arms and ushered her to a far corner of the Den. John couldn't hear what transpired, but he could see the discussion was highly animated. Eventually they calmed Martha and reasoned with her. When they returned to the others, Martha looked bedraggled and exhausted, but seemed resigned to whatever transpired next.

It was agreed that Martha was to be introduced to Randy during the next restricted-lab rounds. Randy was to be informed that there was one more person to join their group. No one knew what his reactions would be, but John, Sarah and Joe agreed that Randy would ultimately allow the addition of Martha.

The conversation turned to whether Randy should know about their plan to use the time machine before Martha was introduced or after. Joe opined that it would be best to inform Randy about the time travel plan before introducing Martha. He reasoned that Randy was reaching his limits on participating in career threatening activities. If he agreed to their use of the time travel machine first and then refused to include Martha, they would at least have a go-ahead on their main mission.

John immediately objected to this line of reasoning. "I've come to know Randy very well. He loves hanging out with his new friends. He will welcome another member to his group. Martha is an especially good addition, because he is working on his sense of humor. One couldn't ask for a better witticism coach than Martha."

"I agree," said Sarah. "With the addition of Martha he will value us too much to refuse our time travel plan out of hand. We will convince him together."

"But you know what we're talking about? Our only interest in him is to use him. We ferret into his life, rummage around for what we can get from him, then, after we use him, we abandon him? It's not right, especially since we would be setting him up to lose everything. By now, we have implicitly or explicitly chosen to risk everything, but we are going to leave him with no choice."

"I agree with your reasoning," interjected Sarah, "but I believe you are referring to a fait accompli, not an open decision. We have already decided for Randy. We did that when we first wormed our way into his confidence in the interest of our time travel adventure. We've placed him in danger. Now it is our duty to protect him as much as we can. If we pull off this outrageously improbable venture, he will be saved along with all of us. If not, he goes down with us. The dirty deed is done." If there is anything such as group guilt, it was displayed on the faces of everyone present.

When John, Sarah, and Joe broached the question of adding Martha to their group, Randy was flabbergasted. He threw up his hands, sighed heavily and clumsily dropped his humongous rump onto a pile of empty boxes. It took all three of them to hoist him back to an upright position. They all knew instantly that when they asked for access to and use of the time machine, he was either going to have a heart attack or simply give in.

Relative to Joe, John and Sarah, Martha was integrated into the lab-rounds group very quickly. In fact, she became Randy's favorite almost instantly. At lunch, they whispered and grinned continuously. When they laughed at one another's remarks, their howling hit such a high decibel level that others in their vicinity glared at them with obvious distain. Randy had finally become a genuine social being, albeit one who had no need for social niceties.

In contrast, John and Martha continued to be estranged. Martha no longer excluded him from her consciousness, or from their group conservations, but she was careful to do no more than acknowledge his remarks. She did not address him directly and made sure they did not sit or stand next to one another.

Finally, during a meeting at the Lion's Den, when John found himself near to her but at some distance from the others, he impulsively grabbed her by the shoulders and gave her a big huge. She did nothing for a moment, but when she gently pushed away and turned to leave, he was sure that he saw a grin forming on the corners of her mouth.

The others heard a mild scuffling as the two embraced, and then parted. Sarah declared, "Thank God that's over."

Joe responded, "Amen."

It was their way of expressing the group's feelings about the welcomed end of the only breach among them.

Now that all five of them were doing the lab rounds, Randy became quite blasé with regard to allowing the gang into restricted labs, with one exception: the secret room within the most restricted lab was off limits. He repeatedly said that he would not let them see the insides of this apparently hallowed place. "It would be the ultimate violation of the trust my professors have in me." He went on to say that it would almost certainly end his pursuit of a doctorate in computer science. Joe, Sarah, John and Martha declared, almost in unison, that they were also resisting their professional lives by, in effect, breaking into the computer science building and gaining entrances into restricted spaces. Randy was unmoved.

As persuasion had failed to gain the group's admission into the most secret area within the most restricted lab, they decided on begging, pleading and, if necessary, forcing their way past Randy into the secret inner lab. The next time they were all in the most restricted lab, they surrounded Randy, and began to bagger him about admittance into the inner lab. He was flustered to be sure, especially since he didn't want to disappoint Sarah and Martha, but he did not yield. Upon breaking away from them, he tried to apply the two cards to the inner lab door before they could interfere, but as he opened the door, they swarmed past him. He tried desperately to grab Sarah and Joe and push them back through the door. This effort not only failed, it allowed John and Martha to flick on the lights and surge past him. Gasping for breath, Randy fell back against the wall near the door. He looked like a man faced with a firing squad. His hands were tied. He could not stop the disaster that would surely end his professional life.

At first the room looked ordinary and disappointing to the foursome who had so rudely barged past Randy. They saw the blinking lights that one would expect in a computer lab. Those lights predominately came from what must have been the mainframe computer. It had several modules, each about 6 feet in height, by 2.5 feet across and about 5 feet in depth. These units were wired together and cables coming from the top of their front surfaces were strung across the ceiling. This mass of wiring converged into a single coil that traversed the ceiling and terminated at the back of a computer terminal.

So, the room had a big computer. No surprise there. But off in one corner was a large, darkened, round container with cables from the terminal inserted into its top. "What's that," asked Martha. Randy rasped, "I can't say." John made a beeline to the light switch by the door and pushed down all of the unengaged switches. Immediately the entire room was fully and brightly illuminated. Now they all could see that the container was actually a chamber with a couple of windows in it and a rounded top. Access to its insides was enabled by a door with a strange and imposing latch. Arrayed around the door was what appeared to be a continuous seal that looked impervious to the escape of any substances no matter how microscopic.

CHAPTER 4

Time Machine

The four would-be time travelers strolled around the room taking in every detail of it and mumbling to each other about how the "time machine" didn't look like they had thought it would.

After Randy got over being pummeled and pushed aside, he showed a level of anger never before displayed in their presence. He yelled at them, berating them for their "imbecilic beliefs about something that is never going to happen!"

"This is not a time machine. It's a piece of junk." He bellowed. "My professors haven't destroyed it because they have siphoned off federal money from various government grants to build it. They don't know what to do with the dilemma it poses for them. If they are asked to verify how the money was spent, they will need something to show the government people. But engaging in this accountability process would mean they'd have to disclose what the machine was designed to do. That would be confessing misappropriating and squandering government money on science-fiction nonsense. They'd be fired and maybe jailed.

So, they keep maintaining this pile of trash until they decide what to do."

"Shocked" would be a way to describe the expressions on the faces of the four science devotees. But it doesn't suffice to describe how they felt after Randy's tirade. They were so obsessed with time travel it had become a part of who they were. Expressions of doubt had been overtly mouthed by each of them, but at a more non-conscious, emotional level, time travel became real and doable to them. They would be in a state of mourning for days.

Even in the midst of all this misery they had to get-it-together in order to soften the devastating blow they had dealt Randy. After recovering from his rant enough to think coherently, they gathered around him and whispered their regrets along with sincere apologies. Randy did not respond. Stripped of his anger, he was reduced to raw depression. He could not accept that they had posed as his friends solely to find and use the so-called "time machine." After repeated offers to walk him home failed to elicit a response, they coaxed him into the hallway, locked the doors of the most restricted lab and left him slumped against the wall.

Days passed with no interactions among the four grad-students. Nor did any of them attempt to seek out Randy. Finally, John and Sarah happened to find themselves on the same campus pathway. They greeted one another mildly and sought a place where they could sit down to chat. After finding a bench nearby they began to dissect the tragedy they and their friends had wrought. In a short time they both promised to find Randy and to personally proclaim that their friendship with him was genuine.

Within a few weeks, Randy was meeting with them at the Lion's Den. At meetings there, the bond among them was as strong as ever, but the swagger, humor and spontaneity that had characterized them was no longer evident. They seemed to be in a perpetual state of grief.

Inevitably, with time, the despondent emotions dissipated and conversations occasionally returned to time travel. Each at one time or another expressed a disclaimer that they had never really believed time travel was possible. But reading between the lines of what they were now saying, it became evident that they all longed for the good old days when, at some level, each harbored the belief that the veil of time could be penetrated.

This revelation reopened the conservation about time travel. Eventually, Randy began to disclose more about the history of the abandoned time-travel project. When asked whether the time travel machine had ever been tried, Randy replied that rumors were all he knew regarding the project. He was not close enough to the professors who ran the project to be trusted with first hand, factual information. If computer science graduate students who were close to those professors were asked about the project, they would simply respond with something to the effect of "That's proprietary information ... I can't discuss it."

Eventually, the four science buffs began to question Randy about the rumors. At first he only scoffed: the rumors were unconfirmed, and were, from a scientific perspective, ludicrous. Yet, the emotional spasms that once accompanied his refusals to provide information about the time machine were progressively tempered and then altogether absent. Randy now believed that the intrusion into the time-machine lab would be discovered and they all would be dismissed from their graduate programs. What good was it to conceal what he knew when they were professionally doomed no matter what he told them about the project?

So, on one occasion, when, for the umpteenth time, he was asked about the rumors, he responded with, "They tried to send a lab rat just one day into the future." Bug-eyes, audible gasps and exhilarated postures signaled that his friends' dormant excitement over time travel was reawakened. They swarmed around him, begging for details. He responded with, "Come on, let's find a private spot to talk."

He led them to a deserted area near campus where some benches had been placed on a grassy knoll near a clump of trees. "First," he said in a rather authoritarian tone, "What I'm about to tell you is a rumor and may not be true at all. Second, even if the rumor is true, it's about another snafu in a long series of failures. Nothing about the time travel project ever worked." Looking at his friends, Randy knew that they were unimpressed with his disclaimer. They were children wanting to know how the fairy tale ended.

"As the rumor goes," continued Randy, "they placed a rat with a id tag in one ear into the machine's chamber and sent it to a place in this surrounding forest. Of course, they checked the chamber after sending the rat. It showed no signs the rodent had been there: no body parts, no flesh or fur, nothing. The next day they gathered at the location to which the rat was supposed to arrive. The arrival time passed and no rat showed. End of story."

His friends looked blankly at him, expecting more, but he said only "that's it … all of it."

Sarah was the first to speak up: "But before we can conclude that the attempt failed, we have to rule out alternative explanations."

"Yeah," said Joe. "Maybe the coordinates for the arrival site were incorrectly entered or perhaps the machine was unable to precisely place the animal."

"Aw, come on!" exclaimed Randy, "A typo? You got to be kidding. And the rat was not precisely sent to the selected spot? If this machine can send a rat somewhere, it can certainly send it to an exact spot."

Sarah broke in, "A rat is fairly small and capable of scurrying off unnoticed by even a careful observer."

"Why didn't they put a bell around its' neck?" interjected Martha, tongue firmly in cheek.

John followed up with, "All of these points are valid. Maybe the rat made the trip but was not precisely placed, or it got away unnoticed, or maybe it was sent to another location."

Randy, who had been confident that his rendition of the rat rumor would convince his friends to give up on time-travel, clasped his hands on the back of his head in apparent exasperation. "I cannot believe this. You'll resort to the most shallow reasoning to rescue the time travel myth." Randy was well on his way to giving up agonizing over their obsession with time travel.

He patiently humored his friends repeated attempts to get more rumors out of him. To appease them he revealed what he considered to be an even more ridiculous rumor. "I heard that on one occasion they put some kind of animal in the time machine chamber and when they hit the switch, the creature disintegrated into millions of bloody bits." But they responded with looks of horror rather than with signs of disbelief. He comforted them by insisting that the "exploded rat" tale was one of the most absurd rumors he had heard. This ploy, and all others Randy contrived, failed to dissuade them from pursuing time travel. They persistently nagged him to help them break into the most secure lab's computer in an attempt to discover its' procedure for time travel. Always he refused, but in a rather mild way that convinced them he would eventually give in and help them with the computer.

One day in the Lion's Den they were chatting about this and that, nothing of any import. Randy was scanning the room as he put in his two cents about whatever topic was being discussed. He noticed a very obese young woman leaning up against the bar across the room. While he was watching her he noticed that others in the room would glance toward her periodically, but look away very quickly. It was as if they had seen an ugly blemish on the convivial scene and wanted to deny its presence. Finally, he was looking at her so often that his friends noticed. When they realized who he was looking at, they became embarrassed.

He could read in their faces what they were thinking. He had to challenge them. "When you were growing up, how many of you had a friend who looked like her?" Everyone cranked their heads down as if to study the carvings on the tabletop, but no one answered. Randy persisted: "Ok, raise your hand if you had a friend in elementary school or high school who looked like her." No hands went up. Randy met this silence with "I don't doubt that you are my friends. But I know that people who look like her and me have few friends because no one ever gets to know us. They don't approach us to find out what we think and feel about important issues. Only when something forces them to approach us do we have a chance to make a friend."

This episode not only created more respect for Randy on the part of his friends, it also reminded them that it was wrong to badger him about invading the time machine's computer. They said nothing more about it for weeks. During this time they seemed to be sinking back into the state of depression to which they succumbed following Randy's revelation that the time machine project had failed. Finally, Randy could take it no more. He got them altogether and announced that he would help them crack the time machine computer. He was immediately subjected to his first group hug.

The obvious first step to learning how to operate the time machine was to access the software that controls it's computer. Obviously, the controlling software would be heavily protected. Randy and Joe conducted a preliminary search and turned up nine possibilities. Cursory attempts to open these nine pieces of software failed. They prevailed on John to help them, but he assured them that he would have no idea which possibilities were more promising, much less be able to come up with needed passwords. So, Randy prevailed on a fellow computer science grad student who was known to be good at cracking passwords. Like others who practiced the fine art of deciphering passwords, the student never inquired about how the information she provided was going to be used. After agreeing to help, she asked for all the information Randy and Joe could provide about the people who regularly used the passwords they wanted decrypted. The list of people known to access the time machine software was rather long: seven professors and four graduate assistants. Randy or Joe or both knew some of these people rather well, and some not so well. It took extensive detective work to reveal some of the hobbies, favorite musical artists and other personal information about these eleven people and their family members. Other interests and pursuits for which the eleven people were known were also submitted. Much information was found for some of the targeted eleven and rather little for others.

When the password cracker received the info about the eleven users of the targeted software, she asked for several days to come up with some possible passwords. The passwords she finally supplied did open some of the nine suspected pieces of software, but the passwords for the others remained mysteries. None of the password-protected pieces of software that were successfully opened proved to be related to control of the time machine. A new strategy was needed, but no one was able to provide it. This was a very discouraging start to the quest for control of the time machine.

More days passed without anyone having a clue about how to crack the password for the time machine-controlling software. Despair was setting in. In the midst of this discouraging time, Randy found a sliver of paper stuck under one edge of the keyboard for the computer in the time machine room. Written on it was what appeared to be a password. His immediate reaction was to dismiss his discovery: the "password" might not actually be a password at all, or if it was, the odds were against it being the password to the software they wished to open. Nevertheless, he used it to attempt opening the remaining candidates for the software that controlled the time machine. When he got to the last of the suspected software, Randy was convinced his discovery was useless. To his amazement, the password worked on this last-resort piece of software. It came up quickly and looked promising. But he didn't want to explore it himself. Instead, he tucked the piece of paper under the keyboard exactly as he found it, closed the software and the shutdown the computer. He had never before felt such exhilaration. Though it was 5:00 AM, he decided to wake up his friends. This couldn't wait.

He contacted all of them and told them to meet him at the Forum, a free speech area on the periphery of the campus. When all four gathered around him, Randy talked excitedly about the possibility that the time-machine controlling software had been discovered. First they had to confirm that what Randy opened actually controlled the time machine. They might be able to do that by playing around with the software to observe whether it had any effects on the time machine. But that would be the easy part. Learning whether they could actually use the machine to send some creature, perhaps another rat, to a different point in time would be the real challenge.

Joe speculated that they would have to get into the code to decipher how to actually test the machine.

"That's a problem," indicated Martha. "We don't have a software expert on our team."

"That's not really a problem ... too much has been made of mine and Joe's preference for dealing in hardware." Returned Randy. "Of course we can understand and write code. Any computer science undergraduate can do that. In fact, many experienced computer users can write code, even if they are not formally trained in computer science. Probably John can write some code." John nodded in the affirmative. "So, let's meet tonight in the time machine control room and see what we can do."

That evening they brought up the suspected software on the control room computer and began to debate about how best to approach trying to get the software to arouse some component of the time machine. The computer screen was full of many presumably active portals to various operations. Some were not readily decipherable, such as an icon on the computer monitor screen inscribed with "Set props now," but others seemed more obvious. "Maybe this software is not purposefully cranky like the Rude Dude," suggested Sarah. "After all, the software we're looking at here was made to control a machine that is behind three levels of security. Could be the software we're considering here is more intuitive and straightforward."

To test that option, they searched the computer screen and found an icon with the inscription "Activate global systems." Martha declared, "Let's try this one." All agreed. When Joe placed the cursor on the icon and clicked the mouse key, lights came on in the chamber and faint sounds were heard. There were spontaneous screams of delight. After shushing one another, they huddled around the chamber in a state of awe and wonder.

Now they knew for sure they had found the software that controlled the time machine. But how to use the machine to transport some creature into another timeframe would be a tough nut to crack. They left it up to Randy and Joe to figure out how to actually use the machine. The two would begin work immediately to tinker with the software and, with unwitting help from their fellow computer science grad students whose minds they would pick, they would figure out how to actually use the time machine software.

CHAPTER 5

The First Time Traveler?

The primary task for Joe and Randy was figuring out what questions must be answered in order to achieve a full understanding of procedures for launching a time traveler. They examined the code written to operate the functions of various hyperlinks displayed on the computer screen. In each case they posed questions regarding what kind of processes were enabled by the code associated with the hyperlinks. If they were not satisfied with their own answers to particular questions, they took the questions to fellow computer science grad students. Should they still not be satisfied with the answers they had obtained, they would have to go back to the drawing board. Asking their professors for help was too scary: it might arouse suspicions regarding what they were trying to accomplish. Their professors might even realize that they had gained access to the time machine and were trying to figure out how to use it.

Eventually, Randy and Joe called a meeting of the gang at the grassy knoll area near the forest where, allegedly, a rat had been sent on a one-day trip into the future. In opening comments, they informed their friends that they had been researching the sequence of events that might end in a launch of a time traveler. After consulting with fellow graduate students, they felt reasonably sure they had discovered a chain of processes reflected in the software code that ended in the initiation of a time travel episode. The sequence they had discovered began a process that checked each stage of the launch sequence leading up to the actual initiation of a launch. A starter hyperlink begins the first check of the time machine apparatus. After this first check is completed successfully, a statement appears on the screen giving the green light to proceed to the second check and a hyperlink to activate the second check appears. This process must be repeated through a total of seven checks. After completion of the seventh check, a green light to begin a launch appears on the screen followed by the launch hyperlink.

When they completed their report, there was silence for a moment. Finally, Martha asked, "Did you try to launch something?"

"Of course not!" returned Randy. "That would be something we would all do."

When queried about their estimates of the probability that a launch attempt would be successful, Joe and Randy simply indicated, "We'll just have to try it and see what happens."

Plans to select the creature that would be used in an attempted launch began immediately. A laboratory rat was chosen for time travel, and, like the alleged original launch attempt, it would be sent one day into the future. Next they opened a discussion about the particulars of the launch. The rat was to be transported to a location not far from where they were presently standing. It was to be recovered the day after the launch by fitting it with a device used by naturalists to track migratory animals. John was to borrow that device and a companion locater-instrument from friends in biology who were studying wild life. Two nights from the present time they would carryout the launch. They would gather in the chamber lab at 11:00 PM and expect to start the launch by 11:30 PM.

Because they knew the topic of discussion would be the launch attempt, the next afternoon they selected a secluded corner of the Lion's Den for a pre-launch celebration. After a few beers dissolved their attempts to suppress intense emotions generated by trepidations about the pending launch and giddy anticipations of it, they began to offer speculations concerning their chances of success. Of course, Randy was the most skeptical. He said the project had been labeled a failure and a potential disaster, if for no other reason, on ethical grounds. Whether or not a rat could be transported into the near future, it was morally unacceptable to risk the life of a human being in the off chance of success at attempts to reach the more distance future or past. And, added Sarah, they had yet to consider whether it would be possible to bring back a person who had been transported into the distant future or past. John shrugged and opined that ethical objections might be mitigated if the person to be transported was willing to accept the dangers accompanying time travel. Martha seemed unable to accept risking a human life regardless of the expressed willingness on the part of a volunteer time traveler to face the dangers he or she would encounter. For Joe, risking a human life in attempting a feat that, if successful, would challenge major assumptions of science, and perhaps change many of them, posed too much of a dilemma. He could not decide. Sarah was of two minds on the issue. On the one hand, there had been a long history of astronauts accepting the risks of space travel. Hundreds of thousands of people, if not millions, continue to be willing to travel in space, regardless of the risk. The same would surely be true for recruiting risk-accepting volunteers to travel in time. Thus, meeting John's criterion for ethical recruitment of time travelers would be no problem. On the other hand, 15 US astronauts had died attempting to travel outside the earth's atmosphere. One was a schoolteacher. Several Russians, an Israeli and a person from India also died. And that doesn't count astronauts killed during training. Inducing people to travel in space or in other dimensions, under the assumption that they clearly accept the risk, becomes more and more indefensible as the odds of survival approach zero. This last pronouncement on attempted time travel left everyone feeling glum. Nevertheless, they adjourned with a commitment to carry out the planned launch of a lesser mammal.

That night sleep for the five friends came late and ended early. Participants in the planned launch blew off classes and other graduate student duties in one way or another. Martha and Joe didn't show up to their graduate classes and duties at all. Randy and Sarah showed up to carry out their grad student obligations, but their minds were elsewhere. John showed a mix of these proclivities: he showed up for the two undergraduate classes he taught, but he failed to report for lab duties. Mainly they consulted their watches, nibbled on snacks and walked like automatons through their day. Even before 11:00 PM all had assembled at a secluded entrance to the computer science building. Once inside, they made sure there was no evidence that anyone else was in the building. Then they headed to the most-restricted lab as fast as walking on cat feet would allow. Once inside the chamber room, Randy and Joe huddled around the time-machine computer and began preparing to go through the launch sequence. John retrieved the rat from his jacket pocket and examined it to make sure the signal emitter was securely around its neck. It also was fitted with a piece of highly luminescent cloth around its' back and chest. Sarah and Martha made separate audio/video recordings of events from different positions. Sarah stationed herself near the chamber to record changes in audio and visual events inside the chamber and Martha stood near the computer to record events there. The rat was placed in the chamber at 11:14 PM.

At 11:20 Randy began the launch sequence. Joe positioned himself close by the computer screen to detect any deviation of computer or chamber reactions from what they had repeatedly observed during practice runs. When the sixth step was completed and the launch hyperlink was visible on the computer screen, Randy looked around the room to see that everyone was ready. As soon as his focus returned to the computer screen, he immediately clicked the launch hyperlink. The computer clock registered 11:26:32 PM.

For a few moments, nothing happened. Then lights briefly flickered within the chamber and an unearthly, low frequency grinding sound permeated the room accompanied at irregular intervals by a high frequency low decibel screeching sound. A few seconds later, the sounds died out and the chamber light came on. Sarah immediately peered into the chamber and calmly reported that the rat was gone. Slowly the others gathered around the chamber and looked inside as if to observe the aftermath of a routine event. For a couple of minutes no one spoke. Then in a voice that sounded vaguely pre-adolescent, John asked, "What's that on the other side of the chamber?" Randy replied matter-of-factly, "That's an escape door. It's there in case a human would-be time traveler changes his or her mind at the last minute. The reluctant traveler could go out the chamber backdoor and proceed a short distance to a door out of the building. It opens from the inside but closes securely and automatically and doesn't even have a handle on the outside."

"Oh," responded John. The others were experiencing equally bland emotions and thoughts. After another few moments during which there were no comments or reactions, Randy quietly announced the obvious: "I guess that we will all know tomorrow night at the grassy knoll." They disbanded and had no contact with each other until they assembled at the knoll near the forest.

John, the last to arrive the next night, showed up at about 11:18 PM. Sarah took charge by defining an approximate circle about the periphery of the grassy knoll and placing each of them at about equal distance from one another along the circumference of the circle. The rat was supposed to arrive at about the middle of the circle, so they all focused on it. Now they were getting tense. 11:26 arrived and passed. No rat. Randy exclaimed with dismay, "The damn machine didn't send the rat to the right place." "Or," muttered Martha, "It doesn't work."

"How can that be?" returned Joe. "There was no sign of it in the chamber after the launch, no hair, no blood, no guts, nothing."

"John," Martha called from across the circle, "what is your location device telling you?"

John fiddled with the device for a moment while turning slowly in a circle and then announced, "I've got a blip. It's coming from the forest." He trotted off in a northeasterly direction while looking down at the dial on the instrument and changing his course slightly as he approached the forest. The others ran after him. Well into the forest, Joe, Martha, Sarah and Randy panned out on either side of John to facilitate looking and listening for any sign of the rat. John shouted that the blip was getting stronger as he turned a bit to his right. They kept pace with him as they penetrated deeper into the forest. Martha suddenly hollered, "I saw something, a flash of light, over there." She was pointing straight ahead. John yelled that his signal confirmed the location she indicated. Sarah told them to encircle the apparent location of the rat. As they closed in on their target John whispered that it was very near. Before they knew it, they were standing around a crouching, trembling, exhausted rat with a strap around its neck and a glowing scarf about its upper body.

"Quick, somebody grab it," suggested Randy in a rasping voice. Nobody moved. "For heaven's sake," said Sarah in a normal tone, "it's just a laboratory rat. They're used to being handled." She walked over to it and gently picked it up. When she raised it over her head they all shouted with extraordinary elation. The time machine had worked.

It was now 11:35. John placed the rat in a small cage and informed the others that he would return after delivering the creature to his apartment. On his way back to the knoll, he stopped by a filling station store for beer and snacks. They spread old beach blankets from the trunk of John's car out on the ground and sat there crossed-legged sipping beer and stuffing themselves with junk food. It was a joyous night. They had witnessed an event that had never occurred before. But it began to dawn on them that they now faced a momentous decision: Which of them would be the first human to travel in time?

All had opinions about making the trip and who was the best candidate to be the first time traveler, but no one wanted to broach the subject. After a few days, Sarah suggested that they meet once again on the grassy knoll where each one of them could candidly indicate her or his opinion. The meeting was scheduled for a holiday week when the campus was all but empty of students. They met on a Wednesday at 3 PM and sat in a circle on folding chairs or blankets. Martha spoke up first. "I'll tell you who won't be going, me!" She went on to say that she thought it was too dangerous and, therefore, no one should go. After a brief silence during which no one seemed willing to speak, Randy, stood up, looked around the circle, and declared, "I'll go."

The other four were incredulous. "What the …" sputtered Joe. "You've been the most convinced that time travel is scientific nonsense. Now you are going to go on a venture that you say has nearly zero likelihood of succeeding and high odds of killing you. I agree with your former position. Time travel is indefensible and suicidal."

"Well," returned Randy rather casually, "I'm still skeptical, but the rat success makes me think a human might travel successfully. And further, I've got less to lose. I think we will be found out and, since I enabled the entire episode by letting you all into the chamber room, I'll be black balled in computer science. Might as well go out in a blaze of glory. Or, if we fail, cover me with the pall of infamy. In any case, I'll be world famous or won't be around to care about whatever people might think of me."

"Let's not forget," interrupted Sarah, "travel to the distant future or past could be very different from sending a rat just one day into the future."

"I absolutely agree," Martha chimed in, "I'm sticking with nobody goes."

"Well, how about you Sarah?" said Joe. "Would you go?"

Sarah replied, "I don't know yet. We need to consider not just ethical considerations, but also logistics. Where would the candidate for time travel be sent and what would she or he take along? The latter must be tailor-made to fit the circumstances peculiar to the time and place the traveler would be sent."

An "Errr … never thought of that." was written on the faces of the others.

Sarah continued with, "Let me bounce it back to you, Joe. Would you go?"

"Yes, I would," responded Joe who had just called the trip suicidal. Needless to say, his friends were astounded.

Randy leaped on this pronouncement: "Wait a minute, you just proclaimed the trip to be indefensible, and now you are declaring that you are willing to go?"

"I was just reminding you of your clearly stated conception of time travel. I don't entirely agree with you."

Randy asked, "Ok Joe, how would you defend your willingness to be the first time traveler?"

"I think it will work and I'm willing to accept the dangers."

At this point, John got up and moved to the center of the circle. "There are some other practical issues we need to consider. All of you are not finished with your dissertations and probably won't be for a year or two. I'm the only one who will be finished soon, actually in less than a month. My research is done and write-ups of dissertation have been tentatively approved by all of the professors on my committee. In fact, a paper based on the dissertation has been submitted to a very respected journal and reviews by editors have been very positive. The professors on my committee are not going to turn down a dissertation reporting research appearing in a publication that will bear their names as co-authors. When my oral defense of the dissertation is finished, I have told my professors that I will be leaving the university to travel around the country in search of a job. They have already provided me with letters of reference and would be willing to communicate with any university's job-search committee members who might want further information. Thus, I can finish my PhD requirements and disappear. So, in sum, I'm ready to go and when I'm gone, no one will miss me."

"What do you mean, no will miss you?" interjected a clearly distressed Martha.

"I mean officials at our university will not miss me. I know you'll miss me … all of you. And I'll miss you while I'm gone, but I expect to return. I truly believe time travel into the distant past will work. By the way, I have figured out where I'd go and what time period I'd enter."

Joe loudly broke in. "Yeah, you got everything figured out, alright." "You really figured out how to eliminate other candidates for time travel while at the same time making a compelling case for yourself as the best alternative."

"Look," responded John, "I can go soon without interrupting my pursuit of a PhD. Not one of you can. I'm also convinced that time travel is reasonably safe. If a small mammal can be sent a day into the future, it follows that any mammal, human or other, can be sent to a more distant point in time. There is little reason to believe that longer trips are less possible or more dangerous. Should I succeed, all of you would feel confident you too could travel in time. And you could make your own trip to another time without sacrificing your careers or worrying about the dangers you might encounter."

A meeting was set at the Lion's Den at 4 PM one day after each had revealed whether he or she wanted to be the time traveler. They brought along their vote for who each thought should be the first time traveler, recorded on scrap pieces of paper. Martha, the only one of them who had declared no one should attempt to travel in time, was to examine the ballots and declare the result. All arrived a bit before 4 and, thus, they entered the Den at almost the same time. A table was selected in a secluded corner. When all were seated, Sarah reminded them that they were to give their ballots to her and no one was to comment on the election at any time during the meeting. She would count the ballots. If the first vote did not result in a majority voting for one of them, there would be one or more subsequent votes until someone received at least 3 votes.

After examining the ballots, Martha quietly announced that no one had received 3 votes. She reported that two candidates had received two votes each. Another candidate had received one vote. Thus, two had gotten no votes. After some discussion, they decided to reveal the voting results on the first ballot. Martha indicated that John and Joe had received two votes each and Sarah one vote. By acclamation Randy and Martha were declared ineligible for further consideration. Neither seemed to care.

After examining the results of the next ballot, Martha declared that there was a winner. Sarah had one vote, Joe one vote, and John the other three. John was to be the first time traveler. There were sighs of relief, and congratulations passed on to John, who accepted them with equanimity. However, Joe seemed ready to explode. He pushed his chair back and got up slowly. Everyone turned toward him with surprise and alarm. Sarah asked, "What's wrong, Joe?" He sputtered that the vote had been rigged. "I was tied for the lead initially and suddenly I get one vote? That can't be. Who's responsible for this atrocity?" Before anyone could respond, Joe slung his chair backward and stumbled in his first few steps toward the door.

CHAPTER 6

Preparation for the Trip

John, Sarah, Martha and Randy sat in silence for some moments after Joe had stormed out of the Lion's Den. Finally, Sarah looked up at John and broke the silence with, "Did we just witness a psychotic break?"

"Looked like it to me," John replied. "But I'm not a clinical psychologist."

Martha offered, "He's seemed ok lately, kind of lost his 'born to the manor' airs. I had come to think of him as pretty stable."

Sarah mused, "You know, I think that he began to covet being the first to travel in time. The rat success must have convinced him that time travel was possible for humans. More importantly, something that has occurred to me, and probably to the three of you, may have dawned on Joe. When you think about it, there is a near zero probability that any new PhD in any discipline will someday produce research results or theory that will continue to be influential long after her or his demise. But, obviously, the first time traveler will be remembered for centuries into the future. Being the first to travel in time is hugely seductive."

By the time she had finished her reflection on what motivated Joe, she was facing John. Randy and Martha also oriented in John's direction. Obviously they were all wondering why John wanted to be the first to travel in time. He started his rationale for wanting to be first with, "Yes, I really want to be the first to travel in time. But what I want out of it may be different from what others might want. I want to go back to the past partly for the thrill of it. It would be the most incredible adventure imaginable. Also, I would like to possibly make the future better by starting beneficial changes earlier. I would provide people from the past with clues to important scientific advancements that could lead to better lives sooner for people in the future. Being famous in my own time would be more a nuisance than a good thing. I'm a private person. I don't like being in the spotlight. However, if decades after people in the past met me, they remembered me as someone who influenced them to advance science, that would be a good thing."

After John finished, no one spoke. Instead they communicated their reactions with warm smiles. Randy was thinking, "This is no ordinary person." Martha responded by tearing up a little, a not uncommon reaction for her. Sarah, the philosopher, admired the ingenious style of his presentation and the skillfulness with which he defended his desire to be the first time traveler.

Martha broke the silence with, "Maybe if we figured out how people voted we can get some insight into what motivated people during voting, especially Joe. I can tell you that I voted for Joe on the first ballot and, of course, he voted for himself."

Sarah volunteered, "I voted for John and I assume he voted for himself." John nodded in the affirmation and Randy indicated that he had voted for Sarah.

"None of this seems too surprising," said Sarah. "I'm betting that Martha voted for Joe to lower the likelihood that John would be the first time traveler."

Martha squirmed a little but said nothing. Randy smiled knowingly.

Martha, in an attempt to draw attention away from herself, asked why Randy voted for Sarah.

"Simple," he replied, "I think she has the even-handedness and ability to think rationally that will be required by the first time traveler."

Sarah smiled modestly and continued the discussion with, "Let's get to the second ballot. Obviously, Joe voted for himself. I voted for John and he voted for himself. Who gave John the third vote?"

"I did," said Randy.

"And," continued Sarah, "who voted for me?"

Martha raised her hand sheepishly. When her friends' facial expressions announced, "go ahead and tell us what we already know," she blurted out, "I don't care what you think. I was making choices that I thought were in the best interest of everyone."

"So," continued Sarah, "what was Joe thinking when he pitched a fit and stomped out of the room?"

"Yeah," offered John, "I don't get it. He acted as if it was a given that whoever voted for him on the first ballot was somehow committed to vote for him on the second ballot. And, of course, in his self-absorbed state, he was sure that at least one other person would vote for him."

Martha regained her composure and offered, "He really, really wanted to be the first time traveler. I'm thinking that, because he wanted it so badly, he felt it had to happen. He must have been sure in his own mind that he would get that third vote. When he didn't get it, he could only assume that we had cheated him."

"His bizarre behavior is consistent with your conclusion," offered John. "But, as he has shown no signs of serious instability, my guess is that he is going to recover rather quickly from his—shall we call it—petit psychotic episode."

"But, will he be an obstruction to the completion of our mission?" interjected Sarah.

"No way to be sure ... we will just have wait and see what he will do," answered John.

Despite John's "best guess," there was tension in the air at their next meeting in the Den. Joe looked depressed and did not participate in their conversations. However, at least, he got it together enough to make the meeting. More importantly, although he was not himself, his demeanor suggested that they were unlikely to witness another angry outburst. Soon the meeting regressed to small talk. As nothing of substance was being considered, John excused himself, saying that he had lab duties to complete.

After John's exit, Joe seemed to brighten up a bit. When they began to discuss plans for an upcoming holiday, Joe spoke up for the first time, saying that he looked forward to going home to see his family. The discussion continued in a more relaxed atmosphere until something someone said cued Martha to make a reference to the launch of the first time traveler into the past. Joe stiffened up. He looked fierce when he muttered, "The rat launch was a set-up. You remember that John came late? He was planting a rat in the woods that looked like the one we launched. Then he snuck back to where we were and pretended to search for the rat with his locator gadget. He tricked us!"

They all looked horrified. Joe was going back into his deranged state. Trying to talk him down, Sarah gently asked,

"But what about the fact that the rat disappeared from the chamber after the launch sequence was completed?"

In a tone an octave higher than before Joe responded with "It was atomized or something like that … it didn't go anywhere."

Now other people in the Den were looking at them with much curiosity. Martha pleaded with Joe to keep his voice down. He sat there trembling for a minute then got up to leave. Sarah followed him to the door. Once outside, she tried to comfort him, but Joe continued his paranoid accusations. "I know that he is planning to fake his launch into the past. He will figure out how to make it look like he has disappeared from the chamber, but he won't fool me." With that he turned and headed away from the Den at a pace that would make a speed walker proud. For the next several days, no one was able to find him.

In the days that followed, preparations for the launch began to take shape. Martha took it upon herself to figure out how to correct the time-machine error in placing travelers at the coordinates selected for a particular trip. When she and John had a chance to talk about it over lunch, she announced that she had a solution to the problem. "I can estimate the degree of error by measuring the distance between the programmed landing location and the actual landing location."

John broke in, "Uh, there's a problem. I didn't mark the spot where our rat actually landed."

"But I did," Martha came back quickly.

"Wow, that's a big 'good for you.' Makes me look less foolish."

"Now the next thing you are going to say is that our rat may have moved from its actual landing spot," continued Martha.

"Not really," said John. "I shot him up with some stuff that would render him immobile for hours. It is the reason for the trembling behavior he showed. Also, though I was a little late to the landing site, I had the headphones on and would have detected any significant movement on the rat's part. The location device has a range of a few miles. There was no significant movement, only a little vacillation that is consistent with the minor movement expected as the drug wore off. It was enough for me to detect him, but not enough to carry him far from the actual landing site."

"Well, 'good for you' back at ya," said Martha with a broad smile. John was grinning at her as well. Both were thinking, "We're a really good team."

At a subsequent meeting the science wonks began to identify other problems that they would have to solve before John's launch. The most obvious was *where* John wanted to go during *what* time period. He answered quickly and confidently, which the others took to mean he had done a lot of mental preparation for his time trip. "I want to go back to New York City in the late fall of 1928, at a time when many momentous events were about to unfold. Hitler was positioning himself to take over in Germany and the US stock market was developing trends that would end in its crash. It was also a time when women were using their new right to vote as a platform for gaining equal rights with men and blacks were being lynched in the South, but were finding a safe niche in the North. In psychology, behaviorism was on track to dominate the field. Physics had advanced enormously because of Einstein's relatively theory and the implications of nuclear fusion for understanding how the sun generates its power. Neuroscience did not exist in the sense it does today. In the 1920s and forward in time, the mind was seen as, somehow, transcending the brain.

Computers and mobile technology, such as iPhones and iPads, were inconceivable. This era was ripe for planting the seeds of the explosive scientific advances that would occur in the future."

After a moment of silence during which the gang mused about John's plan, Sarah addressed John. "Sounds like your love for history rivals your affection for science."

John responded with, "The historical link between advances in science and positive changes in other realms of society is crucial to increasing human well-being. For example, democratization of a society allows the kind of open-mindedness that promotes scientific discovery. These discoveries lead to economic success that opens up educational opportunities for more people. In turn, an educated society protects the essence of democracy: rule by the people and equal opportunity for all."

"Good points. I agree. But I was trying to look at changing the future from another angle," said Sarah. "You mentioned Hitler. If you can provide a hint that might change the course of scientific advance in the future, why can't you provide information about what Hitler actually did during the 1930s and '40s in the hope of preventing his ascension to Chancellor of Germany in 1933?"

A wry smile formed on John's face as he composed an answer to his friend's question. "Well, soon-to-be-PhD in philosophy, I think you know the answer to your own question, but I'll recite it for you anyway. First, let me remind us all that hints I give to scientists in the past may have no effect on science in the future. I do believe that providing scientists of the past with allusions to landmark scientific developments in the future has a chance of speeding up scientific advance. However, the probability of that happening is nowhere near 1.00. Hints to scientists that relate to their burning interests within their own fields of research and theory are likely to be given full consideration. They pride themselves in evaluating whatever is presented to them by reference to empirically derived evidence and well-tested scientific theory. However, changing the course of socio-political movements like Nazism or communism is a different matter. These movements are founded on cherished beliefs that are bound up with strong emotions. What if I tried to convince people of the past that Hitler would soon begin sweeping conquests? People who embrace anti-fascist beliefs would dismiss my assertion out of hand and it would be unsurprising to people who embrace autocracy. Why? Because both groups fervently believe that their own points of view will rule the future. So, don't even think about asking me to preach anti-fascism to pedestrians in Times Square or people congregating at Berlin's Brandenburg Gate. As to the latter, I refuse to go to Germany because I don't speak German, and even if I did, I wouldn't be heard above the din of street fighting between Nazis and Communists." The good-natured chuckling that followed signaled the end of this productive session.

At the next session held at the Lion's Den, John's absence emboldened Joe to once again air his paranoid delusions about the group's selection to be the first time traveler. "I tell you, he's going to fake the launch. When the launch sequence is completed and chamber lights come on, just because he isn't there doesn't mean that he has been transported to the past."

"So," said Martha, "you'll think that he was atomized or something like that?" She and the others were growing weary of Joe's accusations. Mentally disturbed or not, he was becoming a bore and an obstruction to their preparation for the launch.

"Maybe," replied Joe, "or he'll figure out a way to disappear without us knowing how he did it. All he has to do after he sneaks out the back door of the chamber is to carry out his plan to go looking for a job. Nobody will know where he is."

"Well," continued Martha, "other things may happen to human would-be time travelers besides disappearing. Just because rats are transported across time without change to them—or atomized, if you are right—doesn't mean that is what would happen to a human. I tell you what, we could change our minds and send you instead of John. But consider the possibilities of what could happen to a human sent to the past or future. Radical anatomical changes could occur. Body parts could change locations. Your head and your butt could switch locations on your body."

In what seemed to be a millisecond after Martha finished, from the far end the table Sarah was heard to say, "That seems right to me."

Amid rowdy laughter, everyone turned to look at Sarah. She smiled demurely. It felt good to be funny.

Joe's face turned a bright red and his hands were clenched into tight fists. He slammed his beer bottle done on the tabletop, paused for a moment then struggled to make his legs move him away from them. He managed to hobble toward the Den's front door.

Then the guilt set in. Randy said that they should be ashamed of themselves. But his credibility was lowered by the lingering grin on his face. Sarah and Martha were struggling with the same mix of emotions. On the one hand they had had enough of Joe. On the other, they felt they were kicking a friend when he was down. Each pledged to contact Joe within the next few days. They did that, and when they reported back to one another, each described Joe's state of mind in very similar ways. He greeted all of them warmly, but when they apologized, he acted as if he didn't know what they were talking about. He was just glad to see them. Guilt turned to worry that their friend was seriously disturbed.

When Martha described Joe's latest meltdown to John, he promised to consult with friends pursuing clinical psychology PhDs. When he reported back to her, she was disappointed in what he had to say. "My clinical psychology colleagues are in the midst of struggling with changes between the Diagnostic and Statistical Manual 4 and DSM 5. In their opinions, the lines between one category of a disorder type and another category of the same type are no clearer under DSM 5 than DSM 4. But their problems with DSM 5 may be explained by the fact that they have had insufficient time to become familiar with it. Bottom line is that Joe's symptoms don't fit neatly into any personality disorder category of either DSM 4 or 5. Neither do his symptoms fit the criteria for any of the various kinds of psychosis. He is too lucid most of the time. If he presented himself for diagnosis, his symptoms would probably force him into one of the always handy 'not otherwise specified' slots. Would psychotherapy help? Quite possibly it would. It's worth a try if we can convince him that he has a serious problem in need of an effective solution."

Communications among the five friends began to focus on specific logistic issues and problems what must be addressed before the launch. One that threatened the entire endeavor was the fact that they had no method for returning a time traveler to the present. It was decided that John should be the one to nix the launch or not, after taking the lack of a return capability into account. No one was surprised when John declared that being stuck in the past was not desirable, but would be acceptable to him. A less critical, but still important issue, was how to finance the trip.

CHAPTER 7

Check-list to Launch

Sarah opened the meeting at the Knoll. "We need to make a list of all the problems John may encounter that we can anticipate and of all the items he must take with him. And we must find the money that he will need." She paused for a moment to take in all the troubled looks on her friends' faces. "We must dress him in the styles of the period, locate a hotel for him, find a bank for him, and school him in the customs of the time."

"Wow," breathed Randy, "that sounds like a lot."

Sarah responded, "That's all I can think of for now and even these few matters are stated in general terms. We will need to specify each of them in detail. For example, we will need to research what a respectable young man of the late 1920s would wear—probably some kind of suit and leather soled shoes—and get it in his size. At the minimum, his clothes must give him a look that will not arouse suspicion."

"There are many other issues," said Martha. "I'm working on finding a solution to the inaccuracy in placement of travelers. I think I have a solution. When I'm sure, I'll work with Randy in creating a fix. We don't want John hanging from the aerial at the top of the Empire State building like King Kong."

John broke in, "That won't be a problem because construction on that New York City icon didn't start until January of 1930. I want to go back to New York City at the end of 1928."

"Ok," said Martha, "start giving us some details of exactly where you want to go when you get to NYC."

"I want to be not many blocks from the Savoy Ballroom where I expect to spend some time hanging out."

"That's a famous venue for black musicians and singers. Wouldn't you be out of place there?" asked Martha.

"Not at all," John responded. "Blacks and whites mingled there. Among the greatest musicians and singers performed at the Savoy. It was a Mecca of musical innovation. Also, I want to be reasonably close to Columbia University where I hope to find graduate students of that day who are into the sciences."

"That sounds like you are trying to redraw the map of New York City," offered Randy. While looking at the others, he continued, "Is it even possible to find a residence—I assume a hotel—that is close to both the Savoy and Columbia University, not to mention a bank and a safe place for the Time Machine to land him?"

Martha answered, "Since I'm in charge of finding a safe landing place, I'll try to locate an acceptable residence and a bank that are reasonable close to Columbia University and the Savoy."

"I did look at a map for the time period and it appears that Columbia is not far from Harlem and the Savoy is located there. I wasn't thinking about a bank or hotel at the time."

"Yeah, that'd be you," returned Martha. "I'll try to figure it out," she mumbled in a tone that feigned annoyance.

After John left the scene, Randy, Sarah, and Martha lingered for a while. Randy opened a new discussion with, "I'm concerned about John's attitude. He seems to be a little boy unaware of the dangers he will face and acting like he's taking a trip to the big city for the fun of it. This is a serious matter."

Martha responded with, "We've talked about the trip recently. He is fully conscious of the dangers. John tends to be careful in doing whatever he does. Don't mistake his joyful anticipation of the trip for a flippant attitude toward what he will face once in NYC."

Sarah weighted in on the issue: "I've had some of the same feelings as Randy. John is not viewing a deadly serious commitment for what it is."

"Trust me," countered Martha, "I know him better than anyone. He is currently going over every detail of the trip he can conjure up. With our help, he will be totally prepared by launch time."

As discussions of trip preparations continued, Sarah arranged a one-on-one with Joe to assess his mental status. They talked for about 45 minutes during which he seemed to be more his old self. Though he talked and gestured in a languid fashion, he was responsive to what she was saying to him. He seemed mildly depressed but reasonably rational. After consulting with the others, she recommended that Joe be invited to the next meeting about John's trip. They all agreed.

The Lion's Den was chosen for the next meeting during which trip problem solving would be the focus. Everyone was asked to show up on Saturday at 1:00 PM sharp. The place would just be opening and almost no one would be there due to sleeping off the aftereffects of Friday night's festivities. They selected a table in a secluded corner, far from the door.

Martha began a discussion by presenting each of them with a page containing a map of New York City in 1928 and a current map. "NYC hasn't changed all that much since 1928. As you can see from the two maps and the notations I've made on them, any two places that John wants readily accessible are a long walk or a short cab drive away. The Savoy, which is now closed, is located in the heart of Harlem. It's shown in the upper right-hand corner of the maps. The Hotel Theresa is several blocks southwest of the Savoy site. It is no longer a hotel, but was one of the better places to stay in its time. The beautiful Mount Morris Bank Building is a few blocks southeast of the Hotel. Today it's reduced to the original main floor and is in dismal condition. Back in the 1920s it housed the Corn Exchange Bank. John can deposit his funds there and also store any items that he cannot carry around in public. Columbia University, which is west of the other facilities, is a short cab drive away from them. And most importantly, not far south of the bank building, the hotel and Columbia University is Central Park. I plan to land John in it near the Harlem Meer, one of several lakes in the park. From there he can walk a short distance to 5th Avenue and take a cab to the Mount Morris building, or walk there. After completing business there, it is a comfortable walk to the Hotel Theresa."

The next few moments were filled with the sounds of exhilaration and fascination. John was the first to speak: "You have pretty much nailed it, Martha." His comment was followed by applause along with some whooping it up. Bartenders across the room were staring at them.

After the ruckus ended, a lively discussion ensued. John asked, "What if your little algorithm to correct for machine placement error doesn't work? I could end up in the middle of the lake!" Martha calmly replied, "I'm not concerned. The suitcase will be water-proofed and I assumed you can swim." To be heard over the giggling, Martha loudly pronounced, "Actually, I checked. The lake is only four to six feet deep. John can walk out of it ... carrying the suitcase ... over his head."

"But, I'd be such a mess. Can't you guarantee that I won't end up in the lake?"

"No," returned Martha, "but I think I can keep you from landing on some trees and other hazards nearby."

Grinning slyly, John responded, "I don't care about that. I don't mind being banged up a bit, but I don't want to look a mess."

When they returned to serious matters, Sarah reminded them that many critical problems remained to be solved: "Enough money is needed to keep John from ending up a bum on the streets. Part of the money would go to day to day living and part would have to be invested in case we can't bring him back. That's a problem, because, of course, the Great Depression will be happening not long after he lands. I've been looking into this problem and may have a solution. From 1929 to 1934, gold concerns increased in value by a factor of 6. So, $1000 invested in the gold industry during late 1928 was worth $6000 in 1934. If, during late 1928, John could invest as much as $20,000 in gold, it would be worth $120,000 by about 1934 and would remain pretty steadily high through at least 1949."

The others were caught between admiration of Sarah's adroit handling of the money problem and astonishment at how much money would be needed. Randy gasped, "$20,000! Where would we ever find that kind of money?"

Sarah responded, "$20,000 is the minimum investment ... $30,000 would be best. And he would need at least another $15,000 to live on."

"Wouldn't $20,000 back in the late twenties be worth many times more than it is today?" asked Martha.

"Yes, but we are talking about John being gone indefinitely. He will need a lot of money. And that's not all," continued Sarah, "we can't send him there with a bag of gold. For one thing, he'd never drag it out of the lake. For another, he'd be arrested as a gold thief wherever he showed up to sell it. We'll need cash."

Sarah paused for some chuckling and she wasn't disappointed. She continued: "Ideally, he would need currency—bills—that were printed before the end of 1928. I have no idea where we would find that. Sufficient worth in old coins would be too bulky and heavy. Further, very valuable old coins in today's market would be worth face value during late 1928."

There was dead silence for a moment. "I tried to tell you earlier that a successful launch would be the solution to just the first seemingly impossible problem," said Sarah. "Other problems, beginning with getting together negotiable funds, would still have to be faced. As far as I can tell, the money problem may have no feasible solution."

More silence. Joe began to make some noise as he scooted his chair back. That got everyone's attention. Was this to be another conniption? Instead, he calmly announced, "I think I have a solution. I literally have a big bag full of money. It's been in the family for decades. It's mainly $100 dollar bills, and some of higher denominations, that one of my relatives accumulated during the early years of the 20th century. He was somewhat deranged; thought the world was coming to an end by the 1930s. Upon his death, it was passed on to my father who sat on it until he became convinced that it was no longer legal tender due to its age. When I was a pre-teenager Dad gave it to me as kind of a plaything. He thought he had given me a bit of family history that was of little value. I kept it in the attic. Periodically, I'd open up its container, just to have a look. All the time it was getting older. In face value, it's $36,000 and some change. You can have it."

Earlier, the others had thought that they were living in one of the most extraordinary days of their lives. It just got more incredible. Especially in view of Joe's recent mental state, it seemed almost impossible to believe.

Finally, Randy spoke up. "Joe ... look, $36,000 is a lot of money. You don't give that much away on a whim. You need to think about it."

"Oh, I've thought about what to do with it for a long time. Trying to spend it these days would raise suspicions. Bills that old would have been recalled to the U. S. Treasury and destroyed many years ago. And there's another thing. I know that you all think I'm kind of stuck up because my family is rich. Well here's another reason to view me that way. We're so rich you can't imagine how rich we are. $36,000 is chump change for us. It's a weekend trip somewhere. It's a charitable donation so we'll look generous. You are welcome to it. Back in the late 1920s it'll be legal tender."

"Thank you," said John. Joe answered simply, "You're welcome." So ended the most amazing string of events any of them had ever experienced. Only a successful launch would surpass what happened that day.

Getting together clothes for John was less difficult than they had thought. One of John's friends did costumes for plays. While she worked mostly on local plays, she was so well known for her historical expertise that Hollywood had consulted her a few times. Within a week of John's request for clothes apropos to the late 1920s, he had a complete suit, a pair of leather-soled shoes, a couple of shirts and three pairs of pants. He chose from several hats and ties that had the 1920s look.

Schooling John regarding the lingo of the 1920s was a different matter. He easily learned expressions like attaboy, beeswax, big cheese, cat's meow, ciggy, dolled up, earful, gin mill, hotsy-totsy, jake, level with me, necking, on the lam, putting on the Ritz, razz, Sheik, spiffy, stuck on someone, swell, tomato, wet blanket, whoopee, and you slay me. Inhibiting expressions of the 2000-teens was harder to learn. In fact it would be difficult for anyone. Odds were that John would slip up at least occasionally.

Martha expanded her launch preparation duties by thinking of issues that had not occurred to others. One such was that John would need an acceptable ID. When she informed John about the need for an ID he argued that an id would be less important back in the late 1920s. "A lot of people back then had no ids and didn't need them."

Martha replied, "Yes, but you will be putting a lot of money in a bank and engaging in other business. It's best to have a good id."

John replied, "If you say so. I have a friend from way back who forged my first id, a driver's license. He's even better now than he was back then. I could get him to locate a picture online of a New York State driver's license dating to the 1920s."

"Well, maybe he'll do," Martha replied, "but what you really need is a U. S. passport. It will be less seriously scrutinized than a driver's license and is a more credible ID. Can your friend do that?"

"Absolutely. You'll be surprised about how real it will look."

"Will you need money to pay him?"

"Nope, he owes me."

"Ok," continued Martha, "there's another thing. I think you need a new last name. Sarah and Randy agree."

A puzzled John responded with, "Huh?"

"Yeah, your name is weird.'

"And yours' isn't?"

Martha sounded amused when she responded, "Don't you be talking about my name. It's musical; yours' makes people saying it appear to be drunk."

"Alright," moaned John, pretending his feelings were hurt.

"I want to give you a name that is near the top of the list of most common surnames. That way everyone you address will recognize it immediately and may claim they know someone with your surname. It'll break some ice. I thought of John Smith, but I know you'd be out-there looking for Pocahontas." She glanced up from her notes to find him displaying a wickedly mischievous grin. "Yeah, I know you."

She continued, "So, I chose 'Williams' which is number three on the list of most common surnames in the U.S., behind Smith and Johnson."

"What's wrong with 'Johnson?'"

"I had a high school teacher by that name. He was a jerk. Gave me an A-. I know, it's not rational, but there you have it. Now, in case you're still wondering, I wanted a name that sounded pleasant, but not fake. John Williams filled the bill."

"Now this is serious," she continued, "When you're asked who you are, you must answer 'John Williams.' You'll have to practice."

"Now you know I'll screw this up. That's why you're doing it."

"No, that's not it, silly boy. This will save you some hassles."

"So what do I do when I screw it up and use my real name?"

"Just say, 'Excuse me. I have something caught in my throat. My name is John Williams.' They'll believe that because that's what your real surname sounds like when it comes out of people's mouths."

He got up off his seat several feet away from her and pretended that he was coming after her. She jumped up, grabbed her stuff, and ran off. He trotted after her for a few steps then stopped to watch her. She briefly looked back at him. Both of them were laughing. They regressed to their teens when they were around each other, and loved every minute of it.

The lack of a way to bring John back to the present time remained the critical issue. They would know that John was retrievable if they could successfully send him something and get it back from him. Randy proposed sending him an iPod with instructions for retuning it in its 'Notes.' The problem with that would be the implications of using it in public. If people saw him use it and figured out that it was something extraordinary, they might even kill him for it. The solution to that might be fashioning a cover for the iPod so that it look like something people commonly carried in the late 1920s. Joe volunteered to help Randy work on this problem. When John found out about these tentative plans, he revealed that it was his intention to take an iPod with him, along with an iPad, iPhone, and iWatch. When the others heard about what John planned to take with him, there was considerable consternation concerning his motivation for making the trip in time. Was he really approaching his mission with the deadly serious attitude it required? He continued to look like he was preparing for a beach party rather than for a very dangerous and monumental scientific mission.

A meeting was called at the Knoll to address these issues. As was often the case, everyone was there before John arrived. He hurried over to where they were gathered on blankets. Before he could sit down, they were firing questions to him. "Have you lost your mind?" Randy yelled. The others shushed him, but intently focused on John to get his response to Randy's question.

John, as was usual for him when people were on his case, went into his cool, calm and collected mode. "I fully understand the dangers of being found with modern technology on me. Some people would do anything to get it. They would think that they could sell it to General Electric. I'm not planning to be carrying any of these items around with me. Obviously they would go into a safety deposit box at the bank. That was my plan all along. I could go there and ask for a private place to use these devices. Maybe I would be able to lock myself in the room where the safety deposits boxes are located. Oh, and of course I would use headphones. The iPod, covered in a case that would disguise it, is a good idea, but it is much more dangerous than what I planned. I hadn't considered using any of these devices in public. I love these electronic wonders and would unwind by playing with them in private from time to time. I plan to load them with favorite tunes, and movies, and games and so forth. The iWatch, however, could be considered as a relatively safe way to collect information in public. But, the iPod plan is fine. Send it to me with instructions about when it would be retrieved, what information you want on it and where it should be placed so that its location could be precisely specified. I would put it exactly where you would want it placed. Knowing where it is would allow you to bring it back to the present time."

Randy calmed down. Joe was gritting his teeth and looked like he wanted to say something, but he remained silent. Sarah and Martha looked surprised, although they had seen John make these cool-under-fire performances before. Finally, in a tired voice Sarah uttered, "Look let's think more about this. Maybe there is no problem after all." A few days later, at the next meeting, it was decided that John could bring the iPad and iWatch with him—the iPhone seemed redundant with the others—but he would have to pledge never to take any of them out in public. The exception would be the iPod that would be sent to him disguised by its contrived cover.

CHAPTER 8

Countdown to Launch

Randy called John and set up a meeting at the Den for a one-on-one about a technical issue. They huddled at a table in the back of the joint. Randy opened with, "About taking Apple devices with you. You will have a problem with plugging them in. As you may know, NYC used Direct Current during the era you will be there."

"I didn't know that," returned John. "Why?"

"In a word, 'Edison.' He was very powerful and wanted what worked best for his operations."

"Well," Randy continued, "modern electronic devices almost all run on DC, rather than Alternating Current, the standard for these times. Accordingly, modern electronic devices have AC to DC adapters in their plugs that are inserted into wall sockets. But, even if, somehow, today's adapters would allow these devices to operate properly with DC to DC connections, their plugs wouldn't fit into the 1920s wall sockets. I'll need some plugs from the late 1920s to use in charging your Apple devices."

"Where in the world would you find such old plugs?"

"Online. Although not everything is online—millions if not billions of books, documents, and manuscripts have not been digitized—it's truly amazing what you can find on the Web. I've already found the plugs I need and will order them soon. By the way, they are cheap."

"So, how do you know that just wiring an old plug into the battery charger-line will work?"

"I don't know. I'll have to experiment. We have a lot of old electrical devices in our labs and our museum. I know for sure where to find an old DC generator with a set of sockets on it. I'll wire a 1920s plug into the Apple device battery charger-line and run this contraption from the generator to an old iPod. The iPod battery may start charging, in which case everything is cool. Alternatives are that nothing happens or the iPod blows up."

"Randy, this doesn't sound like science to me."

"Hey, we get to go with trial and error sometimes, just like the rest of you do."

"Ok, I get it." John replied. "What do you do if nothing happens or the iPod explodes?"

"If the latter, you'll owe me an old iPod. If the former, it's back to the drawing board. I'll work on constructing an interface for moderating and modulating the current flow between the wall socket and the Apple device. Eventually I'll get it right, perhaps after accumulating a pile of fried old phones and other devices."

About a week passed Randy summoned John to a secluded university parking lot where he displayed a couple of truly ugly masses of unruly wire. Both had an ancient plug on one end. It was joined to a couple of twisted wires running to a blob of plastic. These wires exited the blob and continued a short distance to a plug for insertion into Apple devices.

John was amazed. "This looks awful. Are you sure it will work?"

Randy came back with, "You're welcome ... yes, I'm sure. I tested it on a DC circuit using my own Apple devices." John apologized and heaped praise on Randy for his crucial accomplishment. But when he asked Randy about the steps he had taken to develop the DC to Apple device connection, there was a moment of silence. "I don't even know. I wrote down some notes while I was working, but it was mainly trial and error. Sloppy? Maybe, but sometimes you got to just follow your instincts."

John's final debriefing and a troubleshooting session was scheduled at the Knoll just after he received his PhD in neuroscience and took a short celebratory trip. The first item on the agenda was the launch date. Martha and Randy wanted to launch in a matter of days, perhaps to put an early end to the anxiety that was gripping them. Sarah and Joe wanted to put it off until the fall so that they could be more certain that every conceivable problem had been addressed. When it was John's turn to issue an opinion about the launch date, He said, "I don't care, as long as I'm there for Macy's Thanksgiving Day parade." And he said it while grinning broadly. The others reacted with a lot of eye rolling. Martha asserted, "This is a serious matter, John." Unruffled, John responded with, "I am serious. I'd like to see the parade in its early years."

This flippant response was followed with several lectures about how his deadly serious mission was not a sight seeing tour. After listening not so patiently, John shrugged and mumbled, "I'll go when you want me to go." Sarah got back to the meeting's agenda with a way to arrive at a launch date decision, "Let's look at the weather. We don't want John to arrive during a snowstorm, nor during one of New

York City's infamous hot summers." She pulled an iPad out of her briefcase and a couple of minutes later declared, "Early October looks best, not too hot not too cold. Extreme weather is not likely."

Everybody nodded in the affirmative. Sarah reached back into her briefcase and pulled out a sheet of paper. "This is a 1928 calendar that I found online. How about October 17, that's a Wednesday in about the middle of the month?" Following a brief discussion, the group voted 4 to 1 for October 17. Randy cast the only negative vote. When asked why he disagreed with the group, he muttered, "I don't think we'll be ready by then." Launch time was set at 6:00AM, early enough to ensure that there would be few people in Central Park, but late enough for John to eat breakfast and be at the bank by opening time.

In the next portion of the meeting, Randy, Sarah, Martha and Joe concentrated on grilling John about what he was supposed to do on the morning he landed in New York City on October 17, 1928. "So," Randy began, "what is the first thing you are going to do after landing safely near the Harlem Meer?"

"Thank all of you for getting me there in one piece," replied John.

Sarah asked, "Then what?"

"I'll head east until I come to 5th Avenue. There I'll flag down a cab to take me to the Mount Morris Bank Building."

Joe asked, "And, what do you do there?"

"I'll deposit the money."

"What if they don't take your money?" continued Joe.

"I thought you said they would take it?"

"The odds are they will, but what if they don't?"

There was silence in the room. Everyone had assumed that the bank would accept the money. "Wouldn't you be a little suspicious if you were a banker and someone came into your establishment with a suitcase full of more than 36,000 plus dollars? Maybe the teller you approach will call the bank manager and he'll decide what to do. Maybe he'll want to check with the top US Treasury Department official in the city about whether your money is legal tender. More likely, though, he will wonder, 'What's this guy off the street doing with so much money.' Maybe he will think you're a mobster and call the police."

Faces around the circle reflected various degrees of irritation, most near max level. Finally Sarah raised a question: "Ah, Joe, what are you doing? I thought we had the money issue taken care of and here you are raising multiple red flags.'

"I just want to be sure John is ready for things to go wrong. Nothing ever works out exactly as planned. While I'm confident that the money will be accepted as genuine, it's not a sure thing. What would you do if the money wasn't accepted?"

"I've wondered about that also," returned John. My parents have some jewelry I could take along … they told me I'd inherit it, but I could probably get it now. That would only be good for a short time. I'd have to get a job. Maybe I could convince a hospital that I know enough about the brain to be useful to them."

Randy broke in, "Yeah, that's what I'm talking about. Have some options."

"Ok," Sarah let out the breath she had been holding, "it's reasonable to assume that the bank will accept your money. What do you do next?"

"I'll go west on 125th Street to the Hotel Teresa and book a room?"

"What if there are no vacancies?" queried Martha.

"Uh, hadn't thought of that … let's see I could go back to the Morris Bank Building and ask if they had any apartments to rent … they had some upstairs. I checked online. Or I'll try to bribe them by saying that I will pay a month in advance."

"Reasonable answers," offered Randy. "By the way, how much cash will you have on you when you leave the bank, in what denominations?"

"Haven't thought of that."

Joe offered, "You will need a lot of change for tips, cabs, meals, the New York Times and many other purposes. You had better carry a coin purse."

"Ok, what about bills?" asked John.

Sarah, advised, "The bigger the bills the fewer you should have on you. You should carry only a few one hundred bills, several fifties, many tens, fives, and especially ones. You will need a big wallet. Also, as you learn what it will cost you to get through a day, carry only what you will need on a given day. Flash a wallet full of big bills and you could be in a lot of trouble. Bold criminals are not just a thing of the 2010s. Brazen criminals roamed the streets of NYC during the 1920s."

With a tiny tremble in her voice Martha said, "Maybe you'll need a gun."

John responded in a nonchalant tone, "I don't need that. I'll be alright."

Randy asked, "You sure?"

"Yeah, it's not a problem. I'll be fine. What else you got?"

Joe changed the subject with, "About the grad students you will try to hook up with … You will be dropping hints about scientific breakthroughs that will be far ahead of their time. They may want to check your credentials. What if they ask you for the name of the college you graduated from? If you claim a degree from a college or university that existed during the 1920s, they will be able to check your claim."

"Opps," was all John could come up with.

Martha jumped in, "That problem occurred to me. I hadn't gotten around to telling John about it, but I went online to find a college that closed its doors before 1928. Tabor College in Freemont County Iowa shut down in 1927. It was a respectable little college in the sparsely populated southwestern corner of Iowa. Among its varied departments was one offering a degree in general science."

John was watching Martha as she spoke. He had this "you saved my butt again" look on his face. The others were amazed at Martha's farsightedness.

But Joe reopened the issue with, "Ok, you have a cover story, how are you going to find willing grad students at Columbia to be your audience for revelations about future scientific advances?"

"I'll spend much time on campus beginning soon after I arrive in New York City. I'll be looking for someone who might get me into science discussions she or he has with fellow grad students. I've thought a lot about this issue. I'll look around for people carrying science books who look older than undergraduates. I'm not shy. I'll try to engage them in conversations by referring to the books they are carrying. It will be best if they are already sitting down, but I'll try to stop them if they are walking by. I can spot a nerd a mile away. What do you think, did nerds of the late 1920s look like they do today?" This comment got some chuckles, which improved the heading-to-hostile atmosphere that Joe's questions had created.

John continued, "I'll probably winnow through many prospects before I find one who regularly talks science with other grad students. Hopefully they will meet periodically to talk about science. If not I'll figure something out, like buy them lunch a couple of times a week during which I'll bring up issues in science. What l need is a person who occupies a central position in a social network of science students at Columbia. Such a person may be the leader of a group that meets periodically to talk about science or someone with the clout to organize such meetings. I'll have lots of time. I'll get it done."

After a pause, Randy cleared his throat and asked, "How are you going to pass the time of day? I mean, you have a tight schedule now; we all do. We all have plenty to fill our days. What will you do between occasional meetings with science grad students and evenings at the Savoy?"

"Are you kidding!" returned John. "There are Broadway plays, there are the Yankees, Giants and Robins ..."

"Robins?" asked a perplexed Martha. "I'm a baseball fan, but never heard of the 'Robins'."

"That's an early name for the team that became the Brooklyn Dodgers."

"You've really done your homework," remarked Sarah.

"Yes I have. There are museums, great ethnic restaurants, unique events in different boroughs and that's just what I can think of right now. I'll have plenty to do."

John's friends were getting jealous. Some of them were thinking of calling for a new vote on who gets to take the trip to 1928 New York City. But they got over it.

A few days after this momentous meeting, John left town for parts unknown. His absence provided an opportunity for his friends to consider what was on their minds regarding the trip back in time. Martha and Randy bumped into each other on campus and sat down for some soul-searching. She greeted him with, "You look like you've lost some weight."

He looked embarrassed, and blushed a bit. "I'm … yes I've lost a little." In fact, his famously sagging jowls appeared to be shrinking.

To lessen his discomfort, she quickly switched the topic to the upcoming trip. "I'm still worried and not just about John's possible demise. Concerning that matter, he might die right there in that chamber. I don't think I can handle that. But there is another concern. We could be tried for murder …"

Randy broke in, "Look, that seems very unlikely. Nothing bad happened to our rat or, apparently, the one launched before we broke into the chamber room. The more serious problem is that we may never see John again. I know you care about him. So do I, and I believe the others do also."

"Ok, but I don't think anyone has brought up the possibility that your professors may suddenly destroy the chamber room to hide their misappropriation of government funds used to finance an apparently ludicrous scientific misadventure. He would be stranded in the past for the rest of his life."

After thinking for a moment, Randy responded with, "We would have to keep a close eye on them and, if there was even an hint that they might destroy the chamber, we'd have to stop them somehow, maybe by threatening to make the time-travel project public. Besides, though it would be very hard on us, he may be happy to live out his life in the past."

"If John is gone for several years, all of us will have completed our dissertation orals and moved somewhere else. Who would watch out for John then?"

"I will. I won't leave the campus community until John is back or he has elected not to come back."

"You would do that? How would you support yourself?"

"My parents would support me if necessary, but I could talk my professors into a lab technician job, if I had to. I know their labs. They could use my expertise and could get by with paying me squat. Before I'd let them destroy the chamber room, I'd put ricin in their coffee pots."

"Ok, you're scaring me … but I do feel better," was Martha's discussion ending comment.

The next day, Martha phoned Sarah to discuss her talk with Randy. "Randy has done an about-face. He had never before believed that time travel was possible, but now he is fiercely defending the mission. When I reminded him that his professors might destroy the time machine to cover their misappropriation of funds, he vowed that he'd poison them before he would allow that."

"Yeah, that's weird," answered, Sarah. "It seems unlike Randy. Wonder what's eating him?"

"Well," mused Martha, "I should have prefaced my comments by saying that I told him I was distressed about the possibility that John might die during the attempted launch. Maybe that is what's bothering him. Oh, and I did something dumb. I said he looked like he has been losing weight."

Sarah responded with, "Well, you sort of did the double whammy on him, didn't you?"

"So he's uptight possibly because of dieting or worry about the trip and John's possible demise, or both."

"Not to mention," Sarah continued Martha's comment, "losing his obese persona, which seems to be a great part of who he is."

"I'd better get out of here before you make me feel even more guilty." They laughed and hugged before parting company.

CHAPTER 9

Launch

John returned only a few days before he was to be launched into Central Park of New York City, 1928. He seemed relaxed and showed no signs of apprehension concerning his imminent departure into an uncertain past. During the final meeting before he was to be launched, all preparations were reviewed. Because John was to dress in the clothes that he would wear on launch day, and his all-important suitcase would be present at the meeting, they met at the secluded site where their rat was recovered in the forest near the grassy knoll. They all showed up at about the same time, and headed for the forest. John had a coat over his clothes and the hat he would wear was stuffed into a coat pocket. When they arrived at the meeting site and were reasonably sure that no had seen any of them enter the forest, John took off his coat, put on his hat, and grinned as his friends assessed his look. Joe was inspired to giggle, while Sarah and Randy looked amazed and Martha seemed puzzled. "Whoa!" exclaimed John. "Do I look all that odd?"

"Well," offered Martha, "you certainly don't have a contemporary look."

Joe followed that discouraging remark with, "You look like a character in an old black and white picture of a street bum that we have in our country home."

Trying to be more encouraging, Sarah said, "I have some photos from the 1920s that we used to hunt for your costume." She passed them around to the others. Indeed, John did look like some of the men depicted in the photos, but, somehow, they looked more stylish than he did.

Randy offered, "I think that he looks more disheveled than the men in the photos because their clothes are new and his are not."

There were several head nods in agreement. Martha added that his hat looked like it had been sat on regularly. "However," she said, "It's too late. We have to go with what he has on." The others agreed. John's grin faded. "Well, at least," he thought to himself, "nobody dissed his shoes."

Joe pulled the suitcase forward, sat it on the ground, and asked John to lift it by its handle. He was able to lift it easily, but commented that carrying it several blocks would probably be taxing. Joe then pointed out the crude waterproofing that he had managed to contrive. Upon opening the suitcase, Joe pointed out a waterproof metal case taking up a great part of the middle of the suitcase. "That's the money. Your electronic devices are wrapped in paper and scattered among the clothing packed in the luggage. I put you passport on top of the clothes ... here." He pointed to what looked like a small envelope with a bulge in it. "Be sure to have it in your pants pocket when you arrive at the chamber room. The metal case is capable of taking quite a lot of abuse. Also, I think that the devices will be safe where I placed them, provided you don't end up in the Harlem Meer."

"So what do we do next?" asked Sarah.

When no one responded after the lapse of a several moments, Martha spoke up. "I brought some beer and munchies; let's talk old times." And they did that for a couple of hours.

Because it didn't matter what day they launched John—just the day he would arrive in NYC was relevant—they decided to send him off before the university opened for the fall semester. So, on August 10, a Saturday, at 1:00 AM Randy let them all into the Computer Science building and they made their way to the chamber room. Once there John hugged each one of them goodbye and entered the chamber. The others were distributed about the chamber room as they had been during the rat launch. Before Randy and Joe started the computer software steps that would end with the appearance of the launch hyperlink, they all took a last look at John. He seemed tranquil in his 1928 costume, hat and all, as he stood in the middle of the chamber clutching the handle of his suitcase with both hands. When the launch hyperlink was activated all the initial lights and sounds filled the room, then there was silence and darkness in the chamber. When the lights came on, the chamber was empty.

The four friends who were left behind did and said nothing for what seemed like several minutes. Finally, Martha announced in a mournful tone, "He's gone."

They gathered outside the chamber and peered in. There was no sign that anyone had been there.

"Well, I guess he's in Central Park now," proclaimed Sarah. The others expressed agreement. But Sarah focused on Joe who seemed less enthralled by the launch event than the rest of them. "What do you think, Joe? Did he really go to 1928 NYC or do you have another explanation?"

"No, no, I believe it … he's gone to 1928." exclaimed Joe.

"Just the same, continued Sarah, can you come up with an alternate explanation?"

"Ok, since you asked, after we launched the rat, John acted strangely. You all probably remember that he walked up to the chamber, peered inside and asked 'What's that?' pointing to the back door of the chamber. I explained that it was an escape hatch. If he wanted to, he could let himself out of the chamber while the lights were extinguished, and exit the building through a one-way door, out only. Maybe he parked his car nearby and is making his way out of town as we speak."

"Do you believe that?" asked Randy.

"I told you I believe he was launched ... but Sarah wanted to consider other possibilities."

They left the building a few minutes later feeling surprisingly unfazed by what had just transpired and didn't contact one another for several days.

It was 6 AM, October 17, 1928. John found himself standing in a grassy area surrounded by trees. There was a light mounted on a building nearby that allowed him to make out the Harlem Meer. He heaved an enormous sigh of relief, which attracted the attention of someone standing a few yards behind him. When he turned around he made out the form of a man dressed in more decrepit clothes than his own. The scruffy looking guy asked quite loudly, "Hey buddy, can you spare a dime?"

"Sure," John replied. "I got a dime if you can show me how to make it over to 5th Avenue."

The tattered and dirty man stepped forward and presented his grimy right hand. "Dime first, then I tell you how to get to 5th Avenue."

John dropped a dime and a nickel into the man's hand. His eyes opened wide and his jaw dropped. "Thank you, mister."

After he bit down on each coin to make sure they were genuine, he pointed northeast and declared, "Go this way and you can't miss it. Which way you going, north or south?" John responded that he wanted to go north. "Well then, take a left when you get to 5th Avenue."

As John headed in the indicated direction, the man yelled out to him, "Hey mister, when you coming back here?" John didn't respond.

It didn't take John long to get to 5th Avenue. He was a little worried about the possibility of rain because he could make out some clouds, but that judgment was unreliable due to the still dark skies. After he arrived at 5th Avenue he turned north and walked a few blocks switching the suitcase from one hand to the other every few minutes. He stopped at 116th Street for a respite from carrying the heavy suitcase. It made an acceptable chair while he drank in the sights and sounds of the city. He was surprised at how heavy the traffic was at this early hour. Cars and trucks rolled pass him every few seconds. A few cabs approached him, but when he waved at them to stop, the drivers glared at him for a moment and kept going. The vehicles he witnessed looked scary. All seemed to have big wheels encircled by skinny tires. They tended to have a high center of gravity and be narrow in width, exactly the dimensions that would make toppling over very likely in the event of a collision. Even rounding a corner at relatively low speeds made them lean perilously far to the outside of the turn.

Finally a particularly beat-up taxi stopped for him. As it had no sign on its side, or other indication that it was a taxi, John peered into the interior and spotted what looked like a taxi license hanging from the dash. "Where to?" shouted the driver above the din of street traffic. "Do you know of a diner serving breakfast that is near the Mount Morris

Bank building?" He shouted back in a caustic manner, "You might as well ask me if I know my mommy's name … get in." John opened the back door, tossed in the suitcase, brushed off the filthy seat and dove in just before the driver slammed the floor mounted shift-rod into gear and popped the clutch. John was hurled back and then forward. He stabilized himself by grabbing the back of the front seat and the door handle. The taxi lurched forward until it attained its estimated top speed of about 30 miles per hour. They made it a few blocks before a small truck hit the front passengers' side of the cab with a resounding "WHAM." The cab spun counter-clockwise several degrees before stopping perpendicular to the flow of traffic in its lane. Crude brakes of on-coming vehicles screeched like wounded owls as they successfully skidded to a stop only a few feet short of the cab. As the cab driver ripped open his door and raced toward the approaching truck driver, his mouth was spewing out an impressive ensemble of curse words. Because John assumed that the police would soon arrive, he grabbed the suitcase and slipped out of the back seat.

As he grappled with the truck driver, the taxi driver saw John exit the cab out of the corner of his eye. When he yelled at John, "Hey, where you think you're going?" the truck driver let him go. Now the two combatants stared at John as if they had joined forces against lazy uptown people who cheat hard-working drivers. John ran over to the cab driver lugging the suitcase with one hand and searching his pocket for some change. John pulled out a handful or coins and dumped them into the taxi driver hand. The cabby looked at it with apparent satisfaction, shoved it into his pocket and went back to the push and shove match with the truck driver. As John headed for the sidewalk, he heard the taxi driver yell, "The diner is six blocks north on the right ... you can't miss it."

On his way up 5th Avenue, John turned in the direction of the bank. At this moment, he really felt for the first time that what people in his time called "The Big Apple" was America's biggest city in every sense of the word "biggest." That would remain true for him even if he lived long enough to see some other city—perhaps Houston—exceed NYC in population.

As he approached the diner, it was dawn outside. The sun would soon be fully up. When he entered the diner the clock on the wall read 7:05 AM. He thought, "The bank opens at 9; I have plenty of time." He dumped the suitcase beside a table and collapsed onto a chair. Soon he caught the attention of a middle-age woman wearing a headband with enough embroidered cloth on it to cover the front of her head. Her hair was arranged in what he would later learn was called "bobbed." She ambled over to his table, tilted her weight to her right leg, pulled a pencil out from behind her right ear and, in a hoarse voice, spoke her name and asked "What can I get ya?" Before he could respond, she was licking the pencil lead, readying herself to record his order on a pad in her left hand. John wanted to tell her that the lead she just licked with apparent relish might someday do her in. But, instead, he ordered scrambled eggs, bread, jelly and some sausage. She said, "Want coffee?" He nodded in the affirmative and she shuffled away while continuing to record his order on the pad.

The breakfast was very good. The eggs were soft and fluffy and the bread looked and tasted like it had been baked on site. The sausage smelled a bit strange, but had an excellent taste to it. When she brought him the bill he was surprised that he could pay with the change left in his pocket. She waited patiently as he dug the change out of his pocket. When he spread it out on the table and withdrew his hand, he looked up to find her smiling broadly. Apparently the tip was good.

It now was 7:45 AM, still an hour and 15 minutes until the bank would open. As he walked toward the door, he saw a day-old copy of the New York Times on a chair near the door. He called to the waitress, "Can I have this paper? It's a day old." She called back, "Help yourself." He grabbed it with the hand not clutching the suitcase and exited to the street.

It was a short walk to the Mount Morris Park, which was very close to the bank building. Once there, he found a bench under a big oak tree. When he unfolded the paper to the finance page, he found that the news about the market was good. Hoover replaced Coolidge for the Republican Nomination. Silent Cal had been uncomfortable in the White house. These two Republicans were favored by Wall Street financiers who gave their party a good deal of the credit for the prosperity enjoyed by investors during the 1920s. The Democratic nominee, Al Smith was not liked by moneyed people and, therefore, given little chance to win the election in November. Everything seemed to be hunky-dory on Wall Street. The sports page was all about baseball with the Yankees having recently beaten St. Louis in the World Series. The mighty Babe Ruth was as much a hero in New York City as he was a villain in Boston. The society page was all about which member of a very rich family was marrying into which other well-endowed family. Life seemed good in NYC, at least for prominent members of its population. John promised himself that he would read the Times every day.

As he stood up to head toward the bank, a man approached him looking from side to side as if he was about to do something he didn't want anyone to see. John set the suitcase down and prepared for the worst. When the man was about four feet in front of John, he stopped and applied both hands to pulling open his jacket. John suppressed a laugh at what he saw. Many watches and some cheap looking jewelry were pinned to the left-side and right-side linings of the jacket. The man looked puzzled at his reaction, so John thought for a moment and realized that he needed a watch. He had one in the suitcase, but he wasn't wearing it because he doubted that it looked like watches of the 1920s. "Ok," he said, "how much for that one?" pointing to one that looked like a used 1920ish watch."

The man responded, "For you, today, it's $1.50." When John replied that amount sounded like a lot for the watch he was considering, the man began talking fast about it being a good deal because it was an expensive watch that he was selling cheaply. Then John remembered that he was out of money. He felt his pocket where the change had been, and sure enough, it was empty. Next he felt his coat pockets just in case he had absent-mindedly put some coins in them. He found change in the right pocket. When he lifted the money out he counted five quarters and some nickels. The man extended one of his hands with the watch in it and the other with the fingers curled to grab the coins. "Is this watch set at the correct time?" The man used his thumbs to open his coat again, saying as he did it, "All of these have the correct time." John dropped the money in the man's hand and grabbed the watch. The man looked behind him in both directions, then he took off running at flank speed toward the center of the park. The watch read "8:55."

When John reached the northeast corner of the park he could see the Mount Morris Bank building. It was even more beautiful in real life than in the pictures he had seen online. When he arrived at the bank, he entered through the front door and found the bank quickly. From across the bank lobby, he noticed that a clerk behind the main counter was busily shuffling papers. The young man, properly attired in a coat and tie, glanced up at John, but immediately returned his focus to his papers. When John arrived at the counter, he dropped the suitcase to the floor and leaned on the counter, a mere two feet from the clerk. To John's surprise, the clerk seemed unaware of his presence. John cleared his throat to gain the clerk's attention, but the man continued going through his papers. However, John saw signs of annoyance flash across the man's face. "Excuse me," said John in a voice loud enough to echo about the room.

The man turned to look at John through eyelids squeezed nearly shut. He growled, "Yes?"

"I'd like to open an account."

"We have a minimum initial deposit of $100. Do you have that much money with you?"

"Yes."

"Fill out these forms," sputtered the clerk as he thrust a stack of papers at John and slammed a pen down on the counter. "Take it over there," the man whispered dismissively as he pointed to a table and a chair.

John completed the forms in about 10 minutes, which was fast considering that he had to make up much of the information required by the bank. One of the requests for information worried him, "Indicate your local address." He had yet to register at the Hotel Theresa, so he couldn't indicate a room number. He pondered making up a room number or just writing "Hotel Theresa." The latter seemed safest.

The clerk reluctantly put aside his own papers and picked up the forms John had dropped on the counter. He looked at the forms for a moment with his head tilted back. Then he turned his attention to John, literally looking down his nose at the prospective customer. "Your name is John Williams?"

John answered in the affirmative.

"You list the Hotel Theresa as your local address. How long will you be there?"

"Indefinitely."

Now the clerk looked angry. "Don't be impertinent. Tell me how long you will be there?"

"At least six months."

"Oh, never mind," muttered the clerk. "I'll take your initial deposit now."

John bent over to where he had placed the suitcase, opened the lid, retrieved the box containing the cash, placed it on the counter, opened the lid and spun it around so that the clerk could view its contents. The clerk gasped and staggered backward as if he was about to faint. John swept the cash container to one side and thrust both arms across the counter, grabbing the man by his lapels. The clerk recovered his balance, but his composure was another matter. After a few moments of heavy breathing, he managed to say, "I've got to find the manager." He wondered off down a nearby hall.

An older man wearing a suit with a matching vest and tie arrived at the counter with a skeptical look etched on his face. He stroked his balding, greying head and peered into the cash box. After picking up several of the stacks of one hundred dollar bills and quickly examining them, he announced, "We will have to examine this money more closely. This will take awhile ... is there another matter you could address while you wait?"

"Yes," John replied. "I will need to rent a large safe-deposit box in a room where I can privately examine the items I will store there. Oh, and, there should be at least one electrical socket in the room."

"Yes, we do have the facilities you require. Would you like to inspect that room now?" John answered in the affirmative. The manager explained that he would lead John to a secure safety-deposit room and would take the cash box to a room nearby to exam its contents. John closed the suitcase and picked it up as the manager, intoned, "Please follow me."

Once inside the safety-deposit room, John closed and locked the door behind him and looked around the room. He was pleased to discover that it had two electrical sockets. As the manager had told him that he could choose any box with a key in it, John searched for a large box far from the door. Upon selecting a box, he removed it, pulled out the key and placed it in his pocket. The manager had informed him on their walk to the room that there was only one duplicate to the key for each box. It was stored in his office safe. Should the original be lost, no one but John or, in the event of his death, a lawyer for his estate, would be able to obtain the second key. John carefully filled the box with his electronic devices, his two connections from the devices to wall sockets, some family jewels, and the watch he brought from the future. He returned the box to its place on the wall, locked it, secured the key in a pocket of the suitcase lid, and exited the room.

The manager was waiting for him in the hallway with a stern look on his face. "Mr. Williams," he began, "it is my pleasure to inform you that your deposit is accepted. I am sorry that our clerk treated you in less than a cordial manner. I have had a talk with him and can assure you that all of your requests for service in our bank will be treated in the most professional manner in the future." He held out his hand. John grasped it firmly and squeezed it perhaps too tightly. On the way out of the room, the severely humbled clerk was standing near the door, head down and upper torso bent forward as if he was suppressing an urge to bow. In less than an hour, John had gone from vagrant to a member of the Astor family.

When he arrived at the Hotel Theresa, he avoided a repeat of the scene at the bank by putting a couple of hundred dollar bills on the check-in-counter. It was part of the $500 in three 100 dollar bills, and some smaller currency, that he held back from his new bank account. He asked for and received a corner room on the top floor facing the Mount Morris Park. It cost him twice the $2.50 per day plus tax advertised in the New York Times, but what a view! What a day! Nothing much went as expected, but he had gotten to 1928 NYC in one piece and was excited about the adventures ahead of him.

Before going to bed that night, he put his old clothes in a laundry basket he found in the room and placed it outside his door. Instructions printed on the basket informed him that they would be cleaned, pressed and returned outside his door by early morning.

CHAPTER 10

Settling In

John got up late on October 18, 1928 and showered leisurely. Clothed only with a towel wrapped around his waist, he peeked outside his door where he found and retrieved his clothes. After dressing, he took the elevator down to the main lobby. When he asked a clerk at the front desk where he could get a good breakfast nearby, he was not surprised to hear that the Hotel Theresa Dinning Room offered the best breakfast in the area. Alternatives were also provided, but John elected to try the Dinning room. For less than $3.00 he feasted on Eggs Benedict, a fruit salad, fresh bread, and a bottomless cup of fresh Columbian coffee. He paid with cash in order to get some change and left a generous tip.

At the East 125th exit from the hotel, he asked the doorman to hail a cab for him. Once in the backseat he informed the cabby that he wanted to go shopping and would need the cabby to wait for him while he tried on clothes. The cabby replied, "Yes, sir, but you will have to pay for all my time. Waiting in the cab is the same as driving on the streets."

John answered, "No problem. I'll pay you for your time."

"'No problem'? What does that mean," growled the cabby.

"Ops," thought John. Use of a 2010s slang expression was his first verbal slip-up. John uttered, "Excuse me," in an apologetic tone. "I only meant that your conditions are acceptable to me."

The cabby seemed puzzled, but managed to respond with, "Yes sir," as he cranked the cab into gear. When they began to move into the traffic, he turned his head toward the back seat and loudly inquired, "Where do you want to go?"

John used his own city traffic voice: "I want to visit a clothing store that has the latest styles for men."

"No problem," said the cabby with a grin.

John could see that they were headed for Manhattan. Once there, the cabby pulled up in front of Macy's at Broadway and 34th Street. "Welcome to the world's largest store," announced the cabby with obvious pride. "I'll be waiting for you out here." John handed him some bills and the cabbie smiled in anticipation of more.

The men's clothing store took up most of a floor. As he browsed at leisure, he saw men's two-toned leather soled shoes with elaborate designs engraved into the leather of the toes and heels. He caught the eye of a clerk, pointed out the shoes he favored and was led to a chair where he could try them on. After selecting three pair, total price less than $20, he put on one pair and was ushered to a cashier where he inquired as to whether he could leave the shoes at the register and try on some clothes. With disdain, the cashier carefully pronounced, "I'm sorry, sir, but you must pay for the shoes now. After you pay, I'll keep them here for you."

"Fine," said John as he reached into his pocket, pulled out a one hundred dollar bill and tossed it nonchalantly onto the countertop. Out of apparent deference for big bills, the cashier's eyebrows lifted automatically. While the cashier counted out his change, John noisily tossed his old shoes into a trashcan behind the counter. With obvious annoyance, he grabbed the several bills and coins out of the cashier's hand and stuffed them into his pocket. Immediately he did an about face and headed for the clothing section where a clerk hailed by the cashier was eager to serve him. When he glanced back at the cashier and the shoe salesmen, they were gazing after him with "thanks for your business" smiles painted on their faces.

"Some things never change," he mused to himself as he roamed among the suits, trousers, coats, shirts, ties, socks and belts that defined stylish attire in 1928. But then it occurred to him that he was changing. He was, for the first time in his life, really rich and acting with the arrogance that too often comes with wealth. "I have to work on being who I was," he pledged to himself.

Following some browsing, he picked out a double-breasted blue chinchilla overcoat priced at $35, a double breasted brown tweed suit for $22.50, three wool sweaters for $3.98 each, and for $3.75, a pair of Rough Wear Breeches, puffed out below the waist like riding pants and tightly bound around the knees. After selecting some jackets, pants, shirts, socks, underwear, belts and ties, he felt that he had enough for the occasions he anticipated.

The cabby was patiently waiting for John when he exited Macy's carrying several bags. "Where do you want to go next?" he asked as john eased into the back seat. Because he had recklessly flashed big bills that day, it had occurred to him that he needed to get some blank checks. So, John informed the cabby that he had some bank business to do and asked, "Would you take me to the Mount Morris Bank Building?" "No problem," said the cabby. John didn't respond, but he sighed and thought to himself, "Well at least, I have probably ensured that one worthless, hackneyed phrase from the 2010s will be worn out ahead of its time."

At the bank's main counter John introduced himself and asked for some blank checks. The clerk politely assured him that the checks would be prepared for him by Friday. When asked why he couldn't have them now, John was told that they had to be printed. The clerk, who was not present the day John opened his account, apparently had been told about the initial deposit debacle. He looked frightened. After a few awkward moments, the clerk recovered enough to stammer, "I ... I will deliver the checks to you personally when they arrive on Friday."

John assured him that he could wait for the checks and asked whether a courier could drop off the checks at the Hotel Theresa main desk at least by Monday. "Yes sir," said the clerk with obvious relief. As he headed for his safety-deposit-box room, he was wondering whether he would ever have normal relations with this bank's employees. Once inside the room he locked the door behind him and retrieved his safety deposit box. All of his electronic devices were in good order, although he noticed that their batteries would have to be charged soon. He made a mental note to spend some time charging the batteries very soon.

Back in the cab, he asked whether the cabby would be available to drop him off at the Savoy that evening and pick him up after a few hours. "No sir, I'm off tonight, but I can get one of the other cabbies to pick you up and come back for you." John approved the plan and had the cabby take him back to the Hotel Theresa. On the way, the cabby tallied what John owed him. When they arrived at the hotel, John handed the cabby several bills. After counting the money carefully, the cabby thanked John profusely. "I really appreciate it mister. My name is Robert Jamison ... just call me Bob. All you have to do is telephone the cab company and ask for me. If I'm on duty, I'll be happy to take you anywhere in the city." He penciled the company phone number on a scrap piece of paper and handed it to John who signaled to a bellhop to help with the bags. "What time should I have a cab pick you up this evening for the trip to the Savoy?" "How about 9 o'clock?" "Nine it is, sir. Oh, by the way, I'll need your name so the cabby can ask a bellhop to fetch you."

John stuck out his hand and introduced himself. "I'm John Williams."

John had no idea what to wear to the Savoy. He had a new suit, but thought that was too formal. After some deliberation, he decided on a pair of brown and tan shoes, some olive drab pleated pants, a white dress shirt under a greenish v-necked sweater and a dark brown golfer's cap. When he looked at himself in the mirror he had no idea whether he was "hip" for the times or "square," despite having researched men's clothing for the late 1920s.

Promptly at 9 PM a clean and relatively new cab was waiting for him. As he slipped into the back seat, the cabby twisted his neck around so he could personally greet John with, "Good evening Mr. Williams. I understand you want me to drop you off at the Savoy and pick you up later." John replied in the affirmative and the cabbie headed north on 7th Avenue toward the Savoy. When they turned the corner at 140th and Lenox Avenue the Savoy was lit up like a 75 year-old's birthday cake and the sounds coming from it were among the richest John had ever heard. He told the cabby to drive by the front of the Savoy between 12:00 and 12:15 and he'd be waiting. The cabby asked whether John could meet him across the street from the Savoy where the traffic would be more manageable. John agreed.

He lined up to enter the Ballroom. When it was his turn to pay, he had his 85 cents ready, but the ticket collector stopped him with, "Sir, gentlemen must wear a tie." John explained he didn't have one and prepared to bribe his way in, but the collector merely turned around stuck his hand into a drawer and pulled out a tie. "That will be an additional 15 cents."

John managed to affix the tie under his collar and tie a proper knot despite the crush of the crowd. He finally made his way to a table and slumped down into a chair. Two black men, about John's age, were already seated at the table. Both had looks of amusement on their faces as they sized him up. The bigger of the two stuck out his hand and announced, "My name's Rudolf—call me Rudy—this here is my cousin Fred. Where you from? You one of them college boys?"

"So, that's how I look," thought John as he searched his mind for answer to Rudy's question. "I grew up on a farm in Iowa and went to a small college there."

"Hah" exclaimed Rudy, "I thought you a college boy. And a farm boy? How about dat."

Fred interjected, "Bet you ain't seen this many Negroes in one place your whole life long."

"Especially mixed in with all these white folks," added Rudy.

"Can't say I have," said John.

"Fact is," continued Rudy, "This is the only place in the whole USA where Negros and whites mix together like they one and the same."

John asked, "How about the Cotton Club?"

The cousins responded "No!" in unison.

The background conversation continued with Rudy and Fred revealing that they grew up near Oxford Mississippi where their parents were sharecroppers. They had come north in search of a better life, but were stuck in a one-room apartment. Both were struggling to pay rent and upkeep through odd jobs such as shoe shinning, errand-running and doing yard work for white folks in Brooklyn and Staten Island.

"Is that better than Mississippi?" asked John.

They both blurted out, "You kidding?" Rudy elaborated, "We got no future in Mississippi. Here, at least, we can go to the parks and walk around through most of city. Being broke ain't no good no where, but it's more tolerable here? Maybe someday we get our own newsstand."

They talked some more and drank some more. Soon they were all three pretty much high, and the cousins were broke. At this point, John announced that he had come into some money and would pay for some more drinks.

There were two bandstands so that the music was continuous. When one band took a break, the other took over. This particular night, neither band was well known, but both were composed of black musicians who played so rapidly that the whole room vibrated. John had never seen fingers moving so fast strumming fiddles, stroking strings with bows, pressing keys on wind instruments, manipulating drumsticks and flying across a piano keyboard. The net effect was a sound that you could feel in your bones. Modern electronics could never reproduce it.

At about 11:30, the leader of the band that had just occupied a bandstand announced, "Get ready for the Lindy Hop!"

The crowd erupted in a roar that was joyous and tempestuous at the same time. Almost everyone crowded onto the floor. John tried to stay behind at the table, but Rudy and Fred dragged him by the arms to the dance floor. At first John could just watch the wild yet highly coordinated gyrations that were somehow beautifully synchronized with the beat of the band. Doing the Lindy Hop required a level of athleticism that few people possess. However, partly because he was pretty high and partly because he was exceptionally athletic, John begin to get the beat. Fred and Rudy selected a couple of women to help them demonstrate the right Lindy Hop gyrations. At first John moved his head a little. Soon his torso and arms began to sway with the music and his feet picked up the beat. Then he cut in on Rudy and began to move to the music with Rudy's partner in the lead. After a few minutes John's moves were indistinguishable from those of other dancers. He was doing the Lindy Hop!

About fifteen minutes of Lindy Hoping exhausted the three inebriated young men. They returned to their table and flopped down hard on their chairs. After a few minutes of wheezing to catch their breath, Fred recovered his voice well enough to whisper to John, "You sure you white? I ain't never seen a white boy learn to dance that quick." The question drew some hee-haws from the cousins, but it sobered up John a bit.

"Uh, far as I know I don't have any African heritage, but I've never had my genes assessed."

"You ain't never had what?" asked a puzzled Fred.

"Well," begin John in an attempt to cover up his slip, "I mean I don't know whether any of my ancestors were black."

Rudy chimed in, "Maybe you don't know it, but you sho look like one of us out there on the dance floor."

"Hey," interrupted Rudy, "maybe he another cousin … we got a whole lot of cousins."

They all laughed.

As the midnight hour approached, the crowd began to settle down somewhat. Many who had too much to drink began to hobble toward the main entrance. John began to look around the room and noticed some young women sitting together across the floor. He got up and walked toward them to get a closer look. He had to wait a few moments for the crowd to part enough for him to get a good look at the women. They were uniformly beautiful. All appeared to have European as well as African heritage and each of them was shapely, well dressed, and well groomed. He returned to the table and asked, "Who are they?" while pointing to the women.

"Oh," Rudy began, "they sort of hostesses. You can dance with them if you a regular here and the management knows you. But be careful. Some powerful mens taken a liken to them girls. Some dees mens are white, some Negro, some I-talian, but all of them is rich or mean or both."

"Could you introduce me to them?" John asked in a kind of pleading fashion.

Suddenly sobered up, Rudy replied, "No, we don't know them … we wouldn't want to be seen introducing you to them. But you could come around in the afternoon sometime. That's when things are slow. You could buy one of them drinks. But that's all they do. They won't go anywhere with you."

The warning having not registered with him, John wondered off in the direction of the women. He sat down at a table within a few yards of them and pretended to inspect his nails. John glanced at each of them, but his eyes stopped when they fell on a particularly striking women, probably in her early twenties. Though she looked sad as she delicately touched a drink to her lips, she was phenomenally attractive. Some of the others would probably be rated as equally good-looking, but there was something about this seemingly woebegone individual that touched a sensitive cord within John.

He sneaked closer, getting within a yard or two of the hostesses, where he eased onto a chair. After several glances in her direction he was able to discern that her eyes were hazel, her hair auburn and her skin impeccable, not a blemish or crease ... flawless texture and milk-chocolate in color. Her face was a perfect oval. Her eyes, nose and mouth were in aesthetic sync with each other. But her demeanor was another matter. She looked distracted, perhaps deep in thought. Several of the other girls noticed him and some smiled at him, but his presence seemed not to register on her.

The cabby was waiting for John across the street from the Savoy. He dodged the traffic and made it to the sidewalk where he languidly opened the back-seat door and slid onto the seat. The cabby greeted him in a friendly fashion and tried to strike up a conversation, but John quickly discouraged any verbal exchange by politely communicating his desire for silence. His unusual avoidance of conversation was partly due to his exhausted condition, but it was mostly because of the disappointing end to an otherwise marvelous evening at the Savoy.

Once back at the Hotel Theresa, he tipped the cabby generously and dragged himself to the elevator. By the time he finished a quick shower and climbed into bed, it was a little after 1:00 AM. His dreams that night were a mix of himself gyrating around the dance floor at the Savoy, spurred on by the applause of Rudy and Fred, and of the gorgeous woman alternately smiling at him and yelling for him to leave her alone.

Upon arising at 10:25 AM, October 19, 1928, John again patronized the Hotel dinning room for breakfast. As he nibbled on some toast and jelly and sipped coffee, all he could manage to get down that morning, he thought about making his first trip to the Columbia University campus. "What to wear?" was his first concern. The clothes he had worn the night before passed Rudy's "college boy" test. Fortunately, because his clothes were kind of sweat soaked after his dancing mania at the Savoy, he had remembered to leave them for the hotel laundry before he went to bed.

Back in his room, he shaved, dressed, and posed before a mirror in his "college clothes" to see if he had properly affected the 1928 student look. He judged that he could pass as a Columbia student. Because he felt confident he could easily find a cab back to his hotel, he passed on calling Bob. Instead, he decided to hail a cab to Columbia. Once out of the cab, he referred to a map of the campus he had crammed into the lid of his suitcase. The wrinkled piece of paper showed that the campus was much the same in 1928 as it had been in the 2010s. He walked around a bit trying to determine whether he could see from the books students were carrying with them whether they were enrolled in science graduate studies. Much to his frustration, students were clutching their books as if they were gilded. He was unable to make out book titles, much less determine whether the books students were carrying might have been appropriate for graduate science classes. Finally, he stopped a student and asked to be directed to the library. She turned and pointed to a uniquely shaped building occupying much of the central campus. "That is Low Library." He thanked her and headed for the front door of the enormous and stately building. Once inside he found a directory of floor contents and made a note of where biology books were located. Up the stairs he went, but when he entered the floor where biology books were supposedly shelved, he couldn't find them. After a futile search, he asked a student where he would find the biology books. He was told that the correct location was just a few shelves away. Of course, the books he found in the biology section were unfamiliar to John and, judging from thumbing through a few of them in search of content regarding the brain, he found them to be quite primitive. He roamed around some more in the hope of finding a student to talk with. Many were scattered about the floor, but all had their noses stuck in books. They looked very unapproachable. Nowhere did he find a group of students sitting together talking to each other.

In frustration, he cornered a student and asked where follow students gather to discuss science. The student looked puzzled by the question. After a pause, she offered what could be summed up by the simple phrase "in class." "No," John responded, "I mean, where do students interested in science gather outside of class to talk about it?" After another pause, the student muttered, "I don't know; I'm just a sophomore."

When John crawled into a cab for the return trip to his hotel, the only way he could sum up his day on campus was that finding graduate students informally gathered to discuss science was going to be challenging.

CHAPTER 11

Meanwhile Back at the Ranch

Randy was going to look for something that he really, really wanted to find. He truly believed that John had landed in 1928 New York City, but if he couldn't find John's car he would have to wonder whether Joe's doubts were justified. Because there was no housing for cars in the campus community, John typically parked wherever he could find space, but as often as he could, near his residence. A thorough search of streets near his resident failed to locate the car. Scouring the parking spaces near the Lion's Den, the Psychological & Biological Science Building and the Computer Science Building also failed to turn up John's car. In fact, Randy searched all of the parking lots on campus and nearby with no result. He was worried.

When Sarah called a meeting at the Lion's Den, Randy purposely arrived early. He took a seat where his friends could see him as they filed through the front door. Sarah sat down and immediately asked if he had heard whether anyone had found John's car. "I'm not saying there's anything to Joe's doubts," she said in a conspiratorial tone, "but we need to know whether the launch was really successful."

Randy admitted that he had looked for the car and failed to find it. They both wondered whether the others were suspicious. When Martha showed up soon after Joe, she also asked about John's car. "I wish I hadn't expressed doubts earlier. I believe that the launch was successful. I just have this need to know for sure."

"There's nothing anyone knows for sure. We all can non-consciously misperceive an event: not get it all or distort some of it. We can also misremember aspects of the experience later or subsequently amalgamate it with earlier episodes similar to the experience in question," offered Sarah who immediately saw that her friends had that "don't lecture to us" look on their faces. "Ok," she continued, "I also believe that he is now in 1928 New York City, but, of course, I don't know that with certainty. A little healthy skepticism is a good thing, but let's make sure it is just a little." That seemed to satisfy her audience.

The conversation turned to unfinished business. Martha asked about progress on the multi-functional electronic gadget Randy and Joe were supposed to construct. The device's features were to be designed so that John could use it effectively and surreptitiously while collecting information about New York City before the Great Depression. "Not so incidentally," said Joe, "if we get this new device to John and he returns it to us, we will have highly credible verification that he is in fact in 1928 New York City." Joe went on to report that Randy had a very creative idea about how to house the device so that it would not cause suspicions on the part of New Yorkers who see John use it. "We'll fit it into a 1920's Brownie Camera box. Of course, it will have an opening for a shutter behind which we could place a high-resolution camera with precise focusing capability, including a zoom lens. Very sensitive microphones would be hidden on both sides of the camera. It would do video and stills. We will try to build a special keyboard on the bottom of the camera. It would have half of the keyboard on one side of the camera and the other half on the opposite side. That would make it challenging to learn to use, but, once mastered, it could be used to write script on the go. It would also have a very small microphone that would transmit remotely to a computer inside the camera. John would be able to make comments about what he is witnessing without involving the video camera and the conspicuous pointing of the Brownie box that video recording would involve. Oh, and Randy is working on a touch screen under the top of he box, hidden by a slide away cover. It would allow easy use of numerous apps."

"Wow," exclaimed Martha, "you guys are hatching a marvelous device. Sounds like it would be patentable." Joe modestly interjected that "it was mostly Randy's idea." Randy's shrinking jowls turned visibly red. In an 'aw shucks' voice he claimed that Joe was equally responsible for the gadget.

After Martha finished marveling over the Brownie Box idea, she glanced at her watch and announced that she was late for a meeting. She expressed regrets at having to miss the rest of their meeting and hurried off. There was silence for a few moments as they watched her exit the Den. Then Randy said rather matter-of-factly, "She has a boyfriend." "Really?" remarked Sarah. "I was becoming convinced that John was her boyfriend."

Joe expressed a different opinion: "I had assumed that they were just really good friends, but, now that you mentioned it, they fought like lovers."

Joe added his point of view: "I always assumed they were lovers." This comment started a debate revealing only that Joe steadfastly thought of them as lovers.

"You remember that scene in the Den when they hugged?" asked Joe. "It convinced me that they were lovers."

"Come on, Joe," responded Sarah. "A woman and a man can hug out of friendship. John hugs me sometimes too. You are one of too many men who think that any signs of affection between a woman and a man means they are sleeping together."

At this point, Randy chimed in with, "Nobody hugs me, women or men. And if a woman did hug me, it'd be out of pity." Immediately he was sorry he impulsively revealing his inner thoughts, because his friends took turns hugging him and then tried to group hug him.

"Alright, that's enough!" pleaded Randy. "I get it. You are all my friends. And, by the way, I don't like hugging that much." Instantly they all attempted to hug him again. Everyone in the Den was looking at them. Randy was getting much more attention than he wanted.

After they had all settled down, a conversation about other possible interpretations of John's and Martha's relationship ensued. Maybe they had been lovers, but agree to go their separate ways in view of John's indefinite absence. Maybe they were never lovers, just kindred souls. Or maybe they tried to be lovers and decided they were better off as friends. It was even possible for a woman and a man to have sampled sex and didn't get far because they were not attracted to each other, resulting in a continued relationship that many would label "just friends." Sarah used the "just friends" remark as an introduction into a related issue. "What's wrong with 'just' being friends? We are talking as if friendship is a lower level relationship that doesn't deserve to be mentioned in the same breath as lovers, wife and husband, or relatives. Consider the possibility that friendship is just as good a human relationship as any of the others."

Randy and Joe seemed to resonate to Sarah's thesis. "Yeah, you know," interjected Joe, "I'm thinking that friendship is the purest of human relationships because friends have chosen each other based on mutual interests and compatible traits. By contrast courtship and marital relationships are bound by family and social expectations about what kind of person one should marry and familial relationships are forced on us by law, convention, and biological connection." The other two looked at Joe with renewed respect. Their already cherished friendships looked even better to them.

Randy thought for a minute and then commented, "I have come to accept that you, as well as Martha and John, started our relationships only to get into the secret lab. Maybe even shared negative events can initiate friendships. Chance can also play a role in friendship formation. People can be thrown together by happening to be in the same circumstances, such as finding themselves in the same army unit or, by chance, ending up next door to each other. Even if it's being randomly assigned the same cell in a prison, a true friendship can result.

"Too bad John is not able to hear you today, Randy," said Sarah. "He'd try to recruit you to become a psychologist." They all laughed, but the sound of it was at best a mixture of mirth and sadness.

Joe went to order another round of beer and munches. When he returned they began to discuss their own futures. They knew that Martha's future was uncertain, as she had just begun serious work on writing her dissertation. It would probably be another year before she graduated. Sarah was well into her dissertation, but being a work in philosophy, she was not surprised to find that her committee had differing and changing opinions about the quality and completeness of it.

She said that it could take her from three quarters of a year to more than two years. Frustration oozed from her words and was etched in her face as she talked about her progress toward graduation. Joe was well into his dissertation and fairly optimistic that he could finish within a year. Randy, in contrast to the others, did not have his dissertation research project approved, although he did have a committee. The problem was in part his perfectionism and in part due to declining respect for his committee members, all of whom were involved in the time travel lab. Once high on the deference for authority scale, Randy was becoming openly defiant and even truculent during interactions with his committee. He was anticipating putting them on notice that he would make their double-dealing with regard to funding of the time travel project public if they even hinted that they might dismantle the chamber. The funding was only one reason they didn't want the time travel project made public. They absolutely didn't want their names associated with such a fanciful and seemingly unscientific project. He was clearly committed to staying where he was until John was safely retrieved and all five of them had finished with time travel. When he asked his professors for a paid research assistantship of indefinite duration, it was granted to him without question. That fact confirmed in Randy's mind that his committee and others associated with the time travel project knew he had the goods on them. He had them where he wanted them.

At the next meeting, Martha showed up with her new guy, but left him at the door. When she sat down with the others, they wasted no time expressing their concerns about her new relationship. Randy blurted out, "Who's the new guy?"

Martha was taken aback, but managed to answer, "He's not my 'new guy.' Besides it's none of your business."

Joe continued the inquisition with, "Where'd you meet him?"

"Excuse me," declared Martha. "Haven't I a right to privacy?"

"Look," intervened Sarah, "we are concerned partly because we care about you and partly because of our mutual involvement in the time travel venture. We do respect your privacy, but we are a little intimidated by your new relationship."

"Ok, I can see that," Martha responded, "but let me assure you that I would never disclose anything about the time travel venture to anyone outside our circle. The 'new guy' is just someone I bumped into and found to be interesting."

Joe brazenly dropped the bomb, "Are you sleeping with him?

"You know, I can't believe this. What I do is my own business. All of us have a right to privacy and none of us has an obligation to disclose everything about ourselves even to those closest to us."

Randy persisted in his need to know about the new guy. "What would John think?"

"I know what John would think. We discussed it before he was launched. We agreed to go our own separate ways while he is gone. When he comes back, and I believe he will, we'll very likely take up where we left off."

"Ok, enough of this," Sarah spoke like the de facto leader of the group that she had become, "lets talk about our own futures in the time travel endeavor. For me, I'd now consider going to some other time, probably the past. Maybe I'd visit John in 1928 NYC. I'd like to chat with philosophy department members at Columbia University. It's not only one of the top departments of philosophy in the country, then and now. It has a particularly open-minded tradition. Also, it is one of the most important departments in the history of psychology. One could even say it was the academic birthplace of American psychology. That would give John and I a common pursuit."

Martha took Sarah's rationale for time travel to New York City as a jump-start to revealing her own plans and concerns. "I'd go to NYC 1928 as well, but not now. I wouldn't want my presence to get in John's way. Maybe I'd go there when we get a report on how he's doing, or when he returns to the present time. But, I'd be very concerned about going into the future. We have history books to inform us about the past, but we have only speculation to inform us about the future. Planning would be difficult. Further, traveling to the future is problematic from more than this single perspective. Instead of being the bearers of information about state of the art science when we travel to the past, travelers into the future would be science bumpkins. That is not a position of power. And what about money? We would have no idea about how to answer questions like, "How much money would a traveler into the future need for reasonable assurance of daily survival and in what national currency would the money have to be in?" Depending on how far into the future one went, countries like the USA, Britain, Canada, Australia, New Zealand, China, Russia, India, South Korea, Japan and European Union member nations may or may not still exist. In fact, money in the future might be like web money is today: faux currency represented only electronically."

"Good points," remarked Randy. "But there is an interesting exception to what you say, at least as a matter or degree. If one went to the near future, many of these problems would not materialize. But why go to the near future? Consider Robots. Even today's robots, such as the Google robotic automobile and the robots used to assemble cars, are rather crude. They require human supervision because they do not have sensory systems sufficient to interpret an ever-changing environment, flexible memory that is altered by experience, or the innovativeness of the human brain. Yet, robots are advancing at exponential speed. By analogy, if you emptied Lake Michigan and refilled it a few drops at a time initially, but with an exponentially increasing number of drops added to the lake per unit of time, it would fill more and more rapidly. As the lake got closer and closer to being completely refilled, the rate of refill would be extraordinarily fast. Robots are developing relatively slowly now, even though they are highly capable compared to their early relatives, but in as little as 10 years, robots may become more and more like humans. At that point, they will be able to take over many jobs that humans have performed exclusively in the past. 'How will humans make a living in the future?' is a very serious question for future governmental and industrial leaders, not to mention people who value humans above everything else. Very likely, Hal of 2001: A Space Odyssey, or something like him, will be available to take over your city in the not too distant future. Doesn't that make travel to the near future interesting?"

"Wow, it certainly does," said Sarah. Martha added, "And it looks like even the near future would be a scary place to visit, but I just might risk it."

Joe declared that he'd like to go to the near future because, "I would probably know enough to learn about their advances. That would be thrilling."

"My first choice would be to go to the past," Randy declared. "Maybe I'd choose 1928. It would be fun to hang out there with John. But, more importantly it would be fascinating to devise ways to speed up the introduction of electronics. I might be able to use materials available in 1928 to create some innovations, or, at least stimulate some progress in miniaturizing electrical components."

"Well," Sarah began to sum up their plans for time travel, "I guess we know what we'd like to do. The remaining crucial question is, how are we going to manage time travel with all of us not yet graduated? That's not to mention the question, 'How long will the time machine be available to us? It could be destroyed at any time.'"

"Over my dead body," growled Randy. "I think I have enough on my professors' questionable behavior to keep them at bay for at least the next several years. Even if you all graduate and get jobs in a few years, I'll probably still be here for at least a few more years. But don't worry about me. I've got my assistantship and I expect Joe will share the fortune he will make off the Brownie Box gadget." The giggling that followed this last comment ended the meeting with everyone in a good mood.

Near lunchtime, Joe bumped into Randy in the Computer Science Building a couple of weeks after their last meeting with the gang at the Den. They carried their lunches outside and sat down near a big oak tree about a football field away from the Computer Science Building. Joe announced, "I'm preparing to patent our 'Brownie Box' device. I have it schematically mapped out along the lines we have been discussing. Your name will be on the patent form."

Before he could continue, Randy exclaimed, "Hold on now … you're mostly responsible for it. Only your name should be on it!"

"Not so," Joe replied firmly. "We did it together. Both our names should be on the patent."

They discussed the matter for several minutes and agreed that Joe's name would be first on the patent form, but any proceeds for the device would go to Randy. After all, Joe didn't need the money. The conversation then turned to the originally proposed use of the device. "When do you think we can have the gadget ready for transport to John?" asked Joe.

"I think in less than a month. We can begin testing it in a couple of weeks."

"Good," said Joe, "but we still have a problem to solve."

"And what would that be?" returned Randy.

Joe replied, "We have to transport it so that John will be only person to see the contents of its package."

Randy asked in a puzzled tone, "What do you mean by that?"

Joe responded with, "We know what hotel he's in, but not the room he's occupying. You'll also remember that precise placement of the gadget might be difficult or impossible to pull off. We don't know how close John was to his assigned landing point. Martha probably got him near the intended landing site, but maybe it was a few feet off. That likely means he was not in the lake or hanging from a tree. But we will have to be more precise in delivering the Brownie Box. We will need to place it where only he will have access to it."

Randy thought for a moment and then responded, "You imply that it would be in some sort of package with his name on it. Maybe we could go online to find out what a US mail package looked like around 1928 and mimic it's appearance. It could appear to be sent to John Williams care of the Hotel Theresa, NYC. The building still exists so we could get its address."

"Ok," said Joe. "Your idea seems plausible. But we will still run the risk of someone finding and opening the box."

"I know," Randy replied, "but maybe we can send it to the hotel lobby where a porter or front desk clerk will find it and send it to John's room."

On the way back to the Computer Science building, Randy commented, "Hey, you haven't seen the 1920s Brownie Box I found online. It's exactly the right size for the device. Maybe you can help me integrate the device with the box."

"Yes I can," replied Joe. "By the way, will our patented device fit into the Brownie Box?"

"Absolutely! We can make it a perfect fit. It will be a blend of the past and the future. Won't that be a great marketing ploy?"

"Yes and so cool," answered Joe.

CHAPTER 12

Some Things are Hard to Find

John rose on the morning of November 12, 1928 and dressed in what he regarded as one of his more convincing college student costumes. As he ate breakfast at a diner near the Hotel Theresa, he reviewed his frustrating string of attempts to find a group of Columbia students who regularly discussed science. In about a dozen trips to campus, he had not discovered any such group. He felt naïve to think that, just because he belonged to a group of science aficionados, people like him and his friends would exist on every campus. A troubling thought invaded his consciousness: "If I can't find or create a diverse group of grad students to discuss science, my mission will have failed." His lips must have been moving as he reviewed his worse fears, because when he looked up, a number of customers were staring at him with "are you a weirdo?" looks on their faces. As he got up to make a hasty retreat, he left money on the table and headed for the street to hail a cab.

During the ride to Columbia, he formed a strategy. He would try to find someone, anyone, who was carrying any kind of a psychology book and boldly ask if she or he was a psychology grad student. Maybe this student would at least know some other students enrolled in other science grad programs. This plan was not really new—earlier he had focused on students carrying science books and asked about their disciplines and academic standing—but that had failed. If he found a psychology student, he might better be able to strike up a conversation about a book she or he was carrying and, thereby, establish some rapport. He did have some knowledge of classic books in psychology.

After arriving on campus, he headed to the area between Low Library and the University's Main Hall. With great concentration, he roamed back and forth between these two buildings focusing on the books students were carrying. After nearly an hour of this taxing behavior, he found himself behind a young woman carrying Edward L. Thorndike's *The Measurement of Intelligence*. Without hesitation he hustled past her and, turning to face her, he back-peddled as he blurted out, "Are you taking a class with Professor Thorndike?"

At first she looked a bit alarmed, but managed to respond, "Are you a psychology student?"

"Yes, I am ... or I was. I graduated, but not from here. Do you have a minute that we could talk? I'm very interested in Thorndike's Law of Effect and his work under Professor Cattell."

The young woman was about 5' 4", pale faced, blue eyed and blond headed. Though she was pleasant looking, it seemed that she worked at appearing plain. Her hair was short clipped, her face was devoid of make-up, and her clothes were very baggy. While John waited for her reply, she stood stock still for a minute and studied him toe to head. When she focused on his face, he could see that she was intrigued. "Why don't we sit over there," she said while pointing to some benches a few yards away.

As they sat down, she opened with, "Do you know that Professor Cattell is controversial? He was fired for protesting conscription during World War I. Many academics and members of the public sector were among those who sided with him. He eventually won a judgment against Columbia. I hear that he was an effective and accomplished professor, but there were some who took issue with several of his scientific positions. Some of his eugenics pronouncements have been called racist by academics in various disciplines. Despite these controversies, Cattell has made broad and important contributions. General science owes Cattell a debt of gratitude for saving and reviving the American Association for the Advancement of Science's preeminent journal, *Science*. Professor Thorndike, one of several Cattell students who are counted among the founders of psychology in America, speaks fondly of his former professor. Now, about his law of effect, what is your interest in it?"

John responded with, "His belief that animals and humans learn by doing something was the foundation of behaviorism, a movement that I believe will dominate psychology for many decades into the future. In the many puzzle box experiments Thorndike conducted, when cats perform a response, such a depressing a level that allows them to escape from the box, they generate an effect that is rewarding. That is, responses that are rewarded are learned. Behaviorism can be very useful. Who knows, someday a behaviorist may propose ways to teach monkeys how to control a rocket ship into outer space."

"Now that's very interesting. I'm not a behaviorist, but you are helping me gain respect for them. Oh, let me introduce myself. My name is Sandra Popperman," she said extending a hand to John.

John took her hand for a brief moment and then responded, "I'm John Williams." They talked for maybe thirty more minutes until John had pretty much exhausted his knowledge of the early history of psychology. At this point, Sandra sneaked a peek at her wristwatch. Taking the hint, John made an attempt to extend their acquaintance. "I bet you have classes to attend. Maybe we could meet again. The American Association for the Advancement of Science will be meeting in New York City soon. Maybe that could provide an occasion for talking some more, perhaps with some students from other sciences."

"You know, that might be possible. We have a small group that meets sporadically. We fancy ourselves as student members of AAAS. Of course, we're not real members, but faculty who are members will support our attendance at meetings of the AAAS convention in New York City beginning in December."

"Yes, I knew about the upcoming AAAS meeting. Maybe you could pick, say, three or four members of your AAAS student group to have a meeting somewhere on campus before the convention."

"I'll try," she promised. "Getting people together is difficult, especially if they are studying in different departments, but I'll remind them about the convention and tell them about you. How can I contact you?"

This request caught John by surprise. He didn't want her to know that he was staying at a hotel. That would raise too many questions. He thought quickly and came up with, "Look, I'm out a lot. If I sent a telegraph to your dorm, would you get it the same day I send it?" She replied in the affirmative and prepared to supply him with an address.

"This is better than a dorm address," she said as she tore off a piece of paper and wrote down where to send the telegraph. "It will go to a secretary in the Teachers College building where I do my research and have most of my classes. She will find me as soon as the telegraph arrives."

She smiled and nodded goodbye as she got up to leave. John responded in kind, but had a very broad smile on his face. He was thinking, "At last, I'm in!" For the first time since arriving in New York City he felt reasonably confident that he would be able to get a group of Columbia students into discussions about science. He lingered on the bench for sometime enjoying his prospects.

When John got back to his hotel he put in a call to Bob the cabby with a request for his services that night. Bob was on duty and agreed to pick up John at his hotel about 9:30 that night for a trip to the Savoy. He also agreed to come back for John at 12:10 AM. As it was now one o'clock in the afternoon John felt that he had time to walk to the Morris Bank Building to take care of some business. He walked leisurely down 125th Street toward the bank. When he passed by the Mount Morris Park, he had to linger for a moment to take in the natural beauty of the site. Consequently he arrived at the bank after 1:30. That didn't give him much time to do his business. At the front desk he encountered the clerk who had hassled him the day he had opened his account. The clerk looked up with something of a startle response, but got himself together pretty quickly. "Good day Mr. Williams. What can I do for you?" John responded that he wanted to talk to someone about withdrawing some of his money. "Yes sir," replied the clerk, "Let me get the manager for you." He was on the phone immediately and the manager arrived via the elevator moments later.

"Good day, Mr. Williams. I'm told that you want to withdraw some of your money. Could we sit down and talk about it." John agreed and was ushered to a side room where they sat down at a conference table. The manager got right to the point: "How much would you like to withdraw?" John answered that he would need $15,000. "May I ask about your purpose? Perhaps I can find a better way for you to accomplish your goals."

"I will need the money early next year," John replied. "Today I just want to see about transferring my funds."

"We can manage that for you. It sounds like you are thinking about making an investment. If so, you might want to consider getting a loan from us for the money you need. That way, you will still have your cash reserves here with us gaining some interest while the loan money is invested in whatever market entity you might choose."

"I didn't think of that. Tell me some more. For example, what interest would you charge?"

The bank manager thought for a moment and then responded with, "We are offering 5% right now. As we are giving you 1% on your money even though it is readily available to you, you would effectively be paying about 4% for the money we would lend you."

"Sounds reasonable to me. What about brokerage costs?"

"We have our own brokerage unit. There will be no costs for purchasing stocks, but there will be a small fee when you sell your holdings. You can just call us before three o'clock on a market day to activate the loan and purchase stock for you. What sector of the market are you interested in?"

"The gold mining industry," John answered.

A puzzled look flashed across the manager's face, but he recovered quickly and indicated that he would be happy to carry out John's wishes. He gave John some papers to read,

sign, and return to the bank at his convenience. John left the bank with a feeling of satisfaction. He had gotten a better deal than he expected. He figured that, by 1934, he would have about $90,000 at his discretion, plus the funds he had left in the bank.

John had a pleasant chat with Bob the cabby on the way to the Savoy. He talked about his wife and children and John asked about life New York City. Life for a cab driver's family was apparently better than what many if not most other New Yorkers were experiencing, but there was no way he could compare his experience with that of the very rich people who had used his services. He spoke cautiously because he wasn't sure whether John was among the wealthy. Nonetheless, he was clearly appalled by the excesses of some very rich people. Their tendency to stinginess and ostentation sickened him. Most tipped poorly and a few, in order to impress people on the street, sometimes ceremoniously flashed a big bill for all to see before handing it to him. Most obnoxious was a rich stock market speculator—he made a point of announcing the source of his wealth—who lite his cigar with a flaming one-hundred dollar bill as Bob drove him to Wall Street.

Once out of the cab, John entered the Savoy and searched for Rudy and Fred. They saw him coming their way and leaned back in their chairs in mock amazement. Rudy remarked, "What's a man in a suit and tie doing here? Don't he know this ain't no church. It ain't even Sunday." A few haw, haws later, he was "shaking their hands" like men do in the 2010s. "What's that you doing?" asked an amused Fred. John showed them again and soon they were doing hi-fives. "You've been teaching me some cool dance moves," explained John. "Now it's my time to show you some hip moves."

Fred asked, "What kind of moves?" They ambled to the floor where John demonstrated some hip hop hand gestures. Rudy and Fred picked up this new-to-them hand jive quickly. Soon a crowd formed around the three men and clapped in time with their gestures. They liked the attention.

When they retreated to their seats, Fred exclaimed, "You are one strange white man … ain't never seen one like you before."

"That's right," added Rudy. "You sure you ain't Negro?" They laughed it up and ordered a round of drinks. After they were duly lubricated, Rudy and Fred pulled John back to the dance floor where they taught him some more dance moves.

Once back to their table, something reminded John of the woman who so captured his attention during an earlier visit to the Savoy. He began to scan the crowd in hopes of spotting her. After a few minutes he saw that she was sitting pretty much where she was when he first noticed her. This time he wasn't going to miss an opportunity to meet her. Perhaps emboldened by booze, he walked right up to her and announced, "Hi, I'm John Williams. Could I have the next dance?" She glanced up at him with a look of annoyance that quickly changed to one of indifference. "You've been here before," she began, "so you know I can't go anywhere with you, not even to the dance floor."

The other women tittered at John's look of profound disappointment. He bent down until his face was inches away from hers and whispered, "Can't we just talk?"

This time the other women burst out laughing, but the woman he so wanted to meet drew her gorgeous head back and loudly queried, "Why should I talk to you?" John was stunned by the ferociousness of her reaction to his simple question, but he stood his ground and never took his eyes off her. It registered on him that an instance after she hurled the insult at him, her expression changed subtly. Her eyes communicated that she found him intriguing.

As she continued staring at him, he could see her began to mellow. The other women observed that these two were locking eyeballs for many moments longer than one would expect of strangers upon their first encounter.

Finally, the woman withdrew her gaze and threw her head back into a haughty position. "You wanna talk? Sit down." One of the other women took the cue, jumped up, and motioned for John to be seated. When he settled into a chair, she focused a stern look on him and asked, "You one of them rich white boys thinks he can come in here and take any of us anywhere he wants?"

"No, I just wanted to talk ... get aquatinted," sputtered John, who was amazed at his own awkwardness.

"Oh, you a gentleman ... just want to take me out to tea." The other women laughed loud enough to be heard across the dance floor.

Before he could answer, she announced loudly enough so that at least all of the women surrounding her could hear, despite the noise coming from the dance floor, "Come back tomorrow afternoon. You can buy me a drink and chat all you want." She then turned around toward her friends as if he had vanished.

John weaved his way through the crowd to where Fred and Rudy were getting up out of their chairs to greet him. They looked very excited. "What happened? Did you make a date or did you get a butt kicking?" yelled Rudy across the several feet that still separated them.

"No," said John as he approached his two friends. "But she did say she would talk to me here tomorrow afternoon."

The two men were wide-eyed and open mouthed in response to John's remark. Rudy practically shouted, "You settled for talk? Boy, what's the matter with you? Don't you know how to get women to like you?"

An incredulous Fred exclaimed, "Yeah, you got ta show them you the cat of the walk."

John responded with, "Easy now. I got what I wanted. If we talk, I can convince her I'm somebody worth hanging out with … or not. In the latter case, I'll lick my wounds and retreat. No sense in staying where you are not wanted."

Fred grabbed one of John's arms and Rudy the other. They dragged John back to their table where he got a talking to.

After midnight, Bob was waiting for John across the street from the Savoy. As soon as he got into the cab, John asked whether Bob could take him to the Savoy about 3 PM the next day. The cabby was a bit puzzled. "Not much going on at that time of day," he noted. But he would be on duty and would be happy to take John back to the Savoy.

John slept late the next morning. After brunch in the hotel dinning room he carried the loan papers to the bank where a clerk looked them over and told him they appeared to be in order, but a loan officer would have to examine them. If they discovered a problem, which was not likely, he would be notified.

After leaving the bank, he had some time to kill. The Mount Morris Park beckoned so he walked the short distance to it. Finding a bench, he sat near a tree enjoying nature in the middle of a metropolis. Nearby there were some black kids throwing a scruffy looking basketball at a makeshift rim crudely wired to the top of a wooden pole. He wondered why they were not in school. After awhile, they saw him watching them. One of them shouted, "Hey mister, you play basketball?" John trotted over to them. When he was close enough to catch a pass, they threw him the ball. He immediately took a shot, which neatly passed through the rim without touching it. They looked impressed. When he took another shot with the same result, one of them said, "You good."

After doing a couple of layups, John was asked, "You a Jew?" He screwed up his face in puzzlement and answered, "Not that I know of. Why did you think that?" The kid replied, "Jews good at basketball. I heard they won the city championship."

He played a bit longer, but upon realizing it was time to catch a cab back to the hotel in time for Bob to take him to the Savoy, he signaled for the ball to execute a grand finale. They threw him the ball and he bounced it a couple of times on the way to the rim where he leaped up and slammed dunked it. The contrived rim, made of heavy wire crudely formed into a not-so-round shape, wobbled violently until it slumped to one side of the pole where it hung by one of the few nails that had held in place.

The boys were astonished. One of them stammered, "You ... you ruined our basketball rim!" John apologized profusely, gave them some money, and promised that he would put up a real rim with a backboard, but he had to go. As he walked to 125th street to hail a cab, he looked back at the boys, who were slowly walking away from their destroyed basketball court. He was feeling very guilty. Indeed, he would have to erect a backboard and rim for them.

CHAPTER 13

Getting to Know You

Bob showed up ahead of time to pick up John for the trip to the Savoy where he hoped to have something like a date. He jumped into the backseat of the cab and they headed out into light traffic. By 3:15 they were in front of the Savoy. As he got out of the cab, he asked Bob when he would be back for the return trip to the Hotel Theresa. "I'd like to be home by seven; would six-fifteen be alright?" "Agreed," said John.

Once inside, he looked around the ballroom, finding it nearly empty. There were a few customers at the bar and several employees straightening up, but no sign of the woman who promised to meet him. However, he heard some familiar laughter and went to its source. He found Rudy and Fred at a table in a side room. "What are you doing here?" he asked in an annoyed tone.

Rudy responded, "We here to see you stand up like a man and ask that girl out."

"Yeah," said Fred.

John sat down at their table and sighed deeply. "Look, this is not a big deal. I'm not courting her. I'm just curious about her. Can't you give me a break?"

"I saw the way you looked at her," said Fred. "That weren't no curious look. You want her, so you got to be bold."

"She's not even here. I've been stood up." John's head drooped until his chin was almost touching his chest.

"No, she here. We seen her. Want me to go get her?" asked Rudy.

John pleaded, "Please don't do that. I'll just leave."

"Fred, you keep him here. I'll be back," exclaimed Rudy as he disappeared through the door.

John started to get up, but Fred held out his arms and exclaimed, "Now, I don't want to have to wrestle you!" John thought, "Oh, what's the use. I'll just have to bear this." He fixed the heels of his hands under his jaw, planted his elbows on the tabletop, and prepared for more humiliation.

Soon Rudy returned with his "date" who looked as sullen as before. She plopped down on a chair and assumed a bored look. Rudy placed a drink in front of her and handed another to John. "Now come on Fred. Let these two get to know one another."

They were gone in what seemed like a flash and John was stuck with a situation for which he had no plan. So he asked what any schoolboy would ask, "What's your name?" "Danielle Beaumont," she replied with as little emotion in her voice as in her face.

"Sounds French to me," he offered cautiously.

"That's cause it is."

"I'm John Williams," he continued in a tired voice.

When she didn't respond, he picked up his glass, thrust it across the table toward her and said, "Cheers." She gracefully and quickly lifted her glass and clicked it gently against his. "Cheers," she reciprocated.

After a few moments, Danielle pushed her upper body across the table and whispered, "Now you know what this is about. You buy me a drink and I listen to you brag about yourself."

"Ok, I get it," indicated John. "But I'm not into bragging that much. Why don't you tell me about yourself?"

She replied stubbornly, "No, you tell me about yourself."

"Ok, I like skiing, not on snow … on water."

"You must be a man of leisure. I see a lot of men in here like you."

John came back forcefully, "I told you something about me. Now it's your turn. Tell me something about you that matters."

"I'm black and you're white."

"Ok, that's something about you and something about me. Why does it matter?"

"'Cause you may want to be seen with me and you might take me out somewhere, even to a nice restaurant, but that's as far as you would ever go. It's hep for you 'try anything' rich white men to be seen with a pretty Negro woman. But you ain't gonna be taking me home to meet your parents."

"Hip or hep, it doesn't matter. I have never done what you say rich white men do. If I see a woman who seems strong and independent and different from others, I want to get to know her."

"So, she could be ugly?"

"And I could add smart," he said with a grin. "Alright, pretty too."

Her face softened for the first time. She drew back in her chair and took a first good look at him. With a sly grin on her face she asked, "What about taking me home to see your parents?"

John responded quickly. "My parents aren't around. But if they were, I'd be pleased to introduce you to them. They are always happy to meet people I know."

They chatted amiably for another 40 minutes. Her attitude toward him seemed to have changed radically, but when he asked about seeing her again, she stuck with, "I can see you at the Savoy just about any afternoon." When he asked whether he could telephone her, she said, "Call the Savoy front desk around noon. They can tell you for sure whether I'll be around on any afternoon."

Fred and Rudy were waiting not far away when John and Danielle left the room. Upon noticing the smiles on the date participants faces, the two men were slapping hands and grinning broadly. The cousins dashed over to John with "tell us about it" written on their faces. They were a little disappointed that she and John weren't "going out" somewhere, but John assured them that they would meet again. He thanked them for their advice and encouragement and asked when they would be back at the Savoy in the evening. "We here 'most every night, but sometimes we too broke or tired from work to show up. Both of us live close by and come here sometimes during the day when we got no work. So, the Savoy be like a home to us." They pledged to meet again at the Savoy before the month of November was over. "Neither of us got a phone, but we got a friend who do," said Rudy. He told John the friend's number and asked that he commit it to memory. Fred added, "When you plan to be at the Savoy in the evening, call us that morning. That way we'll get your message and be waiting for you."

On the trip back to the Hotel Theresa John thought about issues as yet unresolved. First, he had to find out where to buy a basketball rim and, hopefully, locate someone who would mount it on a backboard and affix it to the pole in the Mount Morris Park. Second he needed to get back to Sandra Popperman at Columbia University to find out about a possible meeting with science grad students. When he entered the hotel lobby he did what was becoming a habit for him when he was unable to find out where to go when he needed something done: the hotel front desk. The clerk at the main desk cheerfully greeted him with, "Good afternoon Mr. Williams. What can I do for you?"

"I need to locate a telegraph office nearby and also I'd like to know where I might find someone to do a minor construction job. Oh, and I will need to find a sports shop that would have basketball rims."

"We can send and receive telegraphs from here. As to the sports store, there is one a short cab drive away that should have basketball rims. They have all sports equipment. One of our maintenance men does minor construction when he's not on duty here. He's very good and charges reasonably."

"Would he be willing to construct a backboard, attach the rim to it and mount it where I want it?"

"Yes, that would be easy for him. Where would you want it mounted?"

John hesitated for a moment and then reluctantly confessed that he wanted it installed on a pole in the Mount Morris Park. To his surprise the clerk said, "I don't think that's cause for concern. People do little improvements in the park without permission and the Park Service is usually pleased with it, especially if it's useful to park visitors and improves the park's appearance."

"When can I talk to the maintenance man?"

"He's on duty today. I'll can get him here in a couple of minutes."

"About the telegraph service, will the hotel be identified on the telegraph?" queried John. The clerk immediately lowered his eyebrows a little indicating that he was a bit suspicious. But after only a moment's hesitation he indicated, "No, we are just like any other telegraph station, the building quartering the station is not identified. There is a code number on the telegraph that would identify the building housing the station, but only the telegraph people can decode the number."

"Good," John replied. "I'll wait here until the maintenance man arrives."

Before the clerk fetched the maintenance man, he looked around for a moment, and when he found the coast clear, he whispered conspiratorially, "We have a phone in the back for personnel to use. If you want, I can send and receive calls for you. No one who uses that phone says it's a hotel phone."

John winked at the clerk as he pulled out a couple of bucks and laid it on the counter. "Write your name down and the phone number. I'll be using your service."

The clerk picked up the money and smiled broadly as he informed John that he was on duty every week day and he would enlist night and weekend clerks to send and receive calls for John without mentioning the hotel.

When the maintenance man arrived at the front desk, John described what he wanted done and asked if the man could and would do it. "Ralph," as he introduced himself, indicated that it was a relatively simple job that he could easily do. "But," he added, "if you want me to be running errands and toting the backboard to the park where I gotta climb up on a ladder to mount it, that'll be extra."

John jumped on the man's comment and queried, "If I paid you for it would you get together all the materials and the lumber, nails, paint and so forth, including the rim?"

Playing the part of the tough negotiator, Ralph replied, "I can do all of that, but it's a lot of traveling around and shopping for things I'll need. I'd have to stop by the sports shop on the way home and tote a heavy ladder to the park. I don't know. It's a lot to do."

John asked the man to quote how much he'd charge to do the job. Ralph took out a nub of a pencil and a scrap paper to do some figuring. After about five minutes of thinking and occasionally scribbling on the scrap of paper, Ralph announced, "That'll be about $30." After he stated the sum, the man looked like he had bet too high on a weak poker hand. But before he could express a willingness to negotiate the price, John said simply, "Fine. How much do you need now?"

"How about half?" John gave him $15 and asked when the job would be done. He was told that it would take about a week. John ended the meeting by promising to check the park every few days and pay the other $15 at the hotel when the backboard and rim were up. Ralph seemed very relieved.

John, whose mother was a librarian and father was a construction-site manager, was amazed once again at how loudly money talks. During childhood he had wanted for little and truly loved the family beach home his mother had inherited, a possession that none of his friends' families could claim. But he never had enough money to get whatever he wanted. It felt good, he had to admit, but it also made him feel guilty.

When John returned to the front desk he composed a telegram for Sandra. In it he asked whether she had recruited a group of science graduate students to talk about science and, if so, when and where would they meet. He also indicated that he could be contacted at the number provided by the hotel desk clerk. Sandra got back to him that same day indicating that he could call her using a number she provided. She suggested that he contact her between 6 and 8 PM that day. He called at about 7 PM using the hotel personnel phone and they talked about options for a meeting. John, of course, wanted to meet right away, but Sandra thought a meeting nearer to the time of the AAAS convention would work better. They agree on Dec. 10.

As soon as the telephone call ended, John went outside to wait for Bob. When he got out at the Savoy, it was not yet 8:00 PM, early for most Savoy regulars. But he had a mission. Maybe he could find Danielle for at least some conversation before the action started and she, along with the other pretty women, would become unattainable window dressing. In case Danielle wasn't available, he had sent a telephone message to Rudy and Fred, so, at least he could hang out with them. Looking around the not-yet-crowded ballroom he saw neither Danielle nor his friends. So he sidled up to the bar for a beer. Before he could take a sip, he felt a light touch on his left shoulder. When he turned around, there she was, hand on hip, focusing mischievous eyes on him. "You want to buy a girl a drink?" she chortled.

Oh how he wanted to hug her, but he knew he shouldn't. So, he quickly hailed a bartender, and, with the promise of a nice tip, got her a drink in a hurry. They took a table in an almost deserted corner of the room. For a minute after they sat down, he just stared at her with a silly schoolboy grin fixed on his face. She smiled radiantly and slowly extended her hand across the table toward him. He grasped it gently and locked eyes with her. "Wow, you are really cool tonight."

"Cool? What's that to you?"

"To me, it means that everything about you is right."

Her smile broadened and she squeezed his hand. She asked, "Why don't we take a walk?" He was surprised, but pleased. When she guided him toward the main exit to the street, he was even more surprised. He was thinking that he had gained her trust at last.

Unbeknownst to either of them, Rudy and Fred followed them outside but kept their distance. The streetlights were already on, but there were pockets of shadows when they walked down Lennox Avenue toward 141th Street. Rudy and Fred hid in these dark spaces as they followed close behind their oblivious friend and his companion.

Danielle and John rounded the corner at 141st Street. They had walked about 20 yards along the street before John sensed the presence of someone in an alley a few steps away. Just as he had pushed Danielle back to his left, a man in ragged clothing and a dilapidated hat pulled down over his eyes stepped out of the alley and brandished a knife in his right hand. "Gimme your wallet!" he grunted loudly. When John didn't respond, the man stepped to John's left and thrust the knife forward. Fred and Rudy had just rounded the corner when they witnessed a lighting move by John who feinted with his left hand and, with his right hand, chopped the man's right wrist, sending the knife clattering to the pavement and leaving the attacker wheeling backwards in astonishment, grasping his wounded wrist. The would-be assailant regained his balance and scurried away from John as fast as he could move. John turned to Danielle who was in a state of shock. He held her gently for a moment to quell her shaking.

Rudy and Fred slipped back around the corner and looked at one another in amazement. As they hurried back to the Savoy, Fred rasped, "Did you see that?" "I did," said Rudy, "but I don't know if I believe it."

They were still talking about it when they returned to the Savoy. "That was the fastest move I've ever seen anybody make," Rudy remarked as they took a table.

They sat for a few moments with puzzled looks on their faces. Then Rudy said matter-of-factly, "He passing."

"Yeah, he passing," Fred replied. "Ain't no white man move that fast." They laughed fiercely.

But after reflecting for a minute, Rudy said, "But his hair ain't right. It's straight."

"So is yours!" returned Fred and they broke out laughing again.

"And his nose ain't right," Fred continued the assessment.

"Yeah, it's too narrow. I don't know how white folks breathe through them skinny noses."

Fred offered, "Sometimes they noses is long."

"Yeah, but they just too narrow," insisted Rudy.

"His skin looks about right for someone passing," Fred said as an afterthought.

"It's dark, but not black. Looks a little reddish to me."

Fred responded, "Yeah, we commented on that before. But black folks come in all kinds of colors."

Rudy declared, "You got that right."

When Danielle and John got back to the Savoy, she led him to a side room where they sat down and she began to cry. He tried to comfort her with soft words to the effect of "you're safe now."

She sniffled, "He was coming after me."

"I know …."

"How'd you do that?"

John didn't know what she was referring to. Finally, he asked her what she meant.

"How'd you knock that knife out of his hand?"

"Oh, I'm trained in martial arts. I was awarded a black belt in Judo, but I can do a lot of different moves. That feint with the left hand and disarm with the right is patterned after a Jujitsu move." He stopped there because he could see that he was not only supplying more information than she wanted, he was also not interpreting her question correctly.

"I saw he was attacking you and I had to stop him."

She left her chair very quickly, came up behind him, bent down to place her head next to his and hugged him around the shoulders.

CHAPTER 14

Brownie Boxes and Parades

Joe and Randy were all excited about the upcoming meeting at the Lion's Den. They would bring along a prototype of the Brownie Box. Again, the gang met at a day and time of day when there would be few other people present: 1:00 PM on a Saturday. For dramatic effect, Randy and Joe showed up at ten minutes past one. Sarah and Martha were waiting patiently, but made it clear that they wanted a demonstration immediately. Martha declared, "I'm concerned about showing the thing in this place. Somebody might see it or overhear us."

"No problem," Randy assured her. "It looks like what it is, an antique camera."

Joe carefully removed the new gadget from a cardboard box and placed it on the table. No one looking at them from afar would have been able to see it as they all pushed their chairs back and hovered over the table for a better look. Indeed, it looked like an antique Brownie camera. One had to inspect it very closely to discern that it was rigged. The slide-back door on the top was obvious on close examination, in part because they knew it would be there. Also, there was a metal plate on its bottom into which the left and right halves of the keyboard were mounted. A sophisticated zoom lens was recessed into the space originally occupied by the antiquated shutter and lens. Joe turned the Brownie box over for a better look at the odd keyboard and remarked, "I'll bet it's actually not difficult to use once you practice on it a bit."

"We have microphones in every dimension so as to not miss any sounds in the surrounding environment," Randy added with obvious pride. As he slid back the cover of the screen, he said, "Now, let's look under the lid."

They saw a conventional looking screen, about the size of an iPad Mini, but more square in shape. It lit up as the cover receded into a rollup on the back of the box.

"It has an on-screen keyboard for use in privacy. Here, I'll bring up the keyboard," he exclaimed as he tapped the bottom, right corner of the screen. Up popped a familiar looking keyboard. Above it was box into which letters and numbers could be typed.

"If you like a touch screen, you've got it with the Brownie Box. Finally, for old school people, there is a mouse. To replace the keyboard with a mouse, touch the key with a mouse icon on it. Up comes a full size mouse that admittedly looks a little like Mickey, a possible copyright problem. Touch and hold it and you can move its cursor around the screen. When you place its cursor on a desktop icon, releasing and then touching the mouse brings up the content associated with the icon."

"OMG," exclaimed Martha all too loudly. "You've totally merged mobile devices and computers!"

Joe and Randy smiled like two lottery winners.

After a few moments of basking in the warm glow of adoration, Joe reminded them that the Brownie Box was a first-class audio-visual device. It also had excellent speakers, a headphone jack for private listening, and its screen had HD video capability. "Oh, and it has two terabytes of storage space, 10 GB of available memory and a power plug to accommodate my special power connection," added Randy.

After some time over munchies and drinks devoted to absorbing the power and originality of Randy's and Joe's Brownie Box, the discussion turned to how and when it would be delivered to John. Randy indicated that they could make the delivery any time, but he was concerned about placing it where only John will have access to it.

"We can't send it to his room in the Hotel Theresa, because, of course, we don't know his room number, and thus, can't calculate its coordinates. We could send it to his bank, but would the finder know John? I guess the hotel lobby is the best bet. It would be a large space where the discoverer would assume that it was delivered to a guest and, if he or she didn't know John, would turn the package over to the front-desk clerk."

Martha broke in at this point. "I've had fun correcting the landing-site location error. The correction has algorithmic status, if I do say so. If you can get me the coordinates of the Hotel front door, I can put the package with the Brownie Box in it somewhere in the lobby with, say, 90% likelihood that it will not be hidden or damaged."

"Sounds like good odds to me. Since the Hotel building still exists, will its current address suffice?"

"Absolutely," said Martha.

"I'll go online," offered Sarah, "and find pictures of old postal packages from the period so we can make our package look as much like a 1928 postal package as we can." Later she reported that she failed to find a picture of a package, but find enough pictures of postal items to reproduce the marking and stamps that would likely be on a package mailed during 1928.

A week later, the package was sent to the Hotel Theresa lobby for arrival at 3 AM on November, 21, 1928. A bleary-eyed night watchman was trying to read the sports page of the previous day's New York Times, when he thought he saw something move across the lobby. He wiped his eyes and tried to focus on what he thought he had seen. Near the center of the lobby he spotted an object leaning against a stuffed chair. As he had been looking around the lobby for several hours that night and morning, and had not seen the object before, he thought he might be suffering from hallucinations caused by sleep deprivation. Slowly he made his way to the point where whatever-it-was was leaning against the chair. It looked like a postal package. He picked it up and shook it gently. No tell-tell sounds emanated from the package. Not having any further curiosity about the package that seemed to have appeared out of nowhere, he simply carried it to the front desk and placed it on the counter.

When the morning clerk came on duty at 7 AM, he saw the package and thought it looked strange. It didn't have any actual postage on it—just some US postal markings were visible. The clerk looked up John's name on the hotel registry and found his room number. He thought, "I'll wait until Mr. Williams is likely to be awake and send a porter up to his room with the package.

At 9:30 AM John heard a knock on his door. Because he was not yet dressed, he opened the door just enough to see who was there. The porter whispered, "I have a package for you, Mr. Williams." John said, "Just a minute," and fetched some change for a tip. As soon as he had the package in hand he knew what it was and handled it with reverence.

John opened the package quickly but carefully. When he pulled the paper away from its contents he couldn't believe his eyes. "A Brownie Camera! Is this a joke?" he said aloud. But simply picking up the Brownie, and rotating it through 180 degrees, convinced him it was not his grandmother's Brownie that he had played with as a child. For one thing, it was relatively heavy, maybe as much as 2 to 3 pounds. He noticed that it had attachments on its sides for an around-the-neck strap, which was enclosed.

"That will lighten the load," he thought. He was able to see the microphone and speaker openings distributed about the box, and found the power-charger receptacle and power cable. Turning the box over, he got his first view of the split keyboard. "Uh oh, this is going to be challenging to learn," an assessment that cued him to look for instructions inside the box. There he found several pages with pictures to guide quick learning of how to operate the box's many unique features. Looking at the specs yielded a big surprise. He didn't have to read far before he realized that he had been provided with a remarkably versatile tool that amounted to several mobile devices and a computer. Included among the instructions was a note that indicated he must send the device back on December 23. It was to be left in the hotel lobby where it was found, covered with actual postal packaging of the era. The recovery time would be 2:30 AM. There was also a request for his room number so the future deliveries could be more privately completed. Finally, he was asked to specify exactly when it should be sent back to him.

On top, he discovered the cover and eased it back. Up came a screen with several icons on it. At the bottom right corner of the screen was an icon for a keyboard. Touching it brought up a familiar keyboard, except for a key with a mouse icon on it. When he pressed the mouse key, the keyboard disappeared and, to his total surprise, up popped a mouse icon occupying the space where the keyboard had been. When he touched and moved the mouse its cursor moved on the screen. "Chalk that one up to Randy's uniquely playful, innovative spirit," he thought. The entire rest of the day was devoted to learning the many features of the cleverly disguised device. The next day he would take it out for a spin.

Even though he had been up late the night before learning to use the Brownie Box, John arose early on November 22, 1928. After dressing hurriedly, he dropped by the hotel dinning room to cram a muffin down his gullet and guzzle two cups of highly potent coffee. Then he headed for the front desk where he was relieved to find the clerk who had arranged his telephone service. He stuck his head across the counter and whispered, "Sometime in the near future, there will be a package with my name on it in the lobby. Would you inform the night clerks and watchmen that they should just leave the package where it is?"

"Yes sir, Mr. Williams," said the clerk who was flashing his "expecting a big tip" smile. John did not disappoint him. As John walked toward the front door, the clerk called out, "Have fun with your Brownie Camera, Mr. Williams." John was thinking, "I'm going to have more fun than you can imagine."

He headed straight for Mount Morris Park. First he checked on whether the new rim and backboard had been installed. Not surprisingly, it wasn't done, but he couldn't pass near the site of the basketball court without checking. There were children in the park, but most were pre-school-aged kids being carried by their mothers or being pushed in strollers. He took a video of them.

Next he activated the voice recorder and did a few "testing, testing" checks. The recording was clear. When he pulled back the screen cover on the top of the Brownie, he was surprised to see that the device had voice-to-text capability: "testing, testing" had been converted to text, along with the few inane comments he had made to the effect of "I hope I'm doing this right." He shut off the voice to text function.

Elsewhere in the park he encountered elderly people playing checkers on a picnic table. They were cursing the recent rent increase their apartment manager had imposed on them. He thought, "Some things never change." Others were sitting on a bench nearby asking "what is the world coming to?" questions and offering the usual answers. They referred to the new Times Square News Ticker as "putting smutty news up where everyone has to look at it." The proposed new Empire State Building, scheduled to be completed during 1930 "was going to be too tall to withstand strong winds … and people will suffocate on the top floors due to a lack of oxygen …" The gist of it was that the world was changing too fast. John thought, "You ain't seen nothing yet."

John spent the rest of the day roaming up 125th street toward Manhattan. He recorded various street scenes, from vehicle crashes to street merchants fighting over the best spots to place their stands. Then happenstance paid him a favor: he came upon a movie crew filming Babe Ruth riding around New York in a taxi. He took his own video movie of preparations for the next scene. When he attempted to obtain an autograph from Ruth, the large crowd around the legendary player pushed him back. But he did get a good look at the Babe and a short video of him.

On the way back to the hotel, a sign advertising Macy's Thanksgiving Day's Parade reminded him of his pledge to see the famous "Christmas is coming" celebration. He made a note to contact the front desk at the Savoy with a message for Danielle asking if she would be free to accompany him to the parade.

The next several days were devoted to recording as much information about New York City during 1928 as he could manage. He became so engrossed with stuffing the Brownie Box memory with data that November 29, Thanksgiving Day, was on him before he knew it. During this time interval, he had seen Danielle several times at the Savoy. She was excited about going to Macy's parade, even though she had been there before, but didn't get to see much because, "Negroes weren't allow to use the good seats or to push their way to the curb."

Early on the morning of November 29, Bob picked up John at the Hotel Theresa and they proceeded to the Savoy where Danielle was waiting at the curb. She looked brilliant in a pleated white skirt and a matching cotton blouse with a ruffled neckline. Her hair was uncharacteristically curly. She must have gone to a hair stylist. It was arranged so that it was very full on top and in the back. For the first time since John had known her, she was wearing lipstick. Even her smile was new. It was what you would expect on the face of a little girl anticipating Christmas morning.

She jumped in the back seat with John and Bob chugged off to Herald Square in Manhattan. It was only 8:30 AM when they arrived, but the crowds were already occupying the prime spots for watching the parade. Bob promised to be back in two hours, though he warned that he would have a hard time stopping where they wanted him to meet them: at the corner entrance under the big Macy's sign. They would have to be looking for him and prepared to enter the traffic to reach his cab.

Once out of the cab, they hurried down the parade route that bordered on Macy's location while looking for a hole in the crowd. Because the crowd looked impenetrable everywhere, John came up with an alternative to the two of them attempting to plow their way to the curb. He explained that they would plunge as far into the crowd toward the curb as they could go without suffering bodily harm. At that point, he would lift her up to his shoulders where she could see the parade. Her initial surprise at his plan turned to reluctance. She muttered, "What will I do with my skirt?" He replied simply, "Tuck it between your legs before I lift you." They plowed into the crowd until they reached a point that barely allowed room to make their maneuver. He then bent down behind her, grabbed her by the waist and hoisted her above his head until she was able to loop her legs over his shoulders. As he stood up she wrestled with her clothing because it was all tangled. They wobbled for a moment, and then she squealed with delight. "I can see everything," she screamed. There's a Felix the Cat balloon." She was referring to the year's favorite helium balloon. The previous year it had been filled with air, which didn't work well. This year, Felix and his animal friends were able to fly high above the crowd. Each balloon had a tag on it with an address indicating where it could be returned. Macy's offered a substantial reward for return of any balloon that drifted away from the parade site. But sadly, when the balloons were released at the end of the parade, they floated away and burst in full view of the crowd. This bad ending was scary for the children and disappointing for adults. It was resolved that in 1929 the balloons would be deflated by special valves that opened when they were released.

John was seeing little of what was going on in the street. However, his disappointment in not getting to fully see and enjoy a Macy's parade was overridden by the joy of vicariously experiencing Danielle's delight with everything that passed in front of her. She yelled out to him a description of ever animal, band, vehicle and balloon that passed by her. Although he was aching all over from the exertion of holding her aloft for what seemed like hours, his spirits had never been higher. He loved pleasing her with new experiences.

When he finally lifted her off his shoulders and gently lowered her to the pavement, she hugged him and kissed him gently on the lips. With obvious exaggeration born of just having had a wonderful experience, she whispered in his ear, "This is the best day of my life." John felt the same about their day.

Bob managed to get relatively close to the curb at Macy's corner entrance despite a large, though dwindling, crowd still milling around when he arrived. He drove them back to the Savoy, where Danielle refused to get out of the cab until John promised to spend the next day with her. He felt that he still had work to do with the Brownie Box. However, he gave up on doing it alone when he envisioned that he could combine data collection using the Brownie Box with enjoying the warm feelings that came with the mere presence of Danielle. Unfortunately, he wasn't thinking of what to tell her when she inevitably asked about the Brownie Box.

The next day in the early afternoon, a substitute for Bob, who was not on duty, picked John up for the trip to the Savoy. Danielle was waiting impatiently at the entrance. As soon as she got into the car, she grabbed John's arm and pleaded to be told what they would be doing. He told her they would be walking around on 125th street taking in the sights. She wrinkled her eyebrows in apparent disappointment. It occurred to her that today was not going to be as exciting as yesterday. But, she recovered quickly.

When they got to Mount Morris Park, John asked the cabby to wait for them. He replied that he might have to drive around because parking was hard to find. John suggested that he be back for them by 5:30 PM. He agreed and John got out of the cab followed by Danielle. He had concealed the Brownie Box next to him during the drive there, but when he exited the cab and put the strap attached to the gadget around his neck, she was immediately curious. "Oh, a Brownie Camera," she exclaimed. "Can I see it?" He turned toward her so she could have a closer look, but didn't offer it to her. "Alright," he announced, "let's go this way," and he walked off in the direction of the Park's center.

She followed but felt put off. When they were well into the park, he stopped to take pictures of a family having a picnic. They walked some more and encountered a group of people carrying flags of the Soviet Union. Danielle uttered, "Communist" in a way that reeked with disgust. John pointed the Brownie toward the group and, forgetting himself, began to describe the way they were dressed and the signs they were carrying around. Danielle, remarked sharply, "Why are you talking to yourself?" "I'm sorry," he said, but he continued to point the Box at the group. After no more than a few minutes, they saw him and a couple of men rushed at him shouting that they were exercising their constitutional rights and "stop taking pictures of us. We know that you are with the Bureau of Investigation. You can tell Herbert Hoover to go to hell!"

John turned the Brownie away and grasped Danielle's arm to lead her away. Once they were many yards away from the group, Danielle yanked John's hand from her arm and demanded to know what he was up to. He replied lamely that he was just taking pictures. "Let me see that Brownie Camera," she demanded. "There's something strange about it." John could think of nothing to say. Finally he muttered, "I'm sorry. I can't do that."

"What are you," she asked, "some kind of government agent?"

"No, of course not," he said defensively. "But it belongs to some people who don't want me to show it to anyone. I promised I wouldn't."

They spent quite a long time walking around in silence with John aiming the Brownie Box at different scenes in the park. Danielle was clearly pouting. Finally, he pointed to some benches and when they sat down, he apologized once again. When that didn't work he said, "Look, I can't let you examine the camera, but I have something else you can experience that's far more fascinating. In fact, it's amazing. You will never forget it. If you'll forgive me, we will make plans to go where I've stored it." She brightened up, accepted his apology and asked excitedly, "When can I do it?"

CHAPTER 15

Miracles are Happening

John's next trip to the Savoy was special. Louie Armstrong was the featured performer. When he and Danielle entered the ballroom, the largest crowd they had ever seen at the Savoy blocked their view. Using their recently acquired skills at beating crowds, they broke through to the tables nearest the bandstand where Fred and Rudy had saved them seats. Fred shouted over the crowd noise, "He'll be coming out any minute." When Armstrong appeared and fixed his horn to his famously calloused lips, the crowd went wild. Not since a recent appearance by Duke Ellington at the Cotton Club had an audience greeted a musical performer in such an ear-splitting fashion. When they finally settled down, Armstrong literally blew them away. John, who had never listened to an Armstrong performance before, was enthralled. Danielle, Fred, and Rudy had heard him on the radio or listened to one of his recordings, but listening to him live put them into another dimension. If Armstrong could have lasted all night they would have hung onto his every note.

Armstrong performed with periodic breaks until near midnight. After his final appearance, the foursome hung around for a while to revel in the wondrous sounds still coursing through their brains. Before John left to catch his taxi ride home, he whispered to Danielle about his plans to pick her up in the early afternoon on Tuesday. "Are you ready for your special experience?" She didn't have to answer, because he could see the joy of anticipation in her face.

Monday morning John was waiting at the front door of the Mount Morris Bank Building when it opened. He approached the front desk and gave the clerk an envelope with a message for the bank manager. In it he ordered the purchase of gold stock on the first day of 1929 for which the Dow was seriously in the red. Next he spent the best part of three hours in his safety deposit room where he prepared for Danielle's experience. Using the iPad, he fashioned a program tailor-made for her. While he was working on the program, he gave each of his several devices a turn at the electrical wall-receptacles until their batteries were all fully charged. When the program was done and thoroughly checked, he left the bank with an immense feeling of creative accomplishment.

When John arose on the morning of Tuesday, Dec. 3, 1928, he took breakfast at the hotel dinning room after which he called his bank using the hotel personnel phone. He informed the bank clerk that he would be in his safety deposit box room for an extended time that afternoon and would like not to be interrupted for as long as three hours. Looking at the records of safety deposit room use, the clerk indicated, "Yes, Mr. Williams. There is no reason why you can't occupy the room for as long as long as you like this afternoon."

"But, I really don't want to be interrupted. If customers who have safety deposit boxes in the room shows up wanting to get access to it, can you put them off until I'm finished?"

"I would do that, but it's unlikely I'd have to. Let me check the record for your room. I suspect that it is very rarely visited. That would be normal for these rooms." The clerk put down the phone for a few minutes. When he returned he confidently announced, "It has been more than a year since anyone other than you has visited your assigned room. I checked some other similar rooms that mostly store family heirlooms. As I conjectured, these rooms are rarely visited. Many if not most boxes are not opened until the owners' wills are adjudicated. Again, it's very unlikely that anyone will want access to your room. If they did, I would delay them."

John thanked the clerk and made a mental note to leave a tip for him when he and Danielle left the safety deposit box room that afternoon. After he had ended the call, he thought to himself, "I didn't know that mostly family heirlooms are stored in that room. That's a bit of good luck."

Bob picked up John at just after 12:30 PM. He was opening the cab's back door for Danielle at 1:10. By 1:45 they were pulling up in front of the Mount Morris Bank building. At the front desk, John picked up the safety deposit room-key from the clerk and left the lobby for the safety deposit room. Once inside, John turned on the lights and locked the door from the inside. He then pulled the safety deposit box partly out of the wall, placed its key in it and turned the key to the open position. Next he went about giving some ground rules to Danielle. "The experience I've prepared for you involves some equipment that I cannot show you or explain to you."

"You mean, it's like the Brownie Box?"

"Yes. It's different equipment, but must be kept secret, like the Brownie Box." She sighed and said, "Alright."

John placed a chair with its back up against the table and told her she was to sit in it.

"You mean I won't be facing the table?"

"That's right. Your chair will be backed up against the table so that you will be facing the wall. I will turn off the lights soon. A couple of minutes after the room is dark you will see some light coming from behind you, so the room won't be completely dark. When you see the light, we are almost ready to begin. At that point it's very important that you don't turn around."

"Why didn't you just bring a mask to put on me?"

"That would be uncomfortable," John explained. "You should be very relaxed and at ease throughout the experience. The first thing I will do is to put what are called 'ear buds' into your ears. They are small and shouldn't bother you. If they don't feel right, you can adjust them, but don't take them out and attempt to look at them."

"So, I will hear something coming out of the ear buds."

John replied simply, "Yes."

Danielle wrinkled her brow a bit and asked, "The experience is something I'll hear? How will that be as good as what we experienced when Louis Armstrong came to the Savoy?"

"You will see ... trust me." She nodded.

John motioned for her to sit in the chair he had placed for her. He reminded her not to turn around as he extinguished the lights. He had practiced finding the safety deposit box with the key in it by feeling his way from the light switch to its location on the wall. He removed the safety deposit box from the wall and opened it. After quietly lifting the iPad out of the box, he opened it up. Light from the iPad turned the pitch-dark room into a shadowy cave.

He took out the ear buds, plugged them into the iPad and brought up the program. "You'll hear sounds in a moment," he warned Danielle. With the sound control set low, he turned on some music and adjusted the sound to an optimal level: not too loud, not too soft. Then he approached her and gently inserted the ear buds. Raising his voice a little he asked if the buds felt comfortable. She replied in the affirmative.

John then turned on the program. Tchaikovsky's "The Sleeping Beauty Suite" began rather low and tantalizing in tone. Danielle moved a bit when she heard those first notes. In a few moments she seemed totally relaxed. Next she heard some of Norah Jones' best songs. Some Motown selections from the soundtrack of the movie "Big Chill" were followed by some Jay-Z and Beyonce. Other selections included some songs by Paul Simon, sung in duet with Art Garfunkel, Beethoven's 6th Symphony, 5th Movement, a sampling of Bob Dylan's music, and a recording of songs sung by Billie Holliday at the Savoy.

John saw Danielle move with the music and occasionally heard her make a "singing along" sound. She was in different zone, apparently unaware of anything but the music. When the program ended, John gently retrieved the ear buds from Danielle and placed both the buds and the iPad into the safety deposit box. As he secured the box, Danielle became agitated. She practically yelled, "What happened?" As John headed for the light switch, she jumped up from her chair and flung it against the wall. When the lights came on, she cried out, "I don't want it to end!"

John stepped quickly across the floor and embraced her. He assured her that she could hear the program again. But she was hard to console. He hurriedly pushed the box back into the wall and locked it. Danielle had to be practically dragged out of the room.

At the front desk, John dropped three dollars on the counter. The clerk could not believe his good fortune.

With difficulty he led Danielle outside where they sat on a bench to wait for Bob. The first of her many questions was, "How can sounds be so clear?" He explained that there were no background sounds, like at the Savoy, to muddy up the music. She immediately protested, "But there is no background sounds when radios play music." He tried to explain that radios of the 1920s had a lot of static, but that had been eliminated from what she heard. Also the ear buds transmitted the sounds she heard much more faithfully than radio speakers. When she asked how these auditory feats were accomplished, he could not think of an answer that wouldn't reveal too much. So he proceeded to talk around her question until she seemed to be satisfied. She said that she loved all of the music, but she was most intrigued by Billie Holiday. "She has such a unique voice. It's filled with emotion. But, I know about almost all of the performers who have been at the Savoy in the last several years or so, and I have never hear of her." John replied, "Oh, but you will." He did not reveal that the recording she heard had been made at the Savoy during 1937, early in Holiday's career. Just before Bob's cab arrived, he asked Danielle to characterize her experience. She thought for a moment, and then whispered, "It was so wonderful. I've never felt so many emotions in such a short period of time. It was a gentle roller coaster ride. I could have listened forever. Have you got any more miracles?" His broad smile communicated "yes." They held hands on the route to the Savoy, but said little. Before she left the cab, Danielle asked John, "When will I see you again?" She had no way to know that her parting words would one day compose the title of a hit song by the Three Degrees. They made a date for the near future.

On the morning of Dec. 10, John awakened with feeling of apprehension. His meeting with the Columbia University students was about to happen and he had no idea how to behave or what to say. "I'll have to let Sandra lead the way," he mumbled to himself. That made him feel better, but he was still far less than comfortable. Should he initially fail to impress them favorably, he wouldn't have the credibility to ensure that any information about future scientific developments he imparted would be seriously considered. He decided to be cautious during the first meeting, and perhaps during other early meetings. He would have to build his credibility to an appreciable level before dropping informational bombs on them. Then he could hope that it would survive inevitable attacks by group members whose senses of scientific competence would be threatened when they heard what he had to say.

When Bob dropped him off at Columbia University, he headed for The Teachers College buildings hoping that Sandra would be waiting for him at the main entrance. He wanted to talk with her for a moment before he was taken inside and introduced to the group. About 20 yards from his target, he was relieved to see her waving to him. As soon as he was close enough, he asked if they could sit down for a couple of minutes so he could ask a few questions. She obliged and assured him that it wouldn't make them late. The meeting was still ten minutes away and one of the other three was prone to be late. That was just the cue John needed. He wanted some information about the other three before they met. As they settled in on a near-by bench, he began with, "Are any of the three—how shall I say it—a bit pompous, such that I need to be careful lest I fail to pay proper homage to him?"

Sandra laughed delightfully and thought, "I think John and I are going to get along."

"Why yes there is," she replied mischievously. "I've done some research on the three graduate students by finding someone who knows each of them well. Ronald Slaghten's roommate informed me that he views himself as highborn and aristocratic. He goes on and on about being the descendent of European royalty. Since everyone else is beneath him, he is easily offended by anyone who does not unconditionally accept that everything he utters is the last word on the issue at hand. He thinks that biology will undergo a wholesale and highly beneficial transformation by his mere presence in the discipline."

"Oh my," John whispered.

In response to this show of dismay, Sandra assured him that she knew how to deal with Ronald. "I know people like him. When he starts to puff up, it'll be my cue to step in and massage his ego a little. I'll convince him that, in some respects, any pronouncement he makes is the real truth about whatever we're discussing."

She went on to describe Herbert Andersone as a very meek and self-effacing individual. "Herbert, who likes to be called 'Herb,' is described by a friend as a nice young man and very bright. He is not only capable of important insights in math, his own discipline, but also appears able to help others hone and polish conceptions of phenomena in their disciplines. From what I've learned about him, I think he could enrich discussions more often, if he weren't afraid that his advice to others might be seen as 'correcting' them, and thus, demeaning them."

John remarked, "Herb could be an important contributor to our discussions. I'll follow your lead in encouraging him to speak up. And the last discussant is …"

"Andrew Brighart," Sandra continued, "is quite intelligent according to a classmate who studies with him, but mostly due to having been tutored as a child by handpicked scholars. His family has more money than all the rest of us combined, though all of us come from rich families. Andrew has been coddled all of his life which has made him a lazy and sterile thinker. When he does say something, it is usually not pertinent, but others are inclined to nod as if they agree. His discipline is physics."

Sandra got up as she finished the description of Andrew and looked at her watch. "My goodness, we're in danger of being late. Follow me." They entered Main Hall to a conference room in the interior where the others were waiting. John could not tell from their facial expressions whether they were pleased to see him or not. Sandra introduced him to each of the three men. Herbert smiled warmly as he took John's hand and shook it gently. "Hello. I'm Herb." John was equally gracious.

He moved on to Andrew, who looked at him as if he were puzzle for which there was no solution, but he did shake hands vigorously and managed a faint smile. When John approached Ronald, he noticed that this well-dressed, manicured, and coiffured young man moved back a bit in his chair. He looked like someone confronted with an obligation to perform a distasteful act. As Ronald was practically sitting on his hands, John simply said "hello." He then retreated to a seat at one end of the table.

Sandra suggested that, for this initial meeting, they each just simply indicate a major, specific interest in science. They could go into more detail at their next meeting. Sandra took the floor first. "My interest is in the application of more rigorous methods for verifying experimental outcomes in psychology. Too often researchers simply report that research animals did not perform the response of interest when first introduced into an experimental environment, such as Thorndike's puzzle box. However, upon the first correctly performed response of interest, tripping a latch that allows escape, the animals thereafter perform the response immediately upon being reintroduced into the experimental environment. This observation leads to the conclusion that an escape response has been learned. Such a conclusion is tentative. It can be taken seriously only if original results are replicated in other laboratories using procedures like those employed in the original experiment. Results must be so robust that they can be reproduced in other laboratories despite inevitable differences between laboratories and experimenters." John thought, "She is way ahead of her time." Only in his time has the call for replication of results in other than the original laboratory become loud and clear.

Ronald spoke up immediately and loudly: "We always see to it that our results in biology are replicated in others' laboratories."

Sandra responded immediately with "'Always' implies in each and every case. I really doubt it applies to your research or that of all research in your discipline."

Ronald mumbled, "What would you know about real science?"

There was a moment of silence, then Herb spoke just loud enough to be heard: "Sandra has a point. Absolute statements are beyond the pale of science and math. But once we hear them we usually correct them in our own minds."

Sandra suggested that John be next. He declared that his main interest was the human brain, which might often be studied by proxy through the use of animals such as rats and monkeys. Ronald broke in to say that he knew the brain and its functions very well. He could name the brain's parts and the functions of each. The others looked embarrassed. John tried to change the subject by specifying his particular interest. "I'm most specifically interested in the brain operations that lie behind prospective memory." He quickly defined prospective memory. Just as he finished the definition, Ronald blurted out, "That's an action of the mind. What's the brain have to do with it?"

John flashed a desperate look at Sandra who cut in with, "The mind-body problem is a topic for another day." She quickly pointed to Andrew who began with, "Ah, I'm interested in physics, general physics. I haven't picked a topic for my dissertation yet." He stopped there and looked around expectantly in the apparent hope that someone else would take the floor.

Sandra pointed to Herb, who was trying to hide by slipping deep down into his chair. When everyone else turned to look at him, he straightened up and said simply, "I'm interested in pi, the configuration of its digits and its many applications in math." After this short statement, he sunk back down into his seat to signal that he had said all he was willing to say.

With great trepidation, Sandra turned to Ronald, who moved his chair back from the table, crossed his legs and declared, "Like I said, the brain is my interest. My dissertation will be about how the frontal lobes of the brain control higher order functions. My method will employ a procedure that is analogous to the brain destruction described in the case of Phineas Gage. Precise destruction of domestic cats' frontal lobes will be shown to correlate with the loss of specific functions." He stopped there and smiled as if he just described the best dissertation ever proposed.

Sandra looked totally disheartened. She reminded them of the next meeting then turned and fled from the room. John scurried after her. When he caught up with her he declared the meeting to be "not so bad." She disagreed. To her it was a rather complete loss. He talked her into sitting down for a minute to look more closely at what happened at the meeting. "It'll go more smoothly once we get to know one another better. Ronald will be a problem, but we can enlist the others to moderate his influence on our discussions. Maybe we can use the upcoming AAAS presentations to generate some fruitful discussions." She seemed to recover a bit and acknowledged that his idea about the AAAS presentations was a good one. Before they parted, he thanked her again for arranging the meetings with Columbia graduate students.

When John arrived back at the Hotel Theresa, he stopped by the front desk where he dropped a five dollar bill and four ones on the counter. The clerk on duty looked very hopeful, until he was informed that eight dollars was to be given to the maintenance man who was to be told to use it for the purchase of a basketball. Only one dollar was reserved for the clerk. The inflated basketball was to be delivered to John's room when it arrived at the hotel.

CHAPTER 16

All Kinds of Games

As John got out of bed on the morning of Dec. 17 his schedule for the day immediately came to mind. The day before, he had called the Savoy front desk to leave a message for Danielle and contacted Rudy and Fred via Rudy's friend with a phone: "Let's all meet at the Savoy at about 3:00 PM tomorrow." As it was only 9 AM, he had plenty of time to kill until the meeting. For the fun of it, he hailed a cab to revisit the diner where he ate breakfast the day he landed in New York City, 1928. Soon after he entered, the waitress who had served him on his first day in town recognized him and hustled over to where he had taken a seat. "Good to see ya, Mister. How ya been?" John indicated that he had been doing fine. They chatted for a minute before he ordered the same breakfast as he had enjoyed there before. As he ate he reminisced about that first day and how it compared to his current circumstances. On that first day, the relief of having landed safely had been replaced by multiple apprehensions about getting everything set up for life in New York City. After his money had been accepted at the bank in the Mount Morris Building and he had successfully moved into the Hotel Theresa, he felt a sense of relief that lasted for days. Then concerns about his major mission, establishing a discussion group at Columbia University, began to weigh heavily on him. After considerable frustration at failing to find even one grad-student candidate for membership in his science discussion group, he happened upon Sandra. In short order, she found four grad-students who were willing to join in discussions about science. At last he was home free! Not so fast. The first meeting had not gone well. One member of the group appeared to be a nasty, arrogant, obstructionist, while the other two Sandra had found for him seemed reluctant to engage in discussion. He concluded that successful completion of his mission at Columbia University was nowhere near certain, but, at least, it was apparently not in danger of being aborted. He told himself that there was plenty of time.

During the cab ride back to his hotel, John cheered himself up by thinking about the good times he would have that afternoon with Danielle, Rudy, and Fred. Before he made it to the elevators, a clerk shouted out to him, "Mr. Williams, I've got something for you." The clerk disappeared behind the counter for a moment as John approached him. When he reappeared, he tossed a brand new basketball to John. As he caught it his good spirits returned. The arrival of the ball meant that the basket and rim had been installed in the Mount Morris Park. John wheeled around and headed for the hotel door, bouncing the ball every few steps. After a walk down 125th street he entered the park and made a beeline to the site of the basketball court. Because he had heard the schools were off for the day, he was not surprised to find the boys firing their old basketball at their new rim and backboard. With his right hand he slipped the new basketball behind his back and approached them. When they saw him, several yelled out their appreciation: "Thanks Mister!" "We got a real court now." "I'm shooting better." John grinned broadly and signaled for the kid holding the old ball to throw it his way. When he caught it with his left hand he brought out the new ball and threw it to them. They squealed with delight and gathered around him, thanking him, shaking his hand, and making over him like he was a favorite uncle who had been gone for a long time.

John tossed the old ball into a nearby trash barrel and they choose sides for a game. He directed the flow of play for both teams, but let his own team members do most of the shooting. He took a shot only when his team needed to score some catch-up points to keep the point-totals for the two teams about even. They played for what seemed like an hour when John declared the game a tie and bid them farewell, but not before promising that he would be around for other games.

Back at the hotel, John had lunch in the dinning room and fiddled around until it was time for Bob to show up and take him to the Savoy. Bob was on time, as usual. Because of atypically light traffic, they arrived at the Savoy well before 3:00 PM. He looked for Danielle first and, failing to see her, hoped that this was one of those weekday afternoons when Rudy and Fred would be there. Sure enough, he spotted them across the floor seated alone at a table near the main stage. When he approached them, their greeting was less enthusiastic than usual.

All they could manage was "How you doing, John?"

John sat down and asked, "Why the long faces?"

Rudy replied, "We got no work the last two days. Ain't got no money for beer."

"Yeah," sighed Fred, "We hitting some hard times."

"Well the beers are on me … you can make that up later." Neither of them seemed happy about his offer, but they relented. John brought some beers back from the bar a few minutes later, only to find his two friends still down in the dumps. John made two more trips to the bar and several lame attempts at humor. Neither did anything to lift Fred and Rudy out of their glum state of mind. Finally he blurted out, "What's the real problem … come on, out with it?"

"We ain't never going to amount to anything," groaned Fred.

"That's the truth," Rudy announced. "Every time we get a leg up, we get knocked down."

"Don't you have jobs most days of the week?" asked John.

"Well," said Rudy, "that's usually true, but not lately. Problem is, we don't control our own fate. Some days the city needs some help cleaning up the streets or we can work in the kitchens of some restaurants cleaning up, or stock the shelves in some stores. But we don't know when that's going to happen. We need our own business. If we could set up a newspaper stand with some other things to sell, like cigarettes and cigars, candy and pop, then we'd be in control."

John responded, "Ok, let's talk about that. I'm sort of a businessman. What I do is look for some promising investments. I'd be willing to consider investing in your newsstand. What would you need to do first?"

They thought for a minute, then Rudy said, "We ain't gonna take charity. We want to make it on our own."

"I'm not offering charity," John came back sharply. "I put up the money, I get a piece of the action."

"This ain't numbers running or gambling!" Fred came back loudly enough to be heard across the floor.

"I know," returned John. "You want to develop a business selling legitimate products. I'll supply the start-up money. What you will owe me is three percent of your profits."

"You, mean three cents on a dollar of profits?" asked Rudy in an incredulous tone.

"Yeah," John replied with a straight face. "You can pay me more if you want."

"If you that dumb, we be happy to take your money," responded Rudy. They all laughed uproariously.

John reiterated, "What do you need to deal with first?"

"We got to get a license from the city and then we got to find a place where we can set-up the newsstand," said Rudy. The license won't be too much ... 'bout $15.00 a year. The next thing is to find some public property that we can occupy for free. That will be hard, because the good spots will already be taken. Another possibility will be to talk some merchant into allowing us to set-up on his property. Almost certainly that will cost us some part of our profits or some fee we'd have to pay weekly or monthly."

Fred broke in, "I can make the newsstand. I've already figured it our in my head. It will have a counter extending out from the front face of the stand. We can display sample merchandise on it, newspapers, candy, drinks and maybe some other things. Above it will be a cover on hinges that will be raised and supported with props when we're open for business. When it's closed it will hide everything inside. Rudy and I can sit behind the counter and wait for customers. We'll lock it down at night, along with the back door, which will have two locks. Basically it'll be a little house, complete with a shingled roof, where we will wait on customers during the day. Only the cheap stuff will be left behind at night. I know where to find the lumber at little or no cost. Nails, shingles, and some tools will be most of

the construction costs. I figure the bill won't get to $100 …
maybe even half that much."

John's only response was "good." It inspired smiles
from Rudy and Fred. The deal was sealed, but no timetable
for beginning the project was set. Fred stated it simply:
"We'll let you know when we need money for construction
costs. But first we gonna have to find a home for our stand
and figure out where to buy merchandise wholesale … I
already know where I can buy newspapers at the same price
paperboys pay." The three men scooted out of their chairs,
stood up and shook hands. Fred and Rudy took off for parts
unknown. John went looking for Danielle.

He found her sitting alone, sipping a drink near the
dance floor. When he sidled up to her, she smiled softly and
whispered, "Sit down big boy. Where you been all my life?"

"Looking for you, sweet lady. Now that I've found you,
what does our future look like?"

"I don't look far into the future, but when I think of us
I feel like I'm gonna swoon."

"Aw, I like that," whisper John as he leaned over quickly
and kissed her on the cheek."

"My goodness, Sir. What are your intentions?"

"I intend to take you out to a famous restaurant."

"And which restaurant would that be?"

"Lindy's on Broadway."

Her face went slack. All the joy was out of it.

"What's wrong?" asked a truly puzzled John.

"That's a famous restaurant alright. Mobsters and
famous people like Damon Runyon go there. I wouldn't
be welcome. There are places where you can take a Negro
woman. That isn't one of them."

"How do you know that?"

"Because, us black folks, we talk to each other about places where we can go and feel safe and get some respect. I've never heard that Lindy's is one of them."

She felt that she knew him pretty well by then and, therefore, was not surprised at the expression on his face. It was defiance defined. No one was going to tell John he couldn't go wherever he wanted to go and take with him whoever he wished to accompany him. In confirmation of her assessment of him, John immediately declared, "We're going to Lindy's. I'll see to it that you are treated with respect."

"So now you're telling me I have to go somewhere I don't want to go to? Who you think you are, Marcus Garvey without the pigment? White people don't know nothing about our reality, which ain't gonna change without a revolution. White people saying they can get respect for us is not gonna change anything."

John was taken aback. "I won't force you to go. I hope to talk you into it."

"And how you gonna do that?"

"I'll convince you that I know how to handle people who are arrogant and bigoted. I've done it many times."

She stood up, stepped back, put her hands on her hips, and told him what's what. "Now I see exactly what you're up to. You think you can buy your way into any place? Maybe you can, but you can't get people to respect me by waving some big bucks. They'll take your money, but I'll still see them looking down at me."

"Yeah, I've got some money. But I haven't always had money. What I've had since I was a kid was an ability to confront people's ill will and make them ashamed of it. I've used it to get respect for me and for others."

She studied him for a few moments during which her expression changed from anger to resignation. "I still don't believe it's gonna work, but, for this one last time, I'm going along with you. However, if we see some men inside the place with heavy coats on to hide some big guns they're carrying, you're gonna find out just how fast I can run."

John issued an immediate challenge: "Oh yeah? You think you can out-run me?"

She threw her chair aside and raced to the front door, with him hot on her heels. In moments they were both sprinting down the street. After about a block, she stopped and bent over to catch her breath. He pulled up beside her and bent down until their heads almost touched. He exclaimed between gulps for air, "Where in hell did you learn to run that fast?"

She gasped a couple of times and then rasped, "Boy, don't you know? Black people run fast. It's a good thing we can. It's the only way to get away from men in white sheets."

Back at the Savoy, they sat down and engaged in small talk for about half an hour. By then it was nearly 5:30 PM. Bob would be outside waiting for him soon. He asked when would be a good time for them to eat at Lindy's. She said she didn't have to work the next day. "Good, I'll pick you up at your place."

Her eyes narrowed and she hesitated a moment before speaking. "Just pick me up at the Savoy."

"Why not your place?"

She again thought for a moment, "Well, you haven't even told me where you live."

"Not only will I tell you, I'll take you there anytime."

She responded immediately, "So, where is that." He told her and she responded with, "You live at a hotel? If you take me there, the clientele will think I'm your whore."

John thought, "On my. Here we go again."

"Look," he said, "That's not true. People who work there know me. They go along with whatever I want to do. As for the guests, they don't look at me or anyone else. They just mind their own business. They could care less about whoever they encounter there."

She also didn't want a replay of their first spat. In a quiet but firm voice, she repeated herself. "Pick me up here at the Savoy tomorrow evening." He shrugged and agreed to be there for her at 7:30.

When John got out of bed the next day, his first thought was to find out as much about Lindy's restaurant as he could. He got dressed quickly, had breakfast in the hotel dinning room and headed for the front desk. The clerk on duty didn't know more than that Lindy's restaurant was located in Manhattan and was known for its pies. But he said that the dinning room manager often ate at Lindy's and probably could tell John about it. The clerk summoned the manager who appeared after a short wait. He wanted to talk about Lindy's menu and John let him go on for several minutes about the restaurant's best-known dishes. Then John discretely interrupted the man with, "How about what happens there that gets into the news?" The man immediately changed gears and began a recitation about gangsters who frequented the place. Arnold Rothstein was prominent among the mobsters who hung out there. He was said to call the place "his office," although he spent much of his time there outside the front door surrounded by bodyguards as he talked to other gangsters about illegal operations. John thought that Rothstein's name might be useful and said as much to the dinning room manager. The man acknowledged John's interest, but informed him that Rothstein had died a little more than a month ago. This revelation perked up John's ears. Aiming to please, the manager went on about how Rothstein was assassinated by a mobster named George Hump McManus. This tidbit was especially interesting to John. After a few more minutes of relating little of further interest, John politely interrupted the dinning room manager with sincere expressions of gratitude and a handshake. He had all he needed. To address the next item on his agenda, he hailed a cab to a recently discovered haberdashery where he hoped to find some special duds for the evening at Lindy's.

When John exited Bob's cab in front of the Savoy at 7:35 PM, Danielle was waiting at the door. When he saw her, he stepped back in awe. She wore a dress he had not seen before. It was light green with splashes of black here and there. The fit to her splendid frame was perfect. Her make-up was just right: eyelashes and eyebrows were subtly enhanced and her hair was pulled back behind her head by a narrow sash tied neatly into a bow visible just behind her left ear. Her lips were as full as ever, but a deep red tint seemed too subtle to have resulted from the application of lipstick. He opened the door for her and she gracefully slipped into the cab. Bob saw her in the rear view mirror and shyly exclaimed, "My, my Miss Danielle, you look wonderful tonight." It was the first time he said more than hello to her. Her beautifully sculpted smile was his reward.

She didn't notice John's attire until he entered on the other side of the cab. With obvious amusement she exclaimed, "So, when did you join the Cosa Nostra?" He chuckled.

His black suit-coat had oversized shoulder pads, wide lapels and ample pleating. His tie was bound so tight at the neck that its knot was virtually hidden by a collar closed in front with a gold pin. He tipped his bowler hat to her.

Once at Lindy's, they were seated without incident, though some patrons looked at them with barely concealed contempt. The waiter asked what they would like to drink then disappeared behind a partition. When he returned with their drinks, he merely placed them in front of John and Danielle then disappeared again. The next time they saw him, he was talking to the customers who had glared at them earlier. Next, he responded to a signal from patrons at the bar. He huddled with them for a few moments and again disappeared behind the partition. When he returned to John and Danielle he affected an officious look. "I'm sorry, but we are unable to serve you this evening. Please finish your drinks and leave. There will be no charge."

John glanced at Danielle. She was clearly decimated. He repressed an urge to slug the waiter. Instead he demanded to know why they were being told to leave. The waiter at first refused to answer, but relented when John stood up and loudly demanded an explanation. "Sir, please keep your voice down," pleaded the waiter. After a short pause during which John moved closer to the waiter, he explained. "There are some customers—regulars—who … ah … feel uncomfortable that you are here. They asked me to consult the manager about their feelings and he told me I should ask you to leave." John demanded to see the manager. The waiter hustled off and returned in a couple minutes with a tall, middle-aged man who rubbed his baldhead as he approached them. He apologized profusely but ended with "Negroes are usually welcome here, but sometimes customers who come here almost daily don't like it. We have to respect their feelings. I'd be happy to pay you enough for a meal at a restaurant in Harlem."

John stuck his face so far into the manager's that the rim of his hat touched the man's forehead. "Ever heard of Arnold Rothstein?"

"Yes sir, of course. He spent a lot of time here … a very good customer."

"Well I know the man who killed him." John whispered as he moved his head close to the man's right ear. "His name is George Hump McManus. Ever heard of him? He's kind of like family, if you know what I mean. He'll get away with murder. Nobody will testify against him. You want me to send him around to talk to you?"

The manager's ruddy face turned white as snow. He gasped, stepped back and began to apologize once again, but this time it was delivered in a pleading tone. He offered free meals for both of them, anything they wanted. John looked at Danielle. She was nearly in tears as she shook her head side to side in a "no" gesture. John stepped back from the manager, but continued to stare at him menacingly. Then he wheeled around to pull Danielle's chair out for her. As they left, he turned back toward the manager. When their eyes met, the man folded up like a deflated balloon and collapsed onto the floor.

By the time Bob picked them up, Danielle had recovered, but Bob saw the dismal look on her face through the rearview mirror and was distressed. He didn't say anything, but he kept looking back at her. Neither he nor John knew what to say. The trip back to the Savoy was devoid of conversation. When they reached the Savoy, John got out with Danielle and tried to comfort her. She whimpered that it was hopeless; they were hopeless. She felt that what they experienced that evening revealed what they could expect when they went most places together in New York City. John tried to argue to the contrary, but she wasn't listening. She tore away from him and ran to the front door of the Savoy. His heart sunk as the door closed behind her. He feared that their relationship would never be the same.

CHAPTER 17

Science and Its' Malcontents

On the morning of December 19 John was not ready to discuss science with the Columbia group. He was still worried about Danielle and their relationship. In addition he dreaded meeting with the group. The very thought of dealing with Ronald made John fear that he would lose his cool and destroy whatever rapport he had developed with the other group members. After hurriedly dressing in the handiest apparel lying around his room, he ordered coffee and a roll to go from the dinning room and hustled to the front desk to leave a telegraph message for Sandra. It was his hope that meeting with her before the group convened would help him avoid a meltdown that might destroy his mission.

As prearranged, Bob was waiting for him outside the hotel main entrance. Upon entering the cab, Bob said "hello" half-heartedly and then lapsed into silence. John sensed that the cabby was troubled, but, because he was immersed in his own problems, he didn't want to consider anyone else's. They rode the rest of the way to Columbia in silence.

Once out of the cab, John speed-walked to where he expected to find Sandra. To his surprise, Sandra was accompanied by a tall, dark-haired, brown-eyed woman he had not seen before. The two arose from the bench where they had been waiting and smiled at him in a quizzical way. Sandra introduced her friend, Hazel, who extended her hand. John took it and uttered, "Pleased to meet you." As they continued to look expectantly at him, John sensed that he was supposed to comment about them in some way. He noted that Hazel was dressed much like Sandra, in baggy clothes. Like Sandra, Hazel's face was devoid of makeup. She seemed to be a taller, older, darker version of Sandra. "So," queried John, "You two are partners?" The two women's eye-brows furrowed in a way that made John think, "'partners' may not be what they expected to hear." So, he continued, "How long you two been together?"

Sandra and Hazel immediately relaxed. Hazel declared with evident pride, "We just celebrated five years together." John congratulated them and wished them well. "It's great to meet people who have a lasting relationship. I hope it happens to me someday." The two women touched hands before Hazel got up to leave. He and Sandra waved goodbye to her as she walked away.

John asked Sandra if they could discuss the agenda for their meeting before they sat down with the others. They settled down on a bench and John began to talk about his worst fears. Sandra consoled him, but didn't seem to have any suggestions about how to conduct a more orderly, focused meeting. The two of them paused to think for a minute. Finally Sandra said, "How about this? Each of us could speculate about how our particular interests within our disciplines will evolve in the future. Because it's mere conjecture, perhaps we can diminish the threat of having our most prized scientific maxims exposed to criticism. It'll all be about hypotheticals rather than defending our disciplines as 'most important' and our dissertation proposals as 'most original.' Maybe egos will be retracted like turtles' heads withdrawing into their shells."

John expressed approval of her idea and added, "We can become so far removed from our own agendas that everyone could own the ideas being discussed, not just whoever first advocated them during the meeting."

At this point, they looked at each other and burst out laughing. They agreed that nothing so ideal was going to happen at the meeting. However, Sandra's proposal that they discuss the evolution of group members' scientific disciplines had a reasonable chance to succeed.

When Sandra and John joined the others in their Main Hall conference room, they could not decipher Ronald's, Andrew's, and Herbert's states of mind by trying to read their faces. There was a bit of apprehension and a modicum of uncertainty in the air. Sandra wasted no time laying out the agenda of the meeting. "Today we will try to peer into the future. I will ask each of you to speculate about some important advance that you envision for your discipline in the coming decades. In the weeks ahead, we will devote one meeting to each of the five proposed advances. Let's start with Andrew. What future advance would you propose?"

Several anxious moments passed before Andrew uttered a sound. Finally he spoke a few decibels above a whisper: "When I think about the future of physics, I think about the many enigmas we will face. We have acted as if any puzzles we have yet to solve will eventually be figured out by precisely fitting mathematics to physical phenomena. In turn, this assumption on our part brings Niels Bohr to my mind. Some have said that Bohr has a mind for all times.

Einstein finds it difficult to imagine a mind like Bohr's. Bohr does not try to dismiss or explain away the enigmas and contradictions in physics. He works to explain how they are part and particle of physics. In the future, physical events will be characterized in a more probabilistic than absolute manner. Physics will get messier as new sub-atomic particles are discovered. I will talk more on these matters."

Sandra and John looked at one another meaningfully. Andrew apparently was not the empty vessel that Sandra's informant had characterized him to be.

Sandra pointed to Herb next, who was trying to hide, but knew full well that he couldn't escape this moment. He straightened up in his chair and began to talk in a way that signaled he had prepared for his turn. "I want to bring mathematics to everyday life. Don't worry, I'm not talking about everyone being required to take advanced calculus." There were some giggles around the room. Herb seemed pleased at the response to his quip. He continued with, "I'm talking about math being used to bring solutions not only to business and industrial problems. I'm talking about math contributing to making everyone's life easier and more enjoyable. In conjunction with electrical science, I expect to see mathematical advances leading to instruments that everyone can use for enjoyment and for practical purposes. I'm talking about computing machines for everyone."

Looking around the room, John and Sandra could feel the vibrations generated by a meek person's bold prediction. That contrast enhanced the credibility of Herb's proposal.

Sandra selected herself as the next presenter. Her topic was the future of psychology. "I come from a segment of psychology that is completely empirical. Psychologists like Thorndike focus on the behavior of organisms. There is no interest in what goes on inside the brains of cats, rats, or humans. Instead they feel that observing behavior is sufficient to 'understand' various organisms sufficiently to predict what they will do on occasions subsequent to initial observations of them. I expect that this trend will extend into the distant future and lead to the neglect of thinking and feeling."

She then nodded to John, who took the floor immediately and let the cat out of his bag. "I believe that understanding memory in the future will require that we make new assumptions about the brain. The brain must be characterized as more flexible and changeable than we have thought it to be. More specifically, a full understanding of memory will require us to consider the possibility that new neurons are produced in some parts of the brain. Further, the brain must physically change to accommodate the changes in organisms' environments."

Before he could say more, Ronald rose out of his seat, placed both fists on the table, knuckles down, and howled that John was a fraud. "What are you talking about? New neurons growing in the brain is nonsense. All you have to do is look at the brains of people who died at various ages to see that the older the brains the smaller they are. We lose neurons as we grow older. We never gain new ones after we are mature."

John struggled to keep his composure. After a moment he managed to say in a controlled voice, "I haven't spent a lot of time looking at pickled brains, but you are correct that neurons are lost as we mature. However, that does not mean there is no part of the brain that produces new neurons during our lifetimes. It doesn't have to be all or nothing. Many neurons are lost as we mature, but new ones may be produced in a few parts of the brain. I will show that a reasonable understanding of human memory requires that we consider the possibility that new neurons are produced during our lives."

Ronald was the last to speak. Sandra called his name before he had a chance to continue his rant about John's presentation. He scooted his chair back but remained seated. "I want to talk about genetics, especially eugenics. Humans will not survive unless the brightest among us predominate. We must do something about the proliferation of humans who produce little of value, but are more than willing to take what others have created. They will never be among the discoverers, entrepreneurs, and innovators. I'm not suggesting that they be eliminated outright. Instead, they must submit to sterilization. Then they can be placed on reservations where they can exist in reasonable comfort until there are no more of them. I can talk more about this matter in subsequent meetings."

"I also have something to say about the future of genetics. There will come a day in which all humans genes will be catalogued. When that happens we can close the book on human genetics. All that can be known about human genes will be known. Then there will be nothing to study. We can simply observe how the genes control physiology and mentality."

As Ronald spoke, his audience looked around at each other, first in disbelief and then, in some cases, outrage. Sandra saw that a potential riot was about to happen. She immediately stood up and forcefully announced that their next regular meeting would be held on January 3, 1929. At that meeting, they would discuss what they had learned at the AAAS meeting. All sections of AAAS would meet on the Columbia campus except for Geology and Geography. The University had arranged to have AAAS meeting-information tables available to students, beginning on the first day of the convention, Dec. 27. Before anyone could say anything, she picked up her belongings and marched out the door of the conference room. John raced after her. Neither looked back to assess the state of the others.

Sandra stopped just outside Main Hall and began to shuffle, head down, toward the nearest bench. When she sat down, she placed her hands over her face and her elbows on her knees. John sat down beside her, but didn't know what to say or do. After a couple of minutes, she sniffled that her handling of the meeting was disastrous. The fact that she couldn't control Ronald diminished all the insightful comments made by other group members.

John offered, "No one can handle Ronald. He's an arrogant dogmatist, if that isn't redundant." She opened up the fingers of her hand, revealing a tearful grin. They talked until Sandra came around to thinking that the meeting had been a success despite Ronald, principally because all members of the group had come to regard him as someone to tolerate, if not to respect. Paul summed it up: "It appears to me that other group members have presented their own points of view strictly according to the canons of science. In so doing they have separated themselves from the antithesis of scientific thinking, that, someday, all the meaningful scientific questions will be answered. But, according to Ronald and his ilk, for now, we know enough to determine which humans are worthy of continuation and which must be exterminated."

Sandra had been listening intently. After generally agreeing with John's assessment, she began to reflect on her initial assessment of group members. "My informant was, of course, entirely correct about Ronald. Since he was Ronald's roommate and had to spend much time with him, it's not surprising that the informant was accurate.

Also, extreme people are easier to characterize. We hoped that Herb would be a strong contributor, and he has been. However, we apparently fell into the stereotype trap with regard to Andrew. He comes from a rich family who could afford to provide him with the best education imaginable. Thus, he knows a lot, but lacks originality. Wrong! He's apparently a first-class scientific thinker. And, he seems to be a good person."

When they departed, both felt better about the outcomes of future meetings. However, both knew that the coming meetings were going to be contentious. John returned to the hotel and had a leisurely meal. Although it was too late for meeting with Fred, Rudy and Danielle in the afternoon, lacking anything else to do, and being worried about Danielle's state of mind, when Bob arrived, he asked for a ride to the Savoy.

Bob was still glum and said nothing beyond "Where to?" This time John felt the need to ask what was troubling the cabby. Bob replied, "Nothing." But a moment later, he began to spill the beans. His wife was in need of an operation, but they couldn't afford it. He didn't know what to do.

"I tell you what," suggested John. "How about I pay you some tips in advance. You wouldn't get any more tips until the advance is paid off." The concern for his wife overcame Bob's reluctance to accept what, to him, amounted to charity. Accepting "a hand out" was beneath his dignity. They agreed on $150, the amount that would get his wife through the hospital door and into the operating room." John dug the money out of his pocket and handed it to Bob. The cabby looked sad as he contemplated the cash in his hand. He managed to say, "Call me anytime you need a ride. I'll be there to take you wherever you want to go."

Then, remembering that he would sometimes not be on duty or be unavailable for other reasons, he added, "You will have to tip any substitutes I send to drive you around … that won't lower my debt."

When they arrived at the Savoy, he found the ballroom sparsely populated. There was no sign of Danielle, but he did see Rudy emerging out of a side room. They waved at each other and met on the ballroom floor. John stuck out his fist at handshake level and Rudy intuitively touched his fist to John's. "What's happening?" asked John. "Nothing much yet, but I've been talking to a shop owner who might let us set-up on his store grounds. He's concerned that we not sell anything he has in his shop. I think we can manage that."

Rudy went on to say that he had fashioned the frame of their stand. "I've got the side walls, back wall and roof supports done. Next I'll do the front counter and swing-down door. These parts won't be put together until we can move them to wherever we can put up the stand. I think the man we are talking to will make a deal with us. He wants 15%. What do you think of that?"

"Too high," answered John. "Assure him that you won't compete with him, but will draw customers to his store. They'll be attracted to the site by what you have for sale. Then they'll go into the store next door for other things they need. Convince him you'll bring customers to him. Then talk him into 10%.

"Alright," returned Rudy, "but I may need some more money soon to complete the job."

"Tell me how much, and you got it."

"How about $1000?"

John laughed. "You're not gonna get that much. Chop off a zero." Changing the subject, he asked whether Fred was somewhere in the building. "No," replied Rudy, "he's busy this afternoon. He's got work fixing the wiring in a house. He'll probably be here sometime this evening."

John asked about Danielle, but Rudy hadn't seen her. So he left a message for her and later wondered if she had gotten it. Maybe if he stuck around into the evening she would show up.

It wasn't too early for dinner, so he asked Rudy if there was a good place to eat nearby. "No need to go anywhere else. I got a friend in the kitchen. He'll give us some left-over eats."

"Oh, what would that be?" queried John.

"Some barbequed chicken parts ..."

John interrupted, "Which parts?"

"You don't wanna know, but they sure do taste good, even if they ain't fresh. He also probably has some collard greens and other down home things."

John looked a little dubious, but he was also curious. He replied, "Let's do it." They sat down to some leftovers that were better than much of the fresh food he was used to consuming. After about thirty minutes of eating and talking about sports, John left Rudy chewing on something that was hard to identify. He went straightaway to the front desk to inquire about Danielle. There, he was told that she was scheduled to work that night, but it would be another forty-five minutes before her sift began. To kill some time John left the Savoy to roam around the neighborhood. People on the street looked at him with some curiosity, but not much. He stopped at a pawnshop to find a little bracelet for Danielle. The clerk assured him that the one he chose was genuine silver. John had his doubts, but he didn't care. He knew that she liked little trinkets. Outside again, it was growing dark, but he pressed on into the neighborhood. A couple of blocks more and he was stopped in his tracks. He saw Danielle leaving a building about a half-block away. She saw him also and looked anything but pleased. John guessed that he had discovered where she lived. When they met, she asked, "What are you doing here?" He explained that he was just killing time until she showed up for work. They walked together toward the Savoy in silence. Finally, John couldn't stand it. "Why are you acting like this? One bad experience doesn't change everything."

"Oh yes it does," she responded. "You just don't get it. We don't have a future. We can't be together anywhere except at the Savoy. It's a sham relationship. No use to keep pretending otherwise." John was aghast. He knew that she was upset about their trip to Lindy's restaurant, but that couldn't be the real reason she wanted to end their relationship. "What am I supposed to do? Forget you? Stop coming to the Savoy?"

"I can't stop you from coming to the Savoy," she said. "But, we won't be going anywhere outside the Ballroom."

"We can talk when you are at the Savoy, right?"

She thought for a moment, then responded: "Yes, we can talk if I'm not otherwise engaged." He knew that if he could talk to her, he still had a chance.

They reached the Savoy and entered together. She immediately disappeared into the interior of the building and he looked around for Rudy. Failing to find him, John gave Bob's work-phone number to the front desk and asked the clerk to request that Bob be sent to fetch him. In only a short time, Bob was waiting for him outside. When John entered the cab, Bob seemed more his usual self than earlier, but he said nothing. When they arrived at the Hotel Theresa, Bob looked back at him and said only, "Call me anytime." As he exited the cab, John slipped the bracelet he had purchased for Danielle out of his pocket and onto the cab seat.

CHAPTER 18

Getting Things Back to Normal ... Or Not

While John was eating breakfast in the Hotel Theresa dinning room on the morning of December 22, 1928 he was continuing the argument he was having with himself since he arose that morning. He could decide to tell the hotel personnel about the "package" he was putting out in the hotel lobby for pick-up during the morning of the next day. Instead he could just put it out and hope hotel personnel didn't mess with it. After a few more agonizing moments, he decided not to decide ... at least until he took the contents of the package out on the streets of New York City for one more time. So, he hustled back to his room to get the Brownie Box for one last use before he got it ready for return delivery to Martha, Sarah, Joe, and Randy.

It was a mild December day on 125th Street. He headed on foot to the Mount Morris Park. Along the way, he stopped for a few moments here and there to record comments and take some video of events along the street. He hadn't gone far before he noticed that a truck with "BEST CHIRSTMAS DECORATIONS" painted on its side had crashed into a street light pole and its contents had partially spilled out onto the pavement. A crowd rushed from both sides of the street to pick up boxes of Christmas decorations. The truck driver was madly fighting the crowd for possession of his cargo and, at the same time, trying to throw boxes back into the truck. Soon he was overwhelmed and collapsed into a sitting position on the curb. By this time, the sounds of police sirens warned the thieves that it was time to escape with their booty. A police officer's car skidded to a stop next to the truck and he leaped out to begin a futile race after the herd of lawbreakers. He managed to collar a couple of them, but the rest got away with their "free" Christmas decorations. Santa doles out his Christmas largesse in mysterious ways. John recorded much of the robbery episode.

Further down the street John encountered a group of teenage boys harassing a young girl about their age. John pointed the Brownie Box at them and touched the video button. They were teasing her and making sexually suggestive comments to her. She cursed them and yelled that her boyfriend and his buddies would soon be there to "beat you to a pulp." At this point the boys began to touch her and push her. Just as John was about to consider intervention, he heard some shouting and saw that another group of boys was sprinting toward the girl and her assailants. These guys were smaller in number but bigger in size than the girl's tormentors. As soon as the girl's attackers noticed the rescuers, they turned on their heels and ran off in several different directions. It was apparently the boyfriend who stopped to console the girl. His buddies ran after her molesters and were able to catch three of them. They were dragged back to the embracing couple. Punishment was swift and humiliating. The three bullies were forced to get down on their hands and knees and beg the girl for forgiveness. The boyfriend seemed unsatisfied. He huddled with his buddies and whispered orders to them. They immediately grabbed the boys, yanked off their clothes down to their underwear, and hollered "run for your lives." As the nearly nude boys accelerated to sprinter speed, a crowd that had assembled to watch the rescue applauded and yelled their approval. Street justice had been exacted.

Other scenes along the way were more mundane. The Salvation Army was collecting Christmas money for the poor and numerous beggars were asking for a handout. It seemed that pedestrians were being more generous than usual. At the Park, though children were bundled up against the winter cold, they were frolicking on the playground equipment as if it were a summer day. The approach of Christmas was having a marvelous effect on people's spirits, despite the fact that most of those whose lives John was recording were very unlikely to get much from Santa.

On the way back to the Hotel Theresa, John rather arbitrarily decided to tell the hotel personnel about the package. He wanted to be sure that the package containing the Brownie Camera device was located exactly where it had been when it was delivered to him. He had already recorded his room number in the Brownie for Joe and Randy so they could make future deliveries and pick-ups to and from the security of his living quarters.

Fortunately the clerk that John dealt with most often was at the front desk when he entered the hotel. He told the clerk that he wanted to place a package at the same location in the lobby where the first package had been delivered. In so doing, he made up a story about how the person who would pick up the package was given strict instructions that it would be leaning against the same chair on which the

Brownie Box package had been found. Further, the clerk was told that, under no circumstances, was the package to be moved from the spot against the chair. Since the clerk would not be on duty when the package would be sent back to Joe and Randy, John slipped the clerk a five-dollar bill and told him to inform the clerks on later shifts that the package was not to be moved. Also, cleaning and maintenance crews were to be told not to touch the package. When the clerk looked a bit dubious, John pulled some one-dollar bills out of his pocket and shoved them across the counter to the clerk. The clerk's facial expression changed from non-committal to knowing grin. John guessed that the clerk was going to keep most of the dollar bills, but that couldn't be helped. A short conversation with the clerk convinced John that this rather conniving young man would not fail to spread the word about not moving the package.

Next John flagged down a bellboy and asked him to fetch some wrapping paper, postal stamps and string. He gave the guy seven dollars and told him to keep what was left after purchasing the postal materials. The bellhop was delighted but demurred a bit when John told him he had to have the ordered items delivered to his room by 5:00 PM. The boy sheepishly indicated that he could not leave until he got off at six o'clock, which would be after all stores had shut down for the day. John sent him to the clerk to report what he had been hired to do with the sure knowledge that the clerk would allow the boy to leave his post for long enough to complete John's errands. As expected, when the bellhop had finished talking to the clerk, and John had given the clerk the high sign, the boy hustled out of the hotel to get John's postal materials.

John received the postal materials by five PM and had the Brownie Box wrapped and ready for "delivery" by nine

PM. After he placed the Brownie Box package against the chair in the lobby, he checked with the front desk to be sure the night clerk, who was now on duty, knew that the package was not to be touched. The clerk promised that the early morning clerk would also be told that no one was to bother the package. The night clerk indicated that he and the early morning clerk had already been told about being sure that the package was not moved. He got his tip and John left one for the early morning clerk. The clerk's broad grin assured John that all was very likely to go as planned.

The gang had gathered in the time machine room on Dec. 23 for the 3:00 AM arrival of the Brownie Box. Joe and Randy had put the machine through its paces and the chamber was enshrouded in darkness. When the lights came on, the Brownie Box package was situated in the middle of the chamber. Sarah was the first to work the chamber door handle, but when she opened the door, Martha squeezed in just in front of her. When they opened the package, they found the Brownie Box looking as good as new.

Joe called out to the two women, "Be careful …handle it with care." Martha stepped back a bit in response to a mental image of herself dropping the Box. Sarah never hesitated. She immediately bent over, carefully nestled the box between her fingers, and carried it to a table outside of the chamber. There she put it down gently and the others gathered around it. Randy spoke first: "It appears in perfect shape." Joe nodded in agreement. After a pause, Sarah suggested that they cable the box to the computer so that the sights and sounds of New York City, 1928, could be reproduced on the computer monitor with extraordinary clarity and accuracy. Joe and Randy implemented her suggestion in what seemed like a couple of minutes.

When the roar of human and vehicle traffic and the sights of 1928 New York City assailed their senses in full color, high definition, and surround-sound they were nearly floored. "It's like we are there!" gasped Joe. John's typewritten commentary scrolled across the bottom of the screen and occasionally his voice was heard. An hour later, they were still crowded around the computer screen enthralled by their vicarious trip back in time.

"I'm amazed," declared Martha. "The extraordinary clarity is something I didn't expect. I felt like stepping up to the screen and touching Babe Ruth's shoulder so I could ask for an autograph." The others' giggles confirmed that their experience was the same. They all were fascinated by the reaction of the communist protesters to being photographed.

Sarah said, "I'm no apologist for communism—it turned out to be a horror—but it is fascinating that some things never change. As is true today, if you dare to profess views that government considers to be subversive, no matter how benevolent and fact-based your point of view might be, you could well find yourself under government surveillance. Some form of today's NSA has always been around."

They continued to revel in New York City life during 1928 as if they could not get enough of it. However, at one point oohs and ahs changed to something else. Sarah broke into the babbling about what they were hearing and seeing with, "What's that? I think I'm hearing a woman's voice … there's a woman with John."

Joe exclaimed, "Yeah, I hear it." Then they got a glimpse of the woman in question.

"There she is," declared Martha. Danielle appeared head to waist on the screen.

"Run that back," shouted Sarah. Randy did that and stopped the action. There was Danielle in all her splendor.

Randy gasped, "She's gorgeous."

"I think she's black," added Joe.

"She looks like Halle Berry," offered Sarah.

"I think she looks more like Rihanna," suggested Martha. Everyone looked at Martha. She had no explicit expression on her face, but her voice and posture suggested that she was stunned.

To break the awkward silence that followed, Joe chimed in with, "I think she looks like Sonia Rolland."

"Who's that?" said several people at once.

"She was in Woody Allen's 'Midnight in Paris,'" said Joe.

"I didn't see it," said Randy.

Sarah announced, "I did, but I don't remember her." With that comment, Joe, Randy and Sarah ran out of ways to avoid the obvious.

Finally, Randy revealed what was on all their minds: "John has a girl friend." Once again everyone turned to look at Martha.

"So he has a girl friend," declared Martha, a bit testily. "That's his business. It's not his first girlfriend and it won't be his last."

"That's right," said Randy. Before he had time to think about it, he continued his assessment. "After all, you're working on your third boyfriend since John left." Upon making this impulsive remark, he saw the looks on his friends' faces and knew that he had really screwed up. He fell into a nearby chair and, like the others, waited for Martha to address the issue he had unwittingly raised.

Martha sighed heavily and mustered what little patience she had left with her friends' intrusions into her private life. "Like I told you, my relationship with other people is my business. My motivations for hanging out with John and any other man are complex and personal. I'm not even sure why I spend time with one person or another. I do it because it feels right when I'm doing it. I hang out with you guys because I consistently enjoy being with you and learning from you. John is a confidant. We do talk about personal matters … that is until one of us says, 'None of your business!' We're close, but that's all I'm going to say about it." She paused for an instant, and then added, "What kind of relationship John has with another woman is his business." She turned abruptly and walked away. Halfway to the door, she bumped into a chair owing to vision blurred by tears.

The others followed her, leaving Randy to lock up the two most secret rooms in the computer science building. When he got back to his living quarters, he made a note to call a meeting at the Lion's Den two days hence.

John woke up because of a bad dream, which he could not remember, except that something evil was chasing him. It was pitch black in the room, so he fumbled for the switch on the lamp next to his bed. When the light flickered on, he reached for his wristwatch. It was almost 4 AM. He stumbled to the bathroom, flipped on the light switch and, in the bathroom mirror, saw a guy who was not going to go back to sleep anytime soon. The first item on his agenda was to confirm that the Brownie Box had been successfully transported back to his friends. He reentered his bedroom, picked up his pants, slipped in one leg and then the other, buckled up, and looked for a shirt. Finding one draped over a chair, he stuck his arms into its sleeves and his sockless feet into a pair of shoes he found nearby. Then he returned to the bathroom to comb his hair with his hands. Satisfied that he looked presentable, he headed for the hotel room door. Before he got there, he saw his reflection in a full-length mirror on the closet door. He flicked on the main light switch near the door and took another look at himself. His hair was sticking up on the back of his head like a turkey's tail, his shirt collar was halfway tucked into his shirt, and his fly was open. After correcting these problems, he headed out the door to the elevator.

Once in the main lobby he heaved a sigh of relief to discover that the Brownie Box package was gone, but then, he thought, what if someone had taken it. He looked around for the night watchman who he spotted leaning against the reception counter, half-asleep. He jumped when John called to him, "What happened to the package that was leaning against this chair?"

"Uh," muttered the man, "it was there. I saw it there several times. Then suddenly I saw some movement, and it was gone. It's the second time that's happened. Poof, it was gone. But I could have been dreaming."

John had to smile, not just because he felt like he was viewing a scene from a Laurel and Hardy movie. The night watchman's account of the disappearing packages had convincingly persuaded him that the Brownie Box was back with his friends. But it occurred to him that suspicions might be raised if the night watchman told other personnel at the hotel what he had twice witnessed. John told the man that what he saw was their secret. He got the guy to pledge not to tell anyone. Then John thought, "Opps, to seal the deal, I need to tip this guy." He fumbled around in his pants pockets hoping to find at least some change. But instead he pulled out a wad of bills he thought he had lost earlier." Awkwardly, he separated out a five dollar bill and three ones. Seeing the cash, the night watchman became wide-awake for the first time. He couldn't keep his bulging eyes off the cash. John started to hand the bills to the man, but hung onto them long enough to say, "This is our secret, right buddy?" The night watchman vigorously shook his head in a "yes" manner and John dropped the bills into his greedy hands.

John headed back to his room in the hope of catching a few more zzzs. He must have tossed and turned for at least a couple of hours before he fell asleep. When he woke up it was 10:30 in the morning, he crawled got out of bed with a feeling of shame at having wasted a good part of the day. By the time he got himself dressed and down to the dinning room, it was almost 11:00 AM, too late for breakfast. He managed to talk the dinning room manager into scrounging up a stale piece of pastry leftover from breakfast. With that and a carryout cup of coffee, he headed for the front desk to call Bob. It was too early to go to the Savoy, so he told Bob he wanted to go to Playland Park.

The ride seemed to take a long time, partly because of traffic, and partly because Bob spoke only once early in the trip: "You do know that the Park is not open this time of year?" John answered in the affirmative, but indicated that he just wanted to look around. Once there, as he got out of the cab, John told Bob to pick him up in an hour. First on John's agenda was a trip to a refreshment stand near the Park where he selected a soft drink and the lunch of the day, something stuffed between two pieces of bread out of which oozed onions and grease. Not too many steps later, he dumped the concoction into a trashcan and made his way to the giant Ferris wheel. He imagined the view at the top of its rotation and the gentle sway of the seats as it whirled around. Next he took a stroll down the boardwalk and watched people ice-skating. Then he sneaked into the Derby Racers pavilion, settled into one of the racers and pretended to be passing up all of the other cars. Finally he happened by a car ride for children. In his mind he could see kids seated in the cars anticipating being a real car driver and could hear them squealing joyously, just as he had done upon his first ride in a bumper car.

Upon returning to where Bob was to pick him up and finding him not yet there, John's eyes wondered around the street scene. Suddenly he heard a commotion from across the street. A cop was chasing a Puerto Rican teenage boy. The kid tripped and fell to the pavement just as the cop caught up with him. Before he could get up, the cop began to pound him with his nightstick. Horrified, John looked around to see if anyone was going to step in and save the boy. The reaction of the crowd was almost as appalling as the beating. Individuals around him were looking at the cop and the kid, but the expressions on their faces revealed the kind of indifference one would expect of people looking at a familiar scene. A man standing next to John noticed his distress and commented matter-of-factly, "Oh, don't worry. He's just a greaser."

When Bob showed up and John climbed into the back seat, he could not resist giving the cabby a description of what he had just witnessed. Bob's only comment was "I guess you can get used to anything."

Once at the Savoy, John found the ballroom pretty much deserted. Fred and Rudy were nowhere to be found. He guessed that Danielle would also not be in yet. After finding a waiter to fetch a beer for him, he sat down to reflect on his day so far. New York City during 1928 was arguably the most modern city in the world. It was magnificent by any standards, but, like all the world's big cities, it was also the home of human misery. There was beauty, vitality, and an endless supply of fascinating places to visit. It contained Columbia, one of the world's most respected universities, the Museum of Natural History—one of the most revered scientific museums in the world, then and now—and the only English language newspaper in the world that rivaled the London Times. And that's not to mention Broadway, some of the finest ethnic restaurants in the world, and the most loyal sports fans imaginable. New York's people were hardworking, generous, and generally humane. Yet, it was also a showroom displaying all the human frailties.

Before he could resolve the contradictions represented by the city he had come to love, his reverie was interrupted by a soft hand placed on his shoulder. He turned his head to find Danielle smiling down at him. They chatted amiably for sometime, neither bringing up their recent feud. Finally, it became obvious to both of them that they were trying not to notice the elephant in the room. "Look," she spoke in soft tones, "I haven't changed my mind about our future. I don't think we have a longtime future. But maybe we can see each other outside the Savoy, as long as I get to pick the places we go." The space between John's eyelids narrowed just for a second. He was not used to being told that someone else was always going to decide where he would be going. They could share such decisions, but he wanted to have a say about their itinerary. Nevertheless, he repressed his feelings and rose to give her a hug. They were "back together," but their future was uncertain.

CHAPTER 19

Time Travel Issues and Science Debates

Everyone showed up at the Lion's Den within minutes of each other and all were eager to discuss the implications of John's videos. As soon as they were all seated, Joe gushed, "We'll never have to speculate about what happened during a pivotal historical event. We'll be able to go back to any important historical event and record it verbatim, as it actually happened. Chariot races in the Circus Maximus and gladiators battling wild beasts and each other in the Coliseum will be recorded by time travelers just as these events actually unfolded."

"Historians will be in a state of siege, each expert on a critical event arguing with rival colleagues about which of their historical accounts was closest to what actually happened. In each case, it is very likely that no one account of an event will fit what actually happened. History will have to be rewritten," exclaimed Martha so loudly that other Lion's Den patrons heard despite their great distance from her.

"And, oh my goodness, the implications for religion are extraordinary," rasped Martha. What is the real truth about Jesus, Buddha, Mohammed, Krishna, Dalai Lama ..."

Before she could go on, Sarah interrupted in a tone unusual for her. "Are you crazy. A time traveler who returned with 'hard proof' that contradicted central religious beliefs would be strung up or worse. If you travel in time and have an opportunity to record events that contradict religious beliefs, don't do it or delete it if you do it."

"Also," Randy extended Martha's point, "what if the time frames in which preeminent events were supposed to have occurred were visited by time travelers and nothing happened ... the reputed events did not occur? Would you think it wise to report failures to confirm crucial events when you return to the present time? Not if you want to live out the rest of your life in peace."

The looks on all four faces communicated that a previously unacknowledged dark side of time travel was revealed to them for the first time. None of them had thought through the implications of bringing back evidence that cherished beliefs are untrue. "I can hear it now," continued Randy. "The recordings pertaining to deeply held beliefs will be called 'fakes,' and those who produced them will be vilified as heretics and subjected to attempts on their lives."

"Given widespread knowledge of the deficiencies of our senses and memories compared to electronic recordings, how could video made during a period of time—like the one in which John is now immersed—be doubted?" asked Martha.

"Easily," interjected Sarah. "People are capable of believing whatever they want to believe regardless of evidence presented to them. John has said-so many times, in one-way or another. It's what his experience with the psychological literature tells him."

"And some contrarian will argue that 'what happened' is always a matter of subjective interpretation," suggested Joe.

"Awe, come on," interjected Randy. "If we couldn't trust objective recordings of events, we would have no science and none of the practically important results of scientific findings that enrich our lives everyday."

"True," replied Joe, "but many of the people who enjoy the practical outcomes of scientific findings—such as the electronic devices we can't seem to do without—see no contradiction in using products made possible by science and denying the outcomes of science when the results of scientific inquiry contradict their central beliefs."

"Spot on," exclaimed Martha who went on to expand Joe's point. "I wonder, what would happen if people's continued access to all the products they use daily that are enabled by scientific findings was made contingent on their genuine acceptance of crucial scientific findings like, say, the existence of global warming?"

The chuckling that followed this apropos question changed the mood of the meeting. The four friends returned to their beers, munchies and concerns about less weighty matters.

After about 20 minutes of small talk, Martha decided it was time for some mischief. "Let's talk about going to the future."

Joe responded with "All right! I want to go the near future—but not until I finish my dissertation."

"Okay, Joe, let's say you go ten years into the future. Consider what would happen if you ran into yourself."

"Oh, I will avoid myself. I'll stay away from wherever my future self might be."

"Fine, Joe, but I'll come up with a response for you. So imagine that you run into yourself on the street ten years into the future. You might say, "Gees, Joe, you don't look so good. What happened to your hair? Not much left down the middle of your cranium. And what's that hanging over your belt. You're a little paunchy there, huh?"

Joe snarled at her, but he couldn't think of anything to say. "And how about you, Randy?" Her next target grasped the tabletop tightly and his face froze. "You'd probably say, 'Hey Randy. Look at you. You're a mere shadow of your former self. And by the way, who's that beautiful woman clutching your hand?'"

Randy lowered his head, placed his hand over his mouth and blushed. The future of himself looked good to him.

Martha addressed Sarah next. "My goodness, what would you say to yourself? How about, 'Lose those advanced Google glasses. You're swiping the air like you're having a brain seizure. You will never totally reconcile quantum physics with Newtonian physics."

The response this time was rather derisive: some hissing. Nothing much was funny about very serious Sarah.

Sarah didn't change her expression. Her only response was, "My turn." Martha cringed. "Now Martha," began Sarah, "when you encounter yourself on a trip ten years into the future, you would say, 'Hey Martha. Girl you're looking good. And my oh my, are you dating both of those handsome young men walking a step behind you?' The older, and might I say, wiser Martha would reply, 'Yes I am dating both of them, but I'm saving one of them for you.'" There were several disturbing moments of silence, then Martha roared with laughter. The others joined her in the moment of mirth. After the last few chuckles were uttered, Martha announced, "Ok, you got me pegged. The number of men in my life at any given time can vary from 1 to higher digits, but I won't speculate about how high."

Sarah suggested that they get back to past events that that would be fascinating to visit. She began with a list of pre-20th century philosophers who laid the groundwork for 20th century thought: Søren Kierkegaard, Friedrich Nietzsche, David Hume, William James, and Henry David Thoreau. "It would be fascinating to go back to their public presentations and hear them speak about their philosophies ... but I'd have to brush up on my German and Danish." She said the latter without a change in voice tone or facial expression. No one seemed surprised that she might be the master of multiple languages.

Martha took the floor next: "I want to go back to a time between 760 BC to 656 BC to witness the rule of Egypt by black Pharaohs." Her friends looked puzzled. Joe remarked, "I never heard that Egypt was ruled by Black Pharaohs."

"Most people haven't," Martha responded, "but, all you have to do is Google it. It's documented, though some people claim that there has never been an advanced African culture. Well, Egypt is part of Africa, and, if that doesn't work for these people, some of the Pharaohs were from far south of the Mediterranean. Statues and paintings of these Pharaohs showed typical African facial features and dark skin."

Looks of doubt on the faces of Martha's friends faded. However, Randy had a question. "Yes, Randy; what is it?"

"Wouldn't it be dangerous to go back that far when millions of people were brutally ruled by a few despots? If you didn't look like the local denizens, not to mention speak and act like them, wouldn't you be in for a world of hurt?"

"Hmmm," said Martha, "I didn't think of that, but off the top of my head, couldn't I show up dressed like an Egyptian princess? That ought to get me some respect."

"Yeah, maybe," returned Randy, "but when they presented you to the real Egyptian royalty and they didn't recognize you, wouldn't they see you as a rival and chop off your head, or something equally as bad?"

"I'm not coming up with anything 'equally as bad,'" said Martha, "but I think I just learned something important from you. Going to the distant past, or deep into the future, may poise unimaginable dangers to time travelers."

"That's right," offered Sarah. "We can easily conceive of the relatively recent past—there are pictures and a vast literature to tell us what to expect. Or we could ask our great grandmothers. Likewise, we can reasonably predict life in the near future as an extension of life now. In both cases, we could plan for our trips with reasonable confidence, but not for the distant future, or, for that matter, the distant past."

"I agree," said Joe. "I've said as much in regard to my plans for travel into the near future. But as I've also indicated, on a trip to the near future, even people like us—candidates for PhDs in science—would be far enough behind that we might not be able to function effectively in our own disciplines. That would make it difficult to cope, to put it mildly. John doesn't have that problem. He knows where the science of 1928 came from and where it's going. That's powerful. He can regale people from back then with predictions of technological developments in the future. He will become highly credible. And he has other advantages, like knowing that the gold industry is where to put your money beginning in early 1929. Finally, he can speak in a way that people in the near past will find familiar and quickly acquire the clothing that will make him look like everyone else. These advantages appear to be mostly unavailable to travelers into the distant past and even to those traveling into the near future."

"You're onto something, Joe, I never thought of that," said Randy. "Significant advances come a few per year.

We can keep up with them. However, having to suddenly become familiar with ten years worth of critical advances in order to function effectively would be extraordinarily challenging and extremely stressful for most people."

Joe's friends nodded in agreement. At the same time, it occurred to them that Joe had a greater understanding of time travel than they had attributed to him, and possibly more accurate notions about time travel than any of them, including John. It also occurred to them that conceptions of time travel in the 2010s were exceedingly naïve. Sarah put it this way: "Books and movies of the present time have people magically showing up somewhere in time, totally unprepared. But, somehow, they survive and even prosper, though they must fight swarming masses of primitive humans in the past or giant, hideous, multi-eyed, multi-tentacle creatures and robotic demons in the future. If time travel is going to be a scientific endeavor, rather than just fanciful escapism at movie theatres, it must be approached systematically. Every detail of what would be required to survive and accomplish a mission in another time frame must be thoroughly considered, checked and double checked, before a time traveler is launched. I hope we did a good job of that for John."

On the day before Christmas, John got up late. After he had finished brunch at 11:25, he purchased a copy of the New York Times, brought it back to his room and read several parts of it. That got him to almost noon. He knew that there wouldn't be much going on at the Savoy this early, but having nothing else to do, he decided to go there that afternoon. Maybe Danielle would be there. If so, perhaps they could decide on somewhere to go together. If not, Fred or Rudy or both would probably be there. He was very much interested in any progress they had made toward starting their business. So he called Bob to meet him at the Hotel Theresa at 1:00 PM.

Bob was off duty, but he sent a substitute who arrived right on time. When he got out at the Savoy John found the surrounding area less busy than usual. There were few people inside the Savoy, but he did find a bartender. He ordered a beer and whatever they had leftover in the kitchen. When the bartender returned, John quaffed the beer, but stared at the leftovers. He could not decipher what was in the amorphous mass he hoped to call lunch. He cut a little of it off with a knife and fork and cautiously tasted it. Though it didn't look good, it tasted great. He immediately consumed most of the rest of it. When he finished he just sat there, looking around, hoping for company that afternoon. Something like an hour passed and nothing happened, so he decided to give up. On the way to the front door where he could send a message to Bob's cab company, he saw Danielle emerge from the interior of the building. She waved to him and they met on the dance floor. After they embraced briefly, he asked why she hadn't noticed him when she came into the Savoy. "I came early today. This is the first time I've been out-front." John thought her answer to be reasonable, but he was disappointed that she wasn't looking for him. After all, they hadn't seen each other for what seemed like a long time.

They found a table on the periphery of the dance floor and sat down next to each other. After a few moments of awkward silence, they both began to talk at the same time, which left the two of them giggling nervously. His nod to her signaled that she could take the first turn at talking. "I've missed you," she said in a whisper.

He took her hand, leaned forward and spoke in too loud a voice. "I can't stop thinking about you." She looked around to see if anyone was listening. There was no one in sight. They kissed briefly and both relaxed.

"So," said John, "is there anywhere we can go this afternoon?" She replied, "I've been thinking about that. There's a little hole in the wall restaurant in Brooklyn where a man from the Caribbean prepares some wonderful food. I don't know what to call it, but it's delicious. It's a place where you can sit down at one of the two little tables he has available and sample his dishes or order food to take out. I've been there several times. All kinds of people patronize this restaurant and the proprietor welcomes everyone. It's a comfortable place." She went on to describe the interior of the little restaurant in detail.

Even though the thought of eating again so soon was not appealing to him, he wanted to please her. They needed to find places they could visit without experiencing a replay of the scene at Lindy's. "Let's go," he exclaimed with genuine enthusiasm. She looked surprised. It had not been her intention to go right then, just some time. But when she saw apprehension in his face, she said, "Alright."

When a cab from Bob's company arrived at the front door, Danielle gave the cabby directions. When they arrived at the restaurant, John confirmed that the cabby could be back in about an hour.

The restaurant owner and only employee greeted Danielle warmly. "How are you my dear," he said in broken English. She leaned forward and kissed his cheek lightly. He smiled as would a father in response to a kiss from his daughter. He then informed them about what was on the menu for the day. John had no idea what foods he was describing and suspected that neither did Danielle. She listened until he was finished and then asked, "What would you recommend?" He responded in words that they did not understand. John stepped behind Danielle to cue her that she had to decide. Without missing a beat, Danielle pretended she knew exactly what he was talking about and accepted his recommendation. They settled into chairs at the table nearest the counter.

John whispered, "Do you have any idea what you ordered for us?"

She responded in an equally low voice, "I have no idea, but I know we will love it. He always does something special for me and it's always delicious."

They smiled at each other like two teenagers on a first date. He wanted to say something nice to her. Though he marveled at the aplomb with which she handled the situation, he chose to comment on her phenomenal ability to take-in a scene and remember it in detail. "I noticed how well you remembered everything about this place. It's remarkable. I've been to some places numerous times and I could never remember as many details as you can."

She responded simply, "I'm smart."

John replied, "Oh, I know that … I've known that for a long time."

She continued, "I was at the top of my high school graduating class. The Nuns said that I could easily do well in college. But my parents couldn't afford it. Doesn't matter anyway. None of the good colleges in New York City would take a black girl."

John blurted out, "Are you sure of that?" Then he remembered that he had seen no black students on the Columbia University campus. He looked away sheepishly. She demanded, "Well, tell me. What college in New York City would allow me to enroll?"

He mumbled, "I don't know." But he quickly followed that weak response with "I'll try to find out."

"You do that," she said sharply, "but even if you find one, I still will never come up with the money for tuition."

John started to tell her that he might be able to do something about the money problem as well, but the food arrived at their table. It was just as well. He was not at all sure that he could help her get into a college, let alone how to find the money for her. He knew that she would never accept a handout from him.

They ate voraciously until there was not a crumb left, quite a feat for John. It was one of the most gluttonous days of his life. The great food had mellowed them out. They were feeling very good.

After they paid the restaurant owner and praised his cuisine, they saw from the clock on the wall that they had time to kill before the cabby was due back to pick them up. "Let's walk around the neighborhood for awhile," he suggested. She extended her hand and he it took it gently.

Outside on the street they ambled along with no particular destination in mind. Considering the time of year, and some splotches of snow and ice remaining on the street after the last wintery day, it was nice out. Before they knew it, they had ventured pretty far from the restaurant.

Finally they stopped on the sidewalk and John asked, "Where are we?"

"I don't know," said Danielle. But, after several moments of thought she said, "I think I've figured it out. This alley should be a short-cut back to the restaurant." So, they stepped into the alley and began walking toward the next main street, which they could see about a block away. The alley had several intersections with spaces between buildings. They passed one of them and, just as they approached the second, first one and then several teenage boys filed into the alley. They were blocking the way. One of them made a comment to the biggest boy who appeared to be their leader. He waved to some others who were still between the buildings. Then he led a contingent of boys toward Danielle and John. John was not sure what to do. He thought maybe they could make a run for it back the way they came, but when he looked behind him, he saw that some of the gang had doubled back to close off that escape route. He made a quick count of how many gang members were coming at them. He could see at least a dozen.

John motioned for Danielle to get behind him. Now they were surrounded. All of these young hoodlums were leering at Danielle and sneering at John. One of them took a step toward Danielle and growled, "Nigra." Danielle froze, but John was more composed than she had ever seen him before. He stood up straight, hands slightly out from his sides and fingers spread with palms down. His head turned slowly as he scanned each of them briefly. They passed back and forth in front of John and Danielle giving John hard looks but not getting too close to him. Finally, the leader laughed loudly in a forced way. The others joined him in the feigned laughter. After a moment he signaled to the others in a "follow me" manner. They filed in behind him and he led them toward the street from which Danielle and John had entered the alley. They were gone in what seemed like a few seconds.

Danielle slid down the wall she had been leaning against. She remained there for some time choking back tears. John uttered a sigh of relief then bent down to comfort Danielle. She was not to be consoled. "They insulted me! Why didn't you beat 'em up?"

John thought for a moment, trying to frame his answer in a way that would truly reveal his motivations, and, at the same time, relieve her distress. "I'm sorry. I was trying to do the best I could to protect you. I could have taken out a few of them, but there was at least a dozen. Some of the others might have gotten to you. I chose my method from experience. These punks, like others of their kind, are all about saving face. They saw my posture and the way I was looking at them. Any one of them who came at me risked embarrassing themselves in front of their buddies. That's especially true of the big guy."

"I don't care. I wanted you to hurt them!" cried Danielle.

John had to be careful about what he said next. After a brief hesitation he spoke slowly but forcefully. "I'm a student of the classic martial arts. Martial arts are about self-defense, not beating someone up. Some martial arts moves can maim or kill. It's very serious business. You try to protect yourself or someone else. Only in the most serious circumstances would you use a move that might cripple or kill someone. I did the best that I could." Danielle said nothing in response to John's explanation of himself, but the hurt look on her face did not fade.

He helped her to her feet and they headed in the direction they were going before they encountered the hoodlums. When the emerged from the alley, just down the street they could see the restaurant where they had eaten. The cabby was patiently parked in front of the place. John apologized for being late and told him to take Danielle to the Savoy. After she had been dropped off, the cabby drove John back to the Hotel Theresa.

CHAPTER 20

Going to the Meeting
and Reconciliation

On December 27, 1928, John got up late. So he got dressed hurriedly, grabbed coffee and a roll in the Dinning Room and hailed a cab. When he arrived at the meeting site, it was almost noon. He bypassed the registry desk and headed for a table that was loaded with flyers about AAAS and the current meeting. There he picked up a program and a few of the flyers. Next he found a place to sit so he could look through the program. He dog-eared pages containing locations of presentations that looked interesting to him. As he got up to attend his first presentation, a man standing nearby looked familiar. Remembering pictures of Columbia faculty he had found online, the man he was looking at had to be Edward L. Thorndike. He immediately traversed the distance between himself and this revered figure of early American psychology. There he stood for several moments feeling foolish and not knowing what to say. Thorndike explored John's face in search of some clues as to the identity of the obstruction in his path. Finally he asked, "Young man, do I know you?"

John mumbled, "Ah, no sir, Professor Thorndike. I'm a student of psychology who admires your research."

"And what is it that you admire?"

"I regard you as the father of behaviorism. Your techniques for studying behavior will lay the groundwork for methods that will dominate psychology in the future."

Thorndike looked surprised. He frowned a bit as he chose his words carefully. "Well, I hope that I will have some impact on future research and theory in psychology, but I think that your claim on my behalf is overstated. There are many forces at play in contemporary psychology. All of them will have some impact on the future of psychology."

This pronouncement was followed by an awkward moment of silence. John thought that if he opened his mouth to speak, nothing would come out. Thus, he was grateful when the professor announced, "Now, if you will excuse me, I have a meeting to attend."

John immediately stepped aside as if he were a commoner obstructing the path of his king. He made a mental note to think about what he would say before approaching any other famous figure he might encounter.

John spent the rest of that day and the other days of the convention attending many meetings concerning critical issues in the science of that time. Among the themes emerging from the AAAS presentations was that sin and maybe even God could not be reconciled with modern science. To some scientists, astrophysics, quantum mechanics, and relativity theory conflicted with common notions about God. Science did not need God to explain the workings of the universe. John thought this attitude was very interesting as it mirrors that of Stephen Hawking, who said, "science can explain the universe," and "we don't need God to explain" it. It was another case of "Oh how things change, in order to stay the same." However, there is a difference between scientists of the late 1920s and those of 21st century, among whom Hawking is prominent. Hawking did not say there is no God. Some scientists of the early part of the twentieth century at least strongly imply that God does not exist. Also, unlike the scientists of the early 21th Century, Hawking has an enormous database to back up his claims about science and God.

There were also complaints about Freudian psychology. It had not lead to viable methods to deal with the mental problems of everyday people. Presentations at the 1928 AAAS meeting called for a new set of notions—collectively labeled "mental hygiene"— to help people deal with madness and everyday anxiety. Further, psychologists who were spending their time running rats through mazes, and exploring their amorous behaviors, were not producing anything practical. They should, claimed AAAS attendees, be trying to figure out how to prevent crime.

Except for brief encounters with Sandra and Andrew, John had no contact with members of the Columbia science group during the several days of AAAS meetings. Apparently members of the group were attending the AAAS sessions alone and according their own personal schedules. John wondered whether they were as invested in the meetings as he was. More importantly, were their impressions of the meetings similar to his own? He found many of the presentations exciting and, at the same time, iconoclastic. It seemed that the cutting edge scientists of the early 20th century were trying to explain everything by reference to science.

John managed to visit the Savoy every night during the AAAS convention. Part of the reason for this atypical behavior was that he wanted to hang out with Rudy and Fred. He was able to relax around them and was fascinated by the prospects of their start-up business. But mostly he wanted to be with Danielle because he felt that she was slipping away from him.

After the first day of the convention, Bob got John to the Savoy by 7 PM. As he expected, there were few people in the club. He got a beer and sat down at a table so he could think about his future in New York City. Much had been accomplished since he arrived, but there was much to be done. Most important among the yet to-be-completed missions was to drop some heavy hints to the Columbia group concerning future developments in science. At the minimum, he wanted to alert them to the future discovery of the Higgs Boson, discoveries in genetics that had implications for the notion of "race," the development of modern electronic components, and ideas that led to the development of computers. He had to proceed with caution lest he appear to have more information than would be expected of the 1920s scientist that he claimed to be. The Columbia grad students might begin to wonder where he was getting his information. Of course he couldn't tell them that he was from the future. They would think he was insane. Further, he didn't want to be put into the position of selling them on the high quality education he received at little Tabor College, which had gone out of business. He wasn't sure what he would do if they challenged him about the sources of his information.

Before he could resolve these dilemmas, he was startled by a fist thrust at him from across the table. The hand with fingers tightly folded belonged to Rudy who was patiently waiting for John to tap fists with him. John did that and then again with Fred. "Hey boy, 'long time no see,'" exclaimed

Fred, using a phrase he had picked up from John. Once again, John groaned to himself for overloading his 1920's friends with useless catch phrases from the 2010s.

They ordered more beers while the two young businessmen excitedly informed John about the beginnings of their new enterprise. "We're open for business," exclaimed Fred. He looked like a kid who got what he wanted for Christmas.

"Yeah, we're already seeing some profit," indicated Rudy. "We have your share," he added as he reached into his pocket and pulled out a handful of change. He grabbed John's wrist and dumped the coins into his hand. Rudy's manner reflected that of a man discharging an obligation to a friend: inequality in the balance of obligations among friends is uncomfortable. He felt better now that he had paid back some of what he felt that he and Fred owed John.

John was at a loss for words. His first thought was that the coins were a nuisance. He valued them little and didn't know what he was going to do with them. But it didn't take him long to figure out that this payoff was a monumental event for Rudy and Fred. Finally, he sheepishly uttered, "I don't think that these coins will fit in my pants pocket. The pants are kind of tight." He was thinking, "Maybe they could take back the coins and pay me later when the proceeds mount up." But a glance at Fred and Rudy convinced him not to say anything that would devalue the coins. He mumbled, "Thanks." They looked puzzled.

"That's your three cents on every dollar we've earned," announced Rudy with tension in his voice.

John responded quickly and rather loudly, "Yeah, I know. Could I just get a bag or something to carry the coins to my bank?"

Rudy relaxed and Fred reproduced his smile of accomplishment. "I'll get you something to put the coins in," said Rudy as he pushed his chair back and headed to the front counter. He returned shortly with a small cloth bag, the kind with a tie string around its neck. John dumped the coins into the bag and slid it toward the middle of the table.

The conversation that followed was mainly Fred and Rudy telling tales of their business. They already had repeat customers: people who stop by their business daily for a paper, a snack, a drink or some combination of the three. The merchant who had allowed them to set-up next to his establishment gave them permission to pipe into his electrical line. Thus, they had a light inside their little building and one on the outside. They also had a little coal stove to keep them warm in the winter. How did they manage to keep their business open most business hours on most days? They had accepted odd jobs only as these sources of additional income allowed them to equally share keeping their business open during weekdays. They opened on weekends only during afternoon hours and only if one or the other of them wanted to work.

They had talked the better part of an hour when Fred filled a void in the conversation with an impulsive announcement: "Let's go see the shop!" By then it was a little past 8:30 PM and no signs of Danielle, so John agreed to go with his friends to their store. He excused himself and quick stepped to the front counter where he asked a man working behind the counter to ring-up Bob. When the cabby arrived in front of the Savoy he was surprised that John and two other men squeezed into the back seat of his cab. Fred gave Bob directions and, as he drove them to their destination, the three men poked fun at each and jostled one another like teenagers looking to party on Saturday night. Bob had never before seen blacks and whites interacting in this close and casual way. In fact, in his entire career, he had served very few black customers and never had blacks and whites in his cab at the same time. It was an unsettling experience for him.

When they arrived at Rudy's and Fred's business, Bob agreed to wait for them as along as they took no more than 15 minutes. He reminded them that his meter was running. They exited the cab and assembled in front of the small building. Fred and Rudy looked at the neat and clean but unadorned and unsophisticated storefront as if it were the Taj Mahal. Fred went around to the back door where he entered the store, turned on the lights and unlatched the swing-down door over the front counter. Rudy lifted the door up and secured it. Inside, John could see a variety of products, included newspapers left over from a previous day, candy of various kinds, an ice chest for cold drinks, a pot for brewing coffee, cigarettes and cigars, and several others knickknacks and snacks. It looked like a smaller version of the corner store in his childhood neighborhood. It was truly remarkable that two enterprising young men could do so much with so little in such a short period to time. They were natural born business people.

Fred revealed in hushed tones that he had devised an alarm system they could activate and deactivate in a secret way, but he wouldn't reveal how lest someone overhear him. If anyone attempted to break into their store, the alarm would sound and the proprietor who lived above his next-door shop could contact the police. This guy could also shut off the electricity to their business so that, if the alarm went off accidently or during of a failed attempt to breach the newsstand, it wouldn't keep the neighbors up. It looked like they had thought of everything.

After several reverent moments had passed, John was able to tear Fred and Rudy away from the object of their complete devotion and steer them back to the cab. They talked joyously and loudly all the way back to the Savoy. Bob was unable to understand what all the excitement was about. When they bailed out of the cab in front of the Savoy, John went around to the drivers-side door and signaled for Bob to roll down his window. He thanked Bob for his patience and, with some trepidation, asked if Bob would mind turning some coins he had with him into cash.

"What coins?" thought Bob. John had never used coins for rides in his cab. John excused himself, ran inside the Savory and reappeared a couple of minutes later with the sack of coins. He knew that some of Bob's fares paid with coins, so he assumed that Bob could deal with his collection of copper, nickel and silver pieces. He handed the bag to Bob who looked perplexed. John offered, "You could just apply this money to tips until it's used up."

Bob was annoyed. He didn't want more complications added to his already cluttered financial circumstances. "I'd rather cash in the coins and give you the proceeds the next time I pick you up."

John responded with, "Ok, that'll do. You can keep some of the money as payment for your trouble." Now Bob looked a little disgusted. He didn't reply to John's last instruction. Instead he rolled up his window and drove off. John raised his arms out in front of him, palms up and asked himself, "So, what's that all about? What did I do wrong?" He had no answer to his questions.

Back inside the Savoy, John searched for Danielle and found her off in a corner with the other young and beautiful women who adorned the space they occupied. When he approached her he re-experienced some of the emotions that enveloped him on the day they first met. He saw her looking up now and then as he approached. She had to know that he was coming to see her. Nevertheless she kept on talking to her friends as if his impending presence mattered little to her. When he stood just behind and to one side of her, she did look up at him, but her face showed no emotion. "Can I speak to you?" he asked.

"I'm on duty right now," she replied in a flat tone, but seeing the distressed look on his face, she continued, "Oh, I guess I can get away for a few minutes." She pushed her chair back rather awkwardly, and stood up with none of the grace that usually characterized her.

John pointed to one of the side rooms and they walked there without looking at or speaking to one another. He pulled a chair up to the only table in the room and she took a chair across from him. John got right to the point, "What's the matter?"

She replied matter-of-factly, "What do you mean?"

"You know what I mean. You are as cold as the first day I met you. What's up with that?"

She sighed heavily and composed a reply while looking at the tabletop. After a few moments, she exclaimed, "You and I are just not going to work. This is the only place we can go and not face an ugly scene. We're different. We don't belong together."

John's face was distorted into a look of extreme frustration. "How can you say that? We love being together. Just because a few bad things happened doesn't mean we can't be together. It was mainly by chance that we stumbled into some troubles."

Danielle broke in, "You mean, like at Lindy's when the manager told you to leave because I was with you? And how about in Brooklyn when some thugs called me a 'Nigra' and threatened to attack you because I was with you?"

"Ok, there's bigotry out there. I'm not trying to deny it. But bad things can happen anywhere. The man who tried to attack you with a knife was after some fast money, probably so he could buy some booze. Hiding in Harlem doesn't make you safe from people like him. We could have encountered the likes of him anywhere."

Danielle was quick to respond, "Yeah, but that doesn't explain getting thrown out of Lindy's or being attacked by gangsters because we are a mixed couple."

John came back with, "It was a dumb thing to go down that alley. Yes, those young punks are racists, but do you think that they would have left us alone if you were white? Any couple they encountered in that alley would have been treated in much the same way. We can find some places where we can be together. We just have to make better choices."

"Now that's an interesting word you used. Your choices are many in number and high in quality. Mine are scarce and third-rate in quality. Don't project your own circumstances onto me."

John was rendered speechless. She had made a point he could not refute. Tears welled up in his eyes as he reached across the table to cover her hands with his own. When Danielle saw his reaction, she softened. They sat there for several minutes clinging to each other, feeling much but saying nothing.

Finally he released her hands, got up and came around to her side of the table. When he leaned down and kissed her on the cheek, she looked at him in the loving way that he valued above everything else.

After she had dried his tears with her handkerchief, he made a comment that he hoped would get a laugh out of her: "Why don't we go outside and walk around for a bit … we'll stay on the well-lighted portion of Lenox Avenue." She looked up at him and grinned mischievously as she punched him on the shoulder. While they strolled down the street pulling their coats tight around their necks, he talked loudly to counter the traffic noises. "I really believe there are places we can go. Back to Brooklyn … we'll just be more careful next time. And you've seen black folks in Manhattan. We'll find places there that will be comfortable for us."

She listened to him intently, looking up at him now and again to lock onto his gaze. But she didn't believe what he was saying. She just wanted to stretch these sublime moments.

CHAPTER 21

Science, Religion and Reason

On the morning of January 3, 1929 John woke up early even though he had tossed and turned most of the night. He was agitated because he had no idea how that afternoon's meeting with the Columbia group would play out. After breakfast in the Hotel Theresa restaurant, he took a cup of coffee with him to the Mount Morris Park. There he settled onto a bench drenched with sunshine and plotted his moves for that afternoon.

He didn't waste much time on Ronald. There was no way John was going to convince Mr. High and Mighty of anything. But how would he play Ronald? After some thought John concluded that he would not be inhibited by the real possibility that Ronald would explode whenever any group member, especially himself, assumed an unorthodox or unpopular scientific position on issues considered by AAAS presenters. Nor did he spend much time on Sandra. She and he thought much alike and regarded each other as allies.

Herb was a problem because his position on any controversial matter would be difficult to ascertain. The young mathematician seemed reticent to reveal a firm position on any issue. What John hoped to do was to read Herb's emotions. That way he could at least determine whether any position he or other group members took was being understood and appreciated by Herb. A more remote possibility was that Herb's emotional reactions might reveal whether he endorsed any position taken by other group members. Andrew was a different matter. Because he could be a pivotal group member who could help build consensus, John promised himself to support any well-conceived position Andrew took and encourage him to speak about others' points of view.

While John was still unsettled, partly because the cold was beginning to make his teeth chatter, he felt more optimistic about his chances of guiding the group through the lessons to be learned from the AAAS presentations. To warm up and get some brunch, he headed for 125th street to hail a cab. He told the cabby the location of the diner where he ate his first meal in New York City. Upon arrival at the diner he entered the front door and looked around for the latest edition of the New York Times. Having grabbed a copy, he plopped down at the nearest table and began to scan the paper. He found a last report on the AAAS meetings, which he immediately began to peruse. But, before he could get far into the article, the same waitress who had served him earlier was standing next to him, pencil and notepad in hand. He got the impression she had been patiently waiting for him since he last visited the diner several weeks ago. "How are you, mister? I was wondering when you would come in again." He greeted her warmly and asked if she remembered what he ordered the last time he was in. Of course, she did, but sadly breakfast was no longer being served. He asked her to select something from the menu that she thought he'd like. She scratched a note on her pad and said, "I'll have a special meal made up just for you."

The Times post-mortem on the meetings was all about how far science had come and how short the distance it had to go. All the extraordinary advances that had occurred during the early 1900s had convinced many commentators on the scientific scene that most of the important discoveries had already been made.

His meal arrived before he could get further into the Times. The serving was even more abundant than before. Having eaten only a few hours earlier, he was forced to merely sample the massive portions of steak, potatoes, vegetables, bread and soup arrayed before him. Twenty minutes later when the waitress checked on him, she seemed disappointed at his progress. "You don't like it?" she commented in a tone that matched the scowl on her face. Her posture, a hand on a hip thrust out to one side, complemented the sound of her voice.

"No, no!" answered John. "It's delicious, but I was out late last night having a good time, if you know what I mean, and I'm pretty messed up today."

"Oh, I understand," she responded in a manner that said she was very familiar with 'men being men.' He left her an even bigger tip than before and hailed a cab to the Columbia campus.

As usual, Sandra was waiting for him outside Main Hall. They sat down for a few minutes to discuss strategies for getting the most out of the meeting with Andrew, Herb and Ronald. They agreed that they should avoid antagonizing Ronald, but both expressed fears that their effort to that end would likely fail. Sandra concurred with John that they should yield the floor to Andrew whenever possible and do all they could to draw Herb into the conversation.

Once inside their conference room, Sandra and John studied the faces of the other group members. Ronald was, as usual, displaying his well-practiced haughty look. He was ready to punish these Philistines for even the slightest deviations from doctrinaire science as he conceived of it. Herb had a self-depreciating smile on his face and Andrew seemed genuinely pleased to see them.

Sandra began the meeting with questions about how often they attended the daily sessions and what they had learned that was most interesting to them. All reported that they had attended AAAS sessions on all or most convention days. Just as John and Sandra had hoped, all of the others, to one degree or another, saw the most prominent theme of the meetings to be science versus religion. John, Andrew and Sandra had brought along their copies of Times articles covering the AAAS presentations. John opened the discussion by drawing attention to comments by Dr. Harry Elmer Barnes. He argued that, in view of recent scientific advances, there should be conceptions of God and sin that are based on scientific principles and advances. John read quotes by Barnes' from the Times article: "...this newer view of God must be formulated in the light of contemporary astrophysics, which completely repudiates the theological and cosmological outlook of [the] Holy Scripture. ... if a notion of God is needed ... it might work out in the light of ... the study of atoms and electrons by Bohr, Planck and Millikan. It is of little value to attempt to inculcate a view of God so hopelessly inadequate and out of date as that which was slowly and painfully evolved by semi-barbarous Hebrew peoples in the day when [a] rudimentary type of geocentric and anthropomorphic outlook reigned supreme and unchallenged."

Ronald broke in, "I agree with that. Any beliefs that people have are worthless if there is no scientific evidence to support them." For a change, his tone was more matter-of-fact than angry. To continue the surprises, Herb raised his hand timidly, but spoke with conviction. "I must say that these views seem rather naïve. As reported in the Times, this discussion continued with claims that, since science cannot prove the existence of God, we cannot reply on the Bible's notion that 'sin' is any affront to God's will. Being unable to know God's will, it may seem reasonable to argue that we must discard 'sin' in favor of some scientific concept suggested by the idea of 'mental hygiene,' a notion that was often mentioned at the meetings. That would be replacing the unknowable with the nebulous. It is best to separate science and religious belief. Let them go their separate ways."

Ronald was shifting his weight around in his chair as he listened to Herb. "That's nonsense. Astrophysics was mentioned. What we know about the universe proves that God doesn't exist."

"How do you know that?" interjected Sandra. "How do you get from knowledge of the universe to 'God doesn't exist?'"

"Well it's just self-evident!" Ronald's face was puffy and red. Sandra expected that steam would soon come out of his ears and nose. He nearly screamed, "We don't need God to account for the universe."

Before Ronald could say more, Andrew cut in with a look of equanimity and a tone to match. "These are philosophically difficult questions with which greater minds than ours have struggled for centuries. There seems to be no way to reconcile them, or, I would add, any reason to do so."

"I agree," offered John. "Science and religion are different realms. They need not be thought of as contradictory.

Scientists can be sincerely religious and completely devoted to the scientific method."

Ronald responded in a high-pitched tone, "Name some major scientific figures who were religious at the time that their heretical contributions became widely known."

"Copernicus, Galileo, Francis Collins ..." returned John.

"That's outrageous! Copernicus and Galileo were not devoutly religious."

John responded quickly, "Yes they were because they had to be. They were immersed in a religious oligarchy. If they were not religious, they would have been tortured and killed."

Ronald was befuddled. He sputtered some unintelligible words. Instead of responding to John's comeback, he growled, "Who ever heard of Francis Collins."

John had been aware of his screw-up the moment he uttered it, but he hadn't come up with a way around it. After a moment of thought he replied, "Never mind about Francis Collins. He's not yet well known."

John looked around the room expecting that no one would accept his "correction," but no one blinked, not even Ronald. He had used his "get out of jail card" successfully. Maybe it worked because so many bizarre utterances had already aired that mentioning a top scientist who group members would not know, because he was not yet born, merited little concern.

Throughout this verbal brawl Sandra was searching her brain for a way to throw some water on the fire, but not extinguish it. The discussion was fascinating and mind changing, but its value would be erased if she couldn't put an end to the accumulating ill will. Finally she decided on addressing a question to John. She pointedly looked right at him and asked, "You seem to be defending religion. Are you a religious person?"

John was taken aback for a moment because he couldn't determine her intention, but he quickly composed an answer. "I grew up going to church. I was even an alter boy. But, as I matured, I began to think more broadly. By the time I was an undergraduate, I had developed a general sense of spirituality. I am now, and have been for a long time, a spiritual person."

Herb asked, "Have you maintained an association with any religious denomination?"

John replied, "I have not."

"How is your spirituality expressed," asked Andrew.

John thought for a moment and then responded, "I can't say. Even if I could say, I wouldn't talk about it. To me, spirituality is a private thing. It's very emotional and abstract. I imagine that each person's spirituality is unique to her or him. I wouldn't pry into someone's else's spirituality any more than I would reveal my own."

They all sucked in their breath when Ronald raised his hand. To their surprise, the tone with which he posed his question lacked the usual venom. "So you reject organized, doctrinaire religion?"

"No I do not. I respect others' religious beliefs or their other forms of spirituality. They have a right to believe as they wish."

Herb raised his hand. When he hesitated for a moment, they all saw that he was struggling to find a way to phrase his remarks. It was a good thing that there was not a sound in the room when he started to speak, because he began to talk in little more than a whisper. "I'm wondering what you would propose we do when religious beliefs turn into violent behavior?"

"Excellent question," said John. "It's one thing for people to practice their religion among like-minded people, but quite another when they attempt to impose their beliefs on others through violent behavior."

Before he could continue, Ronald interjected, "There has been a history of religious fanatics attempting to forcefully impose their beliefs on others. The Crusades is but one example. In fact, many of the great wars in human history were the works of religious zealots."

"You are entirely correct." John asserted. "What I'm saying is that imposing one's own beliefs onto others by force is never acceptable, whether religion is involved or not. And I would add that imposing one's beliefs onto others is only one impetus for war. Imperialism has probably been more often the incentive for going to war. It was a reason for World War I and it's rearing its ugly head once again in Italy. Mussolini's fascists are spoiling for a fight. It won't be long before they find some country to invade. And he is not the only fascist who threatens to conquer other nations. Adolph Hitler was recently discharged from Germany's Landsberg Prison, where he was incarcerated for attempting to take over the German government. He will not stop …"

Ronald broke in with, "I know all about Hitler. He's a little nobody who was excluded from the German officer's corps because he is low born. His name is a clerical error and his education is third class. You think he will take over Germany? I'll bet you he won't."

"You're on," exclaimed John.

"How about $1000?"

"You've got it," answered John

The others were amazed by this exchange. The discussion had evolved from a shouting match to a reasoned discussion and now it was veering off into a heavy wager. Sandra thought it best to end the meeting while it was still possible to claim that most of their discussion was fruitful. She announced that they would meet "tomorrow at the same time." As had become her habit, she gathered up her belongings and exited quickly. John ran after her and caught up at the steps of the Main Hall. He breathlessly asked, "Got a minute?" She hesitated for a moment then signaled that they should occupy the bench where they usually did post-mortems on meetings.

"What do you think about the meeting?" he asked.

"What do you think?"

"Alright, I'll go first. I thought it was a break-though meeting. I saw some real excitement for the first time today. Even Herb contributed and very well, I think. We are beginning to see some out-of-the-box thinking."

"'Ah oh,' he thought when he saw from her wrinkled brow that she was puzzled. The cause of her consternation has got to be 'out-of-the-box'. Once again I'm forgetting where I am."

He continued with, "I mean everyone was thinking innovatively. They were considering what had never occurred to them before. Minds were opening up in there ... well maybe not Ronald's."

She was nodding in acknowledgement of what he was saying until he got to Ronald. Then she looked remorseful. "It's my fault that he was invited. He's been nothing but an obstruction."

"I disagree," responded John in an assertive voice. "Ronald is a lighting rod. We're sending intellectual thunder bolts his way and that requires original thinking on our part. Without him we wouldn't be touching on topics that most of us have never seriously considered before."

Sandra looked relieved. She smiled as if she had received a complement. In fact, she had. They were in good spirits when they parted.

The next morning John woke up at eight, fell back to sleep, then finally crawled out of bed at a little after nine. He felt like he had fine gravel in his eyes, spider webs in his head and acid in his stomach. All that seemed odd as he had consumed no alcohol the night before and he had gone to bed early. He stumbled toward the bathroom, but halfway there his bare right big toe struck something solid. After hopping around for a few moments, looking like he was under the spell of seizures in his motor cortex, he ended up on the floor rubbing his pulsating toe. When the pain receded, he looked around in search of whatever done his toe wrong. There in the middle of the room was a large and solid looking object. He crawled to it, picked it up and was surprised by its weight. Finally it dawned on him that he was holding the Brownie Box.

Now he was wide-awake. He carried the Box to the light switch near the door, flipped the switch, and began to examine the device. With the box in hand he settled into an overstuffed chair. A few seconds later the Box was up and running. "What to experience first?" was an easy question to answer. He wanted to play videos of his friends. There were several, but first he played the one labeled "Hail, hail, the gang's all here!."

The video began with all of them greeting him at once. There was laughter, tender sentiments, wise cracks about him and finally, in unison, "We miss you!" He wiped his eyes with his pajama sleeve and felt very sad. These smart, loving and rambunctious devotees of science had become his family. For the first time since he arrived in New York City, he thought about going back to the 2010s.

Other video clips were recordings by each of them made in private. Martha spoke of their vow not to commit to each other, because it was very unlikely they would find jobs at the same university. She was rethinking their mutual agreement to remain friends, but nothing more. Maybe they could find some metropolitan area where they could get positions at different academic institutions not so far apart. But that seemed unlikely as positions in strong physics departments were historically few and far between and the same could be said about neuroscience for a different reason: it was a relatively new discipline existing in only a few top universities. These dilemmas were messing with her mind. She was torn between finding a place together, regardless of whether it would be good for their careers and sacrificing their life together in favor of their careers. She needed to talk to him about it soon as her doctorial orals were scheduled for mid-February and she would have to begin searching for a job soon thereafter.

John couldn't imagine getting worse news at a more inopportune time. He had been resigned to seeing Martha only a few times a year, at most. That was hard for him to accept. He didn't want to reconsider it just when his relationship with Danielle was up in the air. He had to put this out of his mind for now. Accordingly, his reply to Martha contained several probably lame attempts at humor and was full of much more optimism about his mission than he actually felt. He didn't even say, "I miss you," though he really and truly did miss her.

Joe's video was on the light side. There was no hint of the rivalry between himself and John that all of the others now openly acknowledged. He was expecting to finish his dissertation research by May and have his orals no later than early June. That would leave him time for a trip to the near future, a prospect that had him totally psyched. He made some personal comments to John that implied they were strong friends. All and all, he was sincerely cordial. This thoughtful message obliterated any lingering antagonistic feelings that John harbored about Joe. In his reply, John confirmed their friendship and wished Joe a great and productive trip forward in time.

Randy reported that he was still working in the computer science college with ample support from several grants awarded to professors who constituted his dissertation committee. His dissertation project was proceeding slowly due to his lack of motivation to finish. He pledged to stay where he was as long as his presence was needed to protect the time machine lab. On that issue, he assured John that the time machine was safe. Then he made a searing revelation: his professors had indicated that they would finance packing up the time machine and transporting it to a secure location. Joe had promised the use of some property in the state of Washington, the deed to which he had been granted by his family. It amounted to an enormous compound having many buildings, including a very large and ornate old house. It also had it's own power sources and water supply. For these reasons and because it was in a wilderness area with a high fence around its perimeter, the property was ideal for housing the time machine lab. After John's return—and perhaps before Joe was launched into the near future— they would make the move. He hoped that John would be around to join them in taking sole possession of the time travel apparatus.

Randy closed by holding up a picture of a young woman and himself. He referred to her as his girl friend. In that picture, and in some frames of the video, Randy was revealed to be half the person he once was. His relatively slim and fit condition, and his attractive girl friend, probably explained the perpetual smile on his face.

John replied that the good life Randy was leading was the most uplifting news he had received in a very long time. "You are my model for achieving happiness and contentment. Can't wait to hang out with you."

Sarah was happy and fully engaged in her pursuit of a doctorate in philosophy. She looked refreshed despite revealing that she was nowhere near finished with her dissertation. "Philosophers," she explained, "tend to be rather picky about everything." But that was all right with her, as she would never submit a dissertation that did not meet her own high standards, let alone those of her committee members. She said she missed John and looked forward to a continuation of their conversations about science. His message to her communicated his admiration for her ability to generate ideas in others that would never have occurred to them without her insights. "I wish you were in the room during the debates that Columbia University graduate students and I are having. We'd be getting to the point more quickly and more often if you were with us."

He once more viewed all of the videos then laid the Brownie Box aside. The next evening John prepared it for redelivery to Randy, Martha, Sarah and Joe, as per their instructions. In it he placed a request for them to return the box to him in no more than a month from the next day's date. That night he placed the Box in the middle of his hotel room. The next morning it was gone. That saddened him. He wished that he had kept the box longer. He could have played the recordings from his friends again and again.

CHAPTER 22

Projecting Science into the Future

In the early afternoon of January 5, 1929, John prepared for another session with the Columbia University grad students. He hoped that he could begin to drop some hints about what would happen in the future of science and applied science. As usual, effectively dealing with Ronald would be his most serious challenge. If he and Sandra could goad Ronald into opposing their positions on science issues, the others would likely become more interested in and thoughtful about those positions. At least that is the way it had worked so far. But there were risks. Ronald's antics and outrageous remarks could crank other students' emotions so high that rational thought would be overridden.

When Bob delivered John to the Broadway side of Columbia campus, he headed to Main Hall hoping to find Sandra waiting for him outside. But when he entered the building, she was just inside the door. "It's too cold to sit outside today. We could talk over there," she gestured toward some chairs nearby. They sit down and she waited for him to reveal his expectations about what might be accomplished during the meeting.

"I think it's time to speculate about the future trajectories of science's several divisions. For example, I want to talk about possible advances in the development of electrical devices, such as radios and instruments that transmit both sound and pictures. I could also consider theoretical advances in the sciences. What would you want to cover?"

Without hesitation, she indicated that her goal would be to predict where psychological theory and research would go in the future. "I see some psychological disciplines as waxing and some as waning. But, what happens now in psychology will shape psychological theory and research all the way into the 21st century."

"That could take the whole meeting, which is fine with me. Why don't I feed off you. We can devote this meeting to psychology." She agreed and they headed to the meeting room.

When they entered their usual meeting place, Herb and Andrew were present, but Ronald had yet to arrive. Sandra started with a brief introduction to the agenda for the meeting. Just as she finished with her opening remarks, Ronald entered and took his usual seat. Sandra looked pointedly at him, perhaps in the hope of getting a reason for his lateness. He responded to her non-verbal communication in tit-for-tat fashion: he folded his arms, pursed his lips and glared back at her.

Wanting to avoid a replay of previous confrontations, Sandra turned away and launched into the implications of the AAAS convention presentations for the future of psychology. "It has been nearly six years since Freud was diagnosed with cancer of the mouth, undoubtedly due to his penchant for cigars. Should he die in a few years, it will still be too soon to declare his theory and psychotherapy dead. His influence will linger decades into the future. Yes, he was a physician, but he often referred to himself as a psychologist. That will be just one reason why his ideas will linger in psychology. He has given birth to a whole new pursuit: treating people with psychological problems by talking to them about the sources of their impairments, rather than sending them to mental institutions or dismissing them as not really sick, just weak-willed. One might question his assumption that the root of a patient's condition was repressed attraction to his or her parent of the opposite gender. However, it would be hard to quarrel with his belief that people with psychological problems were just as 'sick' and in need of therapy as people with highly visible physical ailments. Most importantly, he held out hope to people whose afflictions caused them to be shunned, rather than being regarded with the sympathy and goodwill that characterizes reactions to physically ill people."

Ronald had been squirming in his chair trying to suppress his fierce need to rebut the heresy that assailed his ears. Finally, he could stand it no more. "Freud is a fraud!" he shouted. "He's nothing more than a witchdoctor trying to summon up evil spirits in his so-called patients. They might as well attend a tent revival where a charlatan claiming to be God's messenger is bilking his flock with promises to extract the devil from their souls by merely laying hands on them. It's black magic, not science. People will see this pseudo science for what it is and it will be gone in a decade or two."

Sandra was beside herself. Obviously she was unaccustomed to dealing with ill-tempered dogmatists. After a pause to collect her composure, she sputtered, "Why does everything have to be all or nothing for you? Any all-encompassing theory can be questioned, but why not highlight and use some facets of it? I do not accept all of Freud's theory or all of his methods, but some might be useful." After this response, she fell silent and appeared not able to continue. John waited until he was sure that she would likely not recover for several minutes. Then he slid his chair back to signal that he was taking the floor.

"If we look at Freud with an open mind, as Sandra correctly says we should, we could glen some worthwhile propositions from his theory. Dismissing his general point of view, without considering specific aspects of it, will cause us to miss some valuable insights. That could well be detrimental to the future of psychology. For example, Freud was ahead of his time when he proposed that people harbor thoughts and feelings they cannot dredge up and consider at a conscious level. Someday we will be able to record brain reactions showing that non-consciously we may be attracted to socially unacceptable behaviors, thoughts, and emotions that we consciously believe to be abhorrent. Examples would include showing strong reactions in pleasure centers of the brain when briefly exposed to pictures of people engaging in violent acts or pictures of people stealing merchandise from stores. In a similar vein, someday it may be possible to show that individuals who claim to be egalitarian nevertheless show more positive brain-responses to depictions of people of their own race than to people of another race. Much of our mentality is non-conscious. Alerting us to that reality is Freud's greatest contribution."

Ronald could no longer restrain himself. He grabbed the edge of the table, pulled himself out of his chair and began to pace back and forth on his side of the table. When John saw that Ronald was looking at the ceiling, he reached across the table, grabbed Ronald's drinking glass, and moved it a couple of feet to the right of where it had been located. Several paces later, Ronald had collected his thoughts enough to compose what he thought would be devastating blows to Sandra's and John's arguments regarding Freud. He stopped behind his chair, smiled faintly to signal that he had regained his composure and began with "First, let me say that trying to find good ideas in a bad theory is like trying to find a silver dollar in a garbage dump. It's not worth the effort. Better that the worthless theory be discarded so that more time is available to find previously unrecognized productive ideas suggested by a good theory. And furthermore, the claim that 'most of our mentality is non-conscious' is bunkum. I'm conscious of everything that happens to me and everything I believe. I'm totally aware of what's going on in my environment and in my head. So are most people. If that were not the case, how would we ever be able to operate effectively in our environments?"

Before Ronald could continue, Andrew declared, "In science there is no such thing as a good theory or a bad theory. 'Good' and 'bad' are value judgments that have no place in science. Theories are tools that we use to predict outcomes. Each is valued to the extent that it provides accurate prediction. Some of the best contemporary theories are conglomerations of tried and true prepositions from old theories. It is not in the best interest of science to discard any theory, in whole or in part. In fact, we should keep a close eye on the history of our scientific disciplines so that we can prevent the loss of valuable ideas we may need in the future."

There was pause as all present let Andrew's wisdom soak in. Ronald returned to his seat and reached out to where his drinking glass had been located before he got up to pace and talk. He showed a slight startle response when he failed to contact the drink. Very quickly he rotated his head a few degrees to the right and to the left until he found his drink.

Then something happened that had never happened before. Herb spoke up without even raising his hand.

Addressing Ronald, Herb inquired, "Just now, as you sat down, were you reaching for your drink?"

Ronald replied, "No, I knew where it was. It was where I just found it."

Herb rephrased his question. "When you returned to your seat, was your drink located in the same place you left it when you got up out of your chair?"

Ronald seemed confused. For a few moments he had the look of someone searching his mind. Finally he muttered, "I think maybe it was in a different place."

"So," Herb continued, "when you reached out as you sat down, you were extending your hand to the drink's previous location?"

Ronald sputtered, "Uh, yeah, I guess so." But his face reddened as he thought about the implications of what he had just revealed. After a moment, he declared, "But I knew where it was. I found it right away."

Herb responded with, "You persist in claiming that you were always conscious of where the drink was located and that it was always in its present location. Let's examine that assertion on your part. First, it is contradicted by the fact that, although you first denied reaching to the old location of the drink when you returned to your chair, you have since acknowledged that you did reach to the earlier location. Reaching for the drink as you did is consistent with the proposition that you had a non-conscious memory of the drink's original location. Second, your initial claim you knew all along the drink was always in its present location is contradicted by the observation that you had to search for its new location. It seems very clear that you were not always conscious of your drink's location and that you did have a non-conscious memory of where the drink was located when you left your chair."

Andrew jumped in with, "The point that Sandra and John were making is now clear to me. We scan each of the many complicated environments we encounter to non-consciously record what's there so we can locate components of it when we need to deal with them. Being consciously aware of everything in a many faceted environment would be confusing, even over-whelming. But we have a non-conscious inventory of its major components in case we need it. For example, some time ago I attended a party where I interacted with many people, but not all of those who attended. Later at another location, I saw a woman whose face looked familiar, but I couldn't place where I'd seen it. After I'd talked to her it occurred to me that she might have been at the afore-mentioned party. She confirmed that, in fact, she had been there. What our brains file into non-conscious memory may be useless at the time it is recorded, but it can be very helpful later."

John was sitting back comfortably, trying to suppress a broad grin. When he looked at Sandra, he could see that she was having the same problem. They had tossed out some information regarding their position on consciousness versus non-consciousness, and John had added a cue to where they were headed when he moved Ronald's drink. The latter was all that Herb needed to see where they were going. He brilliantly composed a scenario that revolved around Ronald's behavior and thereby demonstrated the difference between conscious and non-conscious modes of recording information. Andrew translated Herb's account of consciousness and non-consciousness into an everyday example. We could not have done it better ourselves. Two very smart Columbia University graduate students had picked up the reins and guided the horse home. And that was a good thing: Herb and Andrew were the most highly credible members of their group.

John continued their discussion with his take on the future of psychology. He noted that, in 1928, psychology was still dominated by Americans schooled in psychophysics by German physician Wilhelm Wundt who trained under physicist Hermann von Helmholtz. Psychophysics involved, for example, attempts to map out the correspondence between the **physical** decibel-level of a sound and the **psychological** impression of loudness. "However," he predicted, "at the present time American psychology is in the process of shifting toward a focus on how people and other creatures learn. A leading figure in this transition is Columbia University's own Edward L. Thorndike. His presentation at the AAAS meeting was entitled "The relative strength of reward and punishment." The very title indicates the orientation that will likely dominate psychology in the future. We'll call it 'behaviorism.' This position emphasizes learning how all creatures acquire behaviors through cataloguing the rules by which animals learn behaviors. As you may surmise, animals are used as subjects in learning experiments for two basic reasons. First, the environments in which they learn new behaviors can be controlled and manipulated much more easily than would be the case with human environments. And second, animals can be treated in ways that would be unethical if applied to humans. A good example of the latter would be using electrical shock to punish responses."

John was looking around the room as he spoke. What he saw in the faces of his colleagues was looks that communicated, "When are you going to get the important stuff?"

He cut to the chase with "Notice that emotions and thoughts are very much neglected in the behaviorists' approach." Now ears began to perk up around the room.

"Of course, other animals have emotions, but human emotions appear to be unique and more intricate. Further, thought processes may be entirely unique to humans. Animals may one day be taught to communicate with humans and each other. However, not having the brain centers for speech, they would be limited to rudimentary sign language. What animals would accomplish through sign language would be little more than reacting to commands and sending signals regarding the satisfaction of hunger and comfort needs. On the other hand, humans, whether they can speak or not, can learn to communicate in a very broad and diverse way. Humans have a rich inter-life of thoughts and emotions that must be understood before we can claim to have a psychology applicable to them. Sadly, it appears that it will be the better part of a century before attention to the development of viable theory and research into human thought and emotion gains equal status with cataloguing how human behaviors are acquired and extinguished.

"There are many other possible developments to expect in the future of psychology. These include teaching machines in some form or another. These devices will allow students to answer questions about their subject matter and get positive feedback for correct answers and negative feedback for incorrect answers. When it becomes time to explore space, the first astronauts are likely to be animals, such as monkeys. These creatures will be trained to control the instruments of their spacecraft. Human aircraft pilots, and later human astronauts, will learn to fly in simulators that have all the controls and instruments of actual aircraft, but in front of the windshield will be visual displays depicting several different normal and dangerous circumstances to which pilots in training must react."

While John was talking, Andrew was alternately fascinated and puzzled. Noticing these reactions, John suspended his presentation and asked if Andrew had any questions. Andrew's reply was succinct: "How do you know about all of these possibilities?"

John had been waiting for this simple but challenging question. Despite having thought about it, he wasn't sure he had an acceptable answer. The wrong answer could reveal that he was not from the first part of the twentieth century. To avoid that fate, he had to fabricate. "No one knows what will happen in the future. However, based on current trends, one can make some reasonable speculations about what will happen in the years to come. Accordingly, I am not so much predicting the future as projecting into the future based on where fresh developments in science are currently pointing. Some of my speculations will turn out to be correct in some degree and others will be incorrect in some degree, including the nth degree. We 'know' something only when it happens. The trick is to correctly predict what we will know in the future. It's difficult to imagine a more challenging feat to pull off."

Andrew seemed satisfied. He smiled and commented, "I assume that the 'n' in your 'nth degree' is a very large number."

All except Ronald giggled. When the moment of mirth had passed, John answered Andrew with, "You got that right."

Sandra chose this rare jocular moment as the right time to end their meeting. Noting that they had addressed the most thought provoking issues raised by AAAS presentations, she asked if there was any objection to taking some time off. All but John expressed concerns about getting behind in their studies and research projects. They took a vote and it was unanimous: they would take a hiatus of at least a few weeks. Sandra announced that she would personally contact each of them about a date for their next meeting. As the last item on the agenda, she outlined topics to be considered at future meetings. "I think that we've devoted enough time to psychology." A glance around the room confirmed that her assumption was shared by the others. All responded with casual nods in the affirmative, except for Ronald, who appeared to be simultaneously relieved and delighted. "Alright," she exclaimed, "we'll take some time off and, when we reconvene, we'll consider predictions about future developments in the other sciences and in technology."

As Ronald, Herb, and Andrew filed out of the room, Sandra rummaged around gathering up the various materials she had brought to the meeting. John waited until the others were out of earshot before he asked, "Wow, I think that really went well. What do you think?"

"Well," she replied, "I'm a little less bullish about the meeting than you, but I do think it was by far our best. We enjoyed a little levity for a change and I think we saw the beginnings of genuine camaraderie."

"I agree," returned John, "and I would add that everyone got into the discussions for the first time. In fact, the others took over the meeting. That's what we want, right? I saw you smiling when Herb and Andrew daftly picked up the hints and cues we provided and ran with them. I don't think I could have presented the case for non-consciousness as well as Herb did."

"I absolutely agree," affirmed Sandra. "That takes the heat off us and gets everyone involved. Herb must be brilliant. He did so much with the very little we provided him. Andrew, as we hoped, is great at summing up what has transpired and at highlighting the implications of our discussions. But we need to ease up on Ronald. If we create more circumstances during which he can make reasonable comments, we can help him to be a productive member of the group."

"You're right again," said John, "Ronald has been a useful member of the group as someone for us to react against, but I think his value in that way has about run its course. If we can encourage him to open up his mind, he'll be a significant contributor to future meetings."

With that, Sandra stuck out her hand and he shook it. Their collaboration was beginning to be fruitful. And they were becoming friends.

As John headed toward his ride home, he was thinking about shifting his attention toward his relationships with Danielle and pals, Fred and Rudy.

CHAPTER 23

Love and Friendship

John was to visit the Savoy many times in the next several weeks. Bob transported him there most of the time. During one of the first of several trips in January, Bob announced that he had paid back the money he owed John and that he would expect his usual tips thereafter. Bob offered to hand over his records of John's cab rides since their agreement about applying tips toward repaying money borrowed to cover his wife's medical expenses. John declined and, without any prompting from Bob, he wrote out a receipt on a scratch sheet of paper indicating that the cabbie's debt was paid in full. After that, whenever they were together in the cab, Bob abandoned viewing John as his creditor. They began to interact as friends again. It was a great relief for both of them.

John's interactions with Fred and Rudy became confined to the Savoy. As the newsstand business was going well, John heard little about it except when he was paid his share of the profits. So they spent their time goofing around at the Savoy during late afternoons, talking about sports and the latest music on the radio. During evenings at the Savoy, John's first priority was trying to talk to Danielle. The rest of the time he, Fred, and Rudy drank beer, danced, critiqued the other dancers, and argued about which of the band's selections were best for dancing and which for just grooving with the sounds.

But one evening, Rudy and Fred just weren't with it. They were talking very little and smiling even less. Finally, John had to say something about their uncharacteristically dejected mood. Rudy glared at him and growled, "None of your business." Fred just looked defeated. John persisted. After telling him to mind his own business several times in several ways, Rudy flung his chair aside and headed for the front door. John chased after him and caught up just before Rudy left the building. When he placed a hand on Rudy's shoulder a scuffle ensued. "Hey, I'm on your side. Let me help," pleaded John.

"I don't want your help ... even if I did, there's nothing you could do!"

Just as Rudy again turned to exit the Savoy, John took a long shot. "Someone is messing with you. I can help you fix that."

Rudy calmed down and motioned for John to follow him outside.

They huddled in the cold for a moment, folding their arms around their chests to keep from shaking. Rudy looked at John and whispered in a gravel voice, "I know you mean well, but there are some things you can't fix. This has to do with being a black man in New York City trying to make a go of a business. You wouldn't understand the problem, much less how to fix it."

John begged his friend to go back into the Savoy, pick a side room and talk the problem out. Rudy looked defeated, but after hesitating for a moment, he shrugged his shoulders and followed John back inside. They found a deserted room and sat at one of its tables. Rudy slumped down into his chair. His posture suggested that he would be hard to persuade. John guessed out loud. "Some mobsters are leaning on you to pay them 'protection' money. They think that black businessmen are easy targets, because they can't turn to the cops or anyone else for help." Rudy nodded in the affirmative.

To convince Rudy that he could help, John began to relate what happened when he and Danielle ordered food at Lindy's restaurant. He described how he handled insults to Danielle. "For the fun of it, I was dressed like a mobster. I assumed that pose because I found out that mobsters do business at Lindy's. A recent episode at the restaurant made headlines. Arnold Rothstein, who was involved in illegal gambling, got into a wrestling match with mobster George Hump McManus over a gambling debt. McManus got to his gun first and shot Rothstein. True to his mobster code Rothstein died without identifying McManus. I used this information to terrorize Lindy's manager by claiming to be a part of McManus' 'family'. It worked so well, the manager passed out. I can use the same ruse to get these mobsters to leave you and Fred alone."

Rudy's face was twisted into an exemplary look of incredulity. His head was tilted to one side and his eyes and mouth opened wide. "Do you seriously think that your play ground threat will work on some actual mobsters? You'll get us all killed."

"Look, there are some things you don't know about me. The incident at Lindy's is not the first time I've taken on some scary people. I'm willing and able to intimidate these mobsters. Yes, there are some dangers, but I think it's worth it."

Fred was called into the room to join the discussion about John's plan to scare off the mobsters. Fred was as shocked as was Rudy, but thirty minutes of vigorous discussion moved both men in John's direction. John rested his case with a closer question: "So, you are going to let these mobsters take so much of what you earn that staying in business will no longer make any sense?"

Rudy and Fred talked with each other for a few minutes and then turned to John. With faces portraying classis looks of resignation they communicated their willingness to confront the gangsters.

Rudy disclosed that two extortionists had been showing up at about closing time on the first day of the month. "They started out with a spiel about how, for a monthly fee, they would 'protect our business.' These Italian mobsters claimed that Irish gangsters were about to take over the territory where we have our newsstand. When that happened, they would do what they done elsewhere in New York City. They'd demand 20% of our profits. All that we had to do was to pay the Italian mobsters 10% of our profits for protection against the Irish. These two hoods wore coats that were too tight for their bodies so that the people they were shaking down could see the outline of pistols in their hip holsters."

Rudy and Fred thought that they had no choice … they agreed to pay the 10%. But in only a few weeks, the 10% became 15%.

In a strained voice, John asked, "Why didn't you tell me?"

Fred replied, "It never dawned on us that you could do anything about our problem and we still can't imagine there's anything you could do. But I figured you'd find out. Your profits were going down. You probably didn't know that at first, because you don't bother to count the contents of the bags of coins we've been being bringing you. But eventually, when it would be obvious that your take was little or nothing, you'd find out. So now you know. What can you do about it?"

John related how he planned to show up on a night when the gangsters came to collect their 15%. John would be dressed in his mobster garb with a toy gun tucked under his coat in the belt of his pants. He would confront the extortionists with threats about what he and his 'family' member, George Hump McManus, would do to them if they dared to come near the newsstand again.

Fred and Rudy were astounded. "It's one thing to knock a knife out of a bum's hand and another to take on two burly gangsters who are armed with real guns," shouted Rudy who immediately got the "hush" sign from Fred and John.

John answered calmly, "If there is trouble, here's how we'll handle it. The first one who makes a move against me will immediately be preoccupied with trying to catch a breath of air. That'll be your cue to step up. I'll be dealing with the other guy while you make sure the first one doesn't get back on his feet. After we got both of them down, we'll disarm them and I'll tell them about my supposed mob connection. Believe me, I can be very convincing. These guys are highly likely to be very low on the gangster power scale. They'll go back to their bottom feeding buddies and tell them that messing with us is too costly."

Fred and Rudy remained skeptical. However, John's assertion that should they continue to make payoffs they would soon be out of business caused them to accept his bizarre plan.

John needed more information in order to come up with details of how they would manage the two gangsters. "I think

I can remember the layout of your business' neighborhood. If they show up at the same place and time, tell me when and where the payoff exchange is made."

Fred indicated, "There's an alley between two businesses across from our store. They always park their car across the street and stand at the entrance of the alley. They signal for us to come to them. Soon as we arrive to where they are standing and hand them the money, one of them says something like, 'See you next month.' It takes at most a few minutes."

John thought for a moment before he asked, "Is there a side door to one of the businesses not too far down the alley?"

"Yes," Rudy replied. While looking at Fred, he added, "I think the door is about a dozen feet down the alley on the left." Fred nodded his conformation of Rudy's assessment.

"Is it recessed into the wall?" asked John. Fred thought so. Rudy wasn't sure.

"Alright," said John. "Check that out for me and let me know tomorrow night at the Savoy. We'll discuss exactly what we will do."

The next night all three arrived at the Savoy earlier than usual. They found an unoccupied side room and put their heads together to finalize plans for eliminating the mobsters from Rudy's and Fred's lives. "About what time will the extortionists be at the head of the alley on the first of next month?" asked John.

"He waits until we close for the day, which is usually early evening, about 5:30."

"Alright, I'll be hiding in the door-well down the alley by 5:15. When the hoods show up to collect from you, act as you always do, except that your money bag will be filled with pieces of newspaper. When you are a few feet from them I'll come out of the door-well and sneak up behind them. Wait until you hear me say, 'Don't move … keep your hands where I can see them.' Get ready to jump them if they don't comply. Given they comply, I'll tell them to turn around slowly to face me. If at this point they go for their pistols, stop 'em any way you can. I'll hit 'em hard from behind. If they do follow my command, as soon as they are facing me, stick an index finger into the back of the one closest to you. I'll tell one at a time to lift his pistol out slowly with two fingers on the gun butt and drop the weapon on the ground. If they make any kind of funny moves, hit them in the lower back as hard as you can. I'll take care of business on my side. When their weapons are on the ground, I'll give them my spiel about knowing more scary mobsters than they do."

"I'm not sure about your plan," gasped Fred. "It seems like you are saying at some point they will go for their weapons. If that happens it's three unarmed men against two with pistols."

"I think they'll comply," said John, "They will know that they are out numbered and they'll assume we are armed."

Rudy added his own objection, "That's not even to mention whether the gangsters who sent them will believe your story about being connected to famous mobsters."

John confidently answered, "When you hear what I tell them and how I express it, I think you'll believe that their bosses will call a halt to them harassing you." Fred and Rudy looked dubious, but after several more minutes of discussion, they agreed to carry out John's plan.

As February approached, with few exceptions, John and Danielle continued to see one another only in the afternoon or evening at the Savoy. Among the few exceptions was a trip back to the little restaurant in Brooklyn. Again the food was great and, this time, there was no incident. They also ate out in Harlem a couple of times and attended a play at Harlem's Lafayette Theatre. Though John's tried repeatedly, he rarely could coax her to leave the safe confines of Harlem. She also refused to allow him into her home. She said it was not fit for visitors.

Still he persisted. Whenever the subject of their relationship came up, she would insist that they had no future. They could continue as they were, but she would not consider a more permanent relationship. On the occasion of one such discussion, John's frustration overwhelmed him. Without thinking, he blurted out, "We could get married!" Danielle was flabbergasted.

"Are you totally ignorant of racial conditions in this country? Interracial marriages are not recognized anywhere. Even if we did find someone to marry us, our marriage would be scorned everywhere we went."

Her objection was among the several issues John failed to consider when he impulsively declared that they should get married. His friends in the 2010s were expecting him back by sometime in the coming spring, at the latest. He had an obligation to report back to them. They also expected he would help them establish the new location of the time machine. In addition, he could not refute Danielle's objections. After a couple of minutes of very awkward silence, he made another mistake.

"Alright, we could just live together. Lots of people do that. I've known of some couples who have lived together for most of their lives without being married."

"Are any of these couples of mixed race? I also know some couples that live together without being married, but in no case is one black and the other white. And there's another thing. You want to make a whore of me? That's the way to do it. I'm not living with a man who is not my husband. And, in case you haven't figured it out, the only man I'm having sex with is the man I marry."

This declaration was stunning. John immediately understood that she was forever slamming the door on having a lasting relationship with him. They were just dating like a couple of early adolescents. Out of desperation he pleaded, "Let's don't be hasty. Can we just continue until we figure this out?" It was the final blunder. She screamed at him, "We're finished. There is no hope for us!" With that she left him in a state of bewilderment. For several weeks, the closest they got to each other was across the ballroom floor.

In the middle of the following weeks during which he was trying to deal with losing Danielle, he received a call from Sandra asking for a meeting. She seemed not herself. Although she claimed the meeting was about the upcoming sessions with the Columbia students, John suspected that some other agenda was on her mind. He agreed to meet her that afternoon at the cab stop on the Broadway side of campus. When Bob dropped him off, she was several yards away from the stop shivering in the cold. "Look at you. You're going to freeze. Lead me to somewhere warm." She pointed toward the Low Library and they took off at flank speed. Once inside they found a comfortable and warm area where there was no one nearby. They sat down at a table across from one another. Sandra said nothing. She just sat very still looking down at the tabletop. Finally, John asked, "What's the matter?"

"I can't think about the next meetings. I'm too depressed."

John reminded himself, "I'm not a clinical psychologist." But he still couldn't inhibit wanting to help her.

In a soft voice he said, "Tell me what's wrong. I'll try to help."

"Hazel broke up with me," she sniffled.

John's face fell slack. He was trying unsuccessfully to cope with being jilted by Danielle and, somehow, he was going to tell Sandra how to deal with the same problem? He wanted to just get away from there, but when he saw her in such a distraught condition, he had to help her if he could.

"Let's talk about it," he said. "How did it happen?"

"Yesterday, we were having coffee at our favorite place and everything seemed to be going well. But, during a conversation about what's playing on Broadway, she stopped me in mid-sentence and announced, 'I'm getting tired of you.' It hit me like a hammer. I had no idea she was feeling that way. I ended up begging her to stay with me, but that just made matters worse. I accused her of taking up with someone else, but she vehemently denied it. When I started crying and screaming right there in public, she just left me."

This was one of those rare occasions when John could think of nothing to say. He came around to Sandra's side of the table and sat next to her. After several minutes, he whispered to her, "Now, now, breakups happen. It's happened to me several times, including recently. You just have to get through it."

It occurred to him that should he have chosen clinical psychology, given that the drivel he just came up with was as good as he could do for someone in a lot of emotional pain, he probably would have flunked out.

But she stopped crying and looked at him with great interest. "Someone broke up with you recently?'" she asked in a misery loves company tone.

Of all things that could happen at the worse time of his life, Sandra wanted him to help her by talking about his own ineptitude at dealing with a breakup. "Well," he thought to himself, "on this trip to the past, fibbing has become my way to deal with difficult situations. I'll just go with it." He hoped it wouldn't fail him now.

"Yes, it happened not long ago. She believes there's no hope for us. We're just too different. I couldn't convince her, so I have to give up. What else can I do? Sometimes a relationship just doesn't work and you have to move on. Eventually, I'll find someone who wants to spend her life with me, and so will you." Just as he finished uttering this rubbish, he felt like a fool. Now, by once again saying the wrong thing, he was messing up someone else's life. He wanted to pound his head against the wall.

To his amazement, Sandra straightened up and dried her eyes with her shirtsleeve. Looking like her usual self, she announced, "You're right. That's what to do. It just wasn't working for us. I can find someone else. Thank you so much."

They began to speak to each other as they always had. She was back to her usual analytic self. Together, they came up with an agenda for their next meeting, which they set for February 8 in Main Hall. They agreed that he would head a discussion about economics and what that field has to say about the future state of the market. Relying on recent editions of the New York Times, he would talk about a contemporary event that has implications for race relations and she would lead a discussion about women's rights and feminism. Other issues would be considered as time allowed.

When they departed John felt more like his old self again. He chatted amiably with Bob about his wife's recovery and their vacation plans and about sports. More importantly, when he got back to the Hotel Theresa, he was looking forward to getting something to eat rather than continuing to make himself miserable by endlessly anguishing over his breakup with Danielle. The dumb advice he gave to Sandra was working for both of them.

CHAPTER 24

Surprises and Social Issues

The Brownie Box arrived during the early morning of January 30, 1929. John got another "group greet" from his friends back in the future. Each also sent him a personal video. However, because they had communicated recently, there was less said about personal matters. This time, there was more emphasis on time travel issues. Joe was pressing the others to let him go ten years into the future. They had voted unanimously to launch him very soon. From the group's perspective, the most exciting development to be tested during Joe's trip was a new cigar sized device that matched many of the Brownie Box's capabilities. The built-in keyboard, touch screen, some audio-video speakers, as well as some microphones and lens were omitted from the new device. But, it was remarkably capable considering it's small size. It was attached with a standard ballpoint pen-clasp suitable for a shirt or coat pocket. Its upper extremity that protruded from the pocket to which it was attached contained a video/photo lens and a single microphone. A single speaker was on the lower part of the device that would be tucked into the clothing pocket. It looked like a container for a single cigar or, perhaps, a bulbous ballpoint pen or fountain pen. Especially because Martha wanted to go back to ancient Egypt, they were currently working on a process by which the device could be used to send a distress signal should its user be in danger. Most importantly, a controller back in the future could see and hear everything confronting the time traveler. The controller and the traveler could also converse with each other while the traveler was walking around.

So far, the process they had developed required that the controller had to be on-line in the time machine control room to receive a distress call and activate a return of the endangered traveler. That would be labor intensive: one of the gang left behind during a trip into the future or past would have to be at the time machine controls around the clock. As all of them expected to have jobs eventually, they could monitor traveler distress signals only in the summer. Eventually, they hoped to program the time machine to monitor a traveler's auditory communications and uses of an alarm button. A traveler would be returned automatically should voice monitoring detect distress or if the endangered traveler pushed the distress alarm button. Randy and Joe expected that procedures for automatically retrieval of time travelers incorporated in the new device could be installed in the Brownie Box. That was good news for John should he want to return to New York City. That night the Box was placed in the middle of John's room for retrieval by Joe and Randy early the next morning.

John was excited about these new developments. Because he believed that his relationship with Danielle was over and he would be finished with the Columbia-group sessions in a matter of weeks, he planned to request a return trip to 2010s in a month or so at most. He wanted to be with Randy and Sarah when Joe and Martha took their trips.

On the evening of January 31, John met with Rudy and Fred at the Savoy. They went over the plan John had devised earlier until they had it down cold. That made Fred and Rudy more comfortable about what they were going to face the next day, but they still harbored some underlying apprehension.

Typically they were not both at the newsstand at the same time. There wasn't that much for two people to do and each had occasional opportunities to pick up extra cash doing odd jobs. Also, it allowed one or the other to visit the Savoy in the afternoon. When business was slow, sometimes they shutdown early so they could hang out at the Savoy. However, they both were expected to be present when the payoffs occurred. Apparently the mobsters wanted to intimidate both Rudy and Fred so neither would try to convince the other to defy the demand for protection cash. So, on the afternoon of February 1, they would both be at the newsstand waiting anxiously for the showdown with the mobsters.

"Do you think this is really gonna work?" Fred asked Rudy.

"Look," Rudy replied, "we worked hard to get our own business. If we don't stop these thugs, we'll lose everything. Even if we have only a small chance, I want to take it. But you have to decide for yourself. If you don't want to do it, we'll call it off. We can contact John and tell him we're backing out."

Fred wavered for what seemed like a few minutes. His face was distorted into a look of extreme apprehension. Rudy thought he was going to chicken out. But finally, he looked

Rudy straight in the eyes and announced, "Let's do it." They bumped fists.

The next day, as agreed, at about 5:15 John positioned himself in the alley door-well across the street from the newsstand. Some ten minutes later, he heard a car drive into a parking place near the alley. Two car doors slammed and, moments later two very big men took up positions at the entrance of the alley, facing toward the newsstand across the street.

Rudy and Fred were waiting in front of the newsstand. When the mobsters signaled for them to bring the payoff, they headed toward the alley. It was a case of thinking about each step so as to look as normal as possible. By the time they were standing a few feet in front of the hoodlums, their faces were frozen into a look of resolution. The two thugs seemed to be even bigger that they appeared on previous payoff occasions. When they heard "Don't move ... keep your hands where I can see them," the two extortionists appeared surprised and a little alarmed, but they did not move." John then commanded them to turn slowly around to face him. Perhaps because they thought that a cop, or maybe an Irish gangster, was pointing a gun at their backs, they cautiously rotated 180 degrees. But when they saw that the commands had come from one unarmed man in a strange outfit, all hell broke loose. They immediately flipped their coats open and went for their pistols. John's hands shot out striking the thugs' chests as they struggled to deploy their guns. Simultaneously, Rudy and Fred jumped on the men from behind sending them sprawling to the graveled surface of the alley. The two hulks were down and dazed, but not out. Both recovered quickly and fought ferociously. After a few moments of struggle, each managed to get on hands and knees and attempt to stand up. But, because Rudy and Fred held on long enough for John to deliver blows to the hoodlums' carotid arteries, the two brutes slumped into a state of unconsciousness.

Fred and Rudy were breathing hard. Both had ripped and soiled their clothes grappling in the dirt and gravel. But John, who had expended little energy, was breathing normally. However, he did look rather clownish. His flamboyant hat was tilted to one side and its top was smashed in. Also, his coat had been torn open and his shirt had lost its top buttons, rendering his chest hairs visible. Fred and Rudy saw John's condition but were not in a jocular mood. In retrospect, they would get a lot of laughs out of his farcical appearance.

While Rudy and Fred were using their adversaries' own belts to bind their wrists behind their backs, John was massaging their carotid arteries. The men quickly regained consciousness, but continued to be lethargic. Neither offered any resistance. After they were securely bound, John asked Fred and Rudy to help them get to their feet. John buttoned up his coat, threw his hat aside and worked himself into the proper state of mind for terrorizing their captives. As he began to tell the two men what would happen to them and their bosses should they ever bother Fred and Rudy again, John became someone else. The two men began to tremble and shake. The knees of one hoodlum gave way and he had to be hauled back on his feet. The other one looked as if he would regurgitate. By the time John was finished, the two brutes resembled schoolboys harassed by bullies for being sissies.

Rudy and Fred were astounded. After their captives were released and sent stumbling back to their car, Rudy stammered, "I've never seen anything like that before. Who are you?" Fred could find no words to describe what he had just witnessed.

John picked up his hat, dusted it off and reshaped it. As he fitted it to his head his face reflected mild amusement. "What do you mean by 'Who are you?' I'm me, John. I was just taking care of business ... talking in a way these hoods would understand. I think it worked."

Without losing his look of incredulity, Rudy uttered, "There is something inside you, something that's very bad. I don't think I know you."

Fred added, "You are either a great actor, or you're a stone killer. Rudy's right. I've never seen or heard anything like the performance you put on just now."

"Can we just go with the 'great actor' thing?" quipped John.

Rudy and Fred didn't respond to John's flippant inquiry, so he tried again. "Whatever I do that's a serious matter, I'm into it 100 percent. I can't do halfway measures. It's not in me. I assure you that I'm me even if I don't seem to be me all the time. It's the way I am ... I can't change. Believe me, if I have to go to another level sometimes, I'll return to the guy you know. Please be patient with me."

His friends could not think of a response to John's characterization of himself. However, on their way back to the newsstand, they thanked him. After they sat down for long enough to drink a soda, Fred led John to a public phone booth so he could call Bob.

The next day John slept late. After having brunch at the hotel dinning room, he decided on visiting the American Museum of Natural History. Bob was available to get him there by 3:00 PM. While he was dressing for the occasion, a message from the front desk was slipped under his door. It read "urgent phone message for you." He hurriedly threw on a coat as he sprinted to the elevator. A clerk was waiting for him at the front desk. "Someone named Fred phoned you and said that you should call him at the Savoy right away." John was directed to the phone just off the front desk. Once he got through to the Savoy, there was a brief delay before he heard Fred's voice over the phone. "You've got to get here right away. Danielle's gone crazy … walking around aimlessly calling out your name. If something isn't done soon the management will fire her or call the men in the white coats to haul her away." It was 2:15 PM. Bob wasn't due to pick him up until 2:30. He didn't know whether to hail a cab or wait for Bob. He waited for a few minutes outside the hotel where Bob typically picked him up, but after a while he could no longer stand it. He began to yell at the cabs that were passing by. This upset hotel personnel working at the cabstand. It was their job to hail cabs. Before he knew it he was in a tussle with them. Just as the situation was about to get serious, Bob arrived. John dove into the back seat and pleaded with the cabby to get him to the Savoy at top speed. Bob sputtered that he didn't like to take chances, but, seeing John's extremely agitated state, he sped away from the curb and began to weave in and out of traffic. After several near collisions they slide to a stop in front of the Savoy. John threw a twenty-dollar bill on the front seat and exited the cab without shutting the rear door.

Rudy was waiting for him just inside the door. "Come with me … hurry. She's gone mad." Across the ballroom floor, John could see several people trying to restrain Danielle. She was howling loudly and struggling to free herself. When she finally looked his way, she fell silent and stopped trying to break free. The co-workers who were holding her sized up the scene and let her go. Her look of total despair changed fluidly to one of deliverance. She was leaning forward at the waist with her arms at her side, palms facing up. Walking slowly at first, then accelerating into a sprint, she crossed the dance floor in an instant and threw herself at John, folding her arms around his neck and locking her legs behind him. He thought she was crying, but she was laughing with such force that it was difficult to determine which emotion she was expressing. "I thought I'd lost you," she whispered in a broken voice. "But you've come back to me."

Things began to return to normal. Over the next several days, John went to the Savoy every night and during some days. He and Danielle were as close as they had ever been. They spend most of their time together at the Savoy. However, some trips to other places occurred periodically. They returned to Brooklyn for lunch at Danielle's favorite restaurant. The trip was especially pleasant as the proprietor of the little eatery was beginning to see them as a couple. He prepared a special lunch for them that was not on the menu. Afterwards they strolled the streets near the restaurant in total comfort. It was a wonderful day.

On another occasion they visited the American Museum of Natural History. They walked among the skeletal remains of dinosaurs and got up close to stuffed creatures of their earth's present era, some of them seagoing and some land bound. And they attended a lecture on the importance of preserving plants—even those not pleasant to look at or enjoyable to eat—because some of them harbor important medical benefits or may be useful components of future products.

They also walked the streets around the Savoy when the weather was decent, though they never entered Danielle's home. When they were together at the Savoy they would sneak off to a side room to talk, snuggle up together, and when no one was looking, to do a little smooching. In the evenings they would violate a cardinal rule of the house by dancing together many times. Young women employees were there to attract male customers and encourage them to buy food and drinks. Spending too much time with any one male customer was grounds for termination of employment. Danielle and John apparently got by with fraternizing because John was a very good customer. On average, he had patronized the Savoy several times a week, spending quite a lot of money on every occasion.

That Danielle flouted the rules did not go unnoticed by the other young women who shared the same job. Not only did she spend a great deal of time with an attractive and well-heeled male customer, they suspected that she was seeing him outside of work. They would have loved to be in her shoes. Soon they left no chair for her in their corner of the ballroom. Nor would they talk to her. Danielle seemed not to miss their camaraderie but Fred and Rudy knew that would change if she lost John permanently. They had seen her sinking slowly into despair during the short time she and John were estranged.

All through this period there was no talk about the future of their relationship. They were acting as if they could indefinitely continue the way they were. But John knew that was a false hope. He would soon have to return to the future and he did not know how to tell Danielle. Given that she was still adamant about not engaging in a sham marriage with him, he thought she was likely to believe that his disappearance for at least a few weeks would be his way of telling her they were finished. To make matters worse, he was not sure when, or even if, he could return to her. Because the time machine was to be moved and would be used to send Joe and Martha off in time, it might be months before he could return to 1929. In the worse case, his friends who now controlled the time machine might not allow him to return. Though they had mentioned he might go back to 1929, he had already used up his fair share of their labor and use of the time machine. If it were up to him, he would stay where he was, but it wasn't up to him. He had made a covenant with Martha, Sarah, Joe, and Randy that he would return. He could not violate it. Nor could he put off telling Danielle that he must leave her, perhaps for good.

On the surface, John's friendship with Fred and Rudy returned to what it used to be. The three of them continued to hobnob at the Savoy, jiving to the music and talking sports and other man stuff. But sometimes, out of the corner of his eye, he thought he had caught them looking at him like he was about to morph into some kind of savage beast. Pointedly, they never brought up what happened in the alley across from the newsstand. Neither did he. But it was an invisible barrier erected between him and his two friends.

During the week following the brawl in the alley, John visited the newsstand a couple of times, and then a few times in the following weeks. It was more to put his mind at ease than to satisfy any need for reassurance on their part. No one had shown up to threaten them, much less to do something worse to them. Had the hoodlums' bosses not bought his threats, the newsstand would have been burned to the ground by February 2. After he was sure that his friends were not concerned about any retaliation, he stopped making regular visits to the newsstand.

Near noon on February 7 John called Bob for a ride to the Savoy. At 2:00 PM the cabby was to pick him up at the Mount Morris Bank Building. There he would inquire about his holdings and inform the bank manager that he would soon be leaving on a trip and would be gone for an indefinite period of time. But first he stopped by the hotel front desk to effectively check out of the hotel pending his departure from New York City.

When John told the front desk clerk of his plans to take an extended trip, but would not formally check out that day, the young man looked confused. "But sir, if you are going to check out, but not now, can't you come by this desk just before you leave and formally check out? Or, if you know your departure date, I can charge you today for what you would owe up to your departure date."

"The problem is," John replied, "I don't know exactly when I will be leaving. It could be spur of the moment. I'll pay you today for another week and get my dinning room bill up to date, but, since I may have to leave on a moment's notice, there is the possibility that I will depart owing the hotel money. For that reason, I'll make prearrangements with my bank to pay any hotel charges that I may owe." Reaching into his pocket, he pulled out a slip of paper and handed it to the clerk. "My bank manager's name and private phone number is on this slip of paper. You can call him in a couple of hours and he will confirm that any outstanding bill will be paid through his office. I'm going to confer with him after I'm finished here."

The clerk seemed uncertain. However, John was confident that the hotel manager would not be concerned should the clerk contact him about the possibility that John might leave behind an outstanding bill. The manager had shown trust in him before.

One last concern was dealt with quickly. John indicated that, upon his return, he would like to have the same room he presently occupied, but understood that might not be possible. The clerk replied that, should someone be in his room upon his return, he or she would be asked to take another comparable room at a substantial discount. If that didn't work, John would get another room until his top floor, corner room was available. Almost the entire staff, excluding behind the scenes workers, knew that he was a valued customer.

He tipped the clerk and set out on foot to the Mount Morris Bank Building.

When John arrived at the bank's front desk, the clerk on duty recognized him. "Good morning Mr. Williams. What can I do for you?"

"I'd like to speak to the bank manager, please."

"I'm sorry, Mr. Williams. He asked not to be disturbed until after 1:30 this afternoon."

"I understand," John replied, "but I'm leaving very soon and I need to talk to him right now. Please just inform his secretary that I'm waiting to talk to him about an urgent matter."

The clerk picked up the desk phone without hesitating and dialed the manager's number. A few moments later, he announced, "The manager will be right down to speak with you, Mr. Williams."

Before John could settle into a chair in the bank lobby, the bank manager emerged from the elevator.

He walked rapidly toward John with his right hand extended. "Good day Mr. Williams. It's a pleasure to see you again. What can I do for you?"

John told the manager the same story he used at the hotel. When he got to the part where the hotel manager might call the bank to confirm that any outstanding bill John owed the hotel would be covered from his bank assets, the bank manager broke in. "Of course, Mr. Williams. We'll take care of it. I'll send a note to my clerks telling them what to do should we receive that call from your hotel."

John also asked for affirmation that his investment in the gold industry would continue to be handled as per their agreement. The bank manager bent over backwards to assure John that his investment would be safe with them no matter how long he was gone on his trip and regardless of whether he contacted the bank during his trip. He also promised that the small net percentage he was paying for a loan would remain in force at the same low rate. "The way investments are growing, yours may well increase exponentially in worth by the time you return. After all, your money is in Homestake Mining, which is projected to continue it's climb upward in value indefinitely." The manager was talking from experience. It was not uncommon for investors to disappear for years, but by the time they returned, their thousands had turned into millions. John was also assured that the contents of his safety deposit box would be entirely secure while he was gone.

CHAPTER 25

Predicting the Future and Understanding the Past

On the afternoon of February 8, John and Sandra met in the foyer of Main Hall to plan their meeting with Andrew, Ronald, and Herb. Remembering John's earlier comments to her about topics he would like to cover, Sandra suggested that John began the meeting with the present state of the economy and its implications for the market in the near future. John agreed but did not specially disclose what he would talk about. She indicated that she would go second with developments in the feminist movement and John would finish the meeting with a consideration of how white people view black people.

When they entered the meeting room, Ronald was sullen, as was becoming usual for him. The others looked a little fatigued perhaps because, at the present time in the semester, they were facing deadlines for the completion of research projects. Sandra announced the agenda for the meeting and gave the floor to John. He began slowly by merely pointing out some trends and current practices. First he mentioned that, in the last year of the 1920s, stocks were

279

overvalued. They all nodded in a way that indicated they knew of this trend, but didn't find it of much interest. This matter-of-fact reaction reminded John that he was talking to young adults who had long since taken their families' millions for granted. He also mentioned that margin buying was becoming a risky business because, currently, investors had to put down only 10% of the money they were using to buy market shares. The rest they could pay out in installments. They were investing with phantom money for which they were paying high interest. The "so what" looks on the faces of his audience were changing in the direction of boredom. As he observed that new banks were so poorly regulated that there was little monitoring of whether they were meeting minimum capital requirements, he observed that some of his audience were in danger of dozing off.

Despite the indifference of his audience to what he had to say, John moved on to the second phase of his presentation. When he mentioned the 1893 market crash, the Columbia group slipped from nearly comatose back to "so what." Herb commented, "My parents told me about it. Their families lost a good deal of money."

Andrew offered, "I read about it in an undergraduate business class. Some people went broke. Many businesses failed."

John was thinking, "They're making my point for me." But it was clear that the implications of what they were saying had yet to register on them. It was time to pick up the pace. "You're remembering some important points. There were, indeed, many similarities between the conditions that led to the crash of 1893 and what's happening in today's economy. In 1893 there were wildly speculative investments in emerging industries. The best example was railroads. These careless investments led to bank closures and high unemployment. However, in many ways, today's market conditions are more catastrophic than those in 1893. Today's risky margin buying, high interest rates, and poor bank regulation point to a crash in the near future that will dwarf the one in 1893."

Now John's audience was fully attentive. Ronald had moved from indifferent to overwrought. He practically shouted, "So now you're an expert on the economy?"

"No, economic science is beyond my expertise. I'm just commenting on some similarities in general trends between an economic period that occurred not long ago and economic events that are unfolding now. History does repeat itself, partly because we don't learn from the past."

Ronald howled, "Economics is not a science! If it were, there would be a Nobel Prize for it. Because it isn't, we can't use it to predict market outcomes." Ronald looked like he had hammered the final nail into the coffin of John's thesis.

John calmly remarked, "You're right. So far there is no Nobel Prize in economics, but I'll bet there will be some day. Because economic conditions and market outcomes are extremely important determinants of human wellbeing, there will be much attention devoted to them by scientists in the future. For a better tomorrow, we need to start the systematic consideration of economics today."

Ronald came back with, "Well that sounds highfalutin. Why don't we have a science about almost everything. We could be very specific about it. I propose that we have a science about why monkeys hang by their tails. We might make some discoveries that will improve the well-being of monkeys."

Knowing that other group members had become impervious to Ronald's tirades, and seeing that they were unmoved by his current tantrum, John did not grace his current remark with a response. Instead he asked if there were any questions. Andrew looked like he had some questions, but Herb's hand went up first. "What would you invest in as a hedge against this possible crash?"

John paused for a moment to compose an answer. He didn't want to be too explicit. After all, these students came from money. He had, at best, mixed feelings about helping them stay among the moneyed elite. Finally he answered, "The gold mining industry would be a good bet. Gold tends to hold its value." But he did not disclose that his bank manager had put his money into Homestake Mining. Sandra, Herb and Andrew wrote down John's recommendation, but not Ronald. Nevertheless, John assumed Ronald was making a mental note based on lip movements he made almost in sync with John's announcement about the gold industry.

Andrew rather self-consciously asked, "What will happen to the wealth some families have accumulated over time?"

John was thinking to himself, "Another tricky question ... I can reassure them, but should I?" Then he thought, what the heck, I'll just tell them the truth about their future. "The richest 1% of US citizens will continue to hold a higher percentage of the nation's wealth than any other segment of the population, whether you're talking about the professional class, the middle class, the working class or all of them together. The very wealthy will continue to pocket 96 % of financial gains every year for many decades." The sighs of relief were sub-vocal, but John "heard" them anyway.

Sandra took the floor to talk about feminism worldwide. She began with a New York Times description of an incidence in Paris outside the French Senate building. "After a Senator declared that 'a woman's hand, which was meant to kiss, should not be soiled by the ballot' lead to widespread protests, feminists were regarded as obstructionists threating to disrupt the Senate's proceedings. In order to preserve the Senate's decorum, members ordered the police to clear the sidewalks surrounding the Senate building of any suspected feminists. One of the first victims of the order was a woman waiting for her son near the gates of the Senate building. When she declined to 'move on,' three police officers escorted her to the police station. After a two-hour confinement, she was released when she declared 'that she was not a feminist and did not want to vote.'" Sandra stopped at this point, folded her arms and waited for others' comments on the incident in France.

Reactions on faces around the room ranged from indifference to outrage. The latter emotion was confined to John. Andrew was the first to speak, "Well, it appears the woman was breaking French law. When she was told to move on, she should have obeyed." When he looked around the room to see how others reacted to his comment, he sensed that he had missed the point. Herb offered, "She was falsely accused. Just because she was standing outside the French Senate building when women's suffrage was being considered doesn't mean she is a feminist." Andrew nodded slightly to signal that Herb might be on the right track.

While Sandra and the others were speaking, Ronald had been wrenching his torso back and forth, right and left. Finally, he could not contain himself any longer. He growled, "I know what Sandra hopes we will conclude: poor feminists are being mistreated everywhere in the Western world. If we had dealt with the feminists like the French have, we'd still be the nation our founding fathers envisioned. The United States has given women the right to do what they are ill equipped to handle. Throughout most of our history, women have been good wives and mothers who left the business of their families and of the nation to their husbands."

At this point Sandra was about to break in, but John beat her to it. "There are human rights that supersede national laws and practices. It's abominable that one of the world's greatest nations would be so intent on suppressing women's human right to have a role in their nation's course that they would arrest a woman just because of where she was standing. More than half of the world's people are females. Does it seem right to you that the majority of humanity should be subjected to rule of the minority? Early in the history of humans, by virtue of their greater physical size and strength, males provided protection for women and girls. But in these modern times it's clear that physical protection by men is more a ball and chain than a benefit. Women function in almost all the professions, albeit still in small numbers in some cases. Today many women partially or solely support their families. The only reason they don't have full rights here and in the rest of the world is that men fear erosion of their power. It's time to do what's right and what's reasonable: declare that all adult humans must be granted an equal role in the governance of their nations."

Before John could say more, or anyone else could capture the floor, Sandra continued her presentation on feminism. To avoid interruption, she rattled off descriptions of current feminist activity taken from late 1928 New York Times articles. "During a recent meeting at Princeton University about 1000 feminists gathered to promote ratification of the Kellogg multilateral treaty on world peace. In particular, they were supporting a portion of the treaty that renounced war as an instrument of national policy. What does this recent effort on the part of feminists say about the current state of their movement?"

Andrew's hand went up first. "For one thing, it shows that the women's movement has strengthened in numbers, influence and breadth of ideology. During the time of the Civil War and its aftermath, Susan B. Anthony and Elizabeth Cady Stanton helped Negro men get the vote. But, despite that fact, women were not granted the right to vote themselves until 1920. Nevertheless, women have continued to work for the betterment of all people regardless of gender or race. Campaigning against the propensity for nations to settle their disputes on the battlefield has the potential to save millions of lives and prevent the crippling wounds soldiers suffered during Great War of the previous decade."

Sandra tried to hide her amazement. While the men in her group remarked on what she and Andrew had presented, she contemplated the irony of what she had just witnessed. John and then Andrew showed surprising knowledge about and apparent sympathy for the women's movement. Was this just a display of a compulsive need to showoff all one knows about everything there is to know? After all, it is common among academics to spew out any information they have about every topic brought up during conversations. Apparently males, as least those who are academics, have appreciable information about social movements. But why don't they actively support these movements rather than, at best, give lip service to them?

When the conversation among the men lapsed into redundancy Sandra announced that it was time for John to close the meeting with a description of another incidence reported in the New York Times. John hastily took the floor. "There was a shooting at a pay distribution office near a manual labor work site. Apparently one of the men behind the counter dispensing workers' pay thought a holdup was imminent. He pulled out a gun and fired some shots. The article assured readers that there was no cause for concern because no white people were hurt." John paused to let his words sink in, but after the lapse of several moments, faces around the room reflected only puzzlement.

Just before the awkward silence became intolerable, Herb timidly raised his hand to just above shoulder level. He stammered, "Ah, it sounds like if Negroes were shot it didn't matter … um so long as white people were not injured it was a happy ending." He turned red as the implications of his words dawned on him. Others in the room shared his embarrassment. No one stepped up to support or refute Herb's interpretation. Instead they began to fumble with their belongings to signal it was time to end the meeting. Acting on this cue, Sandra announced that the next meeting would be on February 7.

Herb, Ronald and Andrew were out the door in seconds, leaving Sandra and John looking alarmed. "What just happened?" asked Sandra.

John offered, "I think, for perhaps the first time, some basically humane people realized that some human beings are valued more than others."

"Yes, and, I guess, that includes me," responded Sandra. "It's uncomfortable to discover that so much about how we regard people who differ from us in some way is beyond our awareness. Maybe it's time to generate discomfort more regularly."

"That's a good insight on your part," John replied. "But, generating too much discomfort can cause people to deny the biases they harbor. Let's be thoughtful about it."

"Agreed," she said, "and here is something that may generate some discomfort for you. You have been hogging the floor at our meetings." She paused to consider his response to her accusation. Mea culpa was written all over his face. He sat down literally after he was taken down figuratively.

"I'm not shy," Sandra continued. "I'm fully capable of running a meeting and doing most of the talking myself. However, I'm presiding over an all-male group. Even before I knew you well at all it was clear to me that you would have more credibility with the men in our group than I would. I'm willing to accept that because I believe what we're doing is worthwhile." She stuffed her hands into her pants pockets and waited for John's response.

He began with, "I hope you don't think I'm disrespecting you. I'm totally aware that none of what we've done would have happened without your leadership. It's just that I get so into the discussions I can't contain myself. Please, in the future, wave a finger at me or stick you hands in your pockets like you're doing right now," he paused as she grinned good-naturedly. He smiled back at her. "Do whatever it takes to get me to back off."

"Under the circumstances, I think we are doing fine as we are. I just wanted you to know that I was not conceding the floor to you. I'm leading in the best interest of the group. Having said that, in the future I may break in sometimes when you or the other men are talking, if it seems appropriate to do so."

"And well you should," he said. "I'll be watching your reactions more often for any signs that it's time to shut-up."

After shaking hands on it, they turned to the agenda for the next meeting. John took the next ten minutes describing what he planned to cover during the February 7th meeting.

He told Sandra about how he would crash his fists together to illustrate how the Higgs Boson was revealed by action of the Cern Collider. But, of course, he substituted other words for "Higgs Boson" and "Cern Collider." He also would talk about an early conception of how computer software would operate. Then he would discuss epigenetics in plain English. Again, he avoided language that would be unfamiliar to her or anyone else in her time. Finally, he would consider cell growth in the hippocampus and its implications for human memory, without, mentioning the hippocampus or using technical language. All of the implied discovers and innovations would not occur for many years into the future.

When he finished, Sandra was aghast. "Where do you get your information? I didn't understand most of what you said. How in the world would I help the group understand your presentation? If you manage to cover that much in one meeting, no one will comprehend what you're talking about. It can't be done in one meeting. We'll have to have at least two more meetings." She was beside herself.

John was cursing himself under his breath. He thought he was near the end of conveying information about the future, but it was now clear to him that there was more work to be done before returning to the 2010s. He apologized to her again and promised that he would simplify his presentation. Also, he asked her to stop him during the next meeting to ask questions and make comments when it was clear to her that group members were not understanding him.

He tried to get back into her good graces by assuring her that his actual presentation would be easier to understand, because he would go into more detail and give many everyday examples to illustrate what he was trying to get across. When that didn't work, he changed the subject to how she and Hazel were getting along. Sandra indicated that Hazel was showing her more respect and paying more attention to her feelings. They were actually getting along better than ever. She asked about how he and Danielle were doing. He reported that they were getting along very well, but didn't go so far as saying "better than ever." He didn't want to tell her that the status of his relationship with Danielle was tenuous at best.

CHAPTER 26

Things to Come in the Future Near and Far

John got word to Sandra about a date for the next meeting of the Columbia group. She phoned the Hotel Theresa front desk and left a message indicating that the afternoon of February 18 would be good for her and the others. By that date they all would be finished with early semester papers, research-result reports, and tests. He called the phone number she had used and indicated that the 18th would be fine for him. He had several days to prepare for perhaps his most difficult performance.

That night when Bob dropped him off at the Savoy, he was pleased to find that, not only was Danielle on duty that night, but both Rudy and Fred were also there. He strolled up close to where Danielle was sitting and briefly caught her attention. She winked at him, but turned away so as to avoid censure by her bosses.

John headed to where he had seen Fred and Rudy sidling up to a bar. When he took a stool next to them they smiled broadly and aimed fists at him to tap a warm hello. The last couple of times he had seen them they had shown signs of softening their image of him. Apparently, they had forgiven him for the fiasco he had made of their attempt to scare off the mobsters who had come to shake them down. Or they appreciated the fact that his plan actually worked.

They chatted amiably for some time about the prospects for the Yankees, Giants and Dodgers in the upcoming season and about Fred's and Rudy's newsstand. Their business was booming and the Yankees were expected to do well again. A few minutes into the discussion of their business they looked at one another and then back at John, signaling that they were about to make a serious revelation. Rudy began tentatively with a reference to a new location where they might open a second newsstand. "We've found a place in West Bronx near Upper Manhattan. It's a small vacant lot at the end of a line of stores. The proprietor of the shop at the end of the line owns the lot. We could lease the lot or buy it over time. The costs are pretty high: the owner wants $100 a month to lease the lot or $1500 to buy it. We'd build a stand much like the one we have now, but bigger, so it's cost wouldn't be much more than before."

At this point, Rudy paused while he and Fred looked at John expectantly. Taking the cue, John responded mildly. "So, you need some money. Ok, no problem. We can make the same deal we have with the first stand. How much do you need?"

"Ah," began Fred, "We have most of the money and can borrow the rest ..., we'd need only a few hundred from you at most. What we really need ..." he stopped for a moment while he tried to hide his discomfort ... "is someone to sign off on a loan and to be the owner ... how'd the shop proprietor put it ... yeah, the owner of record."

"Alright, I get it," returned John in a tone that reflected his own embarrassment. "They want a white guy to be the owner of record. You know and I know that's not right. You don't have to do it. I think I can find a lawyer who would write you a contract that would make you two the owners of record."

Rudy replied impatiently, "No, you don't get it. We are talking about the way things are, not how they should be. We want to make this deal with this white man. He told us that he had to assure white merchants of nearby stores that he was turning over the lot to a white man. Fred and I would be identified as your employees. Otherwise, he assured us, there would be no deal."

John sheepishly responded with, "I understand what you're saying. I'll get a lawyer through my bank to create a contract that puts you in charge. It'll be set up like a corporation with me as the owner of record. I'll be the managing partner paid 3% of the profits with you two being the majority owners and operators who receive 97% of the profits. Would that work?"

Fred and Rudy looked at each other and then back at John as they nodded their approval. They shook hands on it.

To override the remaining atmosphere of awkwardness, Rudy positioned himself between John and Fred, clasped them on the shoulders and announced that he would pay for the next round of drinks. Thirty minutes later they were interacting as usual, slapping hands, talking trash—John's way of referring to small talk—and commenting on the dancing talents, or lack thereof, displayed by patrons on the dance floor.

As they left, John remarked, "Thanks for getting the first round. I'll pay for the next."

"No problem," said Rudy. "But you owe us some more trash talk."

Even though closing time was approaching, John stayed around after Rudy and Fred had departed in the hope of spending some time with Danielle. Because she had disappeared into the women's dressing room, he waited for her near the front door.

Ten minutes later there was still no sign of her. Reluctantly, he decided to wait outside for Bob to arrive at a previously arranged time that was fast approaching. Just before the front door closed behind him, he heard her call his name. Moments later, she was standing very close. She clasped both of his hands and looked up at him in such an enchanting way that he felt they were alone together, despite the departing crowd milling around them. He bent down to her so he could kiss her forehead and then her cheeks. Before he could do more, she pressed an index finger to her lips and her eyes rolled around to silently inform him that they were in a very public place. He grinned wolfishly and pulled her back inside the Savoy. As they walked away from the entrance, he announced, "I've got to use the front desk phone to tell my taxi driver that I'm not ready to be picked up." In fact, he told the dispatcher not to send a cab and was informed that cabs would be available only until 2:00 AM.

Soon they were again outside on the street in front of the Savoy. She took his hand and began to lead him away. The weather was mild for the time of the year. They chatted about their evening at the Savoy, the coming spring, and places in the city they could visit when the weather permitted. Before long John recognized that he was being shepherded down the street where he had seen her emerge from her residence. Sensing that he knew where they were going, she pulled down on his arm until his head was next to hers and whispered, "You said you wanted to see where I live. Well, we're a couple of blocks away. Are you still curious?"

"Very much so," he replied as they began to walk a little faster. When they arrived at the steps to her front door, he hesitated, unsure what was expected of him. Should he kiss her goodbye at the front door and depart or should he go in and face whatever fate awaited, about which he had no idea. After a few moments, she exclaimed, "Silly, it's alright, come on in." The hallway inside the front door lead to several doors, each, presumably, entrances to separate apartments. About halfway down the hallway, she stopped and fumbled in her purse for a key. After extracting it and opening the door at which she had stopped, she entered and turned around to find him still in the hallway. With mock irritation contradicted by smiling eyes, she stood with hands on hips and issued a command: "Come on in." He shuffled into the apartment like a child who had been granted permission to enter a forbidden space. "Take off your coat and stay awhile," she said as she headed for an area that looked like a kitchen. He obeyed and took a seat at a table near an icebox. She shed her coat, took two beers from the icebox and placed them on the table along with a bottle opener. Then she settled into a chair across from John, who seemed in need of further instruction.

They sipped their beers and talked about nothing for several minutes. Then Danielle got up slowly and, looking back enticingly over her shoulder, headed for a folding partition on one corner of the room. Once behind it, John could see only the top of her head bobbing in and out of sight. He could hear some rustling sounds. A few minutes later she emerged barefoot and dressed in a terry-cloth robe. His face must have given away his emotions because she stopped, looked at him for a couple of seconds and then declared, "You know we can't be married and I will not allow myself to become pregnant until I'm married." She paused to get his reaction. He nodded to acknowledge that he understood her and accepted the boundaries she was drawing around their relationship.

She continued, "Did you bring protection?"

His jaw dropped. He had assumed that they would never make love. After what seemed like minutes, but was probably a matter of seconds, he stuttered, "I ah, ah …. no."

"Me either," she said in a manner more appropriate for referring to umbrellas on a rainy day. "But we could enjoy being close to one another." Forthwith she slipped under the covers on her bed and beckoned to him.

John felt that the "wet cement" he was standing in had suddenly hardened. He could not move. "Come on, now," she said. He took one step and cautiously another. Then he bolted for the bed. When he peeled back the bed covers and prepared to climb in next to her, she burst into laughter. "You can't get into bed with your shoes on and all those clothes." At this point she placed her fingertips over her lips and was reduced to giggling. "For heaven's sake take your shoes and socks and shirt off. Keep your pants on, but take your belt off and empty all that stuff out of your pockets so you can be comfortable."

As he complied with her wishes, he was thinking he must have looked awfully foolish, because she was unable to stifle her giggling as she watched him prepare to climb in next to her.

Once he crawled into bed and pulled the covers over them, she snuggled next to him and kissed him lightly on the lips. He tenderly returned the kiss but kept his hands at his sides. "It's ok for us to touch," she whispered. He responded by slipping his arms around her waist and pulling her close. They kissed, they laughed, they talked about how much they cared for each other and they fell asleep together.

At about 5 AM it suddenly sounded like a horse was running around the room just above them. John moaned, "What's that?"

"That's my alarm clock," she groaned. "The deliveryman upstairs wakes me up every morning at about the same time. His route is all over Harlem and some surrounding areas."

They got up reluctantly and shuffled around the apartment, John in search of something to eat in the icebox and Danielle preparing some coffee. Suddenly it occurred to John that he had things to do that day. First, he had to get a lawyer at his bank to set up a contract that would pass muster with the man whose lot Fred and Rudy needed. He also had to get ready for the next meeting with the Columbia students. He asked Danielle where he could hail a cab.

"This time of day? I don't know. Cabs don't come to Harlem except at night to bring people to places like the Savoy and the Cotton Club, but that's less true the closer you get to Manhattan. However, this deliveryman may get you close to the Hotel Theresa. Why don't you get dressed right away before he goes out to fetch his truck. I'll intercept him and talk him into giving you a ride to where you can catch a cab."

Her mission was successful. Minutes later, John jumped into the deliveryman's truck. As they drove off, he explained where he needed to be dropped off.

"You in luck," said the driver. "I got to pick up some stuff to delivery on 7th Avenue, between 135th Street and 125th Street. That'll get you close."

Indeed it did. As they stopped for the delivery and the man headed for the rear of his truck, John handed him a five-dollar bill. He looked surprised, but he took it.

As John began walking toward 135th Street, he looked over his shoulder for an approaching cab. Finally one turned the corner behind him and was coming his way. He waved it down and told the driver to drop him off at the Hotel Theresa. Once there he thrust the fare and a tip toward the driver and made straightway to the Hotel lobby.

It was too early to phone Sandra about the up-coming meeting, so he sent her a telegram asking to chat with her well before the meeting on the 18th, which was just a few days away. He indicated that they needed at least 30 minutes to talk about an agenda for the meeting. That much time, and maybe more, would be needed to define the roles she and he would play during the meeting and to set a more sanguine tone for the group interactions. She got back to him and agreed to meet 30 minutes before the meeting in the foyer of Main Hall.

That afternoon he met with lawyers at his bank and was assured that the contract he wanted would be legally sound and straightforward to prepare. He signed a cover sheet to accompany the completed contract and had them send a copy to him at the Hotel Theresa and the original to Fred and Rudy at their newsstand address. They would sign and keep the original contract.

John arrived at Main Hall early on the 18th—about 45 minutes before the meeting was scheduled to occur—and found some chairs in a secluded corner near the main entrance where he and Sandra could talk. She showed up about 10 minutes later looking a bit disgruntled. Immediately, she sat down facing him and said "hello" without any corresponding cordiality reflected in her facial expression. If John was put-off by the cold reception, he did not show it. Instead he launched into a summary about what he expected to cover during the meeting. "I'll start out talking about the future of electrical devices, about how their components will shrink in size but grow enormously in capabilities. The implications stretch from sources of entertainment to storing and using massive amounts of data. Then I'll consider some possibilities regarding the nervous system that would have widespread implications. It'll be about growth of new cells in some parts of the nervous system and about a growth process that allows for widespread interconnectedness among neurons and provides for changes in connections."

During John's brief oration about what he would cover that afternoon, she sat there staring at him without any reaction to what he planned to discuss. But, a few moments after he finished, her face softened up a little and she announced, "I understand that the group discussion was your idea and that you had outlined a coherent agenda well before the first meeting. I accept that—in fact I applaud it—the meetings have been extraordinary. I've learned a lot. But, I must say that I've felt a little like your stooge: I'm there to keep the others focused on the topics under discussion and to facilitate your presentations. Beyond that I feel like a non-contributor. I just thought I'd let you know about my perceptions of what we are doing here. I promise I will continue to play my assigned role."

"Look," John replied, "you are indispensable. None of this would have happened without you. I have advantages over others in the group that are not attributable to being smarter or better informed than any of you. Someday I hope you and the others will understand that I have a lot to say that would be news to any audience, because I have sources of information unavailable to anyone else. If you can just accept what I'm saying, I think the remaining group sessions will be very productive. And just one more thing: you have a sharp mind. You could use it for challenging me to clarify and defend what I'm proposing and to induce more insightfulness on the part of other group members." Sandra smiled faintly and put on an "I get it" look.

After everyone had arrived, John first attempted to steer group members away from suspicions about where he got the information he was reporting to them. Also, he hoped that his preface would relieve any threat to their egos posed by conflicts between what he was telling them and information stored in their own knowledge bases. "Let's play a 'what if' game. I'll propose some possible future developments in the sciences and, together, we can consider the practical and theoretical advances that would flow from those developments." The group, with the exception of Ronald, seemed intrigued and relieved.

John began with shortcomings of devices with which they would all be personally familiar. "Present day electrical devices are cumbersome and inefficient. Many are based on vacuum tubes. These relics take up much space and waste considerable energy. Solid-state replacements for vacuum tubes would allow for the miniaturization of electronic devices. I'll give you a practical example. I know that you spend a lot of time hovering around your radios listening to your favorite shows and music. Instead of being stuck in one place to enjoy your favorite entertainment, what if you could take your radio wherever you go? With miniaturization allowed by solid-state replacements for vacuum tubes, you could have your own portable radio to carry with you anywhere. It could have a telescoping antenna and, maybe, push buttons to change stations. Eventually it could be powered by lightweight batteries. That would allow you to carry it to wherever you and your friends gather to enjoy your favorite music and shows, even outside."

Just as John was thinking, "this sounds condescending," Andrew broke in. "I'm sorry, but I'm not able to picture your 'solid state' replacement for vacuum tubes. What would it be made of?"

"Well, the substitutes for vacuum tubes could be made of some kind of plastic, you know, a dense but light weight substance into which electric circuits could be embedded.

Just to come up with a name, call them 'transistors.' They could perform the same functions as vacuum tubes, but be quite small and light weight."

Neither Andrew nor the others seemed satisfied. Before he could go on, Sandra broke in. "How do you know this 'transistor' you propose would constitute the advance you claim for it?" "Ah oh," came to John's mind. Maybe he shouldn't have so fully informed her just before the meeting. He responded with, "I don't know. It just makes sense to me. The smaller an electrical device is, the more portable it is and the less power it would need. An entire factory might be controlled by integrating many of these miniaturized solid-state components into a master unit no bigger than a automobile. It just seems to be the way the science of electrical devices would go in the future. It would be more efficient and would lead to more powerful applications."

Before anyone else could raise troubling questions that might blow his cover, John quickly changed the subject. "Some day there will be electrical machines that will be able to make very complicated calculations very quickly. Imagine a computing device that includes a continuous tape with ones and zeros on it."

Herb interrupted with, "You mean, 'binary?'"

"Yes, that's right." He continued with, "A head sliding back and forth along this tape can access the data on the tape. The head would contain instructions allowing it to arrange the ones and zeros on the tape so that it can use them to complete many different calculations. These calculations can correspond to an almost infinite number of operations ranging from solving complex equations to coding chemical symbols as numbers. It would also be possible to input additional arrangements of ones and zeros into this machine."

"You're talking about a computing machine," exclaimed Andrew.

"Or you could just call it a computer," answered John who was beginning to sense that, at least Andrew and Herb were getting into the "what if" game. In fact, as more questions and comments were offered by group members, it was clear that they were assuming something like "John is now and has been playing a sort of scientific guessing game." They were getting into the game with some enthusiasm.

"With this computer, almost any kind of operation could be digitized," continued John. "For example, letters of the alphabet could be represented as numbers. This means that whole books and massive medical records could be digitized and recorded on discs akin to music records."

Herb broke in to say, "Other alternatives for creating permanent records of data might be recording to magnetic wire or tape." Sandra responded to his comment by suggesting that in addition to storing data externally by use of discs et cetera, computers might have their own built-in memory banks.

Her comment cued Andrew to broaden the discussion. He pointed out that during the 1920s, a process already being called "television"—from the French word *télévision*—was being developed to eventually broadcast images and synchronized sound to home receivers.

As the conversation went on for another forty-five minutes or so, the atmosphere radically changed. Discussions no longer had the flavor of John making other group members look ignorant by providing information they could not process. Instead it became a creative exercise: trying to anticipate the future.

Before euphoria set in, Sandra looked at her watch and realized they had convened longer than ever before.

As it would be a bad precedent to allow meetings to go on indefinitely, she announced that they should adjourn or face the closing of the campus cafeterias before they could grab something to eat. To get them up for the next meeting, she informed them that John would discuss new conceptions of the brain at the next meeting. But before they could clear the room, Ronald spoke up for the first time. "Where did you get these ideas? We don't even know anything about your college education. What college did you graduate from?"

There were several gasps around the room. John had dreaded this question, but he was prepared. "I graduated from Tabor College in Iowa. My curriculum was general science."

Ronald growled, "Never heard of it."

Fearing that he would lose control of his emotions, John wheeled about and headed for the door, followed by Sandra. Just as he was about to exit the building, she caught up with him.

"What's wrong?" she asked.

He answered only, "I can't talk about it now. It'll come up again." Before she could reply, he was gone.

CHAPTER 27

Setting Things Straight

A few days after the fitful March 18th meeting, John received a letter from Sandra. For the most part it was devoted to apologizing about what happened at the meeting. He thought the meeting had gone pretty well. The points he wanted to make were presented exactly as he had rehearsed them and seemed to be understood reasonably well. After John thought about events at the meeting, he became convinced that Sandra felt guilty about her rather cutting remark concerning how he "knew" that transistors would do what he claimed for them. Perhaps it seemed to her that John's fit of pique and quick exit at the end of the meeting was attributable to her remark. In addition, she may have been concerned that Ronald's demeaning remarks about John's supposed education at the little known and now defunct Tabor College were inspired by her remark. To ease any angst on her part, he sat down at the front desk and composed a rather long telegram to her indicating that his anger at the end of the meeting and hasty departure were in reaction to Ronald's tirade, not to anything she said or did. In fact, he continued to regard her as the most important member of the group. She wired him back almost immediately indicating that she understood his anger at the end of the meeting and thanked him for his appreciation of her contributions. She closed with a proposal that they meet again on April 16. He wired her back that the 16th would be good for him.

Throughout the rest of March and the beginning of April John spent an enormous amount of time at the Savoy. Fred, Rudy and Danielle rarely were all there at the same time. That happy coincidence happened at most two to three times a week. There were occasions when only one or two of the trio were at the Savoy in the afternoon or evening. Sometimes none of them were there. In those cases, he was alone for hours with only his thoughts for company.

After a few weeks of his near constant presence both in the afternoon and in the evening, staff at the Savoy began to see John differently. They had regarded him with respect and envy. He was viewed as the dapper young man who, based on his stylish dress and free hand with money, was what most young women wanted and most young men wanted to be. Now he seemed to be a desolate young man with apparently no real friendships. Shallow relationships played out at the bar and on the dance floor were all he seemed to have. To Savoy personnel, his so-called friends were nothing more than leeches that suckered him into buying them drinks. In Danielle's case, John was only an incidental part of doing her job: keeping the customers coming back to spend more money. Never mind that Fred and Rudy shared in the cost of the beer and that only Danielle's explicit behavior fit her role as bait for men with money. Closer observation of more subtle behaviors would have confirmed that Rudy and Fred were true friends and that Danielle was head over heels in love with John.

But personnel at the Savoy were right for the wrong reasons. John was changing. He was sinking into despair, but not because he had no real human relationships. To the contrary, his increasingly anguished condition was because he would soon be forced to leave his friends and lover in Harlem and his new family at Columbia University. He was truly a man torn between two separate lives.

Rudy and Fred were also changing. They had been ebullient about receiving their contract with John, beginning payments toward owning the vacant lot, and starting construction of their new newsstand. Indeed, they finished the newsstand very quickly, despite the fact that it was bigger and more complex, and thus, more difficult to construct. Once electrical wiring was completed, they wasted little time stocking the stand and opening for business. Soon they were trading off, each spending about halftime at the old newsstand and halftime at their new enterprise.

At first, business was booming at the new stand. They were selling more of everything and making bigger profits. They figured that they had paid for the building expenses in only the first few weeks of doing business at the new location. At the rate they were going, they believed that they could pay what they owed on the lot in little more than a year.

Then things began to change. Regular customers would come by their stand, check out their prices and then go down the street and into shops near the newsstand. Sometimes Fred and Rudy saw these now former customers coming out of the nearby shops carrying items they used to buy at the newsstand. That even included newspapers.

To find out what accounted for the precipitous drop in their business proceeds, one day they closed down the old newsstand and they took turns visiting the shops near their new stand. It didn't take long to notice something extraordinary: not in every shop, but across all the shops in the line next to the their newsstand, they found every item they sold offered at a lower price. They were being priced out of business.

The obvious thing to do was to lower their own prices below those in the adjacent shops. They did that but their sales went up only briefly. A new survey of the adjoining shops revealed that shop owners had instituted further reductions in prices of items also carried in the newsstand. Fred and Rudy lowered their prices some more only to find that they were again undercut. It became obvious that soon they would be unable to make payments on the lot or afford to restock for their newsstands.

When Sandra opened the meeting on the 16th of April, 1929, group members seemed to be in an especially good humor. Of course, the exception was Ronald, who was in a worse grumpy-growly mood than was usual for him. He scowled and kept his head down as Sandra informed the group that John was going to converse with them about possible future developments in the science of the brain's generation and maintenance of memories.

John opened with a consideration of what memory is and isn't. He began with a query. "How many of you have forgotten something or other that you felt you should have remembered?" All hands went up; well, except for Ronald who, after looking around at the others' reactions to John's question hesitantly held up one finger. John went on to say, "much of what we think of as 'forgetting' is actually something else. Let's take an example of what may be commonly and incorrectly thought of as 'forgetting.' Suppose you are rushing to class and are stopped by a friend on the steps of your classroom building. She says something or other to you and you nod in agreement. All the while you are thinking about being late to class. After a few minutes you excuse yourself and run up the stairs and into the building. After a week or so, you again encounter the same friend and she brings up what was said on the steps of the classroom building. You haven't the foggiest idea what she's talking about."

There were some "I know what you're talking about" expressions on faces around the room and some chuckling. "So," John continued, "if that happened to you, would you be embarrassed about forgetting a conversation with a friend?" Everyone nodded in the affirmative, even Ronald.

John paused for a moment then declared, "Well, that's really not the case. You haven't forgotten the conversation with your friend; it never became a candidate for long-term memory. You were so distracted by being late for class that the part of your brain responsible for deciding on candidates for long-term memory attended to "late for class" rather than your conversation with your friend. The conversation faded so fast from short-term memory it never got in line for long-term memory."

Andrew remarked shyly, "Once I got drunk at a party." When the others snickered he amended his comment: "Alright, it wasn't the only time I got drunk, but it's rare for me. I was concerned about this occasion because I knew I had been at the party but could recall almost nothing about what happened there. It was unsettling."

"Yours is a common experience. If you pickle the area of your brain that is responsible for selecting what goes into long-term memory, you will lose some of your experiences."

Herb, stuck up his hand quite forcefully and announced, "I have another example. During times when people are fatigued they experience failure of information and events getting into long-term memory. A number of times I've attended all-night study sessions. Sometimes, on the next day, when I tried to conjure what my friends and I studied the night before, I remembered little of what was discussed."

John commented, "You're entirely correct. Fatigue can interfere with getting information and events into memory. Also, information encountered while under the influence of drugs may be poorly represented in memory, if represented at all. I once smoked too much marijuana at a party and, the next day, I couldn't remember much about the party."

Jaws dropped. John had that "oops" look on his face. Before anyone could say anything about his faux pas, he introduced another case of wrongly attributing a failed recollection to forgetting. "Sometimes, what we think of as 'forgetting' is actually a case of confusion." That got the group back to thinking about memory.

"Again, let's take an example. Imagine that you witnessed a crime while shopping at a neighborhood store. A man enters the store, hastily approaches the cash register, pulls out a gun and demands that the owner fork over all of his cash. You get a good look at him, and, when he leaves, you promise the owner that you will give a description of the robber to the police. You leave contact information with the owner. That night you happen to listen to a drama on the radio that involves a robbery at an establishment similar to the one where you witnessed an actual hold-up earlier that day. A detailed description of the robber is a part of drama's script. When the police contact you about the actual robbery, you describe the robber who perpetrated the robbery on the radio."

"Experiences occurring to anyone may share components with other experiences in her or his memory. Over time, a large number of experiences sharing similar components may accumulate in everyone's memory. Any of them could be confused with any other. The result will be memory failures that have nothing to do with forgetting and everything to do with confusing similar experiences stored in memory."

"Just one thing," said Sandra, "what is forgetting?"

"Good question. It's what happens when there is no memory trace of some past event or old information that you once could recall. For example, let's say that one summer during your teens you worked at a beach resort. Years passed during which you haven't thought about that summer. Now your parents ask you about it and you can't come up with anything. It's gone without a trace. If you don't dredge up old memories periodically and think about them they will eventually be erased. Periodically recalling past events and old information solidifies them into memory."

At this point, John paused and looked around the room. All members of the group appeared homed in on what he was saying. Accordingly he prepared to fold all of what he had presented into his final point about memory. "Your brain's sensory systems are not like a sound movie camera that records everything in front of it. By the same token, your brain's memory systems don't store your every experience verbatim. Instead it picks and chooses what is stored into your memory so that events and information that are crucial for your survival and prosperity are maintained in memory for use in the future."

"Storing and maintaining information and events in memory is one of the most daunting tasks faced by the human brain. The component of the brain's memory systems that must deal with selecting what goes into memory and deciding what stays in memory needs capabilities not shared by other parts of the brain. I propose that the module of humans' memory systems responsible for making these decisions requires the regular production of new nerve cells, at least in part to minimize confusions among similar events and pieces of information stored in the brain."

Ronald practically levitated above the seat of his chair. "That's the same old nonsense! I told you before: anyone who knows anything about the human brain knows that it produces no new cells. In fact, as people grow older, they lose brain cells."

John calmly replied, "That's the current dogma; believe it if you want. I believe that, with the development of better techniques and equipment to investigate the brain, it will become possible to demonstrate the growth of new neurons."

Before Ronald could continue his tirade, Andrew cut in. "I'm having trouble trying to conceive of the new equipment for examining brain tissue that would be needed to confirm your proposal. Would a better microscope be a part of what is needed?"

"Yes," John replied.

Herb offered, "That makes sense, but I'm a little skeptical about a significantly better microscope. There is only so much one can do with the magnifying properties of glass."

John responded with, "True, but alternative methods not relying on simple magnifying techniques are likely to develop in the future."

Because John sensed that group members were following what he was saying, he ventured forth with another potentially controversial topic. "The complete interconnection of nerve cells in the brain is vitally important to dealing with the high similarity among experiences in memory and conflicts among some environmental circumstances confronting organisms, including humans. Of course, every neuron has connections to adjacent neurons through proximities of neuronal dendrites and axon terminals. But, if these couplings could not be amplified or diminished rapidly and continually, humans and other organisms could not deal with the enormous variability in their internal and external environments. Accordingly, it appears that some growth process must exist at dendrite to axon couplings so that neurons can alter their connectedness to one another. At the level of a neuron's connection to an adjacent neuron, flexibility is achieved by the short-term growth of spine-like protrusions from dendrites to axon terminals. I am proposing that these spines grow or retract according to whether increased or decreased connectedness facilitates some local process. At the whole brain-system level, spine growth and retraction increases or decreases connectedness between, for example, auditory and visual neuronal networks."

Herb was vibrating with enthusiasm. "So you are saying that the connections between neurons in the brain are not set at birth or shortly thereafter, but are subject to change on a short-term basis according to the demands made on organisms?"

"Well put," John replied.

Andrew followed with, "What you are saying means that the first few of several times you drive an unfamiliar route in New York City, your brain is changing in terms of connections between brain systems so as to accommodate learning a new route."

"That's a very good example," said John. "The more complicated the situation a person faces the more her or his brain changes to facilitate more efficient operation in the situation."

Sandra wisely saw the pause in this more congenial discourse as the right time to call an end to the meeting. "It's getting late. Let's break for today and meet again on

April 25." Everyone signaled acceptance of the next meeting date, except Ronald, who made a point of getting to the door of the conference room before any of the others. This time John hung around until all except Sandra had left the room. They talked amiably and she suggested that the next meeting might begin with discussions about more socially relevant matters. John thought her suggestion was good and explained how he would turn a consideration of genetics into a conversation about race. She liked that idea and indicated that she would focus on the status of women in the future. As time allowed, they could consider other matters.

John turned toward the door of the conference room and was nearly there when Sandra called out, "Oh, John, there is one other thing. I'd like to ask you about the growth of new neurons in the brain."

He turned around and waited for her to approach him. "Yes. What would you like to know?"

"I was wondering, would it be possible to investigate the growth of new nerve cells using currently available methods and equipment."

He thought for several moments and was about to announce that such an investigation would not be possible during 1929 and even decades thereafter. But, upon second thought, he indicated, "Showing the growth of new neurons in humans is probably many decades away. But, but an approximation to that demonstration might be done now using laboratory rats."

After a few more moments of thought, he continued. "Imagine rearing some lab rats in a sort of rat Playland Park. It would he a large area with side partitions too high for them to crawl out, but low enough for researchers to observe the rats' behavior. Inside the closure, you could place apparatuses for them to climb on, crawl into, swing from and so forth. Various three-dimensional objects would be scattered about the enclosure. Different smells would be sprayed on different parts of the environment. It would be a stimulus rich environment."

"Another set of rats, randomly selected from the same litters as the others, would be placed into an impoverished environment. Theirs would be highly confined and bland quarters allowing little to see, smell or explore. Others from the same litters would be raised in the usual laboratory cage environment. When these sets of rats mature, they would be sacrificed. Thin slices of their olfactory bulbs, sometimes called 'smell brains,' would be examined under the most powerful microscope you can find. It's possible that you will see a more dense growth of neurons in the bulbs of enriched compared to both normally reared and deprived rats, with the latter showing the lowest level of density.

One interpretation of results would be that these genetically similar rats developed different neuronal densities in response to different levels of environmental complexity. At least you might be able to detect different olfactory bulb sizes for rats reared in different environments. The rank of most to least neuron density should be enriched rats first, normally reared rats second, and deprived rats last."

Sandra totally got it. She indicated that she had access to a powerful microscope. Having no further questions, she declared, "If I can find the means to do this experiment, I'll do it. In fact, if I can't do it in one of the labs here at Columbia, I'll do it wherever I'm hired, given only that the space and equipment needed is available."

John had never seen her happier.

CHAPTER 28

Getting It Done Before It's Too Late

John was getting antsy. He felt that he had to get back to the 2010s very soon. But before that could happen he had to help Rudy and Fred with their "priced out of the market" problem. He also had to meet with the Columbia group for at least one more time. He had not yet addressed certain critical scientific developments in the future. Further, he knew that not all of his harbingers of scientific happenings in the late 20th century and first decades of the 21st century would be remembered and conveyed to others by the Columbia group. But he believed that the more hints he dropped during group meetings, the more likely at least some of them would result in accelerated developments in the sciences. He could not leave before he had exhausted his list of crucial issues in science for which escalated development would be good for human kind. And he had to find a way to tell Danielle he must leave her and that he didn't know when he would be back.

On the morning of April 25, 1929, the day of the next meeting with the Columbia group, John groggily crawled out of bed and made his way toward the bathroom while wiping his eyes with the knuckles of his index fingers. Suddenly he uttered an oath and began hopping around on one foot and rubbing the bottom of the other foot. He had stepped on something with rough edges. After the pain subsided, he stooped down and picked up a box made of a very hard substance. He was immediately sure that his friends in the 2010s had sent something to him. He opened it with some difficulty and found what had to be the new cigar-shaped substitute for the Brownie Box.

To his surprise, a light on device's business end, where the pocket-clasp was located, began to blink. He jumped back a bit at the next sensory input. Joe's voice came through sharp and clear from a speaker somewhere on the devise.

"Can you hear me, John? I can see you some of the time as you turn the new device over and over. You don't look so good."

John growled, "Your package made a mess of my foot. Send softer packages from now on. Nevertheless, it's good to hear your voice."

Before they continued with their conversation, Joe told John how to hold the new device so that its camera was facing him and he could speak into its microphone. He also told John how to access an important message from Randy.

They chatted for a while and he sent his best to Randy, Martha, and Sarah. After Joe ended his transmission, John turned on Randy's message, which came through loud and clear. "It now looks like we will be able to start moving the Time Machine from the Computer Science College to Washington State during the last half of May. The transfer will begin just as our University's spring semester ends. It will take some of May and much of June to move all of the equipment. In cooperation with the College, I can handle the move. However, I will need Joe to help me render the Machine operational. Unless he wants to delay his trip until August, he will need to launch by mid-May and return sometime in mid-June, at the latest. Martha will have to follow a similar time-table or put her trip off until August. In your case, John, if you are not back by about mid-May, you will not be able to return until August. Any deviation from these time-tables puts too much pressure on me and, more importantly, places all of you in danger. If Martha and you are still on your missions after we begin to pack the Machine for transfer, should either of you face grave danger, rescuing you will not be possible."

When John showed a little late to the meeting with the Columbia group, he found Sandra, Herb, and Andrew looking a bit dubious. Ronald seemed ready to launch some sort of expose'. Sandra ran down what she and John would cover during the meeting and was about to call on John when Ronald stood up dramatically and demanded the floor. Sandra paused for a moment while she pictured herself telling Ronald "go to hell." Then she sighed heavily and slumped into her chair, assuming a posture of resignation.

Ronald turned to John with anger shaping his face and seeping from his voice. "I looked up your Tabor College. It closed its doors in 1927. When did you graduate?"

John's demeanor was cold and his expression unreadable. He was fighting a transition to that other dimension of himself, the one that so alarmed Rudy and Fred. He answered tonelessly, "I graduated in 1926."

"How convenient," exclaimed Ronald in a tone permeated with malice. "You graduated a year before your college closed and you turned up here after its records were placed in deep storage. I checked. Tabor College's records cannot be accessed. What does that make you? You're a huckster who is trying to sell us some nonsense about scientific developments in the future."

The other group members were horrified. Andrew looked up at Ronald from his chair and declared, "How dare you speak to John that way? I've learned more from him than in many of my classes. I don't care who he is or where he's from. I believe he's here to open up our minds about the future."

The normally soft-spoken and regularly eloquent Herb was so discombobulated that he was reduced to stuttering: "Ah, Ah—you ... you infuriate me." After catching a breath, he continued with, "You will never understand scholarship ... you are so lacking in creativity that every scientific notion you possess is written in concrete."

Sandra was more composed. In a controlled tone, She advised Ronald, "There is something wrong with you. You need help."

John was astounded. Although he was sure of Sandra's friendship, he had no idea that Herb and Andrew had such high regard for him. He felt very good indeed ... until he looked at Ronald. Moments ago he stood at his maximum height. Now he looked like a deflated balloon draped over the chair into which he had collapsed.

Sandra debated with herself. Should they continue? Or should she call an end to the meeting. Finally she decided to go on with the meeting, partly because she had no clue what to do about Ronald.

She introduced John who looked around the room as he reluctantly rose from his chair. Andrew and Herb seemed embarrassed. They had been reduced from aristocratic, buttoned down professors-in-training to little children scolded by their parents for being heard rather than just seen. Ronald looked like death warmed over.

John considered calling off the meeting himself, especially in view of the topic he had chosen to begin the session. It might look like he was hitting Ronald with the blow that would do him in. But calling off the meeting might be worse than going on with his presentation. Were they going to call off the meeting, walk out on Ronald and wonder if he survived to the next day? He didn't know what else to do, so he began to talk.

He opened with a discussion of a western Pacific people, Melanesians, with an innocuous consideration of their geographic location. He then passed around a book with earmarks on pages containing black and white photos of some Melanesian people. He noticed some mild startle responses when some of the group first saw the pictures. After a few minutes of passing the pictures around the table, Sandra commented, "They look like Africans."

"Yes, they do," said John. "They look like Africans because they have adapted to an area of the planet that is very similar to Africa in climate and terrain. For this reason, their housing, dress, and way of life are similar to those of Africans. So they resemble Africans in appearance and in other ways, but they are genetically much more similar to Asians, such as Chinese."

"So-called 'race' is not so much a matter of genes. It's more a matter of appearance and culture. Different sets of people around the world who look different, and seem to be dissimilar in life style and culture, may be genetically very similar. Chinese and Melanesians look and act quite differently, but are quite similar genetically speaking.

"More generally, genetic similarities dwarf genetic differences between one so-called 'race' and another. Thus, if two sets of people from very different places on the earth show some physical dissimilarities—for example, Europeans and Africans—the genetic similarities between the two peoples will still be enormous compared to the genetic dissimilarities between them."

Herb broke in with, "Why do Melanesian and Africans look so much alike if they are genetically more similar to people in their own parts of the world?"

"Good question," John remarked. "When we break up people around the world into different races we rely on traits that we can easily appreciate visually—such as facial bone structure, skin color, hair color and hair texture. However, these easy to appreciate traits are mostly due to adaptations to local environments. Let's take skin color as an example."

"Sunlight promotes vitamin D production. The reason it does so for light skinned people living in the north, is that the relatively rare sunlight there penetrates their pale skin readily, allowing the generation of vitamin D promoters in sufficient amounts to protect against bone disorders and various diseases. People living in northern parts of the planet would have vitamin D deficiency if their skin were not light enough to absorb the relatively little sunlight that's available. It's the opposite for people living near the equator. They also require vitamin D promoters, but they need protection from the nearly constant sunlight. If it were not for a lower sunlight absorption rate allowed by their dark skin, they would succumb to skin cancers and other disorders."

Sandra interjected, "So, one shade of skin is not absolutely better than another shade. It's just that one shade is better for health in one part of the earth, but a different shade is better at another location. If a people migrate from one local to another where the sunlight level is different, those among them with skin more suitable for the new location would be more likely to survive and pass their genes on than those with less adaptive skin color."

"Exactly," exclaimed John, whose smile communicated that her comment was apropos. "One variation of a trait is not 'better' than another. In the case of skin color, it's that a given skin shade is adaptive in one local but not necessarily in another. Hair texture is a second case in point. Hair like lamb's wool is good for adaptation to hot climates; straight, full hair is good in cold climates."

"It seems to me that we notice what is immediately apparent about people that we deem to be not like ourselves," offered Andrew. "Then we unconsciously assume that heredity per se—devoid of influences wrought by adaptations to local environments—is behind the differences we observe. It's a short leap from this incorrect inference to assuming that less observable attributes, such as intelligence and character, are also due to genes that we covertly assume to be impervious to environmental effects."

John was seated next to Andrew and across from Ronald. As he patted Andrew on the shoulder to acknowledge his helpful comment, he glanced at Ronald. The perpetually angry young man had been nearly comatose during the first part of the genetics presentation. As Ronald progressively returned to awareness of his surroundings, his face and posture reflected an increasing state of distress. John looked across the table at Sandra. She was also observing Ronald. Neither of them knew what to do.

John was thinking he should finish quickly. Instead of talking more, he passed some colored post cards around the table. Each depicted one or more Melanesians. All showed people who could be easily mistaken for African, but a few showed Melanesians with blond or red hair and even blue eyes. Ronald was startled when several group members laughed out loud. After giving others a few moments of glee, John closed with, "Remember that Melanesians are genetically more similar to Asians than they are to any other people, but they do have some genetic uniqueness."

Sandra was up next. As she collected her thoughts, she noted that a moment of levity helped ease tensions during John's talk about controversies in genetics. She doubted that the others would find anything about her consideration of women's rights and abilities to be amusing.

"I'm going to talk about why women's progress toward equality has been slow. Girls do better in the early years of school than boys, but tend to fall behind boys in high school and are much less likely to attend college. If women do go to college, they tend to prepare for a career in teaching, mostly at the elementary school level, or in some other area, like nursing, that is stereotyped as suitable for women only. Careers in science, engineering, and business are 'off limits' for women."

"Is it that women are inherently less able in pursue careers as captains of industry, masters of law, or leaders in science? I believe the answer is resounding 'no.' Women don't go into these fields because they have been told since they were little girls that they must consider only careers that center on nurturing and caring for others. Females may not do so well as males in math because they are taught very early that it's not for them. They may not think of becoming a scientist because they are discouraged from taking science preparatory classes. They do not even have a passing thought about being an engineer, because it is an exclusively male club. Little wonder females almost never pursue careers that don't involve nurturing and caring for others, or is 'women's work,' such as cooking, cleaning or sewing."

"But the times have changed. Women's successful fight to gain the right to vote has given us a foot in the door. More of us will go to college and graduate school majoring in male-dominated areas. More of us will be like Karen Horney. She graduated with a medical degree in a class dominated by males and went on to train as a psychiatrist who is already challenging Freud's notions about women. Other women pioneers will be beacons calling their sex to professions that have previously been closed to them. Every woman lawyer, every woman physician, every women scientist shows other women that they can do what has been previously reserved for men."

"It may take a long time, but by the beginning of the next century all the doors that have barred women from desirable and challenging professions will be kicked open. Women will be heads of large corporations, members of the U. S. Congress, and officers in the Armed Forces."

As she finished the last sentence, she looked around the room and noticed that Andrew and Herb were suppressing giggles. Ronald was expressionless, but becoming fully attentive, while John had an indecipherable look on his face. Were they viewing her bold predictions as laughable or were they—each in his own way—dealing with discomfort generated by her challenges to male-dominance. She thought, "I don't care," and loudly announced, "Some time near the beginning of the next century, a female representing a major political party will run for President of the United States."

Immediately Herb and Andrew burst into boisterous laughter. John at first tried to muffle his laughter, but could not. Even Ronald managed a clearly detectable smile. Sandra's response was to join the laughter. After the howls subsided, John declared, "And the first black President of the United States will be a graduate of Columbia University!" Herb, Andrew, John and Sandra laughed until the tears came. Ronald seemed puzzled, but managed to snicker a little.

Sandra ended the meeting before anyone could offer an interpretation of the strange reaction to her presentation. Andrew and Herb left immediately, still in a jocular mood. Ronald followed them, but shuffled to the door as if he had aged by fifty years.

As they stood looking at each, John's expression was sheepish; Sandra's was severe. John spoke first. "I really can't explain what happened at the end of your presentation. They laughed during my talk also, but I thought it was mainly in response to the post cards. But in both cases—especially during your presentation—the laughter may have been due to the sensitive nature of our topics. At some level of consciousness, they probably know that they have been guilty of race and gender bias. Because they likely view themselves as unbiased, they reacted strangely when confronted with evidence conflicting with their self-conceptions. One way to deal with the uncomfortable feelings born of challenges to self-perceptions is to laugh about it. That diminishes the importance of the disturbing threats to their self-conceptions."

Sandra, responded, "That's occurred to me also. It's kind of a 'caught with your pants down' phenomenon. All you can do is laugh about it. It offended me at first, but I'm over it. All and all, I think the meeting went well."

"Me also," said John with some sense of relief. "I think we can wrap up these sessions with one more meeting. I'll contact you about it and you can set the time and date."

John went back to retrieve the materials he had brought with him. When he gathered them up and turned around, Sandra was gone. As he approached the front door of Main Hall, something caught his attention out of the corner of his eye. When he stopped and looked more closely, he saw a figure huddled in a darkened corner. It looked like Ronald.

He had walked no more than a few paces toward the figure when he was able to confirm that, indeed, it was Ronald. He was shaking and appeared to be crying. Gently John bent down and whispered Ronald's name. When that got no response, he touched Ronald on the shoulder. Ronald jumped a bit then turned to face John. Tears were rolling down his cheeks. He moaned, "My head is full of rubbish."

John was taken aback. Not knowing what to say, he took hold of Ronald's elbow and attempted to help him to a standing position. Slowly Ronald stood up and was guided to a nearby chair. After John took a seat next to Ronald, he said, "That's not true. You will soon be graduating with a PhD from a highly revered university. Look, don't pay too much attention to what I've been saying. I'm just speculating about what will happen in the future." That was a lie, but oh well. He had long since learned that accomplishing his mission and always telling the truth were incompatible. "You just need to open up your head a little. Not every question has a pat answer. Not every issue is resolved in a straightforward way."

"That's not how I've learned to think. My parents believe that everything can be cast in terms of right or wrong, correct or incorrect. I was expected to apply one end of those continua to every matter that I confront. The group discussions have caused me to acknowledge the mean-spirited dogmatist they have made of me."

John responded with, "What they're doing to you is wrong. You have the right to be who you want to be. You're not going to change them, so, for your own comfort, you could chose to be who they want you to be when you are with them. I presume that won't be very often at this stage of your life. But when you are not with them you can began to become who you want to be. Of course, you will have to decide what kind of person you wish to become. That's something that will take awhile. Once you have decided on who you want be, you will need to began monitoring your thoughts and behaviors so you can catch yourself when you get off course and get yourself back on track. This second phase could take years, but if you vow to change and get started on changing, you should experience some immediate relief from the miserable state you're in."

"What I'm saying is that it's up to you. You decide on going about becoming the person you want to be. But I do have a few pieces of advice. Keep your mind wide-open, get interested in the controversies in your field as well as in the public forum, and never regard a widely accepted finding in science to be beyond questioning."

Ronald was paying close attention to what John was telling him and he seemed to understand John's recommendations. But it was clear to John that he was so severely incapacitated he could not find his way home. John asked where he lived. Ronald mumbled a Manhattan address. "I've got a cab waiting for me. I'll take you to your apartment."

He helped Ronald to his feet. Because the distraught young man seemed unstable, John stood to Ronald's left and extended his right hand to grasp Ronald's right shoulder. Thus, stabilized, John led Ronald out of Main Hall to where Bob was waiting for him at the Broadway entrance to the campus.

As he eased Ronald into back seat of the cab, John explained to Bob that his friend was "a bit under the weather," which was code for 'he's drunk.' Bob nodded that he understood and John recited the Manhattan address.

Once at the their destination, John helped Ronald out of the cab and to the main entrance of what appeared to be a ritzy townhouse. There an unsurprised doorman greeted them and said that he would escort Ronald to his quarters. Apparently Ronald regularly showed up at his resident in a state of incapacitation.

Back in the cab, Bob asked matter-of-factly whether Ronald was drunk. John hedged. After a brief pause, he said, "My friend has troubles. He was drowning his sorrows."

On the way to the Hotel Theresa, John talked about his imminent departure. He thanked Bob for his good service and friendship. Then he indicated that he would return to New York City, but couldn't say when. In fact, he really was not sure that he would be able to return.

As they drove to the Hotel Theresa, he asked Bob how his wife was getting along and was pleased to hear that she was doing well and working at a more enjoyable and better-paying job. Bob went on to imply that he and his wife were out of financial difficulty and were experiencing the best times of their married life. When he got out at the hotel, John came around to the driver's side, cab window. Bob rolled the window down and John passed him the fare and an especially large tip. After Bob lay the money aside without looking at it, John stuck his hand back into the cab. The two men shook hands vigorously and smiled warmly at one another. In parting, John said, "You were my very first friend in New York City. I couldn't have made it without you." Bob stuck his hand out the cab window for one last handshake.

CHAPTER 29

Preparing for Departure

For quite some time, John, Rudy and Fred had been communicating by telephone. From the room adjoining the hotel front desk, he would call a public phone near one of their newsstands and let the phone ring several times. If no one picked up, he could expect a call back in a few minutes. If Rudy or Fred needed to contact him, they could call the front desk anytime day or night and leave a message for him.

On the morning of April 30th 1929, John was up late. By the time he entered the hotel dinning room, it was 10:30 AM. When he finished breakfast, he approached the front desk to ask about messages he may have received that morning. The clerk reached under the counter and produced a note with Fred's name and a phone number on it. John stepped quickly to an opening in the countertop, slipped behind the counter, and entered the phone room. He dialed the number and waited only a few rings before Fred picked up.

"We need to talk right away. We've run out of money trying to match the prices that local merchants are offering for every item we are selling." John indicated that he would meet with Fred and Rudy at the Savoy that evening.

John hailed a cab to the Mount Morris Bank Building where he withdrew several thousand dollars. He transferred most of it to a new checking account in his, Rudy's and Fred's name, and was assured that blank checks would be delivered to his hotel address and to the bank's branch closest to the new newsstand. When he arrived back at the hotel he tipped the cabby generously before asking him for a ride to the Savoy that evening.

The rest of the day was spent trying to map out how he would settle his affairs in New York City before returning to the 2010s. He wanted the last gathering of the Columbia University group to be an assessment of what the meetings had accomplished. Although he was confident in his plan to beat the price-lowering scheme, he had no idea what other obstacles Rudy and Fred would face after his return to the future. And then there was Danielle. What would he tell her? That he would be back, but he couldn't say when? Or should he let her know that they may never see each other again? He would have to decide what to tell Danielle based on what happened the next time they met.

That evening John arrived at the Savoy earlier than usual. Before getting out of the cab, he arranged to be picked up by 12:30 PM. Just inside the door he found Fred and Rudy waiting for him. Both seemed very anxious. To reassure them he adopted a nonchalant demeanor that would make a Wall Street baron proud. He tapped fists with them and motioned for them to follow him to one of the rooms adjoining the dance floor. On the way he signaled to a waiter to bring them three beers. Once they were seated he opened up the lapels of his jacket so they could see that the two pockets inside had stacks of bills stuffed in them. Rudy's and Fred's eyes opened wide and they shifted back in their chairs. "This is part of my solution to the 'we can sell lower than you can' tactic."

"That looks like a lot of money," said Fred, "but every time we go down in prices they go lower. They must be getting financial support from someone powerful who doesn't want us in the neighborhood."

"Maybe," returned John, "but the way to defeat them is to beat them at their own game. You have to continue to lower your prices to undercut them every time they reduce their prices."

"We're selling daily newspapers for five cents and soda for three cents. We're not far from giving 'em away," said Rudy.

John came back quickly with, "And that's not a bad idea. Give good customers a free item and thank then for their loyalty."

Rudy's face communicated skepticism and repressed anger. "Even all the money you got in your pockets won't stop them. They'll find a way to undercut us. We might as well give up."

John's squeezed his eyebrows together as he composed a response. "They have to know that we will not give in. I'll keep putting money into this fight until we win."

Rudy shook his head, leaned forward and looked John straight in the eyes. "I don't get it. Why are you doing this? What's in it for you? You don't need the pennies you are making from our business."

"I'm making pennies now, but I see dollars in the future," John replied. "You two are hard working and you have good ideas. I'm making a business bet on you. Do you want to go with that or not? If you insist, I can walk out right now."

Rudy raised his arms and loudly declared, "Hold on now! Let's talk about this. John, you want us to continue to lower our prices and you're willing to pay for it, that's fine with me. I don't care whether you're doing it for profit or revenge, count me in."

Rudy and John shifted back in their chairs and relaxed. John informed them that the money he had in his pockets, several hundred dollars, should cover their losses for now. He also told them about the joint checking account. Both were amazed. Neither had ever written a check or received one, because neither had ever had a bank account. John explained the ins and outs of banking and suggested that, rather than opening their newsstands the next day, they all meet at the branch of John's bank located a few blocks from the new newsstand. He said he'd be there before nine AM and asked that they bring some kind of identification. Though neither of them owned a car, both had learned to drive using relatives cars and both had passed the driver's test. They flashed their licenses with considerable pride.

The three men had their usual few beers as they watched the dancers and commented on the music. All three ventured onto the floor together on several occasions, each time amusing on-lookers with moves Rudy and Fred taught John, and some John brought with him from the future. John entertained himself while on the floor by imagining how what they were doing in 1929 might affect the future of popular dancing. Before they parted for the evening, John ushered Rudy and Fred to a side room where he extracted the cash from his two coat-pockets and pushed it across the table toward them. When they hesitated, he insisted that they take the money with them. "You will need this cash right away to cover the next round of lowered prices."

Fred picked up one of the stacks of money and placed it carefully into his coat pocket, but Rudy just stared at it for a moment. Then he raised a question. "Man, how you know

I won't just catch a train out of town and live the good and easy life for awhile?"

"You won't," John replied.

"How you know that?"

"I don't. I'm just betting on it."

"You right, I won't," Rudy responded with a grin. "But it sure did cross my mind."

At about 11:00 PM, John managed to get a dance with Danielle. After several turns on the floor, he ordered drinks for them and they sat at a table by themselves. They held hands and whispered sweet nothings to each other for some time. There was also some reminiscing about returns to Danielle's favorite restaurant in Brooklyn and trips to New York's many museums. They had also spent the night together at Danielle's apartment on several occasions since the first time. But the uncertainty of their relationship hovered in the background every time they were together. Even when they were physically close, there was still some distance between them. Before they parted that evening, Danielle asked John to spend the night at her place, but he declined saying that he had to be up early the next morning. When it was time for John to wait outside for his cab, they departed with a kiss and a lingering look deep into one another's eyes.

The next morning, John met Rudy and Fred at his bank's branch near their newly constructed newsstand. They were waiting at the front door up a short flight of marble stairs. "What kept you?" queried Fred, "We've been here for at least ten minutes. The bank opens in a few minutes."

"Ah, my cab was stuck in traffic," John responded lamely.

"We took the EL. It's quick and sure. Hardly ever late. You too good for it?" asked Rudy with a mischievous grin.

"Ah, you hush now," interjected Fred. "You know you'd be taking a cab if you could." As they bumped fists, behind them they heard someone unlocking the door. Once inside, they got the once over from the bank guard who had unlatched the door. "We need to talk to Mr. Samuel Jennings," said John. They were ushered to an office near the back of the bank, where they were led through a large oak door to some chairs arranged in front of an ornate desk covered with papers. As Jennings had yet to make his appearance, they looked around the well-appointed room. It had everything from a library and a bar.

While they waited, John talked about his imminent departure. ""I'll be leaving soon … don't know for sure when … could be any day. And I don't know when I'll be back. So, It'll be up to you two to take care of the business while I'm gone. What we're doing here today will go a long way toward insuring your business has a bright and long future. You just keep on doing what you are doing and you'll be successful."

Just when Fred was going to remind John that the rising prices problem was still unresolved, a door in the side-wall of the room opened and Jennings entered dressed as if he had just come from a meeting with the mayor. He stopped at his desk and glared at them, seemingly taken aback by their appearance. After the passage of a few awkward moments, he picked up a piece of paper at the edge of his desk and read their names from it, then looked up expectantly at them.

"Yes, that's who we are," said Rudy. Jennings' look soured. Ignoring Rudy, he turned directly to John. "I've been informed that you wish to open a checking account."

"Yes *we* do," declared John in a voice just a few decibels below traffic noise. "We're business partners. The account is for our business. I thought my bank's manager—who I understand is the chief executive officer for all branches of this bank—told you who we were and the agenda for our meeting."

Jennings again looked down at the piece of paper and indicated, "Ah, I was told about you, but not about them."

"And what were you not told about my partners?" returned John in a low gravelly voice.

Jennings' eyebrows lifted and his eyes widened. It had dawned on him that he was making a career-threatening mistake. "Yes, I was told about you," he repeated, "and that you had two partners. He also said that I should accommodate your every wish. I'm happy to do that Mr. Williams. Could I see your identification and those of your partners."

All three produced their ids and got approval of them. Jennings now looked a bit haggard, despite his high-class apparel and neatly combed hair. After recovering his composure, he evenly announced that they could pick up their blank checks at the front counter in three days.

Before they got up to leave, John spoke to Jennings as if he were a clerk, "And will each one of us receive prompt and courteous treatment when we come here in the future?"

"Yes sir, Mr. Williams. I will talk to the staff about it today."

As they exited the bank building, John suggested that they go to the scene of the price-fixing problem. Fred and Rudy agreed and they walked the few blocks to the string of stores bordering on the lot containing their newsstand. While Fred and Rudy headed for the newsstand, John proceeded to survey the stores to assess that day's pricing of items also carried in the newsstand. While he was in each store, he asked the proprietors why the cost of soft drinks, candy, newspapers and other items carried by the newsstand were so low. In each case he was told that they were lowering prices on items carried by the newsstand to drive it out of business. More than one of the proprietors added words to the effect of "we don't want that riffraff in our neighborhood." After hearing basically the same explanation at each store, John began to introduce himself as "an Inspector from the New York City Office of Fair Business Practices." He then quickly flashed a badge lent to him by a Hotel Theresa security guard. "This looks like price-fixing to me, which is a city, state *and* federal crime. I'm going to have to report you to the authorities."

The response of the stores' owners was uniform. They begged and pleaded with him not to report them. "Alright," he told them. "I will make an unannounced visit to your business very soon to check on your pricing." He then informed them that they must immediately raise their prices on items also sold at the newsstand to levels well above what Rudy and Fred had charged when they opened their business. He returned to previously visited stores to deliver the same threat.

When John got back to the newsstand, he announced, "Guess what, it's already working. They're now charging more for items you carry than you were charging when you first opened your doors." Rudy and Fred looked relieved, but also puzzled. Fred explained his mystification with, "I thought they would go down to charging nothing for newspapers and such just to get rid of us. Why would they give up?"

John replied, "Well, there are several possible explanations. One is that they were losing enough money to severely cut into their profits. It just wasn't worth continuing the price-lowering scheme. I mentioned earlier that they might give up if we continued to undercut them. Another possibility is that some people in the neighborhood with vested interests—for example, landlords—might have sensed defeat and withdrew their financial support for the price-fixing scheme. In any case, you won. Why don't you take the day off and we'll meet this afternoon at the Savoy to celebrate."

Both Fred and Rudy looked at John with expressions that communicated "not so fast." Fred spoke first. "Alright, maybe I was wrong to think that they would continue until they ran us out of business. But, for them to just give up was not what I expected. They had to know that we were near bankruptcy. Why didn't they just wait until we folded?"

John answered quickly and smoothly. "They never dreamed that you'd come up with enough money to compete with their prices. I think they finally arrived at the conclusion that you would beat them at their own game."

Rudy chimed in with, "Well they probably were amazed to find that we had backing and maybe they bet that we could continue lowering prices for a long time. In fact, we owe all the cash you provided and more. We'll need to tap into that checking account very soon to pay several suppliers. What do we do with any money left after debts are paid?"

"Hang onto it. If there's enough left over, put some of it into a savings account. Remember I'll be gone soon for God knows how long. You may need the money for some other crisis that happens while I'm gone."

Fred and Rudy expressed thanks to John without opening their mouths, but they declined to meet him at the Savoy that afternoon. Fred asked, "How about tonight?" John nodded in the affirmative. Fred and Rudy then headed for the EL. They said they had to visit their suppliers.

John found his cab waiting for him. He asked the cabby to drop him off at Lindy's Restaurant and return for him in about an hour. After selecting a table, he ordered an "everything on it" sandwich and a piece of one of their famous pies. The personnel looked different from those present when he last visited the restaurant. There was no sign of the manager he had intimidated earlier. A man who was in and out of the dinning area seemed to be in charge, so John assumed that the previous manager was not with Lindy's anymore.

After he was returned to the Hotel Theresa he headed for the front desk to send a telegram to Sandra. In it he asked for a last meeting of the Columbia group on May 3. He also hoped that she could meet with him for a few minutes before the meeting so he could indicate what he would cover and find out what she planned to do. Late that afternoon, he received a message from the front desk that there was a telegram for him. He had a bellboy bring it up to him. Sandra agreed to the meeting date and felt certain all would attend, except for Ronald. As this was a serious matter, he came down to the front desk to call Sandra. They spoke for just a few minutes during which Sandra assured him that she would do all she could to persuade Ronald to attend the meeting. But she had seen him around campus and he had the look of a lost soul. Thus, she was not optimistic about getting him to the meeting.

John arrived at the Savoy that evening just as the place was beginning to vibrate. He found Rudy and Fred quickly. The first thing he said to them was "where's Danielle?" They informed him that Danielle had not reported for work that evening. The other girls said she was under the weather.

The three of them brought some beers to a side room where they chatted about sports, music and other matters unrelated to business. After about thirty minutes or so of this small talk, Fred broke a few moments of silence with, "It occurs to me that while we know how to 'talk white'—we have to if we want to do business in this town. But what if we 'talked black' to you? Would you understand?" John seemed baffled, so Fred decided to go about finding the answer to his own question.

"Hey, handkerchief-head," he said addressing Rudy, "I saw you hauling tha other day. You going diddy-wah-diddy to see that frail eel?"

Rudy picked it up with, "Don't be calling me no handkerchief-head, you bull-skating, gator-faced jig. I be getting jelly from your pig meat, liver-lip woman."

Fred returned, "You keep talking about my women and I'm gonna jump salty. Then I find the man and tell him about all that reefer you been selling."

"Look here stormbuzzard, gif up off of me," said Rudy, shifting his eyes toward John. "Why don't you axe this here peckerwood 'bout that pe-ola he's going with."

"Hey Mister Charlie," Fred addressed John, "you need to get u-self some conk buster and try a coal scuttle blonde."

At this point Fred and Rudy were having trouble keeping straight faces and John was laughing out loud. When John regained his composure, he addressed his friends using the talk of his day. "Here now, ace," he addressed Rudy, "You assed out? No, I think you buggin. You got some cheese. Why don't you cop some weed?"

When it was time to part, after John bumped fists with Rudy and Fred, he raised his right arm up and back in a smooth path to just above his ear. At the end of this maneuver he opened his fingers mimicking a Fourth of July skyrocket bursting.

It was a great way to end a momentous day.

CHAPTER 30

Packing Up

On the morning of May 3, 1929, John woke up to a pinging sound that was coming from a shelf in the closet where he had stored his cigar shaped device. He found it and spoke into it's microphone, "Hey, Randy or Joe, what's up?"

"It's Randy," came a voice from the device. "I'm calling to give you a very strong suggestion."

"And what might that be?"

"You should carry this device with you wherever you go. Joe and I have been thinking about it. You could be in danger at any moment. Martha, of course, would be the most likely to face danger so serious that she might have to be extracted on a moment's notice. But who knows what might happen to you. We have recently developed the ability to bring travelers back at the first sign of impending danger without use of the extract button. If you are in danger, just say 'extricate.' The device will pick up your distress call, even if the device is inside an interior pocket of a heavy jacket. In fact, it will pick up any sounds of severe distress and bring you back immediately. This feature is very important. You may suddenly encounter danger and be so

338

engaged in dealing with it that 'extricate' might not come to mind. If you plan to enter dangerous territory, before you go there you can alert whoever is monitoring your activities. One of us will be monitoring your circumstances part of the time. If she or he detects signs that you are about to encounter danger, you will be brought back immediately. If you pin the device into an exterior shirt or jacket pocket so that it's camera lens is exposed, we may be able to see danger approaching before you do. In which case, we'll warn you about it, or if it's imminent we may bring you back immediately. So, whether or not someone is monitoring your activities, if the system detects 'extricate' or serious sounds of distress, you will be extracted immediately. If whoever is monitoring your activities detects danger developing before you do, you will be pulled out."

"Thanks, Randy, and thank Joe for me. I really appreciate your efforts to make my trip safe. I don't expect to encounter serious danger—nothing has happened so far that I would consider serious, but you never know." After he made this remark, John remembered the encounter with the mobsters and thought, "Maybe I have experienced serious dangers ... but I won't worry my friends back in the future."

"You're welcome," Randy replied, "but Sarah and Martha are mostly responsible for these precautions. First, they insisted on the development of safety measures. Also, as you can well imagine, their math and physics backgrounds were vital to helping Joe and I alter the cigar-device software and hardware to make travelers' less vulnerable."

John acknowledged their contributions and added, "I guess Joe was the one to provide the financial backing. I wonder when his fortune will run out. Time traveling is turning out to be expensive."

"Actually, that's not true," Randy replied. "Joe contributed most of the money needed for development of the Brownie Box. But we've patented the Box and the cigar device. Both produced big bucks in advance money from companies that want to produce them. We have received many thousands of dollars so far. But, that will be a pittance compared to the millions we expect to receive when the devices are actually produced. By the way, the versions we've patented are independent of the time machine and can be used to communicate only in the present time. And, in case you're wondering, the move to Washington State will be largely financed by the Computer Science College. They will do anything to get rid of the liability we represent."

After he and Randy had finished their conversation, John retrieved the battered suitcase from the 2010s that he stored in the closet. He wanted it for a trip to the bank after visiting the hotel dinning room. As he ate a plentiful if not healthful breakfast, he thought of what else he had to do before leaving for the future. First on his list was to visit his bank to retrieve all the Apple devices he had brought with him. While there he would inquire about a college scholarship for Danielle. As he knew of no college in New York City that would admit a black student during the late 1920s, he hoped that bank personnel would find one for him. If they found a respected college that would accept Danielle, he would supply up to $12,000 in tuition to be paid out over a four-year period. But, if he was correct and no college would accept a black student, he had an alternative plan. Each college contacted by the bank that declined to accept Danielle would be offered a substantial financial inducement to change its admission policy. The best among those willing to accept the bribe would receive a $3500 inducement upon Danielle's enrollment and full annual tuition payments yearly until she graduated.

He walked to the bank that fine day in early May and immediately went to the room housing the safe-deposit box that contained his devices. He retrieved the key to the room from his pocket. Once inside he opened the safe-deposit box and emptied its contents into the old suitcase that came with him from the future. All the while he was thinking that he must have this suitcase with him during any period when he might need to return to the future. If he had to be extricated under duress, rather than request extraction when in possession of the suitcase, he would be leaving behind secrets that might change the future in unpredictable ways. He had the cigar device with him that day, and planned to always have it with him thereafter. However, he could not leave without the devices. He would have to avoid any circumstance that might lead to an extrication he could not control. That meant, don't take chances; stay out of harms way.

After meeting with the bank officials about the scholarship for Danielle, and finding that they were mildly optimistic about the odds of getting Danielle into a respected college, John setup the transfer of monies to finance the scholarship. Any respected college that would accept Danielle would be paid in four digits immediately. During their discussions, bank officials heavily implied that many pictures of Benjamin Franklin would be more than sufficient to talk college officials into seriously bending their already elastic enrollment rules. John provided bank officials with Danielle's contact phone number at the Savoy. Although he felt that Danielle was likely to suspect he had provided the money, he asked that his name not be disclosed.

All in all, the meeting went well, except for one hitch. When John announced that Danielle could be contacted through the Savoy, one of the bank officials blurted out, "Ah, she must be mostly white." When John gave the guy a hard look, the Vice President who was running the meeting glared at him and pointed to the door. Head down, the offender hustled out of the room.

When he arrived at Main Hall for the meeting with the Columbia grad-students, Sandra was waiting for him outside the building. They sat down on the bench where they initially discussed how to conduct the meetings. John wasted no time raising a crucial question about the day's meeting. "This is the last meeting for probably several months, if not the last one Andrew, Herb, and Ronald will agree to attend. That assumes you might want to have additional meetings beginning at some point in the not too distant future. So, we need to end on a positive note. Got any suggestions about how to do that?"

"Oh, I'd be very willing to have additional meetings," said Sandra, "but I have no idea about the plans and obligations of other group members. We'll worry about that later. For now, let me suggest that we ask each of the other members what he got out of the meetings. At some point, I would also give my take on the meetings. Then you could talk about what the meetings meant to you."

"Good idea," John replied. "And there is one other thing. I have an additional matter to consider. It's about a future development in physics. I'll need only a few minutes to present it and discussion shouldn't take long. You want me to make that presentation first, or at the end of the meeting?"

Sandra thought for a moment, and then answered, "Why don't you do that at the beginning of the meeting. We should end on a lighter note."

Everyone arrived on time and in good spirits. That included Ronald, though he did look a bit bedraggled. His clothing was rumpled and his hair uncombed, but his face was very different. On other occasions his facial muscles were so tight that he looked like he was constantly suppressing a fit of anger. But that day his face was totally relaxed. He resembled a practitioner of Zen Buddhism under the spell of meditation.

After everyone was settled in, Sandra announced that they would begin with one last presentation by John. Then there would be an opportunity to consider what the meetings meant to each of them.

John stood up and walked to the head of the table. He paused for a moment to reflect on what he had prepared to say. After reassuring himself, he began speaking in a confident tone. "Let's play what-if in a way that might allow us to anticipate the future discovery of how fundamental particles gain mass. Suppose that it will become possible to accelerate two beams of protons traveling toward one another at very near the speed of light. When the beams collide"—John stopped for a moment to slam his two fists together in front of his chest; he briefly flinched with pain but continued without missing a syllable—"a new kind of field is created. This field causes remnants of the collision to react like balls rolling on a surface covered with molasses. They slow down signifying that they have gained mass. Thus, this as yet undiscovered field would explain how particles gain mass."

Pleased with his performance, John glanced around the room expecting to see some "ah ha" looks. Instead, he observed looks of rather complete consternation. No one said anything for several moments. Then Andrew spoke up. "I'm sorry, but I don't understand what you are talking about." Herb gestured to indicate that he felt the same way. John's face sagged. He had debated with himself about using notions such as Higgs boson and Higgs field, but the words would have had no meaning for any of them. Had he been trained in physics maybe he could have communicated better about these extraordinary notions from the distant future. But, he wondered whether anyone could have successfully communicated these future developments to people who did not have the terminology, much less the concepts, to understand.

Andrew saw John dismay and tried to comfort him. "If I could conceive of how to accelerate protons to near the speed of light—Einstein's writings imply that nothing could approach such a speed—I might be able to grasp the ideas you are trying to convey. But I cannot. I'm sorry, it's beyond me." Herb again silently indicated that he was also unable to understand what John was trying to convey. Glances at Sandra and Ronald revealed that neither of them were getting his point, though the latter was smiling pleasantly. Not knowing what else to do, John simply announced, "Just remember the little scenario I presented today. I think that some day it will be meaningful to you."

As John sunk down into his chair, both his posture and face reflected his disconsolate state. But he noted that no one seemed upset with him. In fact, all seemed to be in a very good humor. Perhaps they didn't fault him for kicking off their final meeting with an indecipherable presentation. Now if he could just stop blaming himself….

Sandra began reflecting on the entire series of meetings by revealing that, initially, she was skeptical about whether getting together with people from different disciplines to talk about science would enlighten any of them. But prior to this last meeting, she had taken some time to think about what the meetings had meant to her. "I not only gained new knowledge about psychology which may cause me to do some rewriting of my dissertation. I also have come to appreciate what a mind-opening experience it is to learn how people from other scientific disciplines approach studying and understanding issues in their sciences. It now occurs to me that the sciences will cross-pollinate in the future such that there will be no clear boundary between one scientific discipline and another. The first human-like robot—one that can walk, talk and reason like a human—will be a joint product of brain research and electrical engineering, encompassing the fields of psychology, biology, physics and mathematics. I'm betting it will be produced before the year 2020. Finally, accomplishing all of these extraordinary connections between scientific disciplines will be facilitated by a progressive increase in people's intelligence as measured by the Stanford-Binet Intelligence Test. In sum, it seems to me that the curve representing scientific progress in the future will reflect exponential growth."

Following a time lapse of several moments, during which John felt like clapping, Sandra eased into her chair looking like a typical presenter at the AAAS convention: totally comfortable with what they had communicated. Before calling on someone else, she spent a few more moments enjoying the looks of admiration focused on her. Then she turned to Andrew and asked, "What did you get out of the meetings?"

"I got a sense of humility. If you read the Times everyday and the journals in your scientific area, you will get the feeling that we are in the golden age of science. Written between the lines is the assumption that most of what science can discover has been discovered. There will be changes and refinements in the future, but the basic course of science has been set. It is tacitly assumed that scientists of the future will view today's scientists as the initiators of their disciplines who laid the foundations for all of tomorrow's discoveries. While there is some truth to these presumptions, consistent with Sandra's view of scientific progress in the future, it occurs to me that the most extraordinary advances will develop at an increasing rate during the rest of this century. Let me speak in terms of the practical applications that science will produce in the ensuing years. The day will come when giant computing machines will be able to make complicated calculations resulting in, for example, morning predictions of five o'clock traffic jams in large cities and accurate projections of local and national precipitation and temperature levels weeks in advance. In fact, I'll bet that before the turn of the next century, computing machine components will be so reduced in size and weight that individuals will possess personal computing machines small enough to carry around."

At this point, Herb broke in with, "Next you will be telling us that a manned space ship will land on the moon by the year 2000." Much to Herb's embarrassment the response to his outburst was astonishment followed by hearty laughter. In an attempt to rescue his friend, Andrew announced, "Man will go to the moon someday, but probably not by the year 2000."

"I predict a cure for cancer by 2010," announced Sandra. Not to be outdone, Andrew proffered, "I predict an end of heart disease by 1999." These fanciful predictions relieved Herb's discomfort and inspired him to declare, "A vaccine to prevent polio will be available by 1969."

After a pause during which congratulations for venturesome predictions were passed around, Sandra asked Herb to tell them what he had gotten from the meetings.

Herb straightened up in his chair, cleared his throat, and began to talk in an unusually assertive tone. "These meeting have made me rethink the role of my discipline in the future. Math has been viewed as something for the few who love it for it's own sake. That would include me. It also is viewed as an essential tool in the hands of engineers, physicists and chemists, but of little help in understanding the phenomena of other sciences. However, for most people it has been a bitter pill to swallow during school years and something to avoid thereafter. But, I predict that this view of mathematics will fade in the future. It will become clear that nations whose children are taught to love mathematics early in life will become the most successful in the realms of economics and industry. In the process of this change, it will become clear that mathematics has a role to play in all of the sciences. As Sandra implies, it will be important to progress in psychology. To extrapolate, at some point in the future, mathematics will permeate the enterprises of the most successful nations and the methods of the most productive sciences. And finally, by end of the first quarter of the next century, mathematics will allow solutions to such conundrums as traveling in time and contacting intelligent creatures living at the far corners of our universe."

By the end of Herb's reflections on the future, two things were clear: whoever came next would have a hard act to follow, and one of those people was Ronald. It didn't take Sandra long to come up with a way to put off the inevitable. She stood up and announced in too loud a voice, "John, you have yet to say what you got out of these meetings."

Reluctantly, John rose to address what he had looked forward to hearing others consider, but was ill prepared to speak about himself. He could go on for an hour or so, but knew that would kill the good spirits that pervaded the room. Or, he could be very brief, but that might fail to properly show how much these meetings meant to him. After keeping his friends waiting for an embarrassing minute or two while he fumbled with his drink, took off his sweater and straightened his clothes, he began dramatically. "Enlightenment ... that's what these meetings have meant to me. Listening to you and talking with you has enriched my life. I could go on, but I won't. Let me just say that knowing all of you, and learning from you, has convinced me that the future of science is in very good hands indeed. Soon, I must leave New York City and I don't know when I'll be back. I will miss you and look forward to seeing you again."

As John sat down, he realized that he was tearing up, which made it hard to see how the others were reacting to him. But it didn't take him long to find out. As they left their chairs and approached him, he got up to exchange the handshakes and hugs with them. Ronald patiently waited for his turn to embrace John.

Ronald remained standing when the others returned to their seats. When they looked back at him, they were instantly relieved. He appeared to be in a state of serenity.

He began to speak in a low tone. "What did I get out of these meetings? I can put it simply. I must anticipate the next peak of the ever-accelerating change curve. I must keep my mind wide open. That is all I need to know to get started on the path I want to take, rather than the one others have mapped out for me."

The usual post-meeting conference between John and Sandra was most unusual. It would be the last time they would talk for a long time, if ever. John began by crediting Sandra for the success of the Columbia grad-student gatherings. She returned the favor by reminding him that the meetings had been his idea. Amid some good-natured laughter, they both acknowledged that their great teamwork deserved the most credit for the success of the meetings.

Before they parted, John asked about Sandra's relationship with Hazel. "Oh, we're doing fine," mused Sandra. "The problem is that I will be finishing my dissertation in the not too distant future and will be taking a job God knows where. She might not want to go with me, and frankly, I'm not sure I want her to accompany me. She's a party girl and New York City is a party Mecca. I can settle into a small college town. She probably could not. What about you and Danielle?"

"Being unsure about whether I'll ever return to New York City, I've tried to provide for her while I'm gone in a way that may make a different person of her. Should I return, she may not want our relationship to continue. But if and when I do return, I'll try to look you up."

That seemed to be his parting shot. After a short pause, they stood up to say good-by. Before that could happen, John suddenly recalled a final question he wanted to ask Sandra. "Just one more thing. I'm very intrigued by your prediction that intelligence will increase progressively in the future. What's your reasoning behind it?"

"Oh, it's nothing profoundly complex or deeply philosophical. Ballooning advances in the sciences requires that people get smarter over time. Actually, it's mutually causal. Increases in intelligence promote advances in the sciences, and, in turn, advances in the sciences generate increases in intelligence."

They clasped hands and each acknowledged that the other would be profoundly missed.

CHAPTER 31

Going Home

On the morning of May 7, 1929, John's first thoughts upon getting out of bed were talking business with Fred and Rudy and facing up to saying goodbye to Danielle.

After breakfast, he hailed a cab to the original newsstand so he could check in with Fred and bid him farewell. When the cab pulled up near the stand, John asked the cabbie to wait for him. "That's fine with me," said the cabbie, "but the meter is running."

When he approached the newsstand, Fred was busy with one customer and had two others waiting their turn. It looked like business was good. A few minutes later, Fred was able to talk. "You checking on me?" asked Fred in a tone dripping with mock irritation.

"No just wanted to take one last look at your first stand and be assured that everything was going well."

"Yeah," Fred responded. "Business has been good and there has been no sign of trouble ... but let me back off the last thing. I don't think that there is any trouble around the corner, but I did hear a rumor from a customer. He's somebody I've known for a long time. Comes by now and again to spread rumors. Hardly any of them have had a grain of truth to them, but I thought I'd tell ya anyway. This man heard rumors about our fight with the hoodlums and knows that you're in business with Rudy and me. According to him, there's a rumor going around that George 'Hump' McManus is looking for you. It's about you dropping his name to scare people. McManus doesn't like people using him in any way without paying him. Rumor is that if he finds you, he's gonna ruff you up."

John put on a blank face as a part of an attempt to look unconcerned, but he was troubled by this new threat just before his return to the future. "You say this guy is just a blowhard who's not to be taken seriously?"

Fred replied, "I don't take him seriously. Hardly anyone does. But I thought you should know."

"Well, I appreciate that. Thanks for telling me about it. So, how's the business doing?" remarked John with no more trepidation than one would show when discussing the likelihood of rain.

"I'm getting customers who return nearly everyday to buy the same two or three items. I could call some of them friends, because we talk about this and that while I'm fetching their favorite merchandise."

"Would you say that the business is picking up over time?"

"Yes, I would," replied Fred. "When I'm tallying up one week I can pretty much remember how we did the previous week. It tends to be a little more each passing week."

After several minutes of chatting amiably John announced that he had to go because his cab was waiting. "Will I see you tonight at the Savory?"

"Sure thing," Fred replied. "You going to be telling us goodbye?"

"Yes I will," said John. "Will Rudy be there as well?"

Fred answered, "I'll make sure of it."

Back in the cab, John gave the cabbie the West Bronx address of their other newsstand. When they approached the Bronx, John noticed some distant smoke stacks spewing out all manner of dark and ominous waste. He wondered whether people were worried about air pollution.

"Look at all that thick, black smoke," said John loud enough for the cabby to hear.

"Uh huh," returned the cabbie in an indifferent voice.

"Aren't people worried about all the health problems the smoke could cause?"

"No, it's been around for a long time, ever since my grandfather was a boy. It didn't hurt him and it hasn't hurt me."

"Well, what about other kinds of problems. It might cause weather problems, you know, like making it hotter or colder or wetter or dryer or more stormy?"

There were a few moments of silence during which John could almost hear the cabbie thinking, "Why did I have to get stuck with this guy?"

"Uh," mumbled the cabbie, "nobody has noticed any weather problems. If there were some, my grandfather would have told me … people would be talking about it."

Because John and the cabbie could think of nothing more to say about the ugly smoke, it was a matter of good fortune that they suddenly arrived at the Bronx newsstand. John tipped the cabbie and wished him good day. He would find another cab to take him back to the Hotel Theresa.

Upon arriving at the Bronx newsstand, John saw that Rudy was engaged with several customers. He waited patiently until the last of a half dozen customers had been served. "I needn't ask whether business is good. Obviously, it is."

"Sho'nuff," answered Rudy. "It's getting rare that I can sit down and take a rest. What's on your mind, brother John?"

"Just dropping by to see how you and the new newsstand are getting along."

"Well, I toll ya how business is and you can see from the look on my handsome face that I'm doing great."

They chatted for a while about specifics regarding the business: taxes owed, increases in the cost of merchandise, and elevation in their profit margin. When a number of customers approached the stand, John announced that he was going to take a walk around the local neighborhood and would drop back by the stand in thirty minutes or so.

He didn't go far before encountering a change in the surroundings. The neatly maintained residential areas near the newsstand morphed into dilapidated buildings, many of which were being torn down. The fence strung out along the sidewalk ahead of him was covered with graffiti, most of it sexually suggestive. In the distance he could see three men coming toward him. As they approached, he noticed that two of them were in front of the other one. The reason for this alignment soon became apparent: the three men were too broad and bulky to walk shoulder to shoulder. These three brutes, all dressed in suits and fedoras, walked like they were on a serious mission. Before he could say anything, Randy's voice came over the cigar device. "These guys look like they're after you. I can bring you back in an instance!"

"Wait a minute; give me a chance to look around for a way to deal with this situation," John responded in a strained voice. He could see that these guys would be too much for him to handle. Given they were not armed, he might handle two of them, but certainly not all three. Glancing across the street he noticed a construction site that was surrounded by an eight-foot fence with barbed wire at the top. A heavy metal gate secured by a lock and chain was only about 100 yards ahead of him. He thought that he could get to it and leap up to its top, which was about the height of a basketball rim. With his fingers grasping the top of the gate, he could see himself catapulting over it. He was confident that the heavyweights headed toward him would never be able to reach the top of the gate, at least not without helping each other over, one at a time. Before even one of them got over, he'd be long gone. "Ok, I've got this, Randy. I'll cross to the other side of the street. If they follow me, I think I can escape over a gate that is too tall for them. Don't bring me back unless I ask you to."

"That's crazy!" yelled Randy. "Why don't you just let me bring you back?"

"No, don't do that. I have more business here. Wait for my request."

John walked slowly across the street as he watched the approaching men out of the corner of his eye. They never looked at him as they marched past the point were he had been walking. With a heavy sigh of relief, he informed Randy that he was safe. He also told Randy that he would soon be coming back to see the old gang at the Lion's Den. By that night, he would likely notify whoever was monitoring him about when he wanted to be extracted.

He and Randy chatted for a few minutes before John found an opening to say, "see you soon." "I look forward to it," Randy responded, "but there's something else I need to tell you. We are showing too much traffic in and out of the time machine rooms, so we are going to bring travelers back to he present at the edge of the forest above the grassy knoll … you know, the rat retrieval area."

After a moment's thought, John responded, "That's fine with me. It's not far from where I left my car." Because no one had been able to find John's car, Randy started to ask, "Where is that?" but he thought better of it.

John made his way back to the Bronx newsstand before closing time. He checked in with Rudy to be absolutely sure that he would be at the Savoy that night. Rudy asked, "You buying?"

"Sure," returned John. "It'll be my last night there before I leave, so it's on me."

That evening, he showed up a little earlier than usual at the Savoy. Danielle had just arrived, but couldn't talk because she was waiting to check in with her bosses. Rudy and Fred had not yet arrived, so he purchased a beer and brought it to one of the side rooms. He settled into a chair, leaned back and began to plan his trip back to his buddies in the future. Earlier he had concluded that he'd just get up the next morning, get the suitcase with all of the devices in it out of the closet, and, holding onto it with both hands, tell whoever was on duty, "Bring me back." But, upon further thought, it occurred to him that it would cool to leave from the same spot upon which he arrived, near the Harlem Meer in Central Park. "That's it!" he exclaimed out loud.

"That's what?" asked Fred from the door of the room.

"Oh, nothing. I'm just talking to myself," answered John.

Fred looked a little dubious, but he said only, "Where's my beer. Rudy said you are buying." John held up both hands like someone who was being mugged. Quickly he got up and headed toward the bar to fetch enough beers for the first round.

When Rudy arrived, they talked only briefly about sports and such. Mostly Fred and Rudy tried to communicate how much they appreciated John's help and support for their business without sounding like he, rather than they, was responsible for the success of their enterprise. John understood where they were coming from and reminded them of what he had said many times before: their good ideas and hard work was what really made the business a success. Rudy and Fred talked some more about their hopes and plans for the future with John hanging on every word. After some lighter talk, John excused himself, saying he had to talk to Danielle, "But I'll be back in a few minutes to say goodbye."

Danielle was dancing with a Savoy customer, so John took a chair nearby to wait until he could talk to her. He had warned her repeatedly that he would soon be leaving for an unknown period of time. When they were able to retreat to a side room for a few minutes, he asked if he could spend the night with her. Tears began to form at the corners of her eyes. She bit her lip and began shaking her head from side to side. "He whispered, I'll be back … I promise."

When he returned to Rudy and Fred, John started a light-hearted conservation that ranged from trying the latest "hip-talk" on each other to whether John was really black. In the context of the latter, Rudy said, "You know, I could take you if I wanted to."

"Yeah," said John in low growl, "how about here and now." They began to wrestle around the room as Fred acted like a referee. Soon they were laughing too hard to continue. Fred declared it a draw. They ended with all the hand shakes and moves in their hipster repertoires, plus some they contrived for the occasion. Hugs goodbye generated sad faces.

John met Danielle at the main entrance of the Savoy and they walked leisurely toward her apartment. Passersby might have thought they were a young couple on a first date. But, if they had looked closer, they would have seen two broken-hearted lovers. Tears were welling up in their eyes. He could have been a soldier going off to war and she his girlfriend, left behind never to know if and when he would return.

By the time they entered Danielle's apartment, their tears had dried and they were thinking only of the moment. They sat down and talked for a time, trying to recall every occasion they had shared together. John reminisced about how stunned he was when he first saw her from across the ballroom floor. She recalled how hard she had worked not to give him any hope. They remembered their arguments over marriage. John proposed once more, but Danielle could find no words to give him an answer. Instead she responded by bursting into tears again.

To escape the sadness, they began to hug and kiss lightly. Soon they were eying the bed. "Wait a minute, I have to shower first," whispered Danielle. Then she smiled as a mischievous thought came to mind. "Let's shower together."

John grinned fiendishly, but remarked, "How could we do that? The shower is a very small cubicle way down the hall."

"Nobody will hear us at this time of the night," she whispered. "Let's do it." She went behind the folding partition and emerged in a bathrobe. She threw him a towel and exclaimed, "This will have to do for you."

John practically raced to the partition where he ripped off his clothes and stepped out with the towel bound around his waist. They crept out the door and down the hall to the shower. Once inside, they threw the robe and towel out, pulled the curtain shut and turned on the hot water … which came out very cold. Muffled cries got them through the slow transition from cold to hot water. They held each other tightly as they responded to the cold with gasping and choking. Soon their small space was thick with steam. They adjusted the temperature of the water as they gently began to wash each other. They would have stayed there indefinitely had the hot water not run out.

They snuck back to Danielle's apartment, she in her robe, he in his towel, both still wet. Once inside, they finished drying off with fresh towels. He ended up on one side of the room and she on the other. As they looked at each other like two children who slipped out of an upstairs window and down a tree trunk to roam about at night, Danielle was suddenly struck by a strong recollection. Right in the middle of John's comment about how fetching she was, her eyes opened wide and she threw up her hands. Then she raced over to her dresser and got something out of a drawer. Triumphantly she turned and held up a condom. John's reaction was to run over to his trousers and rummage through one of its pockets. He too retrieved a condom. They laughed so loud there was a danger they would awaken the other tenants. Quickly they shushed each other. With index fingers on their lips, they got into bed. That night they cuddled, they laughed, they cried and they made love. They melded together just before they would separate indefinitely.

John woke up early the next morning even before the deliveryman upstairs performed his sunrise cacophony that functioned as Danielle's alarm clock. He rushed to get ready and exit the apartment before she awakened. He wanted to avoid a second goodbye that might diminish the magnificent one they had experienced the night before. Having hastily thrown on his clothes, John slipped out the apartment door and took up a position in the hallway that would allow him to easily intercept the deliveryman. When the man appeared he instantly recognized John and was more than happy to offer him a ride to where he could catch a cab.

Minutes after John was dropped off on a corner where cabs frequently pass, he was on his way to the Hotel Theresa. Inside the hotel, he headed for the front desk where he settled his bill. Before leaving, he reminded the Assistant Manager who waited on him that he would be back and wanted the same corner room upon his return. The young man promised that he would do all he could to see that the room was available for John.

Back in his room, John immediately retrieved the cigar device from his front pocket and called out to whoever was in the time travel room at the time. Joe answered and immediately announced that he was back from his trip to the future. When John asked for a brief description of Joe's trip, he was put off with a promise of a detailed narrative upon John's return. "I'll get everybody together and give all of you an in-depth description of what I encountered." He went on to say, "Of course, my trip won't compare with yours in terms of meaningful events, but I'll do my best." To change the subject, Joe announced that he had finished his dissertation and would graduate at the end of the fall semester. In the meantime, he had gotten a position at a "pretty good little university" within easy driving distance from the new Washington state location of the time travel machine. When he finished with all he was willing to say about himself, Joe paused to signal that John could now give the reason for his call.

"I would like to return to you and the rest of my buddies right away. … Actually, I'd like to launch back to the future tomorrow morning, May 9, 1929 at about 7:30 AM." John stopped to clear his throat and see how Joe reacted to what may have seemed to be a rather brash demand.

"No problem," Joe replied. "We had hoped you would be back soon."

"I plan to leave from almost the exact place where I landed upon coming to New York City in 1928: near the Harlem Meer in Central Park. I assume that you still have the coordinates Martha supplied."

With considerable relish, Joe replied, "Oh, we don't need those coordinates. The cigar device will allow us to locate you with great precision no matter where you are."

John mumbled "opps" to himself. Joe had scored one on him. But that was all right. He could tell from just listening to Joe that their relationship was still good relative to its status when they were vying to be the first time traveler. Before the communication ended, Joe promised he would carry out all of John's wishes regarding time and place of the launch back to the forest above the grassy knoll.

John arose at 5:30 AM the next morning and dressed in his best clothes from the late 1920s. Carrying the old suitcase, John arrived at the hotel dinning room at 6:00 AM and ordered a light breakfast. By 6:30 AM, he left the dinning room, bid the hotel personnel goodbye and caught a cab to the Harlem Meer area of Central Park.

Once inside the Park, he located the spot where he had landed on October 17, 1928, stood straight up with both hands grasping the suitcase handle and asked to be launched. Randy answered and, to make a game of it, began to count down from 10. "10, 9, 8, 7, 6, 5, 4, 3, 2, 1 …" The last thing John heard was, "Hey, mister. Can you spare a dime?"

Immediately he was standing at the edge of the forest above the grassy knoll on the periphery of his university's campus. Down below, he could see two students in sleeping bags sitting up staring at him. Both looked baffled. One of them said, "I swear there was nobody there, then 'zap!' there he was."

The other one responded, "I told you that you drank too much last night."

CHAPTER 32

Hail, Hail, The Gang's All Here

John peered down at the two students for a minute or so, then turned abruptly and entered the woods. He knew a trail that would get him out of the forest at a point near the dead-end street where he had parked his car. Ten minutes later he was feeling around in the front wheel well for a key-box that was magnetically attached to car's superstructure. Quickly he was inside the car pushing the key into the ignition. The first attempt to start the vehicle generated only some low groans from the engine. Several attempts later the engine coughed to a reluctant start. John said to himself, "Good thing I put a new battery in just before being launched."

John parked behind his apartment and entered the back door using a key he had left under a floor mat. Inside he found his long abandoned habitat covered with spider webs and brown dust. After locking the suitcase in a closet, he inspected himself in a full-length mirror. There, behold, stood a very cool dude from the roaring twenties. He didn't even think about changing clothes. After he retrieved his phone, which had been attached to a charger all the months he was gone, he dialed Joe's number. A few minutes later, Joe still hadn't picked up so he tried Sarah. She must have recognized John's number because she picked up immediately. "How in the world are you?" she exclaimed in a delightful tone.

They talked for several minutes. During a brief pause, he was about to suggest a get-together at the Lion's Den. Beating him to it, Sarah announced that she would abandon proof reading her dissertation in favor of calling the others to a 4 PM meeting at their favorite watering hole.

As four o'clock approached, John debated with himself about whether he should show up a little early or a little late. Finally he decided on showing up a little late, after most if not all of his friends would be there, but early enough to avoid being accused of making a grand entrance.

When John arrived inside the Lion's Den dressed in his late 1920's Hep-Cat clothes, be was able to make out the frames of Joe, Martha, and Sarah in a dimly lite corner of the establishment. When they saw him, they yelled his name in unison. Martha immediately shed her chair and run wildly toward him. When she intercepted him, she flung her arms around his neck and rasped, "I've missed you so." They held each other tight for at least a couple of minutes. When he loosened his grip she continued to hang onto him for an embarrassing few moments. After letting go and stepping back, she thought, "Is there something wrong?" His warm smile answered her question in the negative, but still she wondered. Sensing her discomfort, he took her hand and they walked back to where Sarah and Joe were waiting.

Sarah greeted him first with warm words and a hug. Joe shook his hand in a way that confirmed their friendship. Before he could sit down, they demanded that he strut about in his outfit so they could get the full effect of it. "And I thought today's clothes were loud and over the top." Sarah remarked.

"Dude," exclaimed Joe, "you're so flashy I need sun glasses."

Just after they had settled into their seats, Randy showed up. John pushed his chair back, scanned Randy up and down and declared, "Why did you rip-off Randy's face and what did you do with his body?" Randy laughed hardily and gave John a hug.

After his friends had caught John up with what was going on in their lives while he was gone, they wanted to know about his trip. They began with questions about what it was like to travel in time. Sarah asked, "What did it feel like while you were traveling? Were you conscious of streaking through the stratosphere?"

John looked a bit puzzled. "Why didn't you ask Martha and Joe?"

"I did," returned Sarah, "but I didn't like their answers."

"Well, you will probably be disappointed with my answer. I didn't feel anything. The trip was instantaneous and devoid of sensations."

"Yeah, that's what Joe and Martha said. Very disappointing. I thought it would be some kind of existential experience."

"Well, you all learned a lot about my trip from Joe and Randy," John changed the subject, "But I know nothing about Joe's and Martha's trip. Why don't you fill me in.?"

Joe responded, "We really don't have the details about what you did and accomplished on your trip, John. Maybe you could at least answer some questions."

"Ok, ask," said John.

All hands went up, so John had his choice of who to call on. He pointed to Sarah.

"Who was the young woman we saw you with in the park?"

That was the question John most wanted to avoid. He thought about responding with "Next question," but decided that would constitute a bad start. "She's someone I meet at the Savoy, along with some other people."

"Is that all you are willing to tell us?" asked Randy.

"Well, there's not much to tell, but I know what you're after. Yes we did date for a while. But it didn't work out. We both knew that, so we ended it."

"Who else did you meet at the Savoy?" asked Sarah.

"A couple of guys named Rudy and Fred. We became friends and I actually helped them open a couple of newsstands. Their businesses were thriving when I left."

"Black guys?" queried Joe.

"Yes."

"What's life like for black people back in that time?" asked Randy.

"I'd need hours to tell you about that. I'll be writing a sort of free association about the trip. That's where I'll say more about your question."

"How did the meetings with grad-students at Columbia University go?" inquired Martha in a voice devoid of emotion.

"Well, let me see," John replied. From there he went on to talk about each of the Columbia students with emphasis on Sandra and Ronald. He described Sandra's efforts to start the group and keep it going smoothly and how she and he handled Ronald. Herb and Andrew were described more straightforwardly. He told them about Sandra's relationship with Hazel and that Ronald was recovering from a psychotic break. "Because what we discussed in the group was so intricate that it requires detailed consideration, I'll leave it for my written commentary. For now I can say that the hints about future developments in science were successfully conveyed. Of course, I'll spend considerable space writing about those hints. For now, why don't we let Martha and Joe tell us about their time travel experiences?"

"Well," Joe responded. "We've already heard about Martha's trip. It doesn't take long to describe it. Martha, you want me to repeat what you told us, or do you want to do it?"

Martha held up both hands, shoulder high, palms showing and fingers spread. It was her way to say that Joe should do it. "Well, she got back to the time of the Black Pharaohs without a hitch. So there she was, striding gloriously across the desert wearing her carefully researched version of apparel, fit for an Egyptian Princess. We were monitoring her using the cigar device. There were some small pyramids off to her right and nothing but sand everywhere else. Suddenly Randy detected some activity on the horizon. It looked like something moving amid a swirl of sand. As it got closer, Martha could make out that it was several men marching in formation toward her. As they got closer, she and Randy could see that each held a spear in launching position over his right shoulder, as was the tradition of ancient foot soldiers. When it dawned on Martha they were heading straight toward her, she shrieked, 'Eeeeeka! We took that to be a reasonable substitute for 'extricate' and brought her back."

Joe grinned mischievously, but Sarah and Randy failed to suppress some derisive laughter. Martha, who apparently had witnessed this snide reaction to her trip several times before, showed no reaction.

Wishing to save Martha from more teasing, John asked, "How about your trip, Joe?"

Joe reacted with a shoulder shrug and an announcement: "My trip can be counted in days, rather than a few minutes. I don't want to sell it short, so I'll began describing it today and finish up later if need be."

"I decided to visit Chicago ten years into the future. I wanted to be delivered to a location on the campus of the University of Chicago so I could hook up with some students there and sample life ten years from now. I landed at 6:30 AM, during early April, in an isolated area of the campus. No one was around, so I just waited until the students began to show up. A few passersby did notice me, probably because my dress was quaint, but none slowed down to talk with me. Finally, I just followed one of them to a campus dinning room. I got in line with the students and filled up a tray. When I got to the checkout, the cashier hesitated for a minute expecting I'd give her something. I reached for my wallet and pulled out some money—all of it, of course, was ten or more years old—I hoped nobody would notice. When I tried to hand her the bills the cashier looked puzzled. While I was thinking about what to do, a student behind me stepped up and said "He's not a student … he's my guest on campus." She showed her id and asked that I be granted a free meal, which, I found out from her later, was customary for guests of students."

"I sat down with her—her name was … is Joyce—and we talked for a time. I asked where I could find some students who might want to chat about computer technology and other current topics. She said that there was a sort of "free speech" area on campus where one could find people discussing various topics, usually beginning around 5:30 on weekdays during the spring.

"After thanking Joyce, I got a cab to the Palmer House. The next morning, I called a local bank where my family would likely still have money on deposit and asked for a credit card. They took my identification information and said they would send a packet to my hotel by noon of the next day. The next morning, I roamed the Magnificent Mile for several hours, looking for new clothes. It was interesting. I brought a few items in an upscale haberdashery and looked around for someone to wait on me. There were very few employees in the store. A couple of them glanced at me from a distance, but then turned away. Finally, I cornered one and asked to pay for the clothes I selected. They gave me this Goofy look. One said, 'Just use the one of the credit checkout stations. There is one in every department.' I said that I didn't have a credit card. Again I got the dumbfounded look. 'There are no credit cards anymore. Just enter your credit information.' I wondered what the bank would be sending to my Hotel. At this point, I pulled out cash, which made them turn surly. 'We don't do change. We don't accept coins and we have few one dollar bills available.' I said I didn't care and handed one of them more than enough money to pay for the clothes. He sulked off to a nearby office. When he returned, the money he dumped into my palm was less than I should have received based on the posted prices. When I did get the credit packet the next day there was only detailed information about how to use various kinds of credit stations.

About 5:00 PM I caught a cab to the University of Chicago. Sure enough, by 5:30 there were a number of people gathering at the unofficial 'free speech' area. I walked around listening for a conversation among some tech people. Finally, I overheard five people arguing vociferously about the future of computers. I sidled up to them and listened for a few minutes. Eventually they began to look back at me like "Who the hell are you?" While I had their attention, I asked, "Has there been progress on the Universal Quantum Computer?" Now they looked at me like I was from Mars.

'Nobody ever talks about that anymore. Every ten years there have been predictions that it will happen in ten years. It's not happening. It's too expensive and too complicated to manage efficiently.'

That was embarrassing, but I pressed on. 'How about Quantum Key Distribution?' Again they looked at me like I was a lunatic.

'That's becoming a method of choice. It's up and running, although there are problems, such as replacing present network wiring with optical fibers. Where have you been? Everybody knows about this stuff."

Well that took me by surprise. I hadn't thought about being totally unable to anticipate happenings only ten years into the future. I thought quickly and came up with 'I've been in Tanzania doing missionary work.' When I saw a whole bunch of furrowed brows, I continued with '…for ten years.'"

Joe's audience broke up laughing.

Sarah recovered more quickly than the others and asked, "Did they buy the missionary story?"

"You know, I could see that they were believing me, but I was afraid that they'd ask me about Tanzania. I knew hardly anything about that East African country. Fortunately, they didn't press me for more information. Maybe they didn't want to hear about missionary work or were afraid I'd try to recruit them to go on a mission to some God-forsaken corner of the world. I made a mental note to buy a book on Tanzania."

"At that point they accepted me at my word and they began viewing me as someone to educate. The next time I came to meet with them, Joyce was there. She said that she had been looking for me and didn't know where else to find me. We chatted while waiting for others to arrive. Right in the middle of our conversation, she pulled out a joint and began to light it up. She must have misinterpreted the bewildered look on my face, because she pulled out another joint and handed it to me, along with a book of matches. I asked, 'Is it alright to smoke marijuana here?' She answered that it was legal almost everywhere in the USA."

"We talked about trivia as we blew smoke into each other's faces. Finally, I signaled that I wanted to consider some more substantive issues. I asked her how her classes were going. She drew back her head and answered with a question. 'What classes? Universities don't have classes. Sometimes we meet with graduate assistants assigned to professors in charge of our courses, but we don't see our professors, except maybe on the first day of class. Why don't you know that?'"

"Of course, I immediately told her my missionary tale. For a moment I thought she was going to get up and leave, but she stayed put and began to lecture me about how universities and colleges were run a decade into the future.

'As is true here, the relatively few tenured faculty members are primarily researchers. Each also oversees a few courses. Neither professors nor anyone else lectures anymore. Classes are managed by graduate students and part time faculty who periodically meet with undergraduates to answer questions about course material presented online. Some of what is available to students includes short videos of off-the-cuff talks by famous professors, not formal lectures. But most of the information that students encounter is graphic with brief accompanying text.'

"At this point I broke in and asked, 'What about textbooks?'"

"She responded curtly, 'You must have been totally out of contact with the rest of the world when you were doing missionary work.' I shrugged my shoulders in a way that communicated an affirmative answer to her implied question and she continued to inform me about what she apparently assumed should have always been the case. 'Not many years ago, textbook costs were close to 35% of students higher education costs. That got to be too much in everyone's view. Now colleges and universities are assuming the relatively modest cost of presenting class materials online. The graphics are marvelous and the accompanying text is succinct. Here let me show you.'"

"She opened up what looked like a large iPad and out popped an almost holographic-quality figure and accompanying text. It was sort of suspended in space outside the screen of the iPad."

"She described the display something like this. 'This is for my world history class. It shows Napoleon leading his troops into Russia. The accompanying graphs provide information about the size of his forces and his battle equipment. Other figures enumerate the forces and equipment he faced. The accompanying text briefly describes early battles leading to Napoleon's intrusion into Moscow. You can get more information by touching a tag.' She extended her index finger into the display until it contacted a tag labeled 'The affect of weather conditions on troops.' Then bang, up came some more incredible graphics and to-the-point text."

"Before I could get over the demise of lectures and textbooks, she informed me that formal testing was becoming a thing of the past. She argued that students in her time are carefully selected for some level of college or university matriculation. Her description of what students faced in at typical universities went something like this:

'Once you're accepted you complete the course work and any required tests. Tests can be retaken until you are able to answer 85% of questions correctly. Graduation is pretty much guaranteed.' She mentioned that the model for western world education was pretty much the old Japanese model: you sweat your way through elementary school and high school, then, if you have done well, you slide easily through undergraduate education. Her description of graduate school was different in that you don't have formal courses. Instead you have books and journals to read and research projects to complete. But unlike the undergraduate years, during graduate school you do interact with professors, though it's all in the context of research. For a dissertation topic you choose something closely related to ongoing research in some professor's lab. For non-experimental areas, the choice is to pursue something within the purview of a professor who is willing to take you on. You search for a professor who is pursuing something of interest to you—for example medieval literature—and hope you will be granted permission to work with her or him. After she informed me about the new process for pursuing a PhD, I asked, 'What about a master's degree?' Her reply was 'Masters degrees are for the pursuit of careers in instruction, such as teaching biology or law enforcement administration or classes related to any number of other professions.'"

"My interaction with students at the University of Chicago was highly productive. They are very smart and conversations with them were fascinating. As for Joyce, I liked and respected her a lot. It was easy to forgive her for what I regarded to be her only serious fault: her disdain for all things past was widely shared by others I encountered both on and off the University of Chicago campus."

At this point Joe looked at his watch and announced, "It's getting late. I've got more to say, so let's plan to meet here in a few days. I'll call everybody about it."

Much to Joe's surprise, Sarah, John, Martha and Randy stood up and applauded. Of course, everyone in the Den looked our way with considerable curiosity. Joe was disbelieving at first and then profoundly flattered.

John walked out with Joe who was still savoring the reaction to his presentation about the future. "That was amazing," gushed John. "You are a marvelous raconteur. I wish I could do that. How do you remember all of those details and weave them into such an interesting story?"

"Well," answered Joe. "I had much less to remember than you did. I was gone only a few weeks. As for the narrative skills, it's sort of a family tradition. At family gatherings we take turns weaving tales, some of them are tall tales, but most are about interesting experiences we've had. Come to think of it, although we are all good, I was probably the best. It's my most fun thing to do."

As they headed for different paths outside the Den, John's parting shot was, "I'm really looking forward to hearing about the rest of your trip."

CHAPTER 33

Who Goes Where And
When Do They Go?

As John headed down the path from the Lion's Den to his car, he saw a familiar figure off in the distance, seated on a bench. When he got closer, his suspicions were confirmed, it was Martha. She stood up as he approached and he could see that her emotions were a mixture of anger and despair. She wasted no time expressing her feelings. "I know you. I can tell. You've fallen in love."

John responded on as even a keel as he could manage, "You know from what I said earlier, it's over with the woman I met in New York City. You also must remember that you were the one who most insisted that we not think of having a more permanent relationship, because we would have to get jobs in different parts of the country. I accepted that and thought you had also. Now I'm wondering …"

Martha cut him off with, "You were not supposed to fall in love any more than I was … not for a long time. I thought we had an unspoken pack."

"I got hints from Joe and Randy that you've been dating many different guys," returned John.

"So what!" Martha shouted. "I didn't care whether you were dating. None of those guys meant anything to me. But you fell for someone else." She began to cry uncontrollably. John closed the few feet between himself and Martha in an instant. He folded his arms around her and she buried her head into his chest. He held her for a few moments until she stopped shaking."

"Now look what you've done," exclaimed, John. "You've got snot all-over my cool 1920s jacket." She stepped back far enough to make room for a punch to his ribs.

"Ouch!" hollered John while putting on a show of being seriously pained. All the while he was chocking back laughter. Martha was mixing laughter with sobs and giggles.

Finally, she cleared her throat enough to say, "You hurt me."

"I'm sorry. I never wanted to do that. What happened on my trip … well, it happened. I couldn't stop it. It doesn't change the way I feel about you. You are one of the most important people in my life, ever. I don't want anything to change that."

"Well, will you go back to 1929?"

John answered quickly, "I want to go back, but I'm not sure why. I could change my mind, but I don't think so. There is one thing I'm sure about: I'm not going to become a professor anytime soon. I think I will ask Joe and Randy if I can work with them. I want to continue exploring other time frames. Also, I think they can help me develop computer technology to model brain functioning."

As they walked toward John's car, they held hands like a couple of middle school buddies. When they parted that evening, both were sure that they would always be close.

In the interim between Joe's first talk about his trip and the second one, John became more and more convinced that working with Joe and Randy would be best for him at the present stage of his life. He found opportunities to visit with both of them individually and privately. He was pleased to find that both were enthusiastic about working with him. Over lunch one day all three of them sat down to map-out what they hoped to accomplish during their collaboration. It was clear that Randy and Joe were excited about computer modeling of brain functioning. John felt the first sense of genuine comfort he had experienced in many weeks.

At the next gathering in a far corner of the Lion's Den, before Joe continued his narrative about the trip ten years into the future, he asked if anyone had any questions. Instantly Sarah asked, "Why did you come back so soon?"

Joe began his answer with an assertion, "You know, I'm as smart as anyone." Before he said more, glances at each of his friends confirmed that none doubted his claim. "So," he continued, "I just couldn't stand knowing less than nearly everyone I encountered."

In various non-verbal ways, Sarah, Randy, Martha, and John showed that they accepted the reasoning behind his early return.

"The cavalier attitude people in the future have about their predecessors was another reason for returning early. Don't get me wrong. I loved being in the future. But, their apparent assumption that every advance achieved in their time was due solely to their own efforts was more than irritating. Crediting the foundation we provided them seemed beyond their comprehension. Our discussions on the trip convinced me that our generation is at least less likely to award full credit to our own selves, without paying homage to the contributions of our predecessors.

And there were some other things also. After I finished my business at the University of Chicago, I spent major parts of some days hanging out in Grant Park. Crowds were gathering there earlier in the year, possibly owing to an acceleration of Global Warming. I didn't try to cut into other peoples' conversations. I just sort of watched what they were doing from too great a distance to hear what they were saying. But, one day I saw a group looking at me and then whispering to themselves. Finally, one guy came over to me and asked, 'Why do you keep looking at the drones?'

I told him that the drones were interesting to me and that I wondered what kind of data they were collecting as they circled above us. Inevitably, the guy said, 'You're not from around here are you?' Because I didn't want to do the missionary thing again, it took several moments for me to come up with an answer. Finally, I said, 'I'm from Clute, Nebraska.' That seemed ok because I knew that there's only one Clute, in Texas. The guy nodded knowingly and began to fill me in on drones. 'They are mostly collecting information for businesses. They want to know where you are going and what you are doing so they can dump a lot of ads into every place you visit on the web, like Facebook and other social sites, various searches, your home page, emails, tweets, messages and so forth. They also use this information to call you by name and custom-advertise to you using in-store speakers activated by facial or retinal scans.' I thought, wouldn't you know it, Steven Spielberg's movie, *Minority Report*, was spot-on about the future of retail sales.

My response was 'Wait a minute. You mean that most everything about a person is public information for any business to use?'

He answered, 'I'd think that even in Clute, Nebraska'— he glanced at some of his friends who had gathered around us—'people would have heard that there is no privacy anymore. Don't you ever watch TV or read the news on-line?'

'Ok,' I said to myself. 'I guess I've got to fall back on the missionary story.' So I told him and his friends that I'd been a missionary in a remote part of Tanzania, and had just arrived back after ten years.' They bought it just like the students at the University of Chicago.

I was told that it's not just businesses that get info about where people are going and what they are doing. So does the government. I learned that, only ten years into the future, the National Security Agency will have carte blanche to spy on US citizens. So will other government agencies. These government entities won't just be collecting information about private citizens through their smart phones and computers. Electronic eyes installed along interstate highways, at tollbooths, and along major arteries through big cities will collect data about citizens. But the guy said not to worry, because government doesn't mess with most citizens, just commies, protesters, and other miscreants. The guy's friends communicated their agreement with his assessment."

Sarah interrupted Joe with an alarming observation. "You sound like you approve of all this police-state surveillance."

"Hell no," Joe replied. "It's not what I want. It's what I observed."

"Well, it's not written in stone," Sarah replied. "We can begin now to condemn surveillance of citizens and collecting records of people's private business. If it's not stopped soon, it will be entrenched ten years from now."

"Sarah's point is consistent with the whole reason for my trip," John observed. "Some knowledge of likely developments in the future—or projections into the future based on carefully considered extrapolations from the past— would allow us to prevent disasters born of ill-considered technological developments. It would also help to ensure that human well-being is promoted and basic human rights are protected in the future."

"So, should I continue?" asked Joe. His friends enthusiastically answered in the affirmation by words and gestures.

"I'll just talk about some observations I made as they pop into my head. Oh, for example, when I was conversing with the group at Grant Park, I kept noticing that cars would occasionally appear to bounce off each other. But, you wouldn't hear any sound because they wouldn't actually contact each other. My conversation with the group in Grant Park was periodically interrupted by my reactions to these near collisions. One of the people who gathered around me noticed a periodic startle response on my part and asked me what was causing my strange reaction. I told her that I was responding to apparent collisions that were unaccompanied by the usual sounds of car crashes or damage to cars. She explained that many if not most cars in her time were equipped with computerized all-wheel steering that took control of the wheels the instant a collision was imminent. In milliseconds, the cars that were about to collide are automatically steered a few centimeters away from one another. It was a common observation that the cars seemed to have hit an invisible barrier between them. The down side of this safety device, so some people complained, was that drivers over-relied on it. As a result, drivers in the future were becoming less focused on dangers of the road.

Apparently these people had been observing me for some time. Not only did they notice me gawking at the drones and reacting strangely to cars avoiding one another, the also saw me looking with disgust at the clothing, or lack there of, worn by people in the Park and walking past it. I think they thought that I was disapproving of their apparel choices, or worse, of their deficient moral rectitude. That may have been the case primarily because I had revealed that I was a missionary.

Many of the men passing by Grant Park were wearing what might called modern-day codpieces. Unlike the medieval versions that were made out of metal or other hard substances, these men wore sculptured codpieces made of a pliable substance that made their genitalia highly visible under their tight pants. Many of the women passing by wore tight, flexible clothing that generated the same effect."

Martha broke in with, "My goodness, Joe, I didn't know you were a prude."

Joe's eye brows narrowed and he looked ferocious for a moment. "I am not a prude! There has to be some reasonable limit to everything. What about children seeing these adult exhibitionists? There has been enough sexualizing of children in the present era."

"Points well taken," Martha replied. "I believe that people should be able to wear what they want to wear, pretty much wherever they go. But interjecting sex into everything is absurd, not to mention obscene." All of the others nodded in agreement.

Joe announced the return to his narrative with, "I don't have much else, so I'll sort of pick a few things at random. Let's see … ah, one day I needed a newspaper just to look at what was happening and to see if there was an off-Broadway play in town. So, I went to a drug store in search of one … they almost always have papers. After looking around and not finding any newspapers, I asked a clerk, 'Where are the newspapers.' She glanced at me with that same old 'What the …?' look. I thought she was going to ask, 'So, you're not from around here?' but she just screwed up her face some more, like she was looking at a fool. I repeated, 'Where can I find newspapers?' She answered, "In the library, where they store some of the old ones. The Sun Times is out of business and the Tribune is online only."

There were sounds of dismay from Joe's audience. What everybody feared would happen occurred only a few years down the road. John asked, "What about the New York Times?"

"I knew that you'd ask that, so I investigated. A clerk at the Palmer House said that they received a few of the copies shipped from New York City to Chicago daily. And I actually saw a couple of people reading Times editions in the lobby. Also, I saw people reading copies of the Washington Post and the Wall Street Journal. I don't know about other newspapers."

At that point, Joe paused and scratched his head as he tried to think of what else that occurred during his trip that was worth mentioning. When, after a couple of minutes, he couldn't come up with anything, Sarah suggested, "Maybe we could ask you a few questions, so you could rely on recognition recall which is easier than free recall." She winked at John as she posed her question. He frowned at bit in response to her rather unorthodox use of the two basic kinds of recall.

Randy was the first to raise his hand. He asked, "What was most unsettling to you about relating to the people you encountered on your trip?"

"Well, I've already told you that appearing ignorant was a big problem for me. Another thing that bothered me was lying." John began moving his head in a 'I know what you're talking about' manner. "Like John, I had to lie. If I'd told the truth, I'd have blown my cover. There are certain basic questions time travelers will be asked. Count on being asked questions like: 'Where are you from?' Wherever you go in time, people will want to know what you do in life. 'What degrees did you earn?' 'What's your career?' 'What's your hobbies?' and other things like that. You have to give believable answers to these questions. If you can't, you won't be trusted.

You may be asked, 'Are you married?' or 'Do you have any children?' As for the latter, don't pull out pictures from your wallet. If you are from the future, people in the near past will know something is wrong the minute you show them high-density color pictures. If you are from the past, people from the near future will wonder why you have hard copy pictures, because no one does anymore. And a related issue: you may slip up and use slang from your own time. Explaining it will cause you to prevaricate and maybe lead whoever questioned you to think you are some kind of alien."

After several other inquiries, there was a pause that signaled Joe his audience was running out of questions. He asked, "Any more questions?"

Randy raised his hand. "I've got one about Global Warming. Is it worse ten years into the future than it is today?"

"More of the same," Joe began. "The oceans got warmer which led to more bizarre and destructive storms. And the storms along the east and west coasts and the Gulf of Mexico were more damaging because ocean levels had risen. New York City, Boston, Miami, New Orleans, San Diego, Los Angeles, and even San Francisco were planning to create mobile barriers around their ocean-side peripheries. Many had lost some of their territory to the rising ocean.

And it was not just in the USA. For example, residents of London reported being worried about encroaching ocean water. Hong Kong residents were also worried as were most of the Japanese population."

As no other questions were posed, Martha asked, "Got any parting shots?"

Joe answered, "Cool is still cool, but uncool is different." Then he settled back into his chair as if he were finished. His audience began to buzz like people who have been told that there definitely is a fountain of youth, but not where to find it.

Finally, Randy exclaimed loudly, "Dude, you can't say that and think you're finished. Tell us about being uncool in the future!"

Joe thought for a moment before he offered, "It's complicated. It's something I apperceived ... more of a feeling than a conception." He paused for a moment. "It's that not so much is uncool anymore. Ours is a 'do your own thing and mind your business' generation. That orientation seems to have broadened in the future. It will become 'as long as anything I do is cool with you, whatever you do is cool with me.'"

Randy reacted quickly, "It sounds like, after a long life dating to the 1920s, 'cool' is dying out. Maybe it should if it's reduced to 'doing your own thing.' If it's not something people can share, it's not anything." Glum faces around the table communicated that the others thought Randy's assessment was plausible and, at the same time, depressing.

Not wanting to end on a sour note, Joe finished with a broad assessment of the future. "Just so you'll know, the future is much more a good thing than a bad thing. The television news indicated that many cancers had been cured, that heart attacks were occurring much later in life and that poverty was much lower than in the past. The attitude that every human being is worthy will virtually kill-off the self-absorbed conviction that 'I earned everything I got and I'm not going to give any of it to anyone else. If they're in trouble, it's their own fault.' Talking to people in the future led me to believe that they assume some unknown processes contribute to who succeeds and who doesn't. It follows from this kind of thinking that one must share the fruits of one's success with those who are less well blessed by the vicissitudes of fortunate."

As it was obvious that Joe had said all there was to say about his trip, he stepped back from the table so they could cluster around him. Each shook his hand and most hugged him. All knew from hearing about Joe's experiences that good people can become even better when they learn to regard life events as learning experiences.

As the meeting broke up, John lingered to say goodbye to Martha, and Sarah. When he finished with those adieus, he saw Randy and Joe silhouetted in the open front door. Quickly he disengaged himself and ran toward the Den's main entrance. Joe and Randy were already out the door and several meters down the path toward their cars, but John had no trouble catching up with them. "I just wanted to check out a few things with you guys. I take it that the big move to Washington state is under way or will soon be."

Randy answered, "Yes, it has begun, but it will take at least a few weeks to complete. We are going there soon. Will you be coming along?"

"I'll ready to go within a few days, at most," John replied.

Joe said, "Good, let us know when you are ready. We'll wait for a while so we can caravan our three cars to Washington. The time machine computer and integral chamber will go west by truck."

"Great. I'll clean things up here and be ready soon," John replied. "Just one question before you go. I think I know what Sarah will be doing. She will take another six months to complete her dissertation and another year to find one of those rare jobs in philosophy. If she has the option, she'll get as close to the new time-travel computer site as she can. But I don't know about Martha. She's said nothing to me."

Randy volunteered, "We asked her if she wanted to work with us, but she declined. She is about finished with her dissertation and expects to take a job at the best university who will have her, regardless of where it is."

John responded to the news about Martha by twisting his face into a look of helpless dismay, but before he turned away, he posed one last question. "While I'm working with you, will it still be possible for me to take another trip to the past?"

Joe responded, "Oh, of course you can." Randy nodded in agreement and added, "Sure you can."

As John waved goodbye and headed away from his friends, he was thinking, "I'm going back to New York City, 1929."

SOURCES

I began reading in psychological science as an undergraduate and have continued to the present time. During my years as a professor of psychology and researcher, I was known for the large stack of journals on my desk and for walking down the halls of the psych building reading journals and, periodically, bouncing off the walls to keep my balance. Now, as then, I take major journals of the Association for Psychological Science (APS), the American Psychological Association (APA), the Psychonomic Society, and the Society for Personality and Social Psychology (SPSP). In addition, as a longtime member of the American Association for the Advancement of Science (AAAS), I receive *Science*, arguably the world's most respected scientific journal (British scientists have every right and reason to make the same claim for *Nature*). I also read the outstanding popular science magazine, *Science News* (*Discover* is another excellent popular science magazine).

And not all I've learned about science comes from print sources. I've attended many dozens of scientific talks at conventions over the years and gotten feedback from audiences of dozens of my own presentations. *Time Travelers* emerged from all of these years of reading in science and listening to colleagues. As such, it is impossible to recall the source of every reference to science in this book.

None of this is to say that, somehow, what I've learned from other scientists has coalesced into something unique to me. As B. F. Skinner put it bluntly, nothing anyone does or conceives is entirely original with her or him.

Nevertheless being a compulsive hoarder of information about science, I am able to list some of the sources from which I directly took information used in *Time Travelers*. These sources are listed below in an order unrelated to the order of science topics considered in *Time Travelers*.

John's words used to inform the Columbia University science discussants about the scientific significant of the Cern Supercollider event that confirmed the Higgs boson were suggested in part by articles in *Science* (13 July 2012 and 14 September, 2012 both by Adrian Cho). Articles in *Science News* (28 July 2012 and 29 December 2012 by Alexandra Witze and 28 July 2012 by Tom Siegfried) also contributed to John's words.

John's hint to the Columbia students about how computers would operate in the future is based on Alan Turing's brilliant and highly accurate projections about how computer software would operate. Sadly his career was cut short by accusations that he had a homosexual encounter (*Science News*, 30 July, 2012, by Tom Siegfried).

The contributions of Niels Bohr, whose extraordinary mind was much admired by Einstein, are described in *Science*, 19 July 2013 by David C. Clary. Tom Siegfried describes his impact on modern physics in Science News (13 July 2013). The analogy of "filling up Lake Michigan at an ever increasing rate" to the pace at which robots will develop in the future comes from an article in *Mother Jones* by Kevin Drum (May/June, 2013).

Olaf Bergmann and Jonas Frisen have provided an accessible discussion about the limited growth of new neurons in the human brain and the influence of environmental events on the brain (*Science*, 10 May 2013). For information about growth and retraction of spines connecting neurons in response to environmental events, I have relied on research reports by William T. Greenough of the University of Illinois. Using electron microscopes, he was able to actually see and record spines growing and retracting in response to environmental events. His work confirmed the predictions of psychologist Donald Hebb dating back to the 1940s. Hebb accurately surmised that the brain accommodates changes in organisms' environments by continually changing through a growth process between neurons.

It is widely recognized that scientists see overwhelming evidence that global warming is underway. A more controversial issue is whether humans are major contributors to it. There are many sources that report evidence for human involvement in global warning. One of the most credible is a poll of climate and earth scientists. In it ninety-eight percent of the 200 most published climate scientists, and the same percentage of most frequently published climatologists, affirm that humans are the major cause of global warming. This survey can be accessed at the web site below (After finding the site with your browser, click on the figure of survey results to enlarge it. You can then drag it to your desktop.).

h t t p : / / e n . w i k i p e d i a . o r g / w i k i / Surveys_of_scientists'_views_on_climate_change

On All In With Chris Hayes (MSNBC 6/2/14), famed physicist Neil Degrasse Tyson eloquently sums up evidence for global warming and reasons for resistance to it. On a 2013 edition of Hayes' show, the widely known observation that the wealthiest 1% possess most of America's wealth and earnings is extended all the way back to 1920s. The top 1% accounted for all except 4% of gains in wealth during 2013, the first time they corralled such a large portion of gains since 1928.

For Homestake Gold Mines value vs. the DJIA see

h t t p : / / w w w . g o l d - e a g l e . c o m / a r t i c l e / gold-stocks-and-great-crash-1929-revisited-0

Among the sources on memory, epigenesis, and brain rewiring that I consulted in writing *Time Travelers* is Susan Gaidos' succinctly and clearly written "Memories Lost and Found," *Science News* 27 July 2013.

Ed and Carol Diener, who recently retired from the University of Illinois, have not only condemned extraordinarily expensive college textbooks as I did in *Time Travelers*, they are doing something about it. [Disclosure: I am a textbook author.] The two award-winning psychologists are in the process of making materials available to students online that cover a broad range of psychological science topics. If enough psychological scientists contribute to this effort, many pedantic and absurdly expensive textbooks will be replaced with free, attractive, and readily available readings accompanied by excellent graphics.

My projections in *Time Travelers* about changes in the future of colleges and universities may seem extreme and difficult to accept. However, I'm not alone in making dire predictions about the future of our institutions of higher